THE UNDEAD

VOLUME 2

SKIN AND BONES

EDITED BY
D.L. SNELL
AND
TRAVIS ADKINS

Permuted Press
The formula has been changed...
Shifted... Altered... *Twisted.*™
www.permutedpress.com

A Permuted Press book
published by arrangement with the authors

ISBN-10: 0-9789707-4-8
ISBN-13: 978-0-9789707-4-1
Library of Congress Control Number: 2007930570

SLAB OF CONTENTS

THE SKIN...

THE MEAT...

THE BONES...

All the World's Infested:

an Introduction by D.L. Snell

Zombies are taking over the world. Don't believe me? Well, I didn't believe it either until I started editing for *The Undead*. We received enough submissions for the second installment that we could compile an entire third anthology. That's close to four hundred submissions. If you don't think that's a lot, try reading them all. Try dodging their teeth.

In fact, reviewing these submissions is a lot like running from zombies: the crappy ones are shamblers with dirty bites, just some bones held together with rotting green flesh, easy to escape; the mediocre subs are a little faster and a little smarter and a little harder to dodge; and then the really good ones are sprinters, and these are the ones that eventually infect us. But zombies haven't just overrun our inbox at *The Undead*. They have also swallowed a big portion of the earth.

Still don't believe me? Okay. Go to Amazon.com and search for "zombies" under the category "Books." This search should produce upwards of 160 zombie-related titles. Now go to Google.com and execute the same search for approximately 23 million hits. See? Zombies *are* taking over the world. Visit the Ultimate Zombie Book List at www.ZombieBookList.com and you'll see what I mean.

So, you might ask, who started this infection? Who took the first bite? Well, according to "Zombies," an article on the website for the University of Michigan*, the zombie myth derives from Voodoo culture in Haiti, a country south of Florida, USA. Supposedly, Bokors,

Voodoo priests of black magic, can resurrect the dead with a powder called *coup padre*, which contains the main ingredient, tetrodoxin, a poison extracted from the fou-fou, or "porcupine fish." The Bokor sprinkles the powder into the corpse's mouth and creates a zombie. Thereafter, the cadaver obeys the priest's every command.

In the twentieth century, popular culture adapted the myth to the silver screen, with movies such as *White Zombie*, released in 1932. In that film, actor Bela Lugosi plays a Haitian businessman who lusts after another man's fiancée. The businessman hires a witch doctor to zombify his rival, hoping to court the man's wife-to-be. Evidently, Lugosi's character thinks the pick-up line, "I zombified your fiancé," will make a woman swoon; in this case, she keels over. Throughout the 1930s and 40s, most zombie films dealt with Haitian zombie folklore, movies such as *I Walked with a Zombie* and, my personal favorite, *Zombies on Broadway*. Not until the "Hammer Films era" in the 1950's and 60's did zombies begin to eat human flesh.

Possibly the coolest zombie title from the Hammer Films era is *I Eat Your Skin*, released in 1961, but the most recognizable to today's audience is, undisputedly, George A. Romero's *Night of the Living Dead* (1968). Romero forever altered how we look at zombies, creating a creature that embodies the traits of several other monsters: Romero zombies gorge like werewolves, contaminate like vampires, and, more obviously, linger in the realm between life and death like their traditional Haitian counterparts ("Zombies"). Romero's movie engrossed America, fresh from the horrors of Vietnam, because it "acknowledged that the enemy was us and us only... It was, in essence, complete apocalypse... rooted solely in humanity." ("Zombies"). Now *that's* my kind of movie.

So, you might be thinking, all this history is good and great, but what caused this current outbreak? Well, in his afterword for *The Undead*, Bram Stoker Award-winning author Brian Keene claims that the British film *28 Days Later* and his own novel *The Rising* incited the infection. Keene cites several books and movies that followed suit: the films *Shaun of the Dead, Land of the Dead, Dawn of the Dead*, and even Tim Burton's animated effort, *The Corpse Bride*; as for books, Keene mentions *Xombies, Risen, Cell*, and Hellbound Books' best-selling anthology *Cold Flesh*. Keene says that zombies have even infiltrated shows from popular culture, such as *Aqua Teen Hunger Force*, and role-playing games like *All Flesh Must Be Eaten*.

And there's still more to come. *The Undead* anthologies, for example. And Brian Keene's next novel, *Dead Sea*, plus a movie and a videogame based on *The Rising*. Up-and-coming writers such as John Hubbard and Eric S. Brown pump out zombie stories by the plague-load, and even I have a zombie/vampire novel available from Permuted Press, titled *Roses of Blood on Barbwire Vines*. Like Keene says in his afterword, "Zombies are undead. Un-dead, meaning, they can't die."

So, do you believe me now? Zombies *are* infecting the world. They're infesting our imaginations, our publications, and our bookstore shelves. The zombie outbreak is here, now, in our time. All it takes is one trip to www.AllThingsZombie.com, and you're bitten, you're infected... you're hungry. And you want to spread your disease. So you submit a story to *The Undead* because you *know* it will reach an audience. You know your bite will spread. Some people will try to run, but they can't escape the one definite truth: in the end, everyone rots. You might as well make the best of it and eat human flesh.

—D.L. Snell
Forest Grove, Oregon
May 2006

---

* Unless otherwise cited, most of the historical and film information in this introduction comes from the article, "Zombies," from the following website:

http://www.umich.edu/~engl415/zombies/zombie.html

CYCLOPEAN

DAVID WELLINGTON

The Tillinghast Building is Arkham's tallest, at seventy-five floors—seventy-seven if you include the two-story Art Deco step pyramid crowning its top. It was built in the Thirties, not without incident, and like most buildings of the same age, it had problems with mold. Or at least the owners had suggested as much when they hired me.

What I scraped off the dedication plate out front, however, wasn't mold at all. It was mushrooms, believe it or not. Full-formed fruiting bodies with golden brown caps and stems as thick as my fingers. When I tore them away, I saw they were connected to something deeper and larger. The stems grew right through the polished marble, burrowing their way through solid stone.

Genus *Armillaria*, I was pretty sure. The honey fungus. What species I couldn't say. That would take considerable study back at my lab, maybe even DNA sequencing. It might take weeks.

A man in a dark blue suit stepped out of the revolving doors and approached me while I was putting fungus samples in a zip-loc. His clothes were neat and pressed and his hair was perfectly combed, but there was something wrong with his face, a certain roughness like smallpox scars. As he stepped into the shadow of the building, the skin of his cheek glowed distinctly green. Some of it was on his right hand, too, as he lifted a pistol straight out from his shoulder and pointed it in my direction.

I heard someone screaming, but I couldn't think or move or act in any way. I was too shocked.

"Tell them, please. Tell them you can't resist, when it happens." His mouth was smiling but his voice was not. "It isn't the kind of thing you can fight."

I had questions for him—I think I could have asked a question—but in the next moment, he started firing. He made no attempt to aim, and most of his shots went wild. One struck a young woman across the street, and blood rolled down her face.

The noise of the gunshots, huge and terrible, freed me from my paralysis, and I ran down into a SubRail station, into darkness, into safety. Only then did I look at the plastic bag in my hand. Inside, the fungal samples were flickering, dimly, with that same green color I'd seen on the madman's face.

*   *   *   *   *

"They can't be held responsible for their own actions," I insisted. "They've been bent to the will of a larger organism. The ones with the pistols are merely defensive organs!"

The policeman kept staring at me. It was quite unnerving.

"I know it sounds odd. But if you knew what I do about this fungus—"

He didn't tell me to shut up. He didn't have to. He raised one eyebrow, and I couldn't keep talking. His stare had a violence to it that made me feel bruised.

The policeman turned to face the Tillinghast again, and I knew I'd blown my best chance to make the authorities believe me.

They had shoved me—and all the other rubberneckers—behind hastily-erected crowd control barriers. We were a block away from the Tillinghast. If anyone tried to get closer, the inhabitants of the building would emerge and shoot until the streets emptied.

The going explanation was that the building had been captured by terrorists. Except one of the shooters had been a fifty year-old accountant in a sweater set and pearls. She was a well-known accountant who'd worked out of the Tillinghast for decades. Her face had been speckled with glowing green.

Whatever the cause of the violence, there could only be one reaction, of course. More violence. A platoon of armed and armored riot police arrived in short order. They would no doubt shoot everyone inside the lobby.

Ducking under or vaulting over the blue sawhorses, the officers fanned out around the building. Their guns jangled on their backs, and the lunch-hour sunlight burned on their bulletproof visors. They moved silently and in perfect formation, a faceless blob of black plastic and navy-blue nylon. A cheer rose up from the crowd, but that was the only sound.

Squads of the policemen ducked behind parked cars and thundered over the crosswalks. They flanked the main entrance of the building with weapons at the ready. One of them picked up a bullhorn and tested it with a deafening squawk of feedback.

Strange shadows flickered across the street corner. I had the unshakeable feeling that giant birds were wheeling overhead, predatory beasts from out of the unspeakably ancient past. I looked up. So did everyone else.

Half a dozen computer monitors, a few laser printers, and hundreds of multi-line telephone handsets fell from the sky like a beige-toned avalanche. They hung weightless and aloft in a way they were never meant to, as if all the laws of time and space had been momentarily repealed, as if these strange objects were suspended in a medium far more viscous than air. Then the illusion broke, and they fell to the street with incredible speed.

More projectiles emerged a moment later, cast down from open windows a dozen or fifteen or fifty floors overhead. The office equipment fell fast and hard. The first monitor smacked the ground a hundred feet away from me with a high-pitched cracking sound, a noise to set the nerves on edge. The first laser printer struck a riot cop's helmet and caved it right in.

The armored policemen retreated with their heads down and their legs flashing out of time, shouting, "Go go go!" and, "Back get back get back!" punctuated by jangling, cracking bursts as the rain of office equipment followed them to the barrier. They dragged their wounded out behind them—the man with the dented helmet, another with a six-inch dagger of green and silver circuit board protruding from his bloodied side. It was over as fast as it began. A single plastic paper shredder finished its death arc to the street and shivered itself to fragments on the asphalt.

The policeman I'd tried to speak with earlier stared at me with a new expression, a kind of dreadful suspicion. For a long time, he didn't speak. I didn't move.

"You," he said, finally, the word emerging from his mouth with visible recoil. "You said they were making a mistake. You seem to know an awful lot for somebody who just showed up." He started to reach for the baton at his belt.

I reached into my own pocket, thinking my faculty credentials from the University might help save me. Instead, I found a folded sheaf of photocopies, reproductions of some very old building plans. My employer had provided the schematics for the Tillinghast so I would know where to look for mold. I had studied them at length the previous night. I unfolded the sheets of laser paper with sweaty fingers, suddenly realizing what I possessed.

"I know another way into that building," I said.

The cop's face froze in mid-sneer.

*   *   *   *   *

An hour later, the cop, six armored riot police, and yours truly were down in the abandoned part of the Subterranean Railway, slogging through standing water that submerged the railroad ties, trying to find our way through the darkness.

I consulted my schematics again by flashlight. "There used to be a SubRail station under the building. There are platforms and token booths—and a stairwell leading up into the Tillinghast's lobby." That entrance had been closed off to the public for decades, but that just might mean the shooters in the lobby wouldn't be guarding it.

"Who is this guy?" the sergeant of the Riot Cops asked. He was a tall, muscular fellow by the name of Villareal, and he didn't seem to like me very much, or my plan. He also understood that nobody else had a better idea.

Mike Czanek, the cop who had brought me in, scowled around his answer. "A teacher from MU. He works for the guy who owns the 'Ghast, too."

"That's at least partially correct, Officer. My name is Walter Ngo, and I am an adjunct professor teaching botany at the University. To make ends meet, I moonlight doing biohazard assessments. The real estate firm which rents out the Tillinghast hired me to survey the mycological load of the building. They'd had reports of a bad mildew smell in the airshafts, and some people had gone home sick with what looked like hypersensitivity pneumonitis."

"These mushrooms make you sick?" Villareal asked. "Like... *crazy sick?*"

"It's possible," I shrugged. I lacked sufficient data to draw a conclusion. "The building's owners, anyway, were worried the building might have black mold. Abatement on a building this size would cost millions."

"So they were dragging their feet, waiting for the problem to get really serious before they fixed it," Villareal said. "Typical corporate America, right?"

Just then, Czanek said, "Hey, shut up and turn off your lights."

The riot cops acquiesced immediately, Villareal and I a moment later. At first, we were plunged into total darkness, but as our eyes adjusted we saw what Czanek had seen. The policeman must have had eyes like a dragonfly to notice the eerie green glow coming from just around a bend in the tunnel, lining the brick-lined walls with a grotesque gleam. The light gave no warmth, and it did little to dispel the dark. It mostly served to make the shadows longer and more oppressive.

"Foxfire," I said, voicing the phenomenon's most reassuring name.

"Yeah," one of the riot cops said. "Listen, I seen this before. I went camping out by Kingsport last year, out in the woods. Half the trees were lit up this color. Me and Jerry got out of there pretty quick. The old-timers say those woods are haunted, and some of those old guys have seen things nobody ever should."

The other men muttered amongst themselves, clearly frightened.

"There's no need to give in to superstitious nonsense," I assured them. They quieted straight away. "It's simple bioluminescence. The same chemical reaction that allows fireflies to attract their mates. What we are dealing with here is completely natural and harmless."

"Except when it makes rational people start shooting at each other," Villareal opined.

I headed deeper into the tunnel and finally reached the station. The platforms stood before me, flickering with that eerie light that made the dark graffiti on the walls bend and twist into arcane glyphs. I wondered whether any of the artists who had tagged the walls had noticed the fungus growing out of the tracks. Certainly, they couldn't have missed it. The Armillaria had changed that once-human station into something horrible to behold, a cavern of blight.

Stringy dark tendrils like unkempt hair dangled from the ceiling in great clumps. The main rhizomorphs, of which there were hundreds, were black trunks thick as telephone poles, twisting up toward the ceiling and beyond. Ropy twists draped the platforms, branching and branching again like the exposed nervous system of some truly colossal being. Some of the ramified growths adhered to the concrete; others dug in through wide cracks. Centipose clusters of mushrooms sprouted from every available surface, their flattish tops burning cold and green. A smell of mildew, of wet and moldering things, hung in the air as thick as smoke.

As the police fanned out around the station, they stirred the close air, and the growths trembled, the hanging tendrils drifting in our wind. The thicker growths rattled and moved, and it was hard not to imagine them pulsing, throbbing as they pumped nutrients and water and life into the tower over our heads.

"Jesus," Czanek swore. "Where did this all come from?"

"It grew," I told him. "It might have been growing down here for thousands of years. Perhaps millions. The only limit on its size is the amount of food it can find. There are Armillaria colonies out west that cover thousands of acres."

"How do you kill it?" Villareal asked.

It was my turn to raise an eyebrow. "You don't."

"Hey, come on," Czanek muttered, like an old car engine turning over in the cold.

"Oh, you can kill individual pieces of an Armillaria. Any old fungicide will do. Ammonium sulphamate, say, or Benlate. But unless you get every single cell of the colony, it will eventually grow back. Fungi are known for their speedy recoveries, too. Surely you've seen mushrooms sprouting after a rain? Gentlemen, you are looking at the ultimate survivor. Immortal. Omnipresent. It steals the life right out of you and then it feeds on your corpse." I caught myself smiling and stopped at once. People had died today because of this fungus.

"It can't be killed. It'll just grow back. What exactly do you suppose we should do, then, Professor?" Czanek demanded.

"I suppose," I said, controlling my growing impatience, "that we go up inside the building and find a way to rescue the people there. That is your job, isn't it?"

I glanced at the photocopied schematics in my hand. "This way, please, gentlemen," I said, leading the way.

*   *   *   *   *

At the top of a flight of stairs, a very old door awaited us. It unlocked easily, though the deadbolt had rusted a little in its slide. I pushed it open with a soft, muttering creak and stepped back as the riot police slipped silently into the Tillinghast.

The air in the lobby hung perfectly still, not even dust motes twirling in the golden-brown light that seeped in through the glass doors. The smell was, if anything, worse than down in the abandoned station, a sharp reek of vegetable decay and rotten leaves.

Outside, the mid-June day had been warm. Inside the lobby, it was stifling. Dry, too, dry enough to make the membranes inside my nose crinkle, which surprised me a little and got me thinking.

Villareal waved his fingers at his underlings, directing them with hand signals. Mike Czanek and I stood back near the door. Out of the way.

The riot police attacked the shadows of the lobby, pointed weapons into its corners. They clambered over the counter of the newsstand and dug through the janitor's closet.

"Where are they?" Czanek finally asked, breaking the silence. I can imagine what he was thinking, as I was thinking it myself. The shooters were nowhere to be seen.

"Maybe you scared them off," Villareal snapped.

"Well, they're gone, ain't they?" Czanek asked. He walked across the marble floor and touched the push-bar of the revolving doors. They moved a little in their runners and then stopped. "They locked the place up and, what, just went back to work? They figured we were going to just give up?"

"I refuse to think we're dealing with an enemy that stupid," Villareal said. He squinted around the gloomy space as if he might find the shooters given a more thorough inspection. "One of my guys is maybe dead, and Bannicek has to have his kidney out because of these shits."

"Perhaps," I said, "they heard us coming. Perhaps they went upstairs so we'd follow them."

"You can keep any more ideas to yourself, Professor," Villareal said, gesturing with the butt end of his weapon. "You did us a favor getting us in here, but now maybe you should head back." He turned to two of his men. "Mac, Blake. You guys check out the elevator, see if it's working. They want us to chase them, maybe we will."

Czanek stepped over toward the elevator banks, his pistol held in both hands. Villareal shook his head.

"Mike, you're not certified for this operation. You get to escort the Professor home." Czanek started to complain but Villareal held up a warning finger. "Don't make me fill out the paperwork for your sorry ass."

Czanek put his weapon away and started to smile, a cock-eyed grin that made his mustache bristle. "You pulling rank on me, Gus? I thought when we busted balls around here, we went for bad guy balls."

Villareal didn't respond. One of the riot police—Blake, I believe it was—had touched the UP button in the middle of the elevator bank; the left-hand elevator doors slid open. There was no car there, however. The shaft was full of gnarled rhizomorphs, hanging from high above like twisted ropes, dark and heavy with stolen water. Here and there, they had split open, revealing the white bundles of fibrous hyphae inside.

Dangling from those ropes, tangled in their net-like complexity, the shooters, all five of them, hung upside down by their feet. The accountant still wore her pearls, which had fallen across her face. Her white hair was matted with curling tendrils, and her forehead and left cheek glowed a bright and evil green.

The suited man who had nearly killed me lurched out of the shaft. His face had slipped away on one side, revealing a creamy white mycelium beneath the skin. The rot had nearly consumed him from the inside out.

He grabbed Mac and pulled the riot cop inside the shaft. The doors shut behind him with a clang.

The other riot cops shouted and banged at the doors. An enormous rattling, chattering sound came out of the shaft, the resonant echo of automatic gunfire. Someone inside the shaft screamed—then stopped abruptly.

Villareal shouted orders, and his squad pried at the elevator doors with their fingers and combat knives. The doors slid open an inch at a time. Finally, they slid free, and Mac tumbled out onto the marble floor, the doors slamming shut behind him. His helmet was missing.

So was one of his boots. The other cops dragged him onto his feet and slapped him on the back, bellowed questions in his ears. Was he all right, did he need anything?

"It doesn't hurt," he told them. He smiled broadly and added, "It goes in real easy."

I had already noticed the black tendril wrapped around his bare foot, snaking back through the doors and into the shaft. Its probing end disappeared into the cuff of his pants.

I had no time to shout a warning, no time to get anyone's attention. Mac's rifle came up, and he fired a burst of three loud shots right into Villareal's face. As the rest of the squad grabbed at his arms and neck, he laid into them with the knife in his free hand.

Behind me stood the entrance to an emergency stairway. I smashed my back against the push-bar and fell into perfect darkness, Czanek's enormous body slumping down beside me. He kicked the door closed, and together we lay there, listening to our own hurried breathing—and to the shooting—and the screaming that never seemed to end.

*   *   *   *   *

We waited long enough to convince ourselves that we couldn't go back the way we'd come. Mac was still out there in the lobby, having slaughtered all his teammates. He would be joining the shooters in the elevator shaft, if he hadn't already.

If we so much as peeked out through the door, we would make targets of ourselves.

"Trapped," Czanek gargled.

"We can still go up," I said. I switched on my flashlight and waved it at the emergency stairs behind us. They marched upward in endless flights.

"What, and get deeper into this shit?" Czanek took out a white handkerchief and blew his nose volubly. "Goddamn, it smells bad. Like wet towels if you don't hang them up."

I had become so accustomed to the Tillinghast's new odor that it barely registered. Then again, I had devoted my career to the musty and the damp-smelling, to things that grew best in dark, hot, stuffy places. To things that grew best when cultivated in beds of manure. If you have a sensitive nose in my line of work, you soon realize you chose the wrong job.

"I have an idea," I announced. It was only half-formed so far, but it had its merits, I thought.

"Fuck your ideas," Czanek said. "They led us into this deathtrap." He tried his radio again as he had every few minutes since the screaming had stopped. When he failed to raise anyone, he tried his cell phone, then my cell phone, which he had requisitioned.

"Honestly, Officer, I have an—"

He assaulted me with his cold, almost dead eyes. I flinched. "Listen, maybe you just saved my life, so I won't give you a beating. But I don't want you thinking you're in charge, either. Villareal gave me an order, which was to get you out of here."

"Yes, that's fine," I said. "But then he led his men into an ambush. I would imagine his leadership skills to be open to debate, and thus his orders."

I could barely see Czanek in the reflected illumination of my flashlight, but I know his face darkened. He spat on the floor before he spoke again. "You don't have a right to judge them. Those were good men out there. Villareal had a stick up his ass, but I'd rather be in here with that stick than with you." He picked up the radio again and fiddled with its dials.

I withdrew the building schematics from my pocket and brandished them at him, intending to demonstrate why, exactly, his radio calls were failing to give any result. The emergency stairwells were built right into the core of the building. Countless thicknesses of plaster and wooden lathing and steel retaining columns and reinforced concrete stood between his radio and anyone who cared to listen.

I stopped myself before I could give the brutish policeman a lesson in basic electromagnetic physics, however, because I saw something in the plans that had escaped me.

"Look, here," I said, pointing. He looked away. "Look, you can follow the plumbing column all the way to... here. Look! There's an emergency water shutoff valve right there."

"Yeah? So what?"

"So perhaps you cut high school the day they talked about fungi," I said, "so I'll enlighten you. This thing, this organism which has taken over the Tillinghast, has quite a few advantages. You can burn, shred, or poison as much of it as you like, and it can just grow more biomass. It can take over human bodies and use them to kill us. But it's not supernatural. It's a living thing, and that means it has needs. Principle among those is access to water."

Czanek frowned. "So? There's maybe what, three hundred toilets in this building. It can just dip its tentacles in any one of them and take a drink."

I shook my head. "Rhizomorphs, not tentacles. And that would hardly satisfy the Armillaria's thirst. You saw how much growth there was down there. It's going to take enormous amounts of water to sustain something that big. Tons of water every day. It must be tied directly into the plumbing of the building. It must be draining water directly out of the mains!"

Czanek was smart enough to draw a conclusion, I'll give him that. "So if we shut off the water, we hurt this thing. Maybe kill it. Yeah." He grabbed the schematics away from me. "Okay, where's the controls for the plumbing?"

"There are two emergency shutoff valves. One is in the basement. We could have reached it from the lobby, but that route is cut off to us now."

Czanek dropped the building plans. I thought he wanted to strangle me. Instead, he grabbed his handkerchief again and blew his nose.

"Where is the other one?" he asked, knowing full well what the answer must be.

I pointed it out on the diagram. It was in the obvious place, of course. If the building ever flooded, the basement would be inaccessible. So they put the secondary controls as high and dry as possible. In a locked closet on the seventy-fifth floor.

*   *   *   *   *

"What's that sound?" Czanek asked. It had been audible down at the level of the lobby. As we rose higher, it grew in volume. It was an enormous moaning sound, a howling that rose and fell and tattered at the edges.

"It's just wind," I told him. "The temperature is different at the bottom of the building and at the top. Warm air rises and cold air sinks, remember? Plain old harmless wind."

"It's fucking creepy," he told me, which I didn't think was up to his usual level of repartee. But then maybe he was as fatigued as I was by climbing all those stairs.

Even when you're in good shape, you start feeling the burn in your thighs after climbing five flights of stairs. After ten flights, you just want to stop. We were already panting for breath when Czanek signaled for a break. I had to go and make it worse. I knelt down and shone my light along the stairwell wall. I found what I had expected to find: dark runners creeping along the tops of the steps, surging a ways up the wall. Tiny mushrooms clustered wherever two of the runners crossed each other. I had expected—or maybe hoped—that the growths would thin out the higher we climbed until eventually they would disappear. If anything, they were getting thicker.

"Mycologists call these 'boot-laces,'" I told Czanek. He was too busy lying on his back on a cold steel landing to respond. "They're the same thing as the big rhizomorphs we saw downstairs, just juvenile forms."

"This thing, this mushroom," he asked, sitting up a little. "It ever take over people like that before?"

"Not to my knowledge." I opened my knapsack and took out some protective gear, the kind of stuff I normally wear when investigating a possible mold problem. I handed Czanek a paper surgical mask and showed him how to adjust the rubber strap. I gave him a pair of latex gloves and sprayed his shoes with fungistat, then did my own. Hopefully that would keep the rhizomorphs from parasitizing our bodies. Hopefully.

"No, I guess I would have heard of that, huh?" Czanek said. He stared at me and pulled his mask away so I could see how angry his mouth looked. "But somehow you figured it out. You figured out it was a mushroom that made all those people so crazy."

"Are you accusing me of knowing too much, Officer?"

"In my job, we connect dots. That's all I'm doing."

"I knew right away what had happened, yes. Because while the honey mushroom has never done this to human beings before, it has a nasty habit of doing it to other living things. In my profession, we don't just connect the dots. We try to predict where the next dot is going to appear."

He was quiet. Maybe he wanted to hear me out. Maybe he wanted to understand.

"In Oregon, there's a forest. The biggest one of these things lives underneath it. Half the trees in that forest are dead now, and there's no way to stop it from spreading. From the outside, you can't tell anything is wrong, not until the trees start falling down, because they rot away from within."

I drank a little water and handed Czanek the bottle. "An Armillaria colony grows underground, mostly. The mushrooms that you see are just its way of sending spores out to create new little fungi. The body of the organism is a lot less attractive. Imagine a nest of reddish-brown snakes writhing around and around each other. Imagine acre after acre of that, endlessly growing in moist, warm darkness. That's the mother mass.

"It grows by sending tendrils up into the circulatory system of every plant it touches. It grows inside a pine tree or a rose bush or a willow—whatever it can find. And then it turns that plant into a zombie. The leaves, the stems of the plant, all of its organs stop working for the plant and start working to feed the fungus. There's nothing the plant can do. It shrivels and dies from the inside. Botanists call it the *white rot*.

"The trees know it's happening, somehow. They go through a last gasp where they'll flower and make new fruit in the middle of winter, in the desperate hope to achieve something, some kind of posterity. Always, always when it gets that far, the host organism dies."

In the dark, the wind moaned up and down the stairwell around us, making chills run down my arms.

"Jesus," Czanek finally said. "But that's plants. People are different!"

"Not as much as you'd think," I had to tell him. "At least not from the fungus' point of view. Trees and people are both full of nutrients and water. There aren't a lot of trees in Arkham for it to parasitize, but there are plenty of people."

Czanek's eyes were wide. I reached over and tapped his dangling surgical mask. "That cough of yours is getting worse," I told him. "Probably because of all the spores floating around in here. We need to take precautions."

*   *   *   *   *

The air grew thicker. We spoke less often. It was tough drawing air in through the surgical masks, but at least they protected our lungs. After another ten floors, our masks were yellow with spores.

It should have gotten colder as we rose higher in the building. Instead, it got warmer—and drier. All the moisture had been sucked out of the air. My fingers grew white, and the skin around my nails started to crack. My lips burned. There had to be something above us, something big and thirsty.

We kept climbing. Going back wasn't an option. We rested often, but it was never enough. My side began to cramp, and then my legs. Czanek was having an even harder time—his breathing was almost louder than the moaning wind that haunted the stairwell. He pulled himself up the handrail as much as he lifted his feet to climb each riser. His eyes, when they caught my light, were bloodshot, the lids drooped low.

Admittedly, he outweighed me by probably sixty pounds. Admittedly, I was twenty years younger, and I made my living crawling around old buildings and climbing up and down stairways. Admittedly, we were forty floors up, and we'd done it the hard way.

Still. I knew. Czanek was suffering a bad allergic reaction to the spores. Some of them were getting through his mask. Others were collecting in the pores of his skin, in his tear ducts, in his ears. He needed oxygen and a good antihistamine. I had neither to give him.

We had just passed the fifty-first floor landing when he stopped in mid-stride and fell down on the risers. He didn't sit down. He fell down. He was breathing so hard I thought he might hyperventilate.

"Okay, five minute break," I said, trying to sound perky. In the cone of my flashlight, he didn't even bother to glare at me. He reached up though and tore off his mask.

It was the worst thing he could do—and also, probably, something he couldn't resist. At first, it actually seemed to help him as he breathed deeply and a little color rushed back into his face. Then he started coughing. Long, drawn-out honking coughs. He spat thick mucus on the risers and wiped at his mouth and his nose and his eyes. Hurriedly, I opened my water bottle and drizzled water over his face. He sputtered and tried to fight me off, but he could barely lift a hand. I broke out a new surgical mask from my kit and placed it over his mouth and nose. He muttered something I couldn't quite catch, but after a few seconds, he nodded and fitted the strap himself.

His breathing slowed, punctuated occasionally with bad fits of coughing. Eventually, he could talk again. He couldn't get up, though. He said he couldn't climb another step.

"We're almost there," I told him. "Two thirds of the way." But he just shook his head.

We agreed—mostly I offered and he just nodded—that I would leave him there and keep going. I would try to reach the main water cutoff by myself.

If the climb had been bad before, it was horrific alone. I had only half the light I'd been used to. I had no one else to help keep the pace, and I kept rushing up flights of stairs—only to have to stop with a stitch in my side, unable to move for whole minutes. Then I tripped over a rhizomorph and slid down five steps, my chin bouncing painfully as I grabbed for the handrail.

When I'd recovered my footing, I speared the tendril with my light. It was thick—as thick as my arm—and it lay right across the steps. If Czanek had encountered it first, there's no doubt in my mind he would have tripped, too, and that he wouldn't have been able to stop himself as quickly as I did. He might have broken his neck. I lifted my light higher and sighed in unhappiness. The thick rhizomorph was just the first in a larger network. The steps above were draped with dark growth.

I climbed up another flight and watched them get thicker and more densely ramified as I rose. I shone my light up even higher and saw the source of the strange warmth and dryness in the stairwell. There was a knot up there, a mass of rhizomorphs that completely filled the stairwell. The hard, green-glowing body of the fungus lipped over the landing and slouched against the walls, completely obstructing the stairs. It left no room to squeeze past.

I closed my eyes and let my body sway for a while, horror and relief and resignation and defiance warring inside of me. I could give up now—I had an excuse. Then I turned around and headed back down to Czanek.

I woke him up and explained what had happened.

"We cut through it, then," he said, producing a knife from the utility belt at his waist. "We don't just give up."

I shook my head. "There's no way to tell the size of the mass up there. It could be dozens of feet through."

His eyes wanted to surrender. To die even. But his mouth kept moving. "Okay," he said. "Okay. I may not know shit about anything according to you, Professor, but I do know the law. I know fire codes, and I know this building has to have two exits. There has to be another stairwell."

He was right about that. I looked at the schematics and found the twin to our stairwell. It sat on the opposite side of the elevator shaft, maybe fifty feet away. "We'll have to cross through an entire floor of offices," I pointed out.

"So what?"

"So the offices will be full of people. People who, no doubt, have already been parasitized."

He grimaced at me, barely able to keep his eyes open. Then he pushed himself up to a standing posture and drew his pistol. "I guess that's true," he said. "You want to stop now, just stop here and wait to die?"

"Kinda."

Before we could discuss it further, he pushed open the fire door that led into the office space of the fifty-first floor. He stepped through, and I raised my flashlight to follow him, wishing I had a weapon of my own, wishing he wasn't so damned gung-ho. I had no idea what we would find on the other side—what kind of ambush might be waiting for us. I know I was not expecting what I found: a brightly-lit, busy little suite of offices full of happy people busy at their daily work.

*   *   *   *   *

A coffee cup on a desk near me had become the home of a cluster of mushrooms. More sprouted from every recycling bin and trashcan. They grew downward from the acoustic ceiling tile and around the edges of the windows.

Otherwise, very little had changed in the fifty-first floor of the Tillinghast. Fuzzy-walled cubicles made a labyrinth of the space while fluorescent tubes buzzed in the ceiling. Workers at their desks chatted away on their telephones, sent and received emails, made endless photocopies, shuffled paper from inboxes to outboxes, then shredded the contents of the outboxes.

None of them looked up as we entered. A businessman in a college sweatshirt had his feet up on his desk. He was talking steadily and in low tones into the handsfree set of his cell phone while typing something on his computer. Most of his face was green with foxfire.

Czanek leveled his weapon right at the man's forehead and shouted for him to get up and keep his hands visible.

The businessman raised one finger, as if asking for a moment to finish his call. His laser printer rattled out page after page of whatever it was he was typing. The paper filled up its hopper and then spooled onto the floor. I picked up a sheet at random and read:

```
didn't hurt. it just felt like my body kind of
cramped up for a moment and then relaxed, and
when it was done I wasn't in control anymore. I
didn't even know what was happening. it didn't
```

It went on like that, page after page after page. I looked at the man's shoes again where they rested up on the desk. Hundreds of thin white hyphae secured the feet in place like cobwebs holding him down. A twisting black tendril ran up under his pants cuff.

Czanek cocked his weapon. I thought he might actually shoot the man. I got his attention silently and shook my head.

They weren't attacking us. I wanted that to be a good sign. I figured that the shooters in the lobby were the defensive organs of the fungus. These office workers must be serving some other purpose.

We pushed through the office, weaving our way around cubicles where young men and women worked tirelessly at computers and phones. In the aisles between cubicles, printers chugged along without pause, generating ream after ream of densely printed paper. A few more samples, like this from a secretary in a black sweater and tweed skirt:

```
should be angry but where I am now there just
aren't a lot of emotions. It's quiet and dark and
I feel like I'm waiting to be in control again,
though I know that isn't very likely now that
```

Or take the following, which a mailroom clerk handed to me, scrawled on the back of an envelope in black sharpie:

> I pray my family will be okay. They'll miss me but if I went to them now they'd be absorbed and part of this thing too. At least then they'd never die. Or are we already dead, and this is hell?

There was more—volumes more of it. Whenever we heard one of the workers talking on the phone, it was the same thing. I was mystified as to what all this memoir writing was for, as to how it could serve the fungus. It was Czanek who explained it to me, finally.

"It's like the trees that grow fruit in the middle of winter. It's the only thing they have left of themselves."

I was so startled by the revelation that I barely noticed when Czanek tried to pull a young woman out of her rolling chair. She was a petite woman, maybe a hundred and ten pounds, and she didn't fight him at all, but he grunted as he heaved and heaved. He was fighting the rhizomorph that ran up her stockinged leg, and when it finally snapped, he tumbled to the floor underneath her.

"Come on, lady," he said, "help me out here," but she couldn't answer. The black tendril curled and twisted around her leg, and she sprawled across him in one last, spasmodic jerk.

"Oh, Jesus," he huffed, and tried to get up. Her body shifted lifelessly like so much meat on top of him. Finally he managed to roll out from under her. "Come on, lady," he said again.

The skin of her arms glowed a cold green. Parts of it had sloughed off, revealing a creamy white mycelium underneath. She wasn't breathing. There was no doubt in my mind. She was dead—another victim of the white rot.

"Mike," I said quietly, "we can't help them. It's too late."

His eyes met mine, and we stared hard at each other. Finally, he lowered his gaze and nodded. "I guess so."

We both turned then because we'd seen something moving up behind us. The workers had stopped working. They advanced on us, mindless zombies, shuffling forward on legs that gave off an eerie light. Their rhizomorphs trailed behind them like dark umbilical cords.

Czanek raised his weapon. "Stop now, and—"

He didn't get to finish the command. A woman in custodian's overalls had a pot of boiling coffee in her hand. She threw the scalding liquid right in Czanek's face. He went down howling, his gun waving in the air. He couldn't see to shoot.

"Goddammit! Professor, get out of here! Get to the other stairwell!"

What choice did I have? I could hardly defend him against that mob. I ran away.

*   *   *   *   *

There is very little left to tell. I could describe how I mostly ran up the remaining twenty-four flights of stairs. The soreness in my leg muscles was forgotten, thanks to an influx of adrenaline and endorphins. The seventy-fifth floor was an observation deck, and while it wasn't deserted, its inhabitants ignored me, too busy staring out the windows and talking on their cell phones.

I found the janitor's closet easily enough. I found the main water shutoff valve. I was expecting an enormous brass wheel valve, but it was all electronic; I only had to turn a key to shut off the Tillinghast's water supply. It was hard to tell if I'd achieved anything. The mother mass of the fungus didn't scream, nor did any of the countless mushrooms on the observation deck wither while I watched. Fungus is the perfect survivor, and it takes a long time for it to die.

What would happen to all the people in the building I didn't care to think about. They would die, but I didn't want to wonder how much of their minds were left and how much they would feel their internal disintegration. I had done the best I could for them—the *only* thing I could do for them.

As for me, there was nothing I could do. I couldn't go back down the stairs to the lobby. The shooters were still down there. I couldn't signal the outside world because Czanek still had my cell phone. I was trapped.

I wasn't necessarily doomed, though. I wouldn't starve to death, at least. The honey mushroom is unpalatable, but it is edible. I figured I could live up there long enough to outlast the mother mass. It might be days before the fungus finally dried up and withered away, but what choice did I have?

To stave off boredom, I decided to investigate the two-story faux step pyramid on the Tillinghast's roof. It was supposed to be a marvel of Art Deco design. I had nothing else to do, which made it a must-see.

A separate spiral staircase ascended to the pyramid, lined with big plate-glass windows. I couldn't see much through them. A weird brown haze blew in front of the windows and obscured the view.

At the top of the stairs, the pyramid began, a precarious structure of perforated aluminum that rattled in the wind. I had to climb over a very large rhizomorph to get inside. Beyond this barrier lay something truly horrible. I saw the mother mass itself, a twisting, globular snarl of thick reddish-brown tendrils twenty feet in diameter. It squatted on top of the building, lit here and there in round speckles by the sun coming in through the perforations in the pyramid's sides. Ridges of thickly grown mushrooms crested the mass, standing up like wild hair, while a sickly green radiation shimmered over its surface.

I began to turn away in disgust—then realized I wasn't alone in the pyramid. A window washer was climbing along the side of the mother mass, bent over, picking mushrooms off the rugose surface and shoving them in his pockets. I heard a tearing, grinding noise, and I rushed around the side of the mass to find his partner. He had an industrial-sized paper shredder set up next to one of the holes in the pyramid, positioned so that the shredder's output would be carried over Arkham's rooftops. As I watched in horror, he pulled the stem off of a mushroom and dropped the crown into the teeth of the machine. It snarled and choked and then spat out a coarse brown powder that curled and danced away on the wind. When that was done, he took another mushroom from his pocket and started again.

I knocked him aside and pushed over the shredder, but I knew I was too late. How many mushroom crowns had the two of them already ground up and distributed? How many spores had there been in the gills of those crowns?

The Tillinghast's fungus was already dying when I stared out through that slit and watched the cloud of spores hover on the cool air. I had cut off the water supply. I had stopped the possessed window washers, and they didn't attack me.

It didn't matter. The mother mass would take root and grow again in buildings all over the city. Like mushrooms after the rain, they would sprout with new life.

Fungus, after all, is the ultimate survivor.

THE ABBOT AND THE DRAGON

DAVID DUNWOODY

Ben's best friend Jonathan died just before sunrise. As the village pastor read a prayer over him, Jonathan stirred. Ben, kneeling beside him, looked into his friend's eyes and saw nothing. Then Jonathan seized Ben's hand in his teeth, tearing all the skin from the thumb before he was wrestled away and set aflame.

"What will you do, Ben?" his mother asked, wringing her hands.

"I'm infected," Ben replied in a flat tone. "I will leave and go to the wasteland to die."

His mother saw him off at noon. She stood alone.

With him, Ben took a knapsack filled only with bread. The village couldn't spare any water for a doomed boy. He chewed reeds of grass to keep his lips moist, but early into the first day, fatigue started to overtake him. Ben wasn't sure if it was the afternoon heat or the infection. He studied his hand as he walked, to see if its corruption was perceptible to the naked eye.

Ben slept under an outcropping of rock and listened for dragons. He had never seen one in person, but drawings circulated around the village with tales of the monsters in the wasteland. Beyond the walls surrounding the village's hovels, they roamed, half-blind horrors, their very blood churning with the plague that now writhed in Ben's claw of a hand. He also knew that others who had gone into self-imposed exile would be nearby, hungering even for his diseased meat.

*　　*　　*　　*　　*

He caught a small lizard creeping past his sleeping form, on its way to sun itself atop the rock. He crushed it with a ferocity that surprised him and squeezed its blood into his parched mouth. Then he threw up.

The bread was hard, difficult to eat, but he forced dry mouthfuls down to his aching belly. Eyeing the lizard again, he began gathering sticks for a fire.

"Child," came a bold voice. Overhead on the rock stood a gaunt older man dressed in tatters.

"What do you want?" Ben asked.

"I come only to give," the man answered. "I give you release." He fell upon the boy, raising an ivory club.

Ben threw him off and ran. He didn't know in which direction. It didn't matter as long as he escaped the man who was surely a deadsmith: a wanderer commissioned to kill the infected before they transformed. Ben dreaded the change, but dreaded more the thought of dying at the hands of another man. It wasn't the way of civilized people.

Reaching a gnarled cluster of trees, he scrambled up into their midst, grateful for his small size.

The deadsmith peered at him through the branches. "Your mother sent me," he said. "She doesn't want you to suffer." The club swung by his feet, resembling a great leg-bone. The man's knuckles were as white as the weapon they held.

Ben didn't believe his explanation. He tried to imagine the skeletal deadsmith wandering into his modest village, tried to imagine his mother's eyes lighting on that club with a feeling other than sheer revulsion. It wasn't possible. "Leave me alone," he pleaded, twigs scraping his back, rivulets of sweat stinging his eyes. "Tell her you killed me. I'll give you my knapsack as proof. She will pay you well, I promise."

"A mother always knows," the deadsmith said. He walked around the trees, swinging the club at his side. He paced for hours while the sun gnawed at Ben and bits of tree bark peppered his hunched body.

When night fell and all was dark, the deadsmith lit a small fire outside the trees. He sat to warm his hands and wait.

Reaching downward with his foot, Ben tested a lower branch. He gritted his teeth and wormed his way down, freezing every time he made the slightest noise. An hour later, he emerged from the edge of the trees opposite the deadsmith, limbs threatening to give out from beneath him. He inched along on his hands and knees throughout most the night.

*   *   *   *   *

City ruins dotted the wasteland. The cities were much larger and built better than his home; perhaps that was why they appealed most to the dragons. Ben hid himself in the shadow of a crumbling tower and dug the soft centers from his bread before discarding the crusts. He prayed that he would find food here.

Starving as he was, clinging to hope, he didn't sense the deadsmith until the man was just across the street, crouched beside his club, which seemed more and more to be a bone.

The deadsmith opened his mouth to speak, to call the boy. But a low rumble, echoing off the sides of the buildings, startled him.

With a quiet, nightmarish gait, the dragon lumbered around the corner of a tower on two hind legs and sniffed at the dirt. Its weak, shuffling steps moved the earth, and a stench of rot wafted across the road. Around the deadsmith's feet, particles of dirt danced. His limbs trembled, both from the quake and from the thundering of his own heart.

Despite his terror, wonder tickled Ben's imagination. Standing as tall as two men, the dragon had scales that were stained orange and red in splotches, dull and armorlike; it possessed small, dark eyes unlike the fiery orbs of children's scribblings; over those eyes, great crests jutted like horns, flanking a knobbed pate. Fatty haunches sagged as the dragon nosed the earth. With each breath, it billowed the dust and exhaled the plague that had infected mankind. These things had once roamed and hunted in great packs, it was said, venom-like spittle spilling from hungry jaws. Even with a feeble, solitary dragon like this one—one said to have passed from life into death—its constitution still seethed with death for men.

Ben, infected, did not feel kindred to the creature; it would eat him if given the chance. Fortunately, its gaze settled upon the deadsmith. The man turned and used his club to shield his eyes from the sun.

The dragon came at him then, fissures opening in its leathery skin like a thousand screaming mouths; a dark rope of gore trailed between the rotten monster's legs and snarled around its tail. The deadsmith turned his club over and thrust its sharp bottom forward.

The dragon's body opened like an overripe fruit. It swayed, uttered something obscene from its bowels, and fell onto the deadsmith with a heavy splash. Ben's vision shook violently for a moment, then all was still.

He ran, every detail of the terrible dragon burned into his mind. He ran, and he remembered the rhyme sang around the bonfires of his village.

S.BLUNDELL

All the kingdoms forged in flesh
A seat above the Lord.
O'er Heaven angels' horns did sound
But 'twas the Devil who cut them down
And cursed them by his sword.

For lay the serpent in the west
To plot against the dawn.
O'er Heaven reached the arms of men
But blind were they to doors opened
Below—dragons, dragons,
Thus shielded from the sun!

So was told the fall of Man and the rise of the plague.

Ben's parents and their parents before them had not known a world without plague. Perhaps there had never been such a thing. Ben studied the ruins as he climbed through their craters and tunnels. Occasionally, he paused to listen for the deadsmith's pattering feet, but heard only silence. Behind fallen stones, the long necks and curled claws of dragons proved to be only encroaching shadows and dead trees.

A tower at the city's center was remarkably intact. Ben pushed aside the debris barricading the doors and entered.

A pile of soiled rags rose in the doorway with a shrill cry. Ben threw out his arms, only to have them caught by the flailing thing. A hood fell back, revealing a face that was vaguely human—

Infected! Ben's mind screamed.

"Child, child," the thing croaked, "you're safe here!"

Ben stopped struggling, and the man released him to reinforce the doors. He spoke rapidly as if his words had been bottled up for a lifetime. "They don't come here. The dragons. This place is still holy." He was as short as Ben, though thinner, and his hands danced in the shadows. He pointed to a word stitched onto his torn robe: *Abbot*. "I have no food, but I have water. You look exhausted. I have beds."

"I, I, I..." It occurred to Ben that the abbot was alone here.

The sun cut through grime-streaked windows to light a stairwell beyond the doorway. The abbot supported Ben as they climbed.

"Abbot?" Ben said quickly. "I must tell you something." He stopped on a landing and held out his wounded thumb.

The abbot's eyes lit up—not from terror or revulsion, but from wonder, the same way Ben had stared at the dragon.

"Child," spoke the abbot, clasping the bloodied hand in his own, "I minister to the sick. You are welcome here." He pushed open a heavy door. "What is the beast's venom but the last step toward humility and salvation? The body suffers and dies and rises again— but not the spirit. You must free yourself from this notion that you are bound to your flesh. Surely such thinking brought this plague upon us." Though Ben found him difficult to understand, the man spoke with an air of authority.

Down a hall lined with empty rooms, the abbot led him to a washbasin. The water stung, but it was cold, unlike anything he had ever felt. He finally relaxed his aching limbs and loosened his tongue. "Abbot, are they angels?" The man frowned, so Ben pointed to the emblem stitched on his robe, two serpents intertwined around a staff. "Did the Lord send them, as a judgment?"

The abbot fingered the emblem anxiously. "Did He send them? He made the makers of all things. Are they angels? No, but..." He seemed to be puzzling over the question. "We aren't meant to know all the Lord's mysteries while in this flesh."

The door to the stairwell clanged loudly. The deadsmith dragged his bloody club into the hall.

Ben stood behind the abbot. "He wants to kill me," he breathed.

"Sir!" the abbot shouted. "This is a holy place!"

One step closer.

"No harm shall come to the child here."

The club knocked against stone.

"His life is God's to—"

Without a word, the deadsmith swung.

The abbot's head fell at his own feet, still sputtering platitudes. Ben ran down the hall with no idea of what lay ahead. The blood-encrusted deadsmith allowed his bone hammer to mark his slow pursuit: *thunk, thunk, thunk.* The shadows ahead materialized into steel doors. Ben ran into them with all his might and bounced back like an insect.

The deadsmith was not expecting the boy to ricochet and was bowled over with a grunt. Ben became entangled in the man's legs. The deadsmith cried something as they struggled: "You have no life left..." He plunged the club's tapered end through Ben's hand.

Ben tugged at the stuck appendage. He registered pain, but was oddly detached from the feeling. Indeed, it wasn't so much a feeling as the dull recitation of neurons that would soon lack purpose. His body was dying. He pulled his hand from the club with a sucking sound and looked through the meaty hole.

The world groaned and rumbled in his head, and the deadsmith glanced over his shoulder as the dragon hauled its foul ruin into the hallway. It hunched over and squeezed through the door, flaying scales from its shoulders and skull. Teeth gnashed beneath the tatters. One eye rolled like a madman's, and the other was missing, as was the flesh around the gaping socket.

But it pulled itself along on the deadsmith's scent, its nostrils flaring, and the claws of the sightless thing found purchase in the man's back.

Ben retreated to the steel doors. Though turned away from the dragon, he was unable to shut out the rude din of its feeding. He pawed at the wall, felt a button depress; he fell through the doors, and they closed behind him.

Lying in darkness, he felt the floor, the very room, begin to descend. Hell would have him now, it seemed, maybe a gesture of mercy from the Devil.

The room shuddered and stopped.

The doors opened.

Ben saw a new corridor, brightly lit, but not by torches; glassy blue-white stones laid into the ceiling revealed every detail. He shielded his eyes with his good hand and walked. Somewhere, a voice was speaking.

In a room at the end of the corridor, also garishly lit, a face stared at Ben. It was only an image, in some sort of mirror on the wall. It was a man, dressed in the abbot's robes—but it wasn't the abbot. And the robes were a spotless white.

"This is project leader Dan Abbot. I'm making this recording because—I don't know—because we don't know what will be left, but if there are survivors, they deserve to hear this.

"In hindsight, it was nothing but hubris, the rapture of playing God, but at the time we did have a rationale for bringing them back. We wanted to know what ended their time on Earth, perhaps to extend our own. It wasn't until Phase Four, the Cretaceous series, that we found out what killed them. Oh, Christ"—A word Ben had heard, but whose meaning he was unfamiliar with—"we found out. Some anomaly in their blood. The infected die and the dead rise again.

"They were unstoppable. Now the infection has spread to us. Maybe this all was meant to occur. Maybe we as a species reached our peak, and there at the summit waited this plague, as it always has. But there's no comfort in that. Especially for men who thought they'd beaten God."

The image flickered, then the man reappeared and started his speech over. Ben sat cross-legged on the floor, his senses dwindling, and he thought of the old rhyme. It still made no sense.

He heard not the doors opening down the corridor, nor the slow, heavy approach of his devourer.

THE WRANGLERS

ERIC S. BROWN

Red watched the man race across the field as fast as his legs would carry him. The man's breath came in ragged, exhausted gasps. Red knew what he was thinking: if he reached the trees, he might be able to lose the three wranglers on horseback. Red gave the signal, and Hole spurred on his horse in a burst of speed, blocking the man's path.

Of the three wranglers, Face was the closest to their prey. He charged at the man, swinging a lasso above his head even as Red tried to wave him off. Face threw the rope, but the man ducked at just the right moment, and the lasso overshot.

"He's too wild to take that way!" Red shouted.

Face tried to back off, but the man yelled and sprang at him in a rage.

Hole raced to put his horse between the two.

Sitting perfectly still on his horse, Red had gotten out his rifle and was taking aim at the man. He pulled the trigger, and a dart struck the target's neck from the side. The man reeled and collapsed, only a few feet from where Face sat on his horse, still too shocked to move.

The trio of wranglers converged on their fallen quarry. Hole hogtied him, making sure the ropes were tight enough to hold his jaws closed.

Face turned to Red in his saddle. "That was a little too close for comfort, boss. I thought he had me for sure."

"You're dead anyway, Face. Your sloppiness in the pen last week saw to that. All we just did was buy you a little more time at best." Red looked up at the sun, setting behind the mountains. "Let's just get him in the pen with the others before it gets dark."

Face nodded. He and Hole loaded the man onto a horse, and they all headed back to the ranch.

*   *   *   *   *

Red sat by the campfire, puffing on a cigarette. It was a hollow habit since the nicotine had no effect on him. He didn't normally try to breathe except when the old addiction demanded the feel of something warm in his lungs.

Hole and Face approached, on their way from locking down the cattle for the night.

When Red first got into the cattle business, he'd had dozens of "hands" to help him breed the beasts and transport them to the markets. Now it was just the three of them. Everyone wanted a cushy office job nowadays, or to be part of the newly-formed government. No one wanted to get their hands dirty making sure people had food to eat, even though the cattle sold for twenty times the price it used to. It just wasn't glamorous, Red supposed. He had to admit that working with the cattle was dangerous, but he loved it all the same.

Hole and Face joined him at the fire. He could see from the flickering light that Face's companions were working overtime this evening. About a week back, one of the cattle had bitten Face and had given him a disease most people called "the rot." The maggots in Face's flesh practically swam over his nose and lips.

Red was no doctor, but he understood enough about the rot to know that, once it got in your system, it took away or broke down the force that kept you from decaying after you became one of the undead. The disease didn't kill instantly. Instead, it ate you alive, inside and out, and left you open to natural predators, like maggots and worms, until you became nothing but rotting goop.

Some folks figured the rot was caused by an enzyme or a virus in the spit of live humans. Either way it meant a slow painful death if you were bitten. There was no cure. It was just a matter of time until Face would start losing limbs to the disease.

Red grunted, wondering how the hell he would replace Face. The man was a damn good wrangler.

Hole broke the silence. A series of guttural hisses came out of the deep wound that had once been his mouth. To anyone else, they would have been incoherent noises, but Red and Face had worked with Hole a long time and knew what he meant.

Red glared at him, shaking his head. "The cattle's always restless, Hole. I'm sure it's nothing."

"I don't know, boss," Face added, flinging a worm into the fire as his lips moved. "I think putting that wild one in with the others was a bad idea. It's like he's talking to them, riling them up somehow. I could have sworn I heard him yell actual words when he attacked me today."

Red bothered to sigh. "He's wild. What did you expect him to do? Sit around waiting on the butcher's axe like the others?"

"I'm just saying maybe we should put him down is all. We got a pretty decent herd this year anyway."

"Cattle don't talk. That's crazy shit. They have been inbred so much over the years there ain't nothing left in their heads. This new one ain't any different, even if he wasn't raised in the pens. Humans just don't have any fight left anymore." Red saw that Face was far from convinced and ground his cigarette out in the dirt. "Fine. You want to put him down, let's do it." Red picked up the Winchester lying beside him.

"You mean right now?" Face sputtered, sending more worms flying.

Red scowled at him.

Face nodded. "Okay, but like I told you: they're all worked up already. We're going to have to get him out of the pen first, or they might start tearing each other apart. Lord knows how many we could lose if that happened."

The trio made their way to the pen, and Hole readied a lasso as they went. They reached the massive fence, and Hole climbed up the small walkway above the gate to spot the new member of the herd in the starlight. Red could hear the wrangler hissing his complaints before he found his target and started slinging the lasso above his head. Hole snagged the newcomer on the first try. Face leapt up to help him pull the rope. "Now!" he shouted, and Red opened the gate.

A naked, long-haired man caked with dirt and grime charged at him. Face snared the man around the neck with the loop of a handling pole and fought to control the animal as Red slammed the pen's gate.

The human escaped the handling pole as Face jerked back, lost his balance, and careened over the fence. Hole grabbed for him, but wasn't fast enough. Face thumped to the pen's floor, and the cattle poured over him in a rage. As they ripped him apart, the wind carried his screams into the night.

Red had his own problems. The naked man charged him again and knocked them both to the ground. They wrestled in the dirt, clawing and punching at each other—the man sank his teeth into Red's arm. Then his skull exploded, spraying blood and brain matter. Red collapsed on his back as the man's corpse rolled off him.

Winchester in hands, Hole raced to his boss' side. Red looked up at him. "Shit," he muttered, examining the teeth marks in his gray flesh. "I screwed up this time, didn't I, Hole?"

Hole said nothing, a sad expression on his face.

"Hole, I want you to end it for me."

Hole shook his head, lowering the weapon.

"Dammit, Hole! He bit me. I can feel it. I got the rot just like Face had. Don't make me waste away until you can scoop me up off the pavement."

Hole lifted the rifle, hesitated, and then lowered it again.

"The business is yours now, okay? Just do it already!"

Finally, Hole nodded and braced the rifle against his shoulder. He hissed something, and Red said, "I know."

The shot echoed off the sides of the pen as the humans howled and screamed inside its walls.

Casual Friday

MATTHEW SHEPHERD

Derek's nose hurt.

It was the Vicks. It was blocking the smell, sort of, but after several days of using it, he was sure it was disintegrating his septum. He'd read about it on the Internet, all these people with no cartilage in their nose because of Vicks, because of the stench.

Derek touched his nose. It felt firm. Maybe a bit wobbly. He gently probed the inside of his nose with his little finger and yelped as he pulled it back out, a bit of blood on the tip. The stinging made him sneeze.

"You okay, Derek?" Todd's voice was gravelly and a bit choked. Derek didn't turn around. He knew Todd would be swivelled in his chair, facing him from the opposite cubicle, his head lolling to the side like it always did. Todd's voice whined on. "You got a cold, Derr-ek?" The smell got worse when Todd talked, his voice pushing the stench right across the cubicles, past the VapoRub. He imagined death, wafting on Todd's breath, a little foul cloud seeping up through his nostrils.

"Fuck off," Derek muttered, looking at his computer screen. A flashing Biocall reminder blinked down by the time clock, but he ignored it and kept punching in numbers; there was a mountain of work in his inbox. His fingerless gloves were slowing his typing down, but if he took them off, his hands would get so cold he wouldn't be able to type at all. He sneezed again.

"Summer colds are the *worst*," Todd droned on. "Hey, your Biocall thingy is blinking. Better take your Biocall, or you'll get sick.

Or sicker. I remember a couple years ago, before my accident, I got this cold that lasted like three months. Like, all summer. It was so nice outside and I had a cold. Summer colds are the worst. Aren't they the worst?"

Pushing back from his desk, Derek spun in his chair and looked at Todd. Todd's unblinking eyes, Todd's piano-key tie dangling from Todd's scrawny broken neck, Todd's insipid smile, teeth showing yellow through the spreading rotten hole on Todd's cheek. "Shut the fuck up, Todd. If I have a cold it's because it's fucking freezing in here." Derek thumped his chest, covered in a thick sweater, and he pushed his wool hat back a bit. "And it's freezing in here and I'm losing the cartilage in my nose because of you fucking *shamblers*."

Todd's eyes widened in shock. The right one had some sort of spreading cataract thing; it was glassy and bloodshot at the same time, while the left one still gleamed with human intelligence. "Mr. Claiiiirborne," Todd bleated, "Derek is using hate language."

"Fffffffffffffuck." Derek spun back around and started punching numbers into the computer. This would be the third warning, if Clairborne followed up on it, third warning and a week's suspension, and he needed the money. The smell was making his head pound; the pain in his nose was like a tendril squeezing his brain. The government said the Animant virus wasn't airborne, but Derek could feel it in the air. The office was infected. The *world* was infected.

Inevitably, Clairborne turned up. "Derek, my office." He looked tired: bags under his eyes, a slouch in his heavy step. His eyes slid over to Derek's monitor. "And your Biocall reminder is flashing. Have you taken it?"

Derek shrugged and opened his desk drawer, removing one of the foil-wrapped pre-loaded Biocall syringes. Rolling up his sleeve, he found a clear space in the squirrel-tracks of old puncture sites and jabbed the needle in, wincing as he pressed the plunger.

"Biocall's no joke," Clairborne said dully. "Can't have you dying on us." He turned, and for a moment Derek thought he'd forgotten, but Clairborne's hand slowly motioned him on. "Office, Derek."

Derek followed him as he shuffled—human-shuffled, not the drag-legged gait of the shamblers—back to his small office near the elevator. Clairborne closed the door behind Derek and crossed to the far side of a small pre-fab desk. A small globe sat on the corner of his desk, shaking slightly on its pivot as Clairborne eased himself into his chair.

"*Differently animated*, Derek," Clairborne said quietly. "Not 'shamblers.' How can I get that through to you?" He wasn't wearing a sweater like Derek, but a Mr. Rogers-style cardigan stretched around his oversized torso, and instead of a wool winter cap like most staff members, he had an Irish tweed cap perched on his broad head. A daub of Vicks made his upper lip shine. "You can't call them 'shamblers.' You can't call them 'deadies' or 'brain-eaters' or 'rotguts' or 'corpsicles.' *Differently animated.*"

"Mr. Clairborne," Derek said, leaning forward in his chair. The chair squeaked. "Mr. Clairborne, I'm sitting out there with a f—a freaking *sweater* on, in *June,* with this stuff disintegrating my *nose.* You're in—all respect, sir, but you're in your office here, you don't have to smell them all day, you don't have to hear the *noises* they make. Sometimes Raines just *groans*, sir. He just lets out this fu— freaking *moan* that makes me feel like my guts are going to freeze in my belly. He's all the way across the room, and I can hear him. How come you don't talk to him about the noise, huh? How come it's always *me*?"

Clairborne rubbed his eyes. "The smell's gotten into the air conditioning, Derek. I can smell them just as much as you can. I'm as cold as you are. But the cold keeps them from rotting, from spreading disease. There'd be an epidemic in here if we didn't keep the office at forty degrees Farenheit. The Biocall can kill whatever low-level diseases the slow decay produces, but if they began to really rot, we'd all just drop dead in our tracks."

"But—" Derek began.

"I need to keep this department running," Clairborne said, pushing a pencil across his desktop. "I'm... there's a lot of pressure coming down. From the top." He looked into Derek's face, and his eyes were hollow, deprived of both sleep and success. "I can't take another one of those strikes, the building surrounded by *them*, waving signs, with that smell..." His head drooped for a second, then rose again. He looked strangely fragile despite his huge frame. "We're all just getting by here, Derek, and you calling them 'shamblers' doesn't help. Doesn't help at all."

There was a slight scraping sound somewhere in the room, and Derek realized it was his teeth grinding. The thumping he heard was his right foot, tapping the floor as his leg twitched like a spastic jackrabbit. "This isn't *fair*," he said, hating the whine in his own voice. He sounded like the kind of kid he used to beat up at school.

"As you know, Derek, we offer sensitivity training—" Clairborne began. Derek's head jerked up from his examination of his leg, and Clairborne drew back when he saw his expression. "—which is optional," Clairborne finished. "But in your case, I think it might help you adjust."

"I don't need to 'adjust,'" Derek said. "I need those *things* out of my department. I need to work in room fuc—freaking temperature. Those things are... my cartilage is being destroyed." Derek poked his nose. "My *cartilage* is being destroyed. Yours is too. Soon we're not going to have noses." He pointed at the door. "They're taking our noses. Are you just going to sit there and let them *take our noses?*"

Clairborne blinked. A "ding" echoed from his computer, and he slowly peeled the foil off a Biocall syringe from a dirty mug on his desk and stabbed his bicep. Clairborne looked down at the syringe for a second, then pushed the plunger. "Maybe you need some personal days," he said.

"Screw it." Derek left the cramped office, left Clairborne with the syringe dangling out of his arm, and slammed the door behind him. "Screw it," he said again, crossing the frigid office. "Screw it," he said, slouching in his chair and pecking at the keyboard. "Screw it."

"Screw what?" Todd's voice, choked and obsequious.

"I'm not talking to you," Derek said. He glanced at the clock. Ten a.m. Break soon, and he could step out of the building, take the sweater off for a few minutes, enjoy the sunshine and relatively fresh air. Then push through to lunch, then... God. How the hell could he make it through the rest of the day? And then Friday? And after the weekend, the week after that and the week after that and—

Coffee.

He spun around and bounded out of his chair, ignoring Todd's glaring cataract, stalking across the room to the coffee table. The pot was empty, no surprise, so Derek filled it at the water cooler, poured the water into the machine, took out the old filter and grounds, put in a new filter and—

—an empty aluminium can.

"Hey, Singh," Derek said, his voice shaking a bit. "There's no goddamn coffee."

"No money in the coffee fund," Singh said without turning around, "no coffee."

Derek looked in the coffee fund jar. It was, indeed, empty. "Fucking shamblers," Derek said out loud.

"Don't call us shamblers." Hughes, a tall gangly man with a gash bisecting the right side of his face, stood up and walked from his cubicle, a full head taller than Derek. Hughes tapped his own chest with a grotty finger, the nail yellowed and starting to pull free of gray flesh. "We have *feelings*."

"What happened to the coffee fund?" Derek said, gesturing at the empty jar. "You—you *people* never contribute to the coffee fund. Now we don't have coffee. I want coffee."

"We don't *drink* coffee," said a pudgy dead woman named Deborah or Barbara or something. She walked over, her hair combed to cover a huge missing patch of scalp and skull. "Why should we contribute to the coffee fund when we don't even drink coffee?"

"I contribute to the coffee fund, but I don't drink coffee," Singh said, again not turning from his computer, his fingers a blur as he processed another report. Derek felt a quick flush of warmth. He normally didn't like Singh: his cute little accent, his holier-than-thou diligence. But maybe the kid was all right.

"See?" Derek said. "*Living* people contribute to the coffee fund. Even if they *don't* drink coffee."

"But Singh drinks tea, so he uses the machine for hot water," Deborah-or-Barbara insisted. "We don't drink anything. At least Singh is using the machine."

"Yeah," Hughes said. "And besides, you're supposed to contribute to the coffee fund when you have a coffee. So the number of people contributing doesn't make a difference, just the number of people drinking coffee and not putting their quarter in the jar."

Derek tried to back away from Hughes and the dead woman, but the coffee table was behind him. The smell was getting to him, making him dizzy. "This place was better before they hired you," he said. "At least it was warm. At least it didn't goddamn *stink*."

"If it isn't kept real cold in here, you're gonna get a whole lot sicker, and it's going to stink a whole lot worse," Todd said amiably, wandering over to join the conversation.

"We can't smell," Deborah-or-Barbara said helpfully. "But I can see how it might be awful for you. I'm going to get you one of those plug-in things tomorrow. Or I think I have some potpourri at home. Would that help? It's not like I'm using it." She gurgled something that should have been a laugh, and tossed her hair. Derek saw a bit of wet red flesh under her comb-over and felt his stomach flip.

"I'm glad that's settled," Todd said brightly, and walked away. Hughes glared at Derek then went back to his desk, and Deborah-or-Barbara smiled before she left.

Derek took a step over to Singh's cubicle and leaned in conspiratorially. "It's the fucking government," he muttered. "Goddamn equality legislation. Those things shouldn't be working with us. They should be in camps, they should have their own factories or something. They don't belong with humans."

Singh kept typing. "It's economics," he said blandly. "The company doesn't give a wet shit about whether you're happy. Returners will work for one-third what a human labourer demands. They don't need to eat much, they don't need medicine, they don't take sick days, and they never sleep. They're a bargain at the price. Equality laws let us keep *our* jobs, not the other way around."

"You've got to be kidding me," Derek said.

"I'm not," Singh said, finally turning from his monitor. He had two black plugs in his nose. "If it weren't for the equality laws, we'd be on the street. You know how much the company spends on Biocall? If it were up to them, this place would be all deadies, all the time."

"What the fuck is in your nose?" Derek asked.

"Incense cones. I know all you guys like Vicks, but that shit will rot the cartilage right out of your nose."

Clairborne was chugging toward Derek with a sullen, flat step. "What's this about you harassing other staff members about the coffee fund?" he asked.

"They're not contributing," Derek said. "It's not fair."

"Watch it," Hughes said from his cubicle.

"It's the fucking *principle*, you stinking corpse," Derek snapped at him, then looked at Clairborne, painfully aware of the large man.

"Go home," Clairborne said. Derek opened his mouth, and Clairborne held up a hushing hand. "Just take the afternoon off.

Tomorrow's Friday. If you need tomorrow too, you just let me know, and then you've got the weekend to think about this. Okay?"

"This..." Derek began. "This is so..." He turned on his heel and stalked into the elevator, wishing there was some way to slam an elevator door. He mashed his thumb on the DOOR CLOSE button and watched the elevator display count down. Down, and down, and down.

It was a nice enough day for early June, sun shining and birds chirping somewhere in the ambiguous distance. Derek hopped on the bus—*human driver, human passengers, an oasis of sanity*, he thought—and went back to his house, a small suburban bungalow that his mom had left behind when she passed on. Derek thought of her every time he went up the walk, past the weeded-over garden she'd once tended.

Through the knots of dandelions, a village sprouted: a small church, a school, a little supermarket. Towering over them was a garden gnome, a bearded Godzilla in the tiny town. Derek stooped, looking at the little village, wishing he lived in it. No shamblers. No stench.

He went into the house, stepping over a few pizza boxes in the front hall. A beer. A beer, the couch, some TV... an empty fridge. Not *empty* empty, but beerless. Derek leaned on the door, staring into the vast white emptiness, and sighed.

There was juice, or tea, but there had to be something... something to take off the edge. Derek rummaged through the cupboard above the stove, hitting on the half-bottle of cooking sherry his mother had kept up there before she died. Derek filled a tumbler, went to the living room with the glass in one hand and bottle in the other, and turned on the TV.

It was all dead. It was all afternoon talk shows, and it was Returners wall to wall—Returner guests in zero-degree studios, talking about their life after life; a news interview on the Second Leasers, a Returner religious group; a scientist talking about the mysteries of Returner physiology; a financial advisor talking about the global stock market post-Returners... Derek tossed the contents of the tumbler into his mouth, swallowed and grimaced, clicked the television off, and threw the remote at it for good measure. "They took the TV," he said to his glass. "They even took my fucking TV."

He filled the tumbler, drained it again and stared at the dead television.

He woke up when the doorbell rang. It was dark outside, which meant it was late—after nine? His tongue felt thick and fuzzy from the sherry, and his feet were oddly heavy as he stumbled to the door. The sherry bottle was lying by the couch, empty. When had he drunk the rest? He opened the door and recoiled—Todd was standing on the stoop, head drooping to the side, rotting hands extended with a gift-wrapped book in them.

"Hello, Derek," he said cheerfully.

Derek took his finger off the front stoop light switch. The last thing he needed was a better look at Todd, at the glassy eye and the horrible hole in his cheek.

"You're *stalking* me," Derek said. The stench hit him like a hammer, and he reeled back a few steps into the house, which Todd took as an invitation.

"You're funny," Todd said. "I just felt bad about how things happened at work today. I took the bus over to bring you a gift." He thrust the present at Derek, who took it and—anything to get Todd out of the house sooner—fumbled the wrapping off. A shambler stared at him from the cover, one eye missing from its socket, grinning and vaguely recognizable. *Dead Geek Walking*, the cover read.

"It's the latest Wheaton book," Todd explained. "He has so *much* to say about how our peoples can interrelate. I think if you read that, you might under*stand* how our *feelings* are the same as yours, even if our *bodies* are—"

Derek felt the pain in his nose, a budding headache from the sherry, and a sudden wrench in his mind. "I don't want your gifts, Todd. I don't want to *read* about shamblers. I don't want to *think* about shamblers. I just want some fucking privacy in my own house, okay? Now go the hell away."

"You're processing a lot of *anger*, Derek," Todd said. He was trying to look Derek in the eyes, propping his head up with one hand to compensate for his snapped neck and atrophied muscles. He took a drag-step forward. "You need to share your feelings…"

The book bounced off Todd's forehead, gouging out a small chunk of flesh with the bottom of the spine; it fell to the runner carpet in the hall. "Get out," Derek hissed. He picked up the small end table that he put his keys on, holding it legs-out like a lion tamer. "Get the *fuck* out of my house."

Todd hesitated. "Derek, I'm going to talk to Clairborne about this. I think you need *sensitivity* training."

Derek stepped forward and poked Todd with the table legs. "Get out," he repeated. "Get out, or I'll beat the shit out of you. You're trespassing."

Todd stepped backwards out the front door, standing on the stoop and grinning like an idiot. Derek set down the end table. "I'm here as a friend, Derek," Todd said. "Do you know what I think?"

Derek stepped forward to slam the door. "I don't care what you think."

"I think this is about your mother," Todd said. "I think you haven't processed your emotions from her death."

"Get off my stoop."

"I think that you resent us because we came back while your mother didn't." He spread his arms wide again. "You need to feel love, Derek. Hug me."

Derek saw red, blood pounding into his *living* brain, his *living* blood burning in his veins. "Get off my goddamn *stoop!*" He grabbed Todd's outstretched arms and swung him to the side. Todd fell back, making a quiet "awk!" as he thudded onto the garden, a thud accompanied by a strange *shlupping* noise.

Todd lay there, staring at his chest, the point of a church steeple sprouting from where his heart would be.

"Errr." Todd stumbled to his feet and began to turn in circles on the lawn, reaching around his back for the base of the model-village church. "What did you do to me?" he asked, his jaw hanging open in shock. "What... is there a *church* on my back?"

"Holy fuck." Derek felt a cold flood wash through him. The neighbours would hear this, would look out and see a shambler impaled on a church stumbling around Derek's front yard. "I just wanted to get you off my stoop," he said, stepping down, hands extended. "Look, I'll pull the church out, just don't start yelling or any—"

"*You!*" Todd hissed, pointing at Derek. His voice cascaded up into a shriek. "You *wanted* this to happen, you *hater!*"

"Todd, I just wanted you off my property," Derek said, taking another step toward him. "Let me just pull that fucking thing out, and we'll forget all this, okay? We'll just... go back to normal."

"Hater!" Todd tried to leap backwards, away from Derek, but the weight of the church unbalanced him—Todd twisted in mid-air, falling sideways back onto the garden, arms flailing. There was a hard crack, some sort of breaking noise, and Todd jerked once and was still.

Derek approached cautiously. Something red was coming through the side of Todd's head, something red with a domed tip. "Uh... Todd?" He rolled him over on his back. Todd lay atop the church, steeple sprouting out of his torso, and his head was impaled by the garden gnome. The gnome's hat ran straight through Todd's skull, its impish grin protruding just below his ear.

He looked like modern art.

"Jesus," Derek whispered. He looked up and down the street. All the houses were dark, no cars, no people in sight. Was it possible that nobody saw? "Jesus," he said again, running his hand back and forth across his head. It was an accident, but nobody would believe that. Everyone knew he hated Todd—hell, *everyone* hated Todd. But an argument at work, forced leave... nobody would ever think this was an accident.

He had to get rid of the body. Another glance around: street still quiet. He had to—his eyes fell on the large wheel-out garbage bin at the end of the driveway.

Friday was garbage day.

On garbage day, a large city truck came by, and with a huge fork, it dumped the bins into the back of the truck; it collected garbage for the whole city and dumped it *en masse* into a landfill.

Could it be that easy?

Derek ducked into the house, grabbed the area rug from the front hall, and threw it over Todd. It looked a bit weird, but at least it wasn't a body. From the kitchen, he retrieved garbage bags and duct tape from the junk drawer. Working as quickly as his shaking hands would let him—all house lights off, in the pale glow of the streetlights—Derek wrapped Todd's body in plastic, taped it around the head and ankles, dragged it over, and hoisted it into the rolling garbage bin. He threw the area rug in on top of it for good measure. The neighborhood was still quiet.

Derek's heart was a triphammer in his ears. Was that all there was to it? He tried to think things through the haze: tomorrow, the truck would dump his bin in the back, and everything would be mixed together in the landfill. Even if somebody saw the body in the landfill, there'd be no way to tell where it came from. Would there?

There was no point in staying on the street anyway. Derek ducked back into the house, got changed, and tried to sleep.

Friday morning, he was still awake. He was awake when the garbage truck came up the street. He was awake, eyes open, ears practically twitching, as the fork on the truck lifted his bin and dumped it. He was awake when absolutely nobody cried in panic, awake when the truck did not come to a screeching halt, awake when the morning continued as it had every Friday for months before.

"I don't believe it," Derek said, lying in bed in his pajamas, looking at the morning sun through his Venetian blinds. "I finally caught a break."

It was with a smile on his face that Derek brushed his teeth, with a song in his heart Derek ate his breakfast, with a spring in his step Derek caught the bus and hustled off to work. It was the thing to do: show that he was a team player, that he wasn't a "hater," certainly not a shambler-loathing maniac. And it was now an office without Todd, somewhere ever so marginally more pleasant to work. Somewhere just a little less... loathsome. A fleeting doubt crossed his mind—what if Todd had told someone where he was going? But no, Todd had no friends, even among the shamblers. Derek was probably the closest acquaintance the pathetic dead bastard had. He was better off dead. Dead again. Re-dead. Derek shook his head to clear it and stepped off the bus.

A crowd was gathered around the middle of his floor when he stepped out of the elevator, and Derek felt a surge of panic. What if they somehow *did* know? What if they were meeting to confer on what to do next? But no, somebody glanced at him and turned back to the conversation, not interested in him at all.

Derek stepped closer, hearing snippets of conversation, in the middle of the scrum of people... Clairborne, his voice sounding oddly... *choked.*

"So I was hanging there," Clairborne said, his eyes dull, a livid red rope burn around his throat, "and I came to, one of the twenty percent, and I'm thinking, 'I really didn't think this through.'"

Derek jerked back in horror. The crowd around Clairborne—all Returners, all shamblers, all reeking and rotting and stiff in their movements—laughed. Deborah-or-Barbara patted Clairborne on the back.

"How did you know you'd get lucky?" Hughes asked.

"I just wanted to end this," Clairborne said. "The uncertainty, the responsibility. I honestly didn't think I *would* come back. I just didn't... I didn't want to deal with this shit any more."

"How do you feel now?" a spindly little shambler asked, a bespectacled kid Derek had rarely seen before.

"Calmer," Clairborne said. He looked around at his audience, noticed Derek standing over by the elevator, and half-waved. "Didn't think you'd be in today," Clairborne said.

Derek felt his throat close. "*Glllk*," he said. He swallowed hard. "You're going to be... I mean... I'm going to answer to... a..."

"No," someone said. Derek turned: Singh was behind him, standing straighter, a black tie knotted around his neck. "I'm in charge of the department now," Singh said. "Management had... *concerns* about Clairborne being emotionally ready to come back. He's just dropping by before he takes a few weeks paid leave for counseling."

"I... he..." Derek looked around him. Nobody else seemed shocked, upset. He pulled off his wool cap. "*Paid* leave? He gets *paid* leave?"

"You're off today," Singh said. "Disciplinary. Come back Monday. Then maybe we'll see if you can continue here." He held a foil-wrapped stick toward Derek. "Since you've visited the office, you'll need a Biocall shot. Regulations."

Derek felt the cold air catch in his throat. "I thought..." he said, whispering urgently, "I thought we were in this *together*." He glanced around the room. "We're not like them."

Singh looked evenly at Derek. "We'll talk Monday about your attitude," he said. "I hope to welcome you back to the team as a positive contributor."

"Don't..." Derek glanced around again. His sweater felt too tight, his head dizzy. "Don't pull this management shit on me, man."

"Monday," Singh said. He pushed the elevator button, and the door opened. "Monday," he said again, finality in his voice.

"Monday," Derek repeated, and stepped into the elevator.

"Hold that!" Clairborne stuck a meaty head into the doors as they were about to close, forcing them open and hurrying into the elevator beside Derek. "I bet this is a surprise," he chortled, as the two were heading down to the mezzanine. The raw, angry rope burns on his neck hadn't healed. They never would. "Bet you never expected to see me like this. *I* didn't expect to see me like this. But it's comforting, isn't it? Knowing the company will keep us on, even if we're differently animated."

"Comforting," Derek said, his tongue cotton in his mouth.

"As long as it's cold, as long as it's cold enough that I don't rot away, I can stay on here," Clairborne said. "I can work in this office for the rest of eternity. And if you die, so can you. Isn't it great? It's like the future is all laid out for us. Nothing will ever change." His smile was empty, vapid, ghastly. "We can just keep working here forever."

Derek didn't speak or smile back. He stood as still as he could, eyes unblinking, heart thumping softly in his chest, gazing at the numbers on the elevator display as they counted.

Down, and down, and down.

Agent Red

PHILIP HANSEN

Sqwwwaaaaaawwwrrrrkkkk! "...slick. Say again, inbound..." *Rrrzzzzzawwr!*

"Fuck your mother, El Tee," Mack growled, "fix that goddamn radio or just hump it into the bush."

Bzzzzshhhhhhh! "...nine, eight, seven... Copy? Copy? Echo squad? Copy?" *Rrrzzzzaaassskkkppppp!*

"This place stinks," Navarette said, looking over his shoulder.

Echo squad was camped out in a small open-air bunker near a muddy river. Twenty-five yards away, a decrepit fishermen's shack squatted like a dried snail near a decaying dock. Secured out of sight under the dock was a rubber raft.

"It's a dead place, don'cha know," Skinny said, a faux Jamaican accent echoing from his pale cracker throat.

Mack pinched his face up tight, a parody of a grin. He had heard the line a hundred times. It was funny eight weeks ago; now it was just fucking annoying.

El Tee dropped to one knee in the mud and pulled his radio out of the holder. It whined in protest.

"Did they say *slick*?" El Tee grunted. He racked the radio against his helmet a few times. It made a sound like a dying cow.

Skinny rolled his eyes and flipped a small cell phone out of his BDU cargo pocket.

Mack gave him a quick look that said, *If you say, 'Can you hear me now?' I'm going to shoot you in the face.*

Cheep-cheep! "Dog squad, ten-nine that radio traffic from command." *Cheep-cheep!*

Cheep! "SLICK! SLICK!" Masterson's voice screamed over the tiny handheld. "Inbound F-18 fast mover has painted the target. Target crawling with undead. Find cover. Find some *fucking* cover!" *Cheep-Cheep!*

Mack looked around. *Cover? This rathole isn't cover. What does he expect us to do, put on a grass skirt and hide in the fisherman's shack?*

"We wouldn't need cover if Smart was still alive," Navarette growled. "All our gas masks were in his pack."

"Fuck his mother," El Tee said. "Smart knew there were *Sharks* in the water." El Tee made biting motions, showing all his teeth.

Mack pulled up his binoculars and looked out through the gun slits. Across the river was an old warehouse, most of the windows shattered by time and wayward children. At the top of the hill sat the remains of a parking garage and a couple apartment buildings. The skeleton of a half-constructed high-rise apartment complex rusted next to a ten-story construction crane.

Mack pointed to the apartment buildings. Navarette nodded. They would have to haul ass up the hill and across open ground to get to the buildings in time, but they were the best source of cover.

Mack handed the binocs to Skinny. "*Roamers?*"

Skinny scanned the surrounding hills with the binoculars, his head bobbing around like a broken Pez dispenser. "All clear, Boss Man. Watch the high grass for *Decaps*." A *Decap*, one of the living dead with no legs. The clever fuckers liked to hide in tall grass.

Mack rolled his eyes and grunted. *Decaps in the high grass*, he thought. *Fuck your mother. I would rather run buck-naked across a minefield with a pole shoved up my ass than deal with that hairy voodoo shit.*

"Everyone grab ass your rucks and be ready to roll out. El Tee?"

El Tee did a little cowboy twirl with his field radio, slid it back into its holster, and strapped it down.

"Let's go," El Tee said. "Everyone move on three."

"Three," Mack said, kicking open the bunker's rusting door.

Echo squad barreled out in single file and then spread out when they hit a dirt road. Navarette's M249 Squad Automatic Weapon

(SAW) whipped around left and right like it was sniffing at the murky swamp air. Leading from the bunker, the dirt road intersected with a cracked paved road. Scrub weeds grew up through the cracks; the rest of the world could go screaming straight to hell and the weeds would still be there, happy to take over the planet once again.

To the right, a rusty metal bridge spanned the mud river. The road to the left wound down below the hills and buildings, ending in an abandoned airstrip several miles away. Mack knew this without checking the map. He could see map grids in his head.

They crossed the cracked blacktop and waded into the tall grass. Mack kept one eye on the abandoned construction site at the top of the hill. There was still no movement, no enemy in sight, but the mp3 player in his mind played back the soundtrack of the undead, composed of low moans.

He chanced a look up, imagining he could hear the whine of the inbound jet with its deadly payload, sure he could hear the metal twang of safety straps blowing away as four sixty-pound AR-210 bombs cycled up to active. He had seen them loading the AR's back at base, the ordnance geeks chalking little sayings like "Bite This!" and "Choke on me!" on the nose cone of each bomb.

When they hit two hundred yards into the tall grass, Skinny screamed and disappeared. His 1911 sidearm barked twice, and he sprang back up. His eyes had gone white, bulging out under his goggles like a pair of boiled eggs. "*Decap* motherfucker grabbed my leg. Fuck. Fuck this. Fuck this."

Echo squad formed up on Skinny's forty-five. At his feet lay half a rotting corpse, its head all popped jellyfish from Skinny's .45 caliber 1911. Blue-green entrails snaked away from the corpse and wound around the tall grass.

Navarette nudged Skinny with the nose of his SAW. "You bit?" the big Indian asked. Navarette was all business.

"Nnnoo..." Skinny said, twisting around to look at the back of his leg. His digital cammo was covered in grime where the corpse had grabbed him. No blood, just caked with dirt.

Around them came the low moaning cry Mack had been dreading: the quiet howl of the animated dead.

"Fuck your mother," Mack whispered.

Around them, the tall grasses began to move. There was no wind.

"It's a trap," El Tee said. He motioned with his hands to the left and to the right. Navarette was already moving, hunched down low and leading off with the deadly barrel of his SAW. Mack and El Tee followed. Skinny, still trying to brush clotted slime off his BDU's, suddenly realized he was getting left behind.

"Someone mail me a clue." He holstered the 1911 and trotted off after his squad. He flipped out the little yellow cell phone again.

Cheep-cheep. "Masterson. Time." *Cheep-cheep.*

Cheep-cheep. "Less than five. Haul ass, I'm going below." *Cheep-cheep.*

Skinny shaded his goggles with one hand. Nearly a mile away was another tall apartment complex. Masterson stood up from his hiding place on the rooftop, waved, and then disappeared into a stairwell.

With Masterson taking cover from the incoming AR-210's, Echo Squad would have no sniper cover; Richard "GOD" Masterson was no longer watching their backs. Skinny crouched low and humped back up to the others.

Navarette glanced back at Skinny and grinned. The Indian loved the little white boy. He was stupid and he was trouble, but he was also fast with a gun. Quick-draw fast, and steady as polished steel.

Behind them, the grass shuddered, and the dead moaned and wailed.

*   *   *   *   *

The squad stepped out of the tall grass at the top of the hill, appearing out in the open like Shoeless Joe Jackson stepping onto the Field of Dreams.

Navarette looked behind them. The high grass rustled. "*Decaps creeping up on us, Mack.*"

Mack pinched up his nose, his face going all straight angles. Only his stubbly jaw showed, the rest hidden under his helmet, his black lens goggles pulled down over his eyes. He looked like Judge Dredd, the stone-faced futuristic lawman from one of the four-color comic books Skinny carted around in his pack. El Tee might be in charge, but when it came to giving out orders in Echo Squad, Mack *was* the law.

"Under the skeleton and into Cabrini Green," Mack said. He pointed past the construction skeleton of an unfinished apartment building. On the other side was a ten-story tenement-style apartment building surrounded by a chainlink fence. Even from a hundred yards, they could see a billboard proclaiming, "Coming Soon! A New Monumental Mart!"

They started moving in less time than it took Mack to point the way. Navarette was point man, his SAW pulling him forward. Its name was Nicole, named after the nagging Italian princess he had married after Special Forces Underwater Operations School. He could still see her black hair blowing in the Key West breeze, the sun turning the ocean spray into flecks of diamond. A postcard moment.

Time was working against them. Five minutes away (4:55 and counting), their last F-18 E/F Super Hornet was *In the Pipe* and *Five by Five*. Her name was *Pity the Fool*. And her pilot was Lance "Penguin" Charlier. They needed to be under cover when the Penguin dropped the four laser-guided AR-210's. Under some *serious* mother humping cover.

Echo Squad moved silently under the rusted steel girders, expecting trouble and finding none. Two-by-two, they cleared the area, Navarette and Mack moving first, El Tee and Skinny following. Mack hung onto an old M16A2 rifle with the M203 Grenade Launcher. A center hit with the M203 would leave you wondering why your head was lying on the ground seventeen feet from your toes. Skinny had a tiny Belgian P90 assault machine gun (capable of laying down nine hundred rounds a minute from an overhead fifty-round clip) and the El Tee stuck with a pair of flat black Desert Eagle .50 caliber handguns. After the first shot with a Desert Eagle .50, the recoil would twist your arm so far off the mark that a second shot would catch nothing but wind, but whatever you hit with the first shot was already three shades of dead, so it was *frosty*.

All of them had backup guns. These days, there was no such thing as too many guns.

Huddled behind the loose planking of construction scaffolding, Mack saw the first *Roamers*.

Six of them formed a loose group right on the other side of a man-sized tear in the chainlink that surrounded the condemned apartment building. They were dead. They were, as Skinny was fond of saying, "All messed up."

The leader corpse may have been a doctor. It wore a dirty white lab coat, splashed with copper stains, over a pair of green scrubs. A stethoscope hung around its neck with the little silver dongle cleverly tucked into a front pocket. It had lost one shoe and one sock. Mack could see a shiny copper penny in its one loafer.

Even from fifty yards away, Mack could tell it was long dead. Somehow, its neck had broken, and the head hung at a ninety-degree angle from the body. Broken neck or not, its lips were curled back in a hungry snarl.

The group of *Roamers* ("*Never* use the Zed word," Mack had said once, sure that Skinny would get the joke. Zed for "Z." "Z" for "Zombie." "Zombie" for "Fucked up dead guy trying to kill you and eat your Skinny ass.") shuffled around in front of the entrance.

They moved in a ploddingly slow, seemingly harmless manner. Except for the eyes. The eyes were still alive, moving around. Looking up and down, left and right, always in motion. Always moving around. *Roaming* around.

Mack looked at Navarette. They spoke in fractured sign language. Navarette made a little cross with his fingers like he was warding off vampires. Navarette said, "Hospital?"

Mack checked the little checkerboard map in his head. He made little walking fingers and then held up three fingers. Mack said, "Three blocks away."

Navarette nodded. The doctor corpse may have wandered away from a hospital. That could be what they were looking for... a hospital, a football stadium, a shopping mall. Someplace with thousands of creepy fucked-up dead guys. In other words, a *hive*.

"No such thing as six *Roamers* without a *hive*, Mack," Navarette said.

Mack nodded. *Roamers* were like rabbits: there was no such thing as just one rabbit, and there was no such thing as just one zombie. "No time. We go in there, or we get puked on by the bad ass Penguin."

"Make a sound like a cow," Skinny said, moving up right behind Navarette.

Navarette grunted, "Mooo..."

"I've got this, Mack," Skinny said.

"You're on point then."

Skinny patted Navarette twice on the back and then stepped out from under the cover of the construction site onto an overgrown two lane blacktop. The sun shined down on him, all warm and inviting. A slight breeze made the loose ends of his Army-green dew rag flutter like pale strands of seaweed in an ocean current.

Skinny had dropped his oversized backpack, leaving it with Mack, Navarette, and El Tee while he dealt with the six *Roamers*. He wore a black multi-pocket ammo vest over his forest green digital cammo BDU pants and jacket. The bottom of his BDU pants were bloused, paratrooper style, into the top of his scuffed black Army boots.

He ducked into a triangular opening torn into the chainlink fence and then dropped to one knee, aiming the short barrel of his P90 at the six *Roamers*. They picked up on the movement right away, turning toward Skinny. Their normal shuffle-step living dead walk gave way to a more determined step-and-drag. The lead corpse, the doctor, let out a howl that would have frightened away a hungry mountain lion.

Skinny took aim and fired a short burst.

Thrrrbbbbrraaattttt!

Six rounds hit the Doctor center mass, knocking it to the ground where it started thrashing around like an overturned turtle.

"Crap."

"You missed, white boy," Navarette's voice echoed into Skinny's radio headset.

Two corpses took the Doctor's place. The first was a woman in a ragged blue EMT outfit. Her intestines had been torn out, leaving a raw, maggot-filled hole like a giant mouth. Her face was pale yellow, the flesh desiccated. Clots of long blonde hair clung to her skeletal head. Skinny aimed down the sight and fired another short burst.

Brrraaatttt!

The EMT went down, half her head disappearing into a pink mist. "Cha-Cha!" Skinny said.

The second corpse was male, dressed in a flower print one-piece hospital gown. In one hand, it gripped the chrome pole of an I.V. stand. The empty saline bag swung as it moved, the plastic tubing attached to the corpse's arm and filled with dried blood. Flower Print moved fast, using the I.V. stand like a crutch, his naked feet making a dry crunching sound on the loose gravel. He was almost on top of Skinny.

"I think he wants you to give blood," Navarette taunted over the headset.

Skinny ignored the big Indian. "I'm sensing a motif here, Mack. This bunch is all hospital-looking and chummy."

Thukka-thukka-braaatttt!

Skinny fired off a long burst. Flower Print's kneecaps exploded, and his legs crumpled backward, the joints suddenly reversed like the back legs of a dog. It snarled at Skinny. *Pain or rage?*

When Flower Print tried to move again, its legs fell apart, severed at the knees; it slumped forward, pulling the I.V. pole down on top of it. Only a few feet away, it tried to bat at Skinny with the pole like a long silver claw. The pole thumped against the ground, drawing sparks from the cement sidewalk. Skinny fired a single round at it point blank.

Grrraa-aaattt! The P90 growled. Flower Print's forehead caved in like rotted fruit. Blood, hair, and brains reached out from the back of its head in small pink chunks like fleeing amoeba.

I really need a better job, Skinny thought. *Three down.*

Skinny looked around. Two unmoving dead bodies and two more *Roamers* hung back near the entrance to the abandoned apartment complex. They were shuffling from foot to foot in anticipation of their Skinny meal, but they hung back.

What are they waiting for? Roamers don't wait. They eat and stink up the place. What isn't right here? Two Roamers left, two dead bodies. Two. After one comes two, after two comes three...

"Break, break, break!" Skinny shouted into his headset. "Mack, I've got problems. I lost one of the *Roamers.*"

"On your six," Mack said back. The flat sound of his voice was muffled and distorted through the headset, like it was coming from under the midnight hood of Death himself.

Skinny spun around. The Doctor corpse was right behind him, rotted hands almost around his neck. Skinny pulled up the barrel of his P90 and pulled the trigger at point blank range.

Click.

"Crap. I'm out." Skinny dropped to one knee and rolled forward, slamming against the legs of the Doctor, knocking it over like an olive-green bowling ball taking down a fleshy pin. He rolled a second time and came back up on one knee, pulling another clip from one of the front pockets of his black ammo vest.

The Doctor moaned and started to push itself up by its arms. It turned its head and looked directly at Skinny, narrowing its phlegmy yellow eyes.

"Mmm... eee-t-t-t," it hissed.

Skinny rapped the new clip against his helmet twice and then ejected the spent clip from the P90. He slapped the new clip into place.

Ka-Chink.

Lord, that has to be the finest sound on the earth. Please let me live to hear it again.

A rotted smell, like the burning of a wet dog wrapped in a black garbage bag, assaulted him. Four dead hands grabbed his shoulders. The dead hands of the other two *Roamers*.

"Crap."

Skinny fell onto his back, the P90 dropping and rapping hard against the blacktop. The two Roamers were dressed in faded gray coveralls like automotive repairmen.

Or janitors, a voice in Skinny's head observed.

They both had friendly oval nametags. One read "Bob" and the other one "Neal." If they hadn't been trying to tear off Skinny's head and his right arm, he might have laughed.

Laugh anyway, Skinny boy, the little voice said. *It is the last joke you will ever hear.*

Skinny lashed out with his right arm; he found the P90 right where it should be, tethered to his side by twenty-four inches of tactical combat strap. He got a good grip on it and swung it up hard, smashing in Bob's head like a rotting pumpkin.

Neal had Skinny's left arm pinned to the ground with both hands and was chewing on his BDU jacket, tearing off chunks of the green and brown digital camouflage.

Not missing out on the free lunch, the Doctor jumped onto Skinny's legs. Something cracked.

"Fuck!" Skinny screamed. "Mack, Navarette, El Tee!"

No one answered, but he could hear the bark and whistle of El Tee's Desert Eagle. In slow motion, the bullet left Matrix ripples in the air. It tore into Neal's arm, severing it at the wrist. Neal fell back onto its ass, gawking at the stump of its hand in disbelief. Its eyes went all wide and it started to bawl blood-red tears like a four year old with a broken toy.

His arm free, Skinny pulled the P90 up to his chest and charged the rod, putting a live round into the chamber. He flipped the switch from burst to full auto and fired down the length of his body, where the Doctor had Skinny's bootlaces dangling from its teeth like skinny licorice.

The bullets tore into the Doctor's arm, shoulder, and chest, flipping the corpse end over end. Skinny sat up and fired again.

On full auto, the Belgian P90 can hammer out nine hundred rounds a second from an overhead fifty-round clip. Skinny let the Doctor have the full clip. The corpse was twitching and bouncing around as if an invisible cat were batting at it like a fuzzy ball at the end of a string.

Skinny was screaming when the clip ran dry. He hadn't heard himself screaming, but there was a sound coming from him, a high-pitched alien sound from the deep primal part that still feared what it couldn't see in the darkness.

His body ran on automatic. He ejected the clip, grabbed another from a front pocket in his ammo vest, rapped it twice against his helmet, and then slapped it in place.

Ka-Chink.

Skinny had lived to hear the sound again. He charged the rod and took aim.

A heavy hand fell on his shoulder.

"Go easy," Navarette said. The edge of Navarette's slight accent slipped over the top of Skinny's howling cry like a bad check going into an envelope. Skinny stopped screaming and pointed his rifle at the ground.

Mack and El Tee swam into Skinny's tunnel vision. Mack kicked the Doctor corpse in the leg.

"Looks dead enough. Let's go."

"What about *him*?" El Tee waved his flat black Desert Eagle at Neal. It was snuffling dead snot and crying big blubbery baby cries.

"The AR-210's will get it," Mack said. "Make like a tree."

Navarette looped his free arm around Skinny's chest, and they hobbled toward the abandoned apartment complex. Skinny's right leg was twisted at an odd angle above his torn boot. Every time his foot hit the ground, he got a feeling in his knee like live squirrels were gnawing on him. He bit his lip hard enough to draw blood and let Navarette drag him along, looking like stepbrothers in a three-legged race.

What is funnier than a rubber crutch? the little voice said as Skinny's bones ground together.

"A pay toilet in a diarrhea ward," he whispered through clenched teeth. Navarette smiled and nodded like he had heard both sides of the joke.

Mack and El Tee were already at the blocked entrance, hacking away at the boards with small field hatchets.

Navarette dropped Skinny on the sidewalk and pulled another shiny chrome hatchet from a second backpack looped around his arm. He had been carrying Skinny, Skinny's pack, his burly SAW, and his own pack. Navarette was three kinds of muscle.

Skinny grunted a little when he hit the sidewalk.

Navarette held up the little axe and made *chop-chop* motions. "You want me to cut it off?"

Skinny gave him a grin like a bear.

"Thought it might hurt less." He held up the axe again, turning it slightly so it gleamed in the sun. "Last chance."

Skinny squinted at him, pinching up his face in his best Mack-on-a-bad-day impression.

Skinny's face suddenly went blank. He had caught the shadow of something on the mirror surface of the small axe. It was the shadow of the incoming F-18 E/F Super Hornet.

They had run out of time.

*   *   *   *   *

Lance "Penguin" Charlier was flying too low and too fast. He did a quick bank around a skyscraper and leveled out above the rooftops of the city center. Echo squad was down there somewhere, mixed in with the *Roamers* and *Freaks*. He rolled his eyes at the thought. *Freaks* were those little non-military civilian groups that tried to survive in the city of the dead, living in shopping malls and skyscrapers. They didn't usually last long.

"Incoming," he said to himself.

Pity the Fool, the F-18 E/F Super Hornet jet fighter, had lost her Communications system months ago—she had been shot to hell by a couple of rogue Russian Migs at the beginning of the whole mess—

and there was no one left to fix it. He flew quiet now. It was him and his poor crippled girl and miles of empty blue sky.

They wouldn't be flying the F-18 at all, except she was the only bird they had that could hold the modified AR-210's.

Twice, Penguin tapped the glass screen controlling the missile guidance system. The four AR-210's were showing red for "Ready." Flashing text in block military letters said, "LASER ACTIVE. FIRE?" *Pity the Fool* couldn't hear, but she could still see fine. She had homed in on Masterson's laser targeting pointer.

Penguin said, "Red for Ready. A for Active. F for Fire. Bombs away." He tapped each of the red AR-120's on the glass Heads Up Display (HUD) twice. Three of them cycled back to green and then went dark. He could feel the F-18 E/F shudder slightly as three of the AR-210's dropped into the city center. One of them stayed red.

"Fuck your mother," Penguin grunted. He twisted his head around, snapping his black helmet visor into place as he turned to avoid the sun's glare. The fourth AR-210 was still there, shaking and rattling. It hadn't let go.

He double tapped the fourth bomb on the HUD. It went from red to green and then went dark. He twisted around again. It was still there, shaking worse now and causing the whole jet to rattle with it. He saw the red nose-cone and the white chalk where the ordnance tech had written, "Headshot!"

The bomb started thrashing around, banging against the housing and slamming into the wing.

"Oh, shit."

Then it exploded.

*　　*　　*　　*　　*

Navarette saw Skinny's face and dropped the axe. He swung his SAW around on its tactical combat strap.

"Clear," he growled.

Mack and El Tee ran to one side, El Tee turning his face away and holding onto his black SWAT-style combat helmet with both hands. Mack squinted under his goggles, his jaw square.

Navarette unloaded the full one hundred-round magazine into the boards blocking the entrance to the apartment complex. Brass rained down around Skinny. Wood chips, sawdust, and gunpowder smoke stung his face. When the magazine ran dry, Navarette grabbed Skinny by the front of his jacket and crashed headlong into what was left of the wood planks.

It was a scene from The Incredible Hulk. Navarette plowed through the smoke like a big green monster, Skinny thrown over one shoulder in a firemen's carry.

The only thing missing, Skinny thought, *is the big explosion right behind us.*

Behind them, there was a big explosion.

The apartment complex shook, cheap white plaster raining down on them like an upturned bag of flour.

"G-g-ground," Skinny said from over Navarette's shoulder. "Get us off the ground."

Dark shapes moved in the white plaster dust. The lobby was filled with *Roamers.* Hundreds of them.

Navarette didn't stop moving. He plowed across the lobby, heading for the fire stairs. He slammed right into the crowd of Roamers, pushing into them like a New Yorker without a subway token.

Pale hands of rotted flesh reached for Navarette. For a moment, the big California Miwok Indian transformed, becoming a huge green Mississippi water snake. Skinny felt the muscles in Navarette's back moving, felt the grip of his tattooed body-builder arm around his narrow waist; Skinny's mind sensed what his eyes could not comprehend. Navarette *had* changed. His breath hissed from his lungs and his legs melted together into a green and black blur. Navarette wasn't pushing through the pack of growling corpses—he *flowed* through them, serpentine fashion, as if they were ripples in a quiet pond.

And like that, they were on the other side.

Navarette kicked the metal 'Push to Exit' bar on the fire stairs, and the door swung open on the empty stairway. He took the stairs three at a time, Skinny bouncing up and down on his back.

"M-m-mack," Skinny said. "El-l T-t-tee."

"Forget them. They're gone."

Navarette was all business.

The building shook with a triple thump as the air-to-ground AR-210's hit their target.

*   *   *   *   *

The AR-210 is a modified air-to-ground chemical agent deployment system developed by Iraqi scientists. In the right hands, it is a weapon of singular mass destruction, capable of deploying 210 pounds of compressed chemical agent in a quarter mile area. Similar to a fuel-air missile, when the AR-210 detonates, it sucks up all the oxygen in a quarter mile area—mixing it with its chemical payload—and then explodes it outward in a rapidly moving cloud of poison gas. Once successfully deployed, an AR-210 bomb creates a low-lying fog bank that takes hours to disperse.

Dubbed "Agent Red," this powerful neurotoxin is best known for its blood-red color. Agent Red is deadly to all known life forms. Agent Red also has a strange side effect: it *dissolves* necrotic flesh.

*   *   *   *   *

The shockwave almost knocked Mack off his feet. He caught his balance long enough to smash the butt of his M16 against the forehead of a white-faced corpse dressed in a lacy lolita-goth costume. Mack and El Tee were totally surrounded in the small lobby. Mack could see Navarette hauling ass through the dogpile of corpses, but he couldn't catch a break from the melee to follow. Every time he pushed a drooling *Roamer* back or knocked one down, three more took its place.

Mack had run out of .223 rounds and was pushing and swinging wildly with his M16A2, using it as a club to protect El Tee from the clawed hands and moss-encrusted teeth of a hundred hungry corpses.

El Tee's eyes went blood red, and he smiled. A blood vessel somewhere in his brain had burst. He crossed his arms over his chest and started firing the dual .50 caliber Desert Eagles Wyatt Earp style. Each shot took down a *Roamer,* and they never got back up. Heads exploded and spines broke. Black blood splashed his face, and drops of it sizzled against his smoking guns.

"I never liked you!" El Tee screamed.

Mack crunched the fallen corpse of a small Mexican child under his boot heel. "I know."

"When I get to *Hell*," El Tee laughed, "I'm going to kill Smart again for losing those damn gas masks."

Blood-red tentacles of gas slithered through the smashed lobby doors. A low moan started up from the crowd of *Roamers*. It built into a howl and then rose in pitch until they were screaming. Slowly, the Roamers started backing away from Mack and El Tee, (who never stopped firing, dropping the ghouls with one bullet-boy precision shot after another.)

"They know," Mack said.

"Time to die, motherfuckers!" El Tee taunted as a swirling rope of red smoke wrapped around his knees. Engulfed in a cloak of red smoke, El Tee died, his eyes bloodshot and his lungs filled with the Agent Red neurotoxin.

Mack waited, holding his breath as the cloud of Agent Red washed over him.

I can hold my breath, Mack thought, *for a long time.*

The *Roamers* broke ranks and began to run, some of them running into the slow moving bank of poison gas. When they hit the gas, they melted. Gobs of steaming flesh boiled away from their bones, splashing the floor like pools of vomit.

In less than a minute, the horde of *Roamers* were dead. Melted like toy soldiers in a microwave. Mack walked outside, stepping over the body of El Tee, whose dead flesh had started to bubble and sizzle like bacon on a hot plate. He looked for the sun. It was there, hidden behind the fogbank of pale red gas, and it looked down on him like a crimson eye.

Staring up at the sun through his black combat goggles, Mack took a deep breath and died.

*   *   *   *   *

When they hit the fifth floor landing, Navarette set Skinny down and looked out through a dirt-encrusted window. He knew that five floors below, the bodies of his best friends were melting.

The three AR-210's dropped by *Pity the Fool* had struck their target dead center and had flooded an area nearly two square miles with the acidic Agent Red gas. At the center of the bombardment, the zombie *hive* woke up and started screaming in pain as Agent Red smothered its *Roamer* worker bees.

The gas seeped into the buildings and flooded the empty streets. Swarms of zombies poured from the ruined buildings and subway tunnels surrounding the apartment building where Navarette and Skinny had taken shelter. The streets were alive with thousands upon thousands of the walking dead. Shuffling into the ruby sunlight, the zombie horde was bathed in the thick red fog.

Flesh turned sunburn red, bubbling and melting, falling onto the black pavement in sheets, like the skin from burned tomato soup. White bones showing through melting flesh, the first *Roamers* dropped to the ground only to be stepped on by the next wave of undead. Shuffling at first, and then walking, finally running in mad panic, the *hive* tried to flee only to be melted into reddish pools like strawberry ice cream on a hot summer day.

The moans and screams shook the windows.

Navarette reached over and shook Skinny's black 1911 out of its holster. He squinted a bit to clear his vision, because somewhere inside him, the flood was building, and he knew there would be waterworks. Oh, yes. There would be waterworks and sadness and a deep tunnel sliding down and away and down again into a pit of black-faced despair, but for right now there was still business to take care of.

He pointed the 1911 at Skinny's face. "You bit?"

Skinny did a quick check of his jacket and his leg where the *Roamers* had torn into his clothing. His hands came away clean.

"Clean! I'm clean."

"Good. I didn't want to shoot you today," Navarette said.

Navarette was all business.

SOMETHING FISHY THIS WAY COMES

JOEL A. SUTHERLAND

They shouldn't have started with the dog.

That was the beginning of the problem.

Every parent on planet Earth knows you don't start with the dog—you start with the goldfish. If that goes well, you move to the hamster. From there, you proceed with what I'd call a mid-size pet, such as the iguana or the guinea pig. And finally, should mom and pop decide you're responsible enough to take care of another life for an extended period of time, you finally get the animal you wanted all along.

The dog.

My parents started with the dog.

The dog died.

And that's as good a place to start as any other, I guess. Oh, sure, I could go further back, describe my childhood and my family, but that's major league boring. Mom and dad were like porcelain dolls: pretty on the outside, hollow on the inside. They forever tried to do good, but they forever ended up doing bad. And Amy has always been your typical little sister, with her cooler-than-thou attitude fueled by the boiling hormones of all the guys in my school and their worship of the new grade nines with their knee-high hooker boots and tissue in their bras, trying to be just like Britney or Christina or whoever. It disgusted me and Amy knew it and she loved it. We'd yell at each other and, naturally, my parents would take their little princess' side. Sounds kinda like your family, doesn't it? So I won't put you to sleep with a waltz down memory lane.

I'm no Brad Pitt, so I won't describe my physical appearance, all chicken legs and noodle arms and milk-white skin, a popcorn face with a cherry-red mop.

And if there's one thing I learned in high school before it was overrun and burnt to the ground—just *one* thing—it's that I. Hate. Shakespeare. So I certainly won't open by painting a rich and eloquent picture of the setting, no "Two households, both alike in dignity, / In fair Whitby, Ontario, where we lay our scene, / From ancient" blah, blah, blah, blink, yawn, snore.

Show me a comatose reader, and I'll show you a failed writer. That's why I started with Spot kicking the doggie dish and chasing the golden school bus all the way up to K-9 heaven. I hope I've grabbed your attention.

Although, there is no "you." Not exactly, not anymore; therefore, there will never be a reader. Not unless *They* suddenly learn to read, which, from all I've observed, is highly unlikely.

So why am I—sitting alone in the public library for the past six weeks and counting—bothering to write down the story of what could be my final living days?

That's what I hope to find out.

Before it's too late.

* * * * *

My parents are backwards people, so it's fitting that they gave me pets in a backwards order. Straight to the dog, and like I said, the dog died. It was a golden lab, such a typical pet for a teenage boy, and it was run over by a car, such a typical death for a young dog.

Mom and dad admitted their mistake—*of course we shouldn't have started with the dog!*—and brought home an iguana. Two days later, they brought home a guinea pig. A day after that, a hamster. Guess what? They all died. Iggy was crushed by an ill-placed bag of groceries; G.P. saw an open freezer as an excellent opportunity for a feast, until the door was closed for the night; and Hammy, God bless him, took a joy ride straight to the garage through the Centralvac.

Most parents would cut their losses at this point, move on, realize their kid is cursed, buy him an Xbox. But my parents gave it one more go.

They gave me a goldfish.
The goldfish died.
Surprise, surprise.
Thing is, Goldie didn't stay dead.

*   *   *   *   *

Ah, my parents, ya gotta hate em. They knew that our dilapidated shanty they called home had walls so thin you could rub a deep-fried cheese stick on one and—*presto*—you'd have a new window. Yet they always had Serious Talks about me in the room next to mine without keeping their voices down. And Saturday nights after a meal of oysters, chocolate fondue, and two bottles of wine were even worse.

They said I watched too much T.V. They said I ate too much junk food. They said my grades weren't good enough. They said something should be done about my acne before it scars. They said I should take up a sport. They said I should learn to play a musical instrument. They said I picked on my sister too much. They said I was kind of weird. They said I kind of creeped them out. They said I was starting to remind them of that kid in *The Omen*. They said they were relieved they didn't name me Damien, ha ha. They said they wished that I would befriend some of the kids they had introduced me to, because pets obviously weren't the way to go.

Yes, that's right, my parents set up play dates for me. Puke! Total rejects, every last one. First was Harold, the kid that liked to kick himself; then there was Zeke, the dish monkey from Pizza Hut that ate the crusts off the dirty plates; and let's not forget the aptly named, needs-no-introduction, Snot-Nose Sammy. This trinity of good times was followed up by the Twitcher, the Biter, the Cusser, and the Outdoor Masturbator. I mean, where were my parents finding these nuts? *Whitby Mental Health*? Did I mention that I'm fifteen? Play dates? Seriously? C'mon!

Besides, I used to have a friend. Dillon lived next door, and his parents were never around, which in my opinion made them excellent parents. It also made Dillon's house the ideal place for us to burn G.I. Joes and shoot each other with roman candles. Mom and dad didn't like me hanging out with Dillon, just because he shaved his eyebrows once and he wore a shirt that said, "I'm With Stupid" with an arrow pointing at his crotch. My parents said he was a bad influence, but he was my best friend. Plus, his older brother would buy me cigarettes.

I wonder where Dillon is now? No doubt he's shuffling mindlessly down a blood-soaked street somewhere as his flesh rots and his skin peels off like an onion, using some corpse's dismembered hand to slap itself in the face.

Years ago, Dillon dared me to drink a full bottle of Soya sauce, and when I finished puking my salty-scented guts out, I dared him to eat some duck brain from the butcher's. Dillon chewed on it thoughtfully, shrugged and said, "Tastes like chicken." I think he kinda liked it. So I'm sure he's making out just fine.

*   *   *   *   *

Goldie was a really cool fish. I started out by putting him in one of those glass bowls that cartoon characters sometimes wear on their heads as space helmets. He swam in circles and ate fish food, which got really boring really quick. So I sold my dad's Viagra to Dillon and bought Goldie an expensive tank, one with a plastic rock and a sunken pirate ship. It even had a light if I ever wanted to watch Goldie swim in circles and eat fish food in the middle of the night.

Soon after the fish was introduced to his new home, something amazing happened: Goldie began to grow. In just a few days, he was almost twice his original size! A light bulb lit up above my head, and I immediately moved Goldie to the downstairs bathtub for a little experiment. Four days later, Goldie had doubled in size again! I realized that the more room he had for swimming in circles and eating fish food, the bigger he would get.

Since he was still only slightly bigger than a jalapeno popper, I decided I needed more room for my freak fish to expand. I scooped him up, took him outside, turned on the hose, filled up the turtle pool, tossed Goldie in, and went to bed. I was so anxious to check on him in the morning that I couldn't sleep all night.

That's why I was awake when the meteorite fell from the sky and landed with a splash in my very own backyard.

*   *   *   *   *

When something that cool happens, you expect your life to change for the better. Like everyone at school will come up to you and ask you tons of questions, even Jessica Peterson, the girl with the really big ones that sits in front of you in Geography and who probably doesn't even know you're alive, and the local media will knock on your door and your parents will tell the journalist that they're so proud to have a son like you, one that made such an important discovery—only the thirteenth meteorite ever discovered in Ontario!—and NASA will pay you tons of money for your tiny hunk of space rock, and then you can move to Mexico and leave your parents and your sister and school and Canada and the cold and your shitty old life behind.

All I got from that damned meteorite was a dead goldfish.

Goldie was floating belly up in the turtle pool. The meteorite had struck him square on the head and covered him in some gross-looking green ooze. No way was I going to pick up that filthy mess with my bare hands, so I grabbed a couple of dead branches and carefully—oh so very carefully—squeezed Goldie between them like chow mein between two giant chopsticks. I went inside and tiptoed to the nearest toilet, but just before I dropped my fourth ill-fated pet into his porcelain casket, a crazy thought ran through my head: *Something's not right about all this. Something's, uh, fishy. Maybe I shouldn't flush Goldie down the toilet. Maybe I should take him over to Dillon's so we can strap him to an egg rocket and send him one hundred feet straight up into the air. That would be awesome.*

But no, Goldie was a cool fish. He deserved better than that.

With a *plunk* and a *flush*, he was gone.

*   *   *   *   *

Goldie came back bright and early the next morning. He crawled into my room, pulling his legless body towards my bed with his wee little flippers. It would have been cute if it hadn't been terrifying. His once golden scales were now a sickly-hued pukey-green-yellow, his once black eyes now bloodshot-red, and he left a trail of mucus behind him that would have made Snot-Nose Sammy extremely jealous. He was making little fish moans that made the hair on the back of my neck stand at attention. His lips were covered in blood and something else—human brains. With a nauseating lurch, my bladder released, drenching me in my own warm piss.

Goldie kept coming. I couldn't move as terror and panic wrapped their wriggling tentacles around me, pinning me under my sheets, where only moments ago I had been enjoying a slightly naughty dream about Jessica Peterson and her big ones. All that remained of the warm and fuzzy memory was a little morning wood. The only thing on my mind now was the fact that my goldfish was going to eat me. Goldie kept coming.

He reached the edge of my bed and stopped. Thank God! But my relief soon vanished as Goldie began flapping his body about like a... well, like a fish out of water. One flap, two flaps, three flaps. With every flap, he flapped higher and higher. Four flaps, five flaps, six flaps. Back and forth, higher and higher, back and forth, higher and higher! Seven flaps, eight flaps, nine flaps! Then one more final flipping flap and Goldie was up on my goddamned bed!

He rolled onto his belly, and his menacing, vacant gaze fell upon me. His sticky mucus soaked through my sheets and moistened my toes.

Without wasting any time—but moving excruciatingly slowly—the cursed fish crawled up my leg, past my wet crotch, over my belly, and onto my chest. He bared his tiny fangs and moaned in ecstasy as he lurched in for the kill. I pissed myself again, cursed the extra Dr. Pepper I drank before bedtime, and finally got my ass into gear. I grabbed the pillow from under my head, slipped out from under Goldie, and smothered him under my feather-filled cushion of doom. The fish thrashed and snarled, but I held the pillow tight, determined to suffocate him. Seconds passed, then minutes, but Goldie kept on kicking. Realizing that for some Godforsaken reason that wasn't going to work, I ripped my alarm clock from the wall and brought it down on top of the pillow again and again and again until the hard crunching sound turned into a wet smacking one.

I paused.

Nothing.

No sound, no movement.

Slowly, I lifted a corner of the pillow with a trembling hand and peered underneath it.

I had turned my pet goldfish into mashed tomatoes and orange peel.

Never before had I been so proud of myself.

* * * * *

It didn't take me long to figure out what was happening. A meteorite, carrying some weird space disease, had crash landed on Goldie's head, killing him, but later reviving him, turning him into a freaking zombie fish intent on eating my brain. Furthermore—and this really worried me—it had looked like Goldie had already feasted.

A quick check into my parents' room confirmed my suspicions. They were both sprawled out, motionless in bed, tiny fish bites on their foreheads and scalps. A powerful emotion enveloped me, but I wasn't sure what it was. Was it sadness? Relief? Joy? Terror? Whatever it was, I think I would have pissed myself again if I hadn't already pissed myself dry. I wrote the mystery feeling off as shock and moved on.

As I approached my sister's room, I was startled by a loud crash of shattering glass. I ran through the open door and quickly looked around. The room was empty. There was blood on the bed, and a small mucus trail on the ground. This didn't look good. Wind tussled my mangy red hair, and I noticed all that was left of the window were a few jagged shards of glass around the frame. I ran to the broken window and peered out.

Amy was creeping across our backyard, heading straight for Dillon's house. No way would I let my zombie sister eat my best friend's brains!

From her pile of chick lit books, I picked up one with a bunch of hotties on the cover, painting their toenails. Once I had cleared the glass from the bottom of the window frame, I dropped the book, climbed up and readied myself to jump. I paused. The ground looked really far away. But if zombie Amy could do it, so could I. I tensed my muscles in anticipation. And then I paused again.

I stepped back down into my sister's room, opting to walk downstairs and use the door instead. It was the sensible thing to do. But first, I realized, I would need a zombie-sister-killing weapon.

I grabbed my bloody alarm clock.

*   *   *   *   *

As I passed through the kitchen, my tummy rumbled. I stopped before reaching the door and looked longingly at the food cupboard. I glanced out the window and saw Amy, frothing at the mouth, still shuffling towards Dillon's house. She had scaled the fence that separated our yards, and I watched her through the chain-link. Then, and thank goodness for this, she toppled over into the large hole that Dillon had been digging to make his own swimming pool.

After rolling around in the dirt for a while, she began to scrabble at the steep sides of the pit, looking for a way out. That would take her some time, which gave me the opportunity to down some breakfast. I know it was stupid, but hey, I'm a teenage boy; zombies aren't the only ones who can't control their feasting urges.

I grabbed a box of Pop Tarts and tossed a couple in the toaster. As I waited for the orange-glowing wires inside to work their magic, I glanced outside to check on my sister's progress. To my surprise, Dillon was actually awake in time for school. He was standing before the hole, holding a garden hose, obviously in the mood for a swim.

The toaster dinged. I tore into the first Pop Tart and was overcome with the sweet tastes of pastry and icing and exquisite cherry filling. I laughed as Dillon covered the nozzle with his thumb and sprayed Amy in the face with a Mach Three jet of hose water. But then Hell's Bells rang right behind me: the sound of heavy footsteps and the morbid moan of a zombie.

The Pop Tart fell from my fingers as I picked up my alarm clock and spun on the spot. Mom, back from the dead and looking none too pleased about it, was within grabbing distance. I darted past her, narrowly escaping her clawing hands, and ran outside.

Blind terror gripped me even tighter when I saw that Amy, obviously unimpressed with Dillon's antics, had escaped from the hole and had pinned him to the ground beneath her. With a gut-wrenching crunch, she bit into him and ripped his throat clean out of his neck. Covered in my best friend's blood, she slurped up Dillon's throat like it was nothing more than a strand of spaghetti and she was one of the dogs in *Lady and the Tramp*.

I ran and ran and ran, stopped at the end of my street, hummed a hurried rendition of eeney-meeney-miney-moe, turned right, and then I ran and ran and ran some more.

*   *   *   *   *

Running sucks. You get all sweaty and huffy and puffy, and all you accomplish in the end is that you're farther away from where you started.

After running for God knows how long, I came across a nice looking park, one with trees and swings and garbage that was actually placed in garbage cans, so I knew I was far from home. The Pop Tart was giving me cramps, so I decided to rest on a nearby bench. Bending my body like a professional contortionist, I was able to sit down without touching any white bird crap. It was a little awkward at first, but it didn't take long for all the excitement of the last twelve hours to catch up with me. I slipped into a deep, peaceful sleep.

Some time later, I woke up to a beautiful bird's song. A robin, the orange-breasted bird of spring, circled overhead. Spotting some prey, maybe a worm or a grub, it dove towards the earth. To be more specific, towards my bench. To be precise, towards me. As it rapidly neared, I realized it wasn't singing, but moaning in some terrible zombie bird language, and I was its prey.

I had no time to lose. I jumped to my feet and began whipping the alarm clock by the cord in large circles over my head. When the bird flew within range, I swung the weapon straight for it. A hit! The bird's body went limp and careened backwards through the air.

It landed in the middle of a band of wandering zombies. Previously lost and aimless, they now looked in my wide-eyed, shell-shocked, crap-in-my-pants direction. There were fifteen of them; Amy, as usual, had gotten around. I looked at my alarm clock—it didn't have many more bashes left before it fell to pieces.

Reluctantly, I turned and ran again.

*   *   *   *   *

Late last August, my dad demanded to know how I, jobless, penniless, and completely void of ambition, had spent my summer. I quickly crunched some numbers.

Turned out I spent on average three hours a day watching television, five and a half hours a day watching movies, and a whopping seven hours a day playing video games. That left eight and a half hours to eat, sleep, answer the call of nature, bug my sister, and occasionally get up to no good with Dillon.

My dad told me I wasn't living; I was slowly dying. I think he was pretty close: I was a human zombie.

But who's laughing now? Thanks to my laziness, I have the uncanny ability to get inside my enemy's mind. I can think like a zombie, act like a zombie, become one with the zombie. It's why I've survived all alone in this nightmare of a world for so long.

Being alone—it's something else. And I mean, being *really* alone. First you love it, then you hate it, and then you love it even more. But then you turn on the television and find nothing on. Absolutely *nothing!* I'd give my left nut right now for fifteen minutes of C-SPAN. So to pass the time, I've been writing. Not only this journal, but jokes, too.

Here are some of my best:

Q. How does a zombie feel after pulling an all-nighter?
A. Dead tired.
Q. After which movie did the zombie demand his money back?
A. *Dead Man Walking.*
Q. What did the zombie say to Albert Einstein?
A. "I'd like to pick your brain."
Q. What did the zombie eat at Red Lobster?
A. The waiter.

Man, these would have killed Dillon.

Oh, wait...

Awkward.

*   *   *   *   *

I ran and I ran and I ran until I started to get pretty good at running.

I ran past burning houses and overturned cars and dismembered corpses and frantic journalists and dying soldiers and hordes of mindless, flesh-eating zombies.

I ran all the way to my high school, hoping it would be zombie-free and, more importantly, that I hadn't slept through my afternoon spare. I love my afternoon spare.

School, however, had been canceled for the day. From the way things looked, probably for the next while, too.

Flames had engulfed the old building, the sky thick with ash and smoke. The memory of the first Canada Day I was allowed to light my very own burning schoolhouse came rushing back to me, and I realized one of my oldest fantasies had just come true.

Amid the chaos and the screaming were my classmates, running to and fro, engaged in a battle royale. It was like an undead version of *The Lord of the Flies*. It was awesome. Vincent, the football captain, A+ student and all-around asshole, was eating Johnny's brains like so much cotton candy. Two members of the school drama club were ripping the principal to shreds, and my respect for them went up a notch. Mr. Richardson, the Economics teacher, had grabbed Sally Drumfeller and was chewing on her face, even though she was a zombie, too; I was pretty sure Mr. Richardson would have been fired for that in the pre-zombie world.

And then I saw her. Zombie Jessica Peterson. I boldly sneaked a peek at her big ones. She was still hot. She was roaming in my direction, moaning and groaning and spitting-up all over. So she *did* know I was alive! This was a happy moment in an otherwise shitty day. Too bad I couldn't stick around.

Nope, my high school was obviously not a safe place to be. I had to find a quiet place where I could hole myself up for a few days. A place I could go unnoticed. A place I was sure I'd be alone.

I turned and ran for the public library.

*   *   *   *   *

I used to hate libraries, and I'd still never admit to calling one home, but it's not all that bad. I've had just about all I could ask for. After landing a flurry of karate kicks, I cracked open the vending machine and have had three square meals a day of Fritos and Dr. Pepper. The puppets in the storytime room have provided hours of entertainment as I reenacted my favorite episodes of *Trailer Park Boys*, like the one when they kidnapped Rita McNeil and forced her to harvest their pot. And I've discovered that properly placed paperback books can double as blankets and pillows when you're absolutely desperate.

A bunch of quotes are on the walls of the library. Most are pretty dumb, some make no sense, but there are three that I like. They are: '*When I step into this library, I cannot understand why I ever step out of it,*' (Marie de Sevigne); '*We read to know we are not alone,*' (C.S. Lewis); '*A good book is the best of friends, the same today and forever,*' (Martin Tupper).

I'd like to meet these quotable people and chat over corn chips and soda. This is what I'd say to them: "I bet you're jealous of me now, Ms. de Sevigne. That is, if you're not a zombie, which you probably are"; "Your quote is a cruel irony, Mr. Lewis"; "Mr. Tupper—or Marty, if I may—you hit the bullseye."

You see, the library's books, when not providing me with warmth in the night, have provided me with friends. There's Mack Bolan, the one-man army of restitution with the cold blue eyes and a heart of gold. There's Fuzz, Ziggy's look-alike dog from the comic strip anthologies, whose bark is worse than his bite. There's Captain Underpants, who... well, who cares what he does? I just love that name.

I've even enjoyed some quote-unquote classics. William Goldman. Joseph Conrad. Even Shakespeare. *The horror!*

The first few days I was here, I saw the odd zombie amble past one of the windows, but they never noticed me. Soon, they stopped passing by altogether. I haven't spotted a single zombie in weeks. I think I'm the last human survivor, and I guess the zombies have gone looking for brains somewhere better than Whitby, maybe Mexico. Even still, I'm hesitant to go outside, fearing a trap. Can zombies plan traps? I don't want to find out the hard way.

I'm trying not to think about what I'll do when I run out of carbonated beverages and toilet paper, but for the time being, I've got a crap-load of books, and I'm surprised to say I've never been happier.

* * * * *

I've never been more miserable.

Mom and dad showed up today. And my sister. And Dillon.

Those two were even holding hands. Yeah, that's right. Zombies, holding hands. My sister and Dillon, holding hands.

And what's more, the whole lot of them were *singing*. "Kumbaya," or some garbage like that.

I crouched behind a stack of Louis L'Amour westerns, hoping that the cowboys, Indians, and fair maidens would block me from my family's view.

They walked deeper into the library, scanning the stacks of books and periodicals, looking for something. Me? How did they know I was here? My mind raced as fast as my heart was beating, like a jackhammer trying to drill itself out of my chest. Thin streams of sweat trickled down my ribs. I felt faint, but I tried not to breathe too loudly.

They stopped once they reached the middle of the large room. I wanted to get up and run, run far from the library, and never return. And then my mom opened her mouth and spoke.

"Clayton?" she said. Her voice echoed around the room, bouncing off books and careening down deep aisles. I hadn't heard my name in what felt like a lifetime. It knocked me off guard.

"Clayton?" she said again. She didn't moan. *She didn't moan.*

"It doesn't look like he's here," Dad said in perfect non-zombie English. "Shucks."

Amy gently patted Dad's shoulder. "There, there, pop. We'll just have to keep on looking."

"He's bound to show up sometime," Dillon said with great difficulty through the gaping hole in his neck.

What the hell was going on here? I mean, seriously, what the hell?

They took up their song again and walked towards the exit. Relief washed over me, but so did confusion bordering on hysteria, and my body trembled. Before I could get it together, my nose let out an ill-timed little peep, a dreadful mix of a sneeze and a snort.

My family stopped. They looked at the Louis L'Amours dead-on.

"Clayton?" my mom repeated, an audible note of giddy anticipation rising in her voice.

They circled my hiding place. I had nowhere to go! This was it! This was the end! Oh, cruel world, to end my life in the library!

The four of them jumped on me, wrapping me up in their groping arms. My dad was the first to put his hungry lips to my skull.

And kissed me. My zombie dad kissed me. A big, wet, sloppy one. My dad has never kissed me, not even before he was a zombie, back when he was just a dad.

I felt like puking. I pissed myself instead. Damn you, endless supply of Dr. Pepper! Damn you, weak bladder!

"Ah," cooed Amy. "Somebody's so happy to see us he's lost control of his plumbing." She smiled at Dillon, and his neck-hole seemed to smile back.

"Don't worry, sweetie," said Mom as she ruffled my unkempt hair. "I brought you some clean underwear!" Out of her pocket materialized a pair of Calvin Klein tighty-whiteys. Mom beamed from ear to ear.

"Get off me!" I shouted. "Get away from me!" I pushed them away and jumped to my feet. This was surely a trick! Why were they torturing me so?

"What's the matter, brother?" asked Amy as she and the rest of these fiends exchanged confused looks.

"You're zombies! You're here for my brains!" I said.

Bret Jordan 2006

They all laughed heartily. "Yes, we're zombies," said Dad, "and we're here for your brains."

"I knew it!" I shook my index finger at them triumphantly.

Dad continued, "But we're also here for your bones and your skin and your heart and your soul! We're here for all of you! We're taking you back home. We're going to be a family again!"

I lowered my finger and slowly exhaled. A deep crease furrowed my brow as I quickly went over the facts. My family and my best friend were zombies, and they openly admitted to that. They had disappeared for a few weeks, along with all the other zombies. Then they came back. They could speak coherently again (even—to some extent—Dillon, the throatless wonder.) They could walk upright again. And most importantly, they hadn't eaten me yet. The one thing that made the least amount of sense, (and that's saying something,) was that they seemed to be filled with love for each other, and for me. I sighed in exasperation.

My mom reached out and took hold of my shaking hand. "Come home with us, sweetie. I'm going to bake a batch of my chocolate chip cookies!"

My head throbbed. My tummy rumbled. I didn't know what to do.

"And to celebrate, I'm buying chimmy chongas for everyone!" said Dad.

Without looking back, I left the library and stepped out into the afternoon's fading light with my loving zombie family.

But I sure as hell didn't join in "Kumbaya."

*   *   *   *   *

So that's my story. Does it conclude with a happy ending? Absolutely not.

They came back, all right. Everybody. My neighbors and my classmates and my teachers and the cops and the lawyers and the doctors and the waiters and the garbage men and the journalists and the hockey players and the bankers and the hobos and the hair stylists and the rock stars and the florists and the librarians and the birds and the bees and the goldfish and even Jessica Peterson and her big ones.

They all came back, and they were all happy. Joyous. Euphoric. It made me sick.

My family was thankful to be alive. Every day was a blessing. And they hugged and kissed each other way too much. But nobody, not a soul, knows what happened when they disappeared. They can't remember where they went or how they returned. All they know is that they're so very fortunate to be back, and Jesus loves them.

When I make gagging sounds after someone says something mushy, which happens all the time, my family shares a chuckle and looks at me with sympathetic eyes. And somebody invariably says with a shrug, "Ah, I guess you just don't understand. You're not a born-again zombie." Every time I hear that, I feel like punching a teddy bear in the face.

What's worse, Dillon's no longer a bad apple. Just yesterday, I shot him with a roman candle, and he scolded me for it, saying, "Hey, hey. Time out, mister. Someone could lose an eye." These new zombies have no sense of humor.

If I thought I didn't fit in before this whole fiasco, I was dead wrong. I don't fit in now. Oh sure, everyone tries to include me, tries their damndest to make me feel like one of the gang. But I can see it in their eyes: it's clear that I'm not one of them. And these zombies no longer eat brains, so I guess I can forget turning into one myself.

As long as I stay here, I'm not living—I'm slowly dying.

I've packed a backpack with Fritos and Dr. Pepper. I've squeezed in a few good books. I've got my notebook and a couple of pencils. And just in case, I'm armed with my bloody alarm clock.

I figure I'll head south. If I'm going to move, I may as well move somewhere warm.

I wonder what Mexico's like this time of year? How long would it take to walk there? Is the country frequented with meteorite crashes? Do they speak English, or Mexican? Will the senores and senoras be zombies, too? Do they have public libraries? So many questions explode in my head like kernels in a heated bag of microwave popcorn.

New question: do they eat microwave popcorn in Mexico? And can I get it with salsa?

I guess there's only one way to have all my questions answered.

I step out the door and head down the street, a crisp fall wind bristling my skin. I walk; there's no need to run.

And if I ever get lonely, I can always get myself a dog.

The Hill

ERIC SHAPIRO

I'd call Kelly crazy, but what would that make me? After all, I'm the guy who's with him. That could possibly make me worse than he is. But at least I had the presence of mind to stay in the car.

Fifteen minutes since Kelly left. With each passing second, I become more nauseous. I'm thinking of hopping in the back and stretching out, but it would rob me of my sight. And what if one of the tortoises comes up to the car?

It's a habit I can't shake, calling them tortoises. My sister used to call them that, and then my mother started saying it, and then it kind of stuck. Maybe it was wishful thinking, comparing the things to a known animal, one that's known for being harmless.

Until my last day on Earth, I'll never forget the first time I saw one. I knew something was wrong when Mom didn't send us to school for three weeks. Christmas break ended, but before we knew it, right in the first week of February, everybody's parents started keeping them at home. And when I say at home, I mean it literally—we weren't allowed to step outside.

From talking with our friends on the phone, we got scattered bits of information: there was something in town, and in the neighboring towns, and also in the neighboring states. It had to do with a nuclear problem. And things that crawled along the ground. And no matter what you did, you couldn't kill these things.

I was twelve; Allie was nine. But both of us were becoming grown-ups.

It wasn't the cabin fever that made me restless; it was the lack of television. Though I begged and begged, my mom wouldn't explain why we could only watch the movies we owned. And after three weeks of watching the same crap, I felt my mind beginning to split. So I ran to the patio window and tore at the thick curtain. It was hard to tear off 'cause Mom had nailed it to the wall. But even though I almost lost my fingernails in the process, I managed to rip the fabric.

Same old yard: slanted green grass, upside-down baby pool, rusting swingset. Had all the grown-ups gone insane? The world looked the same as it had the last time I'd seen it. And I was intent to go outside and run around. I needed to get my blood moving, needed to run and skip and jump and scream my head off.

Mom was upstairs sleeping, but I still didn't waste any time grabbing my shoes. No need to risk her waking up. I slid the glass door open and ran outside in my bare feet. The grass was so unfamiliar to me; its coolness made me quiver.

Everything was the same, goddamn it. The backyard, the side of the house, the front yard, the sidewalk, the street. Except no cars were driving by. And no people were walking. And all the windows had boards or cloth in them.

I can't remember what I was thinking when I ran all the way to the library. Sometimes I shake when trying to recall that stretch of time, but it's entirely gone. Who knows whether I was juiced or scared. The next thing I knew, I was at the library by the corner of our street and Brand Street. I'd always hated going there before, but given the current circumstances, I was kind of glad to see the place still standing.

But what were those enormous rocks scattered about the hill on the library's north side? From my position on the sidewalk, the rocks were far away, but their color was still striking: a choppy mix of red and pink, with faded white dots splashed about. Their shape was clear, also: kind of dome-like, but curling inward near the lower rim.

I strained my eyes to see what they were. Stupid me, I was failing to make the connection between what I was seeing and what I'd heard about the "crawling things." Maybe the experience of being outside had me in a state of sensory overload.

Then I realized what I was looking at. These strawberry domes were hardly rocks—they were shells. A couple lifted off the grass, revealing yellowish stumps along their bottoms. The stumps would move a bit, carrying the shells along some inches, and then creak downward and disappear again. I didn't like the looks of those legs.

From behind me, I heard a single word, one that I wish wasn't so common. Then I wouldn't have to hear it so often. The word was "boy." The voice that said it sounded full of lice and maggots.

When I turned around, the first thing my brain processed was the face. It was a human face, no question about that. Two eyes, two ears, one nose, one mouth, and a full head of hair. But it was only four or five inches from the ground. Surrounding it was one of those reddish shells.

I remember feeling my arms as I ran. I kept half-hugging myself, making sure I still had arms. No doubt I had legs; they were right underneath me, carrying me along at the speed of a meteor. With every inch, I scanned the surrounding grass and pavement, looking for those domes, seeing none, hoping I wouldn't see any more.

God, did I cry when I got home. I hadn't known I had so many tears in me. My head just kept grinding them out, along with quite a bit of mucus. The images in my head were too rude, too harsh. It hurt me to know that my eyes had seen such a thing—to know that *anyone's* eyes had seen such a thing.

My mother, you had to admire her strength. We sat at the kitchen table that night, me with my moist face, her with her pale one. I demanded answers, but she just shook her head.

Oh, God, her head.

All I could do was think about people's heads, sticking out from underneath big turtle shells.

The face I'd seen, it looked so ordinary. Female, I think it was. The hair was long, and might have had a bow in it. Was she wearing glasses? I can't recall. Ornaments or not, she was human. Or at least partially so.

"Tell me, Mommy," I said through my tears, knowing I was too old to call her that, yet knowing it touched something deep within her, and that it just might be the thing to make her crack.

"*Listen*," she snapped, scaring me with her eyes, "if I tell you what they are, you won't have a mind. Do you hear me, Michael? You won't have a mind. Mine is hardly left, and I'll need you to look after Allie."

Things got terrible after that. Mom started doing one weird thing after another. She'd sometimes be in her closet for hours at a time, not so much screaming as talking real loud, struggling to form whole sentences, but only managing to produce dull fragments:

"There can't be..."

"There WON'T be..."

"I'll go, I'll go, I'll go..."

I love her so much for sparing my mind. Yet, despite her condition, I wanted to know what was in her head. Asking her again, though, would hardly be any use. She couldn't really talk anymore. It was almost as though she tricked herself into no longer being able to speak, so that the God-awful info would never make it to our precious ears.

Allie and I started sleeping in the same bed. Where we were close before, we were now like a unified soul. Though we couldn't articulate as much given our underdeveloped vocabularies, we managed to express that we were there for each other, that we would always be there for each other. This sentiment became especially strong after Mom used the hammer on herself.

* * * * *

That was over three years ago, and tonight I can't be there for Allie. I've long wondered what would happen if it was ever my well-being against hers, and now I know the answer. Though I'll live in guilt, at least I'll live.

Better Kelly than me, I tell myself. Better him to brave the hill, and better him to die if he fails to rescue Allie.

These things (they call them "Low Walkers") have been getting smarter over time. The military once thought it stood a chance, but after a spectacle of countless explosions, they found the tortoise population wasn't getting any lower. No, it was just increasing. Rumor had it there were whole strawberry deserts in the West.

What they do is, they go to people's porches. And then they climb on top of one another, six or seven in a pile. The top one on the pile uses its mouth to twist open a doorknob or bash in a window. Sometimes the piles go as high as twenty. They can get into all kinds of places this way. And once they have a person in their grip, they hang on with a tightness that can only be described as industrial. Allie's arm was no match for that turtle's teeth.

Where they take people, God only knows. There's no flow of information, no media mechanism to inform us. The things have effectively taken over, reducing humans to something like rats—a species that usually hides in its homes, only to scurry out rapidly in search of food or drink.

Kelly was making out with Allie when the tortoises came in. They were down in our basement, and the beasts cracked their way through the sump pump. They'd been tunneling underground, apparently. Sometimes, before this happened, I dreamt of them, deep underground, faces black with soil, white rings betraying their eyes. Maybe I'm telepathic.

That's doubtful, considering I can't see how this will pan out. We're parked at the foot of the library's north hill, where the local population likes to lurk, and Kelly just went out there with his pair of handguns. He doesn't go anywhere without them. Me, I'm unarmed. My only weapons are my eyes; they keep darting toward the door locks.

The worst part is the words they say. None of them are less than twenty feet from the car, but I can hear them. Random words, like the remnants of an intellectual consciousness:

"Favorite."

"Go away."

"The nighttime comes."

Buggy though they are, the words sound human, and that's got to be the hardest part for me. What goes on within their minds? Do they converse with humans before they chew them up?

Kelly says he shot one in the head once. It wasn't attacking him or anything; he just snuck up on it to see what would happen. The skull shattered like a human's would, and rosy blood flowed out, and the face got all melted, but still it walked. As a matter of fact, Kelly says its pace picked up when it went away. And it screamed a bit. And muttered, "You made me frown."

"Where'd they come from?" I once asked Kelly. I'd heard all the half-assed theories from my other neighbors, but he seemed like he might have something good.

"Mutation," he answered, his eyes toward the floor. "Nuclear accident. It's the only angle that works."

I have to admit that I like that theory. Though it hardly calms my nerves, it does have some logic going for it. But how can it be that they don't die?

My thoughts screech to a halt. An image of beauty has graced the center of the windshield. It's Allie's face! Did the son of a bitch actually find her? Holy shit! My heart flies upward in my chest. And a smile—an actual smile—twists up my face.

"Allie!" I scream, honking the horn. I do so with the heel of my hand, flattening my skin 'cause I press so hard.

She smiles back. Oh, thank God! They're not as vicious as we feared. My sister's face is so becoming when she smiles. If I have any hope left, it's all due to her.

Then I twist on the lights and Allie's gone.

My brain twists into a pulsing question mark. With a half-frozen hand, I reach for the passenger side lock. I feel so weak that pulling the lock up is like manually extracting a tooth. When it finally comes up, I pause before reaching for the door handle. I get a bit of air in my lungs, tug the handle, and click open the door.

A strange smell hits my nostrils, a combination of human juices and alien sewage. I want to shut the door as much as I want to go see Allie. Compassion wins out; I step into the frightening air.

Once I arrive at the front of the car, my heart instantly lets up. Allie is present; she's just fallen to her knees. I race over to her and kneel on the ground, leveling our heights.

"What happened, Allie? Did they hurt you?"

When she looks up at me, I catch a subtle flicker within her eyes. Their surfaces have tears on them. "I was so happy to see you," she breathes. As her breath touches me, I feel a sickness in my chest.

"I'm happy to see you, too," I say. "Where's Kelly?"

"They're breathing on him now," she goes, and I suddenly know what my mom meant about your mind leaving.

"They—?" I start, but then Allie hugs me with all her strength, cutting off my air.

"He'll be okay," she says. "He'll be okay. He'll. The walk. To tangle."

I try to say my sister's name, but I'm having trouble remembering what it is. So I settle for returning her hug. As I wrap my arms around her, my mind becomes a blackish cloud. There's a hardness all along her back. I knock on it to make sure it's real.

My sister then taps my back with her fist. The sound is similar, though less acute. My cloud grows darker. Allie's knocking back.

THE FINGER

MATT HULTS

1.

Through some ironic twist of fate, the phone call from the morgue came while Jim Cooley sat watching *Frankenstein* on one of the cable channels.

"It's me," Stuart said when Jimmy picked up the receiver. "I got one. How fast can you get down here?"

Jimmy straightened up in his seat, letting the half-eaten bag of Crispy Pork Bits fall to the trailer's floor. "Hot damn, Stu, are you serious? When'd he come in? Where'd they find him—"

"I'll fill you in on the goddamn details when you get here," Stuart interrupted. "Harrington just went out to lunch, so we have less than an hour to do this."

Jimmy grinned. "We're really going through with it?"

"I guess so. Meet me at the back loading dock by twelve-thirty, or the deal is off!"

He hung up.

Outside, thunder rumbled like the footsteps of an angry god.

Jimmy continued to smile as he replaced the handset, then slapped his hands together with a whoop of delight. "Hot shit!" he cheered. "The little bastard did it!" He jumped up from the couch and grabbed his jean jacket off the wall hook as he hurried out the door.

2.

Three inches of rainwater sloshed along the gutters and burbled around the storm drains as Jimmy guided his rusty Mustang down the alley that serviced the back side of the Hewitt County Municipal Building. The parking area at this end of the lot boasted twenty spaces, but only two vehicles occupied the asphalt: Stuart Wyllie's dented red Honda and a 1988 Ford that made up the third unit in the HCPD's trio of squad cars.

Jimmy parked next to the sunken driveway that gave access to the lower loading bay of the building and got out. The rain continued to come down like a busted water main, soaking his shoulders and hair as he ran to the back door.

He rapped on the steel. "Yo, Stu, open up, man!"

He knocked again when no one answered, letting his gaze flick to the old squad car as he waited. A smile crept onto his face when he thought of how he had etched his initials in the vinyl on the rear of the driver's seat back when the car had been new.

The door clicked and flew open.

"What the hell?" Stuart asked. "I never told you to knock!"

The kid glanced around like a mouse in a cat kennel as Jimmy stepped past him, into a green-tiled hallway outside the morgue office.

"I'm due back at the hospital as soon as Dr. Harrington returns," Stuart reminded him. "We don't have much time!"

"Don't shit yourself," Jimmy told him. "Now what do you got for me?"

Stuart eased the door into its frame before speaking, and when he did, he kept his voice low. "Mexican male, no ID. Sheriff Pickett said a trucker found the body under the I-30 overpass around four o'clock yesterday morning. He's guessing the guy was an illegal thumbing his way north."

"Kick ass!" Jimmy cheered.

"Keep your voice down!" Stuart hissed, glancing up and down the corridor.

"Yeah, yeah—what else?"

Stuart ushered him inside the empty office, toward a door across the room. "We got him fresh," he said, snatching a manila folder off the desk as they passed it. "Harrington pronounced the cause of death as heart failure two hours after they brought him in, and we just got the toxicology and blood work reports back from HCMC: negative across the board; aside from being dead, he's as healthy as a horse."

"Ah, man," Jimmy said, "this is friggin' *perfect!*"

Stuart pushed through the door of the autopsy room and led the way past the central operating table and body hoist. Jimmy shivered as the first drops of adrenaline hit his veins. His neck hairs prickled on end the way they did in his childhood, when his mother would drag him to the doctor's office with an ear infection or pneumonia. Cold sweat sheathed his palms as his eyes drifted over the various items in the room: the table, the scales, the stainless steel containers. The drive over had been easy enough—even a bit exciting—but now the reality of what awaited him began to sink in.

Stuart unlocked another door, and they stepped into the cooler. Six stainless steel storage lockers took up the far wall, but only one displayed an information card in the holder on the door.

"This him?" Jimmy asked.

Stuart gestured toward the locker. "Be my guest."

Jimmy reached for the handle but stopped short before his fingers touched the metal. He glanced at Stuart, at the purple latex gloves he wore; with a smirk of self-admiration, he slipped the cuff of his jacket over his hand. "Can't be too careful."

He opened the door and rolled out the retractable table.

The corpse had already been packaged in a black body bag for its trip to the Hewitt County Medical Center, where it would await cremation if nothing came up on a fingerprint check, or if nobody claimed the body.

Still using his jacket cuff, Jimmy unzipped the top third. With a final glance at Stuart, he reached up with both hands and parted the two halves of the bag to reveal a bloodless stump where the man's head should have been.

"Holy Christ!" He snapped his hands back and leapt away. "Son of a bitch!"

Stuart cracked a grin for the first time since their meeting.

"Real hilarious, asshole! I thought you said his ticker crapped out?"

"It did," Stuart laughed. "After he got hit by a truck."

"Damn!"

"Hey, at least we don't need to wait for the dental x-rays."

Jimmy shook his head, still squirming from the surprise like a snake trying to work itself out of an old skin.

Stuart's smile faded as he glanced at his watch, then to the door. "Okay, let's get this over with. We're pushing the limit here."

He placed the manila folder on the dead man's chest and flipped it open. A second later, he produced an ink tray from the pocket of his lab coat.

Jimmy lingered at a distance for another moment, then moved forward again. He glanced at the shredded mess of torn muscle and broken bones in the bag—all that remained of the cadaver's neck—then refocused on Stuart as he held up the man's right arm and dabbed his blue-gray fingers on the ink-soaked felt of the tray. The top form in the manila folder contained two rows of sequential square boxes, each labeled for the digits of the human hand. Starting with the row marked "Right," Stuart pressed the man's fingers into the appropriate spaces one at a time, rolling them from side to side to transfer their impressions. He repeated the procedure for the left hand, all except for the smallest finger.

For that box, he dabbed his own left pinky in the ink and rolled it on the paper.

He took the original fingerprinting sheet out of the file—the one Dr. Harrington had completed when the Sheriff first brought the corpse in, Jimmy guessed—and he crumpled it into a wad, using it to wipe away the excess ink from his hand. Finished, he stuffed the soiled paper in his pocket, slipped the new form into the file, and gathered up the folder.

"I still say it should be your print on that paper," he commented. "This was your plan, after all."

"I got a record," Jimmy said. "You don't."

"Yeah, yeah. Anyway, that's my end of it. Your turn."

Jimmy reached into his back pocket, extracting a sandwich-size Zip-Loc baggy and a dirt-flecked pair of pruning sheers.

He met Stuart's eyes... then looked to the cadaver's left hand.

To the smallest finger.

His heart hesitated as he positioned the tool's cutting edge between the first and middle knuckle. Then, after one last glance at Stuart, he squeezed down on the sheer's handle with both hands as hard and as fast as he could.

Shick!

Stuart grimaced as Jimmy lifted the severed digit from the table, holding it between thumb and forefinger.

"You really gonna eat that thing?" Stuart asked.

"I ain't gonna *eat* it," Jimmy corrected as he slipped the finger into the Zip-Loc bag. "I'm going to do like we talked about and just... *chew it a little.*"

"This is nuts," Stuart said.

Jimmy eyed him. "Hey, we're in this together, man. Don't start getting fidgety on me! Just keep thinking about that old lady who burned herself with the coffee from McDonalds. What'd she get for her lawsuit... a million? Two million?"

"Actually, I think it came closer to three."

"Exactly! Now imagine what a big-ass chain like Smokey's will have to shell out when I find a human *finger* in my food!" He clapped his hands together. "Hot damn, boy! Even split fifty-fifty, we'll both be rolling in it! I'll make sure a couple of guys from the worksite are there to see me spit it out. Then those patty-flipping pricks will have to pay through the roof for emotional stress."

Stuart's expression remained as serious as ever, but Jimmy noticed a renewed gleam of determination in his eyes at the mention of the money. "Just remember to cook it," the kid said. "You gotta simmer it in the chili for at least three hours at one hundred and eighty degrees so the spices will permeate the flesh. That'll give any prosecutor in the country an uphill battle to prove it wasn't in the mix from the start. Especially since Smokey's meat supplier just got busted for hiring illegals. I Googled the case settlement last week and..."

Jimmy shook his head and laughed.

"What?"

"Nothing," Jimmy answered, heading for the door. "I just knew hanging out with a nerd like you would pay off eventually."

3.

Jimmy waited three days, just like they'd planned, allowing the police time to do a fingerprint check on the Mexican. When no word came from Stuart to abort the mission, he drove to work on the fourth morning with the finger in a Styrofoam cooler full of ice on the passenger seat.

With the lid on, the white rectangular box hardly looked worth the three-dollar price tag. But Jimmy couldn't help seeing the container as something secret, something important, and during the drive from the Shell station he imagined himself on one of those TV medical dramas transporting an urgently-needed donor organ.

He arrived at the job site just after nine, coming to a stop amid the larger pickups and SUVs of the regular work crew. Construction had been suspended for the last few days due to the rain, but today the steel skeleton of the new Park Street mini-mall bustled with activity.

Before getting out, he peeked in on the finger. It lay in the Zip-Loc bag like a half-curled worm. Smiling, he closed the cooler's lid and got out of the car.

The ground remained soft and moist from the recent rainfall, and Jimmy's feet made loud smacking sounds in the mud as he walked to the construction company's mobile office. He noticed Tom Ryder, the foreman, talking with two of the subcontractors working the same site, clapping them on the back as he always did during conversations, acting like a father congratulating his sons on a well-played little league game. Jimmy ducked into the trailer to clock in before the man spotted him.

He found Jeff Densi, the lead mason, out by what would become the entrance to the mall's parking lot. Jeff crouched beside his brother, Roy, near the first of two walls that divided the lot from the sidewalk. When seen side by side, the two looked like the working-Joe equivalent of Laurel and Hardy.

Jimmy waved hello as the men looked up.

Jeff had been kneeling alongside the guide wires that outlined the wall's base, and he stood up as Jimmy approached, maneuvering his bulk with ease. He returned the greeting eagerly enough, but his features appeared grim. "You're a half hour late, Cooley. What gives?"

Jimmy put on his apology face. "I'm sorry—"

"I gave you a break with this job," Jeff went on without pause. "You wouldn't have it if my regular bricklayer hadn't wrecked his back."

"I know, sir—"

"With your work history, you'd be lucky to get hired at a firecracker stand, let alone anywhere else. I took you on 'cause I didn't have another choice."

Jimmy nodded, trying to look humble. "It won't happen again, man. I just couldn't find my lunch box this morning... I think Meg must've taken it with her when she split."

Jeff had been glaring at him with what Jimmy had come to know as his 'business look,' but at the mention of Megan, his face softened. "Your woman left you?"

Jimmy nodded.

"Shit, pal, I'm sorry to hear that."

Roy had stopped his work to listen, leaning on his shovel like a farmer watching his crops grow. "Women," he said.

Jimmy shrugged. "Like you said, I'd be damned if I could hold a decent job for long, and that doesn't look too good on a home loan application... She must've just got fed-up with living with a loser."

Jeff waved his comment away. "Hell, kid, I didn't mean it like that. Don't be so hard on yourself."

"I guess."

The big man hooked his thumbs in his suspenders and simply nodded, looking uncertain of what else to say.

"Here comes Slappy," Roy commented, breaking the silence. He tipped his head in the direction of the company trailer, and Jimmy spotted the foreman making his rounds.

Jeff clapped his hands together and gestured at the wall base. "Let's get back to it," he said, sounding relieved to have gotten off the subject of Jimmy's muddled love-life. "I hope everything works out for you, Jim—I really do—but we got a schedule to keep."

Jimmy nodded. "Don't worry about me. Besides, I got a plan to get her back."

"Yeah?" Jeff asked.

Jimmy looked at the Smokey's restaurant across the street and thought about the finger in his car.

"Why don't you boys join me for lunch, and I'll tell you about it."

4.

Just before lunch, Jimmy went to his car under the pretext of retrieving his wallet. Using his body as a shield, he reached into the cooler, snatched up the Zip-Loc bag, and slipped it into the pocket of his jean jacket.

Jeff and Roy had already started across the road to Smokey's, and Jimmy caught up with them as they fell into one of the lines behind the bank of registers along the counter. The lunch rush had the small building packed to capacity. He wiped his brow in an unconscious reaction to the crowd, and his hand came away covered in sweat.

He stood in line, pretending to count his pocket change as he waited to order.

Jeff bought three cheeseburgers, fries, an apple pie, and a Coke.

Roy went for a fish sandwich and a fountain drink.

Jimmy got a soda and a bowl of chili.

They grabbed a booth at the back corner of the main dining room as a trio of teens vacated their seats to leave. Jimmy pulled the plastic top off the paper bowl of chili as Jeff and Roy sat down on the opposite side of the table.

"I hear they got a new titty bar over by the air base," Roy said, sipping his drink. "Seeing as you don't got no current attachments, Jim, maybe you'd like to check it out sometime?"

Jimmy had steeled himself to keep cool, to just act normal so the others wouldn't get suspicious, but he suddenly found himself speechless as he focused on how to execute the plan.

"Dammit, Roy," Jeff said. "Can't you see the kid's just had his heart ripped in two?"

Roy shrugged as he bit into his sandwich. "Just thought seeing some skin might cheer him up, is all."

Jeff's bushy mustache twitched under his nose. "You ever think about anything else?"

Roy paused his chewing for a moment then shook his head.

Jimmy reached into his pocket as the two men exchanged looks, splitting the bag's seal with his hand. He had to force a neutral expression as his living fingers found the dead one. Then, with the finger cupped in his hand, he picked up the packet of Saltines that had come with his order and tore open the plastic. "Check out the peach by the register," he said, crumbling the crackers. "I'd like to see her in one of them places."

The men looked over their shoulders, and he dropped the finger into the chili with the crackers, stirring it under with his spoon. Initially he'd planned to take a few bites before getting to business—to make the lunch seem more authentic—but the thought of swallowing a single drop of the food after the finger had been mixed in made his stomach flop.

Get a grip, Jim. Think dollar signs.

He churned the chili, feeling the finger's weight against the plastic utensil. Then, with a furtive glance to make sure Jeff and Roy had their attention on their own meals, he scooped the finger into his mouth.

It slid off the spoon, onto his tongue, taking up far more space than he liked.

Don't think about it, dumbass, just do it!

And he did.

He bit down, feeling the rubbery texture of skin, the hardness of bone. The heat from the chili had yet to penetrate the cold from the ice, and as his teeth came together, a frigid liquid spurted against the inside of his cheek.

His empty stomach seemed to fill with a putrid green liquid and his body fought to expel the object. But just as he prepared to spew it onto the tabletop, Jeff and Roy turned away, facing the front of the store to look at the menu.

They won't see it! his brain raged. *They have to see me spit it out!*

So he held it in his mouth, feeling its horrid presence.

And it moved.

He'd raised his hand, about to slam it down on the table to regain the men's attention, when he distinctly felt the finger uncurl, its nail scraping the side of one molar.

Every nerve in his body seemed to short circuit from the shock, and he stiffened in his seat, unable to move. Then the finger did it again, squirming like a half-dead worm trapped in a storm puddle, just as someone said, "Hey there, Jimbo!"

Slapping him on the back—

Gulp!

—causing him to swallow!

He felt the finger slide down his throat like a thick bite of licorice, pressing hard against his insides.

Oh, shit!

He clutched the table with both hands, tensing his neck muscles in a last ditch effort to stop the dead man's digit from reaching his stomach. But then he felt one last squeeze deep inside his chest and knew it was already too late.

"Jimbo," he heard Tom, the foreman, say from behind. "You all right, man? Damn, I didn't mean to surprise you like that."

The others set their food aside when Jimmy failed to respond, Jeff leaning in close, asking him what was wrong. Tom offered him a hand, but he pushed it away.

"Outta my way, you back-slapping asshole!" He leapt from his seat and raced for the bathroom.

5.

He elbowed his way through a group of teenage girls blocking the hall that accessed the restrooms, then shouldered the door open, only to slam it shut again and slap the lock into place. He caught a glimpse of himself in the mirror as he did, and for a heart-stopping moment, he thought he'd come face-to-face with an albino psychopath.

Without wasting another second, he turned away from the mirror and crammed his own finger down his throat in an effort to puke. He reached as far back as he could, stabbing tender flesh and poking his tonsils.

He gagged a few times, but nothing came up.

"Dammit," he shrieked. "This can't be happening!"

He slammed his fists on the sink top and punched a hole in the plastic cover of the paper towel dispenser. He tried hitting himself in the stomach a few times, but when that didn't bring up the finger, he took his frustration out on the wastebasket in a flurry of kicks.

Huffing out of exertion and fear, he leaned against the sink and paused to collect himself.

"Think, dipshit! Think!"

His breathing had just begun to ease when the door to one of the two toilet stalls clicked and slowly swung open. A moment later, a balding middle-aged man wearing a business suit and wire-frame glasses stepped out, clutching his unzipped pants at the waist. Without making eye contact, he edged toward the exit like an overweight tourist who'd fallen into the lion pit at the zoo.

Jimmy gaped at him. "Can't you see I'm having a moment here, pal?"

"I don't want any trouble, mister," the man quickly replied.

A dull silver cell phone poked out of the breast pocket of his shirt.

Jimmy saw it and lunged at him.

The stunned patron blubbered out a string of half-coherent pleas as Jimmy seized him by the lapels of his jacket and plucked the phone from his pocket. The man's pudgy hands flew up to ward off Jimmy's attack, leaving his pants and underwear to collapse at his feet.

"Please, mister, don't hurt me!"

But even as he said it, Jimmy unlocked the bathroom, shoved the phone-owner into the hall, and yanked the door shut again before the man's bare ass hit the floor.

Jimmy flipped open the phone and dialed Stuart's number.

"Hello?"

"Stu, it's me—"

"Jesus, Jim," Stuart gasped. "I've been trying to get a hold of you all morning. Listen, don't—"

"I swallowed it, man!"

"What?"

"The finger! The fucking thing's in my guts!"

Stuart's reply came out as one word. "*Wathefugitshididyou-dothatfor?*"

"I was hungry!" Jimmy bellowed back at him. "What do you think?!"

"Jesus, this figures!" Stu moaned.

"What the hell does that mean?"

"It means Sheriff Pickett came by this morning and told Harrington not to ship the corpse over to HCMC for cooking, that's what! Some homicide detective called about him last night, and he's on his way here right now to ID the body. If he's right, our illegal amigo might actually be a Navaho serial killer!"

"I don't give a damn!" Jimmy replied. "I need you to pump my stomach!"

"I don't know how to do that!"

"You're the goddamn medical expert here, you gotta do *something!*"

"Shit... I don't know... Just give it some time. It'll pass through you."

"I don't want it to pass through me, you idiot! I want it *out!*"

Suddenly a fist pounded on the bathroom door. "Open up!" a formidable voice ordered.

"Jim, we're in deep sewage here," Stuart said.

"Yeah, thanks for the tip!"

Jimmy snapped the phone shut and shoved it into his jacket.

"I said open up in there!" the voice ordered.

Rather than go for the door, Jimmy kicked through the window at the back of the room and jumped into the alley, landing in a filthy puddle of runoff from the dumpster.

6.

He went to a roadside motel off the interstate rather than chance returning to his trailer, and he spent the better half of the evening waiting for the police to show up.

Finally, around 2:00 a.m., he lay down on the bed. Sleep came in short spurts, but only out of exhaustion, and during the times when he dozed, he dreamed of the finger sloshing around in his stomach, refusing to digest.

Or trying to crawl out the way it went in.

Jimmy moaned at the thought, not wanting to recall it.

He'd chugged a whole bottle of FiberAll for dinner, followed by half a package of Exlax that he picked up at a small market adjacent to his hideout. So far, neither had freed him of the thing.

Earlier, he tried to call Stuart, but the bastard never picked up. On the contrary, his stolen cell phone rang about two dozen times, its display glowing with the names and numbers of callers he didn't dare answer.

He finally drifted off to sleep as the first red rays of sunlight bled over the horizon.

7.

When Jimmy awoke, he went straight to the bathroom.

The day had come and gone while he slept, and he felt confident that the long rest had given the meds time to generate some results. Much to his disappointment, he spent nearly twenty minutes on the toilet straining/praying to shit out the finger, secretly fearing that he'd crap a whole hand.

Back in the bedroom, the television droned. He'd left it on last night to escape the burbling sounds produced from his gut, and now some sitcom gave way to the ten o'clock news.

"Our top story: a morbid case of burglary at the Hewitt County morgue—"

Jimmy bounded back into the main room with his pants trailing behind him.

"—involving the theft of an unidentified corpse."

The newscaster explained how the county's medical examiner had found the morgue's autopsy room in disarray earlier that evening, a discovery that led him to a second scene of destruction inside the cooler. There, the perpetrator(s) had stolen the decapitated remains of a body held for forensic testing as part of a murder investigation by authorities upstate. According to sources, the room's stainless steel door had been torn off its hinges.

Jimmy dropped down on the end of the bed as he listened.

The events of the last few days spiraled through his mind, chased by the dread of whatever new miseries the future might hold, and all at once, he clutched his midsection and ran for the bathroom.

The lurching started even as he leaned over the sink. He seized the faucet handles to stabilize himself while the tremors passed through him, then sagged in despair when the convulsions concluded with nothing more than a foul-smelling belch.

He rinsed his mouth and was about to leave when he glimpsed movement in his peripheral vision. He glanced to the left, facing the room's tiny window.

And saw a dog staring back at him.

Two yellow eyes glinted in the dark, reflecting the light from the bathroom, and Jimmy leapt backward in shock even as his over-stressed brain realized that the eyes had to be at least six feet off the ground.

The window exploded in a hailstorm of glass.

Blood-splattered arms reached through the frame.

Jimmy shrieked as the attacker clutched fistfuls of his shirt, each hand a skeletal mess of torn flesh and exposed bone, as if the person outside had recently clawed his way out of a grave—or through a stainless steel door. Then, in a split-second of hyper-awareness, he saw that the assailant's smallest left-hand finger ended in a clean, circular stump.

Oh, Jesus, he thought, *it can't be!*

He punched at the restraining limbs, struggling to break free. Several of the meatless fingers tore through his shirt, and he mewed in disgust when the cold bones touched his skin.

The man leaned through the window, into the light, and Jimmy's shouts died in his throat.

Unlike before, the corpse was no longer headless.

At the point where the man's neck should've started, a railroad of thick stitches connected the severed head of a coyote to the human skin of his torso.

Jimmy shook his head, unable to escape the glare of the animal's yellow gaze as it stared down at him over a lipless snout filled with jagged white fangs. It pulled him to the edge of the window, inches from its reeking flesh, where a legion of maggots explored the bare patches of skin that dotted its fur.

"It was an accident!" Jimmy heard himself repeating.

The stink of formaldehyde wafted out from the thing's dripping maw when it opened its jaws, and a new degree of terror pushed Jimmy's mind to the edge of insanity as the monster started to laugh.

"Yee-nadlooshii!" the undead nightmare declared, speaking each syllable with perfect clarity despite the mouth that produced them.

Its putrid breath gusted into Jimmy's face, but the creature's ghastly physical composition no longer compared to the terror of facing an intelligent being with supernatural strength and a malevolent spirit.

Suddenly, the back of Jimmy's head crashed into the wall.

A swarm of fireflies swirled across his vision, but when they cleared, he saw the monster towering before him, still only halfway through the window, holding two equally shredded halves of his T-shirt in its bony hands.

Jimmy patted his bare chest, just then realizing that he'd braced both feet against the sink in an effort to escape the creature's grasp and must have torn clear through his clothes!

The coyote-headed horror roared, spraying spittle through the air.

It gripped the edges of the window frame, and with the gunshot noise of cracking timbers, it yanked a five-foot section of the wall into the night.

Sparks hissed from a severed electrical line, and the bathroom lights went out. A ruptured pipe shot water at the ceiling.

But Jimmy was already through the door and across the bedroom, fleeing from the building in nothing but his boxer shorts.

Behind him came another thunderclap of destruction, another downpour of rubble.

Outside, in the parking lot, a blue convertible sat idling in the space reserved for the room next to Jimmy's, trunk open, front end facing away from the building.

Jimmy jumped into the driver's seat without even touching the door and left twenty feet of burnt rubber smoking on the asphalt as he peeled away from the motel.

8.

Stuart's house emerged out of the murk.

Jimmy drove the stolen car right up on the lawn and left the engine running when he hopped out and hurried to the door. No lights glowed in any of the windows, but he pounded on the door and thumbed the ringer.

When no one answered, he kicked open the door.

Inside, he found Stuart sitting in the living room with a double barrel shotgun.

What remained of his head was still dripping from the ceiling.

9.

Jimmy pushed through the police department's front door at ten minutes to midnight.

Deputy Vern Ferguson was eating a late dinner behind the long counter that separated the lobby from the offices, and Jimmy ignored the kid's muffled commands to halt as he tried to speak through a mouthful of ham sandwich.

"Hey!" the young officer shouted when Jimmy let himself through the partition.

Sheriff Pickett sat at one of the desks in the open central area of the building known as the bullpen, and even from a distance, Jimmy noticed the frown beneath his storm cloud of a mustache.

And he wasn't alone.

A tall Native American man in blue jeans and a suit coat (*cop casual*, Jimmy called it) stood to the left. A roadmap of fresh cuts crisscrossed the man's face, some linked by dozens of black stitches that looked all too reminiscent of the patchwork monster he'd faced at the motel. The sight stopped him in his tracks, and he had to refocus on what he'd come here to say.

"Want me to cuff him?" Ferguson asked from behind, but the Sheriff merely motioned him back to his food.

"Sheriff, we got trouble," Jimmy said.

Pickett stood, repositioning his pistol belt as he did. "Oh, I don't doubt that," he answered. "After what you pulled yesterday—"

"Forget that shit! I'm the reason that dead guy disappeared from the morgue today!"

Pickett let out a short bark of laughter and raised his hands as if surrendering to Jimmy's statement. "What a surprise!" he added with sarcastic flair. "Tossing a feller outta the john with his pants around his ankles and stealing his phone wasn't enough fun, was it? Ya just had to find something more interesting! All right, then, Cooley, enlighten us... What the hell did you do with a half-mutilated corpse?"

Before he could answer, Pickett's eyes narrowed to two suspicious slits that focused on Jimmy's boxers.

"You didn't fuck it, did you?"

Jimmy stared at the man. "What? No! Jesus, Sheriff, I ain't like that. I just ate one of the fingers—"

Pickett's bushy eyebrows seemed to fly off his forehead. "Christ almighty, son! Now you're mixed up in cannibalism?"

Deputy Ferguson laughed, expelling spurts of orange cola out his nose.

Pickett glared at the younger officer like an executioner with one hand on the power switch, ending the amusement. He then redirected his attention at Jimmy with equal intensity.

"This is Detective Riverwind," Pickett said, motioning to the Native American with the lacerated face. "He's the one you're going to have to make friends with if you don't want to spend the next decade in prison."

A phone rang at the desk. Vern answered it.

"Now listen up, Cooley," Pickett continued. "If it wasn't for the detective's investigation, I'd can your ass right now, and Judge Morton would put it on the shelf 'til winter. So if you have some serious information—and I mean it better be a goddamn treasure map with a big fuckin X at the end of it—then start talking."

"Hey, Sheriff!" Ferguson said. "We just got a call from that rescue shelter over on route nine. The neighbors say some nut job broke into the place and hacked up all the animals with an ax. Sounds real messy."

"Wonderful!" Pickett exclaimed. "Has the whole world gone crazy?"

"I think it would be best if I questioned Mister Cooley alone," detective Riverwind said. "Do you mind?"

It was the first time he'd spoken since Jimmy arrived, and the power of the man's voice sent a shiver down his spine.

Pickett waved them away. "You can have him!"

10.

A scarred, coffee-stained table sat in the center of the police station's only interview room, and Riverwind gestured for Jimmy to have a seat as he closed the door.

"Look," Jimmy said once they were alone, "this is a waste of time, man. That psycho you're after ain't dead! He's walking around right now, looking for me!"

Riverwind nodded, but didn't reply. He took off his jacket and draped it over the back of his chair.

"The 'psycho' you're referring to is a Navajo witch," the detective explained, now rolling up his sleeves as he talked. "My people call them Skinwalkers because they have the power to assume the shape of an animal to avoid our detection. Seven days ago, I beheaded the one you encountered, trapping its spirit inside its body, but the confrontation left me severely wounded and unable to fully dispose of the remains."

Jimmy gaped, looking to the man's ravaged face and recalling the coyote-headed corpse ripping out the bathroom wall of the motel.

"I could tell you the whole history of how they came to be," the detective went on, "but as you said, there isn't much time. All you need to know is that by consuming the Skinwalker's flesh, you've given it the power to thwart death and seek a new body."

"Me?!" Jimmy gasped. "But how—"

"Your friend Stuart isn't very good at keeping secrets," Riverwind answered. "He told me about your little scheme when I questioned the morgue staff about the disappearance of the Skinwalker's corpse. He mentioned how you'd inadvertently swallowed the creature's finger. Now it's using your energy—your *life force*—to stay in our world until it can transfer its spirit into your body."

"So how the hell do we stop it?" Jimmy asked. "I mean, you can stop it, right?"

"There are two options. One is to completely destroy its physical form, either by force or simply by waiting until the creature's body decomposes. The only problem is that you're now linked to the Skinwalker by the same magical bond that reanimated it, which will allow it to follow you wherever you go. It will anticipate our moves."

"Great! So it could be here any second?"

The man nodded.

"What's choice number two?"

"I cut off your head."

Jimmy blinked. "What?"

Riverwind reached behind his back and pulled out a knife large enough to reflect Jimmy's whole face in the blade. It glinted with the overhead fluorescents.

He jumped to his feet. "You can't kill me! You're a cop!"

"Decapitation separates a host's spirit from his life force. You and Mister Wyllie have left me no choice."

Jimmy shivered as a sudden pang of understanding ripped through his brain. "You killed Stuart!"

"An act of necessity," Riverwind admitted. "I had to be sure he wasn't lying about which one of you ate the finger."

"You stinking motherfu—"

The detective slashed, and Jimmy leapt backward. The tip of the blade plowed a red trench across the skin of his chest.

Jimmy dropped back in his chair and kicked upward as the wild-eyed detective lunged over the table. This time, Jimmy was faster. His heel slammed into Riverwind's face, popping loose a score of fresh stitches and peeling back a section of cheek.

The man roared in pain, clutching the wound.

Jimmy ducked under the table and scrambled to the door, throwing it open as six consecutive gunshots blared through the building.

He froze in the doorway.

Across the main room, past the bullpen, the Skinwalker rammed the front desk, demolishing the boards like a runaway wrecking ball. Pickett stood less than ten feet away, frantically reloading his sidearm.

The creature reared up on the hind legs of a horse, displaying the new additions it had made to its body. Jimmy recalled Vern's mention of an attack at the nearby animal shelter, and he now knew the fate of those various creatures.

Or parts of them, anyway.

The Skinwalker had transplanted its torso onto the body of a horse, looking like a mythological Centaur out of mental patient's nightmare. Four new arms sprouted from its sides, each freshly skinned and glistening with red muscle. Two of those newer appendages looked to be human, but the last set clearly came from something bigger.

The monster's coyote head snarled, now topped with deer antlers and flanked on each side by the heads of a mountain lion and a goat. Each scanned the room independently from the other, seeking new prey.

Deputy Ferguson emerged from the rubble of the desk and squeezed off five shots from his service pistol before the creature turned and struck out with its powerful hind legs, shattering his skull. Blood sprayed the wall.

Jimmy watched it happen with a dreamlike detachment, unable to react even when the beast plunged two of its hands into the deputy's chest and tore open his ribcage.

"Move your ass, Cooley!" Sheriff Pickett shouted.

Jimmy flinched at the force of the man's voice, glancing over his shoulder just as Riverwind's knife hacked into the doorframe beside him.

The detective surrendered the knife where it imbedded in the wood and yanked Jimmy backwards by the hair, even as his other hand drew a gun and fired three shots into Pickett's chest.

The Sheriff collapsed into a heap.

The Skinwalker roared.

As it charged forward, Riverwind hauled Jimmy into the interrogation room and slammed the door.

Jimmy pulled the knife from the doorframe when he passed it, but Riverwind slammed the pistol-butt down on his wrist.

The knife clattered to the floor.

"Now we end this!" the detective declared.

A moment later, the entire forward wall of the room bowed inward, shattering the sheetrock and splintering the wall studs. A hand tipped with eagle talons punched through the door paneling, snaring a hunk of Riverwind's skin before he got clear.

The detective howled in agony, losing his grip on Jimmy's hair as he strove to slip free of the hooks in his back.

Jimmy elbowed the man and made his escape, scooping up the knife.

He spun around to face the trapped Navajo officer.

"Kill yourself!" Riverwind hissed.

The door to the room and most of the wall had fragmented into a spider web, and Jimmy watched as a furless bear's paw reached through one of the cracks and clutched the man's face, instantly crushing his lower jaw into mush.

Jimmy stumbled away, shivering when he saw that the man's eyes still gazed with awareness. When the creature released him, Riverwind raised the gun to his head and ended the pain.

The entire building seemed to shudder as the monster pressed forward.

Ceiling tiles rained to the floor.

Jimmy edged into the corner of the room as he watched the wall crumble, knowing he only had a matter of seconds before the creature exploded inside and did whatever perverted mystical bullshit it wanted to do with him.

Which left him only one choice.

He reversed his grip on the knife and stabbed it into his stomach.

Outside, the Skinwalker bellowed with rage. Jimmy closed his eyes, blocking it out, then suddenly saw himself through the Skinwalker's vision, viewed from the other side of the door—he plunged his hand into the wound to search for the finger.

An alien world of pain exploded inside his abdomen, and he had to reopen his eyes to be rid of the Skinwalker's viewpoint. A pale blob of intestine slipped out past his wrist.

Darkness began to creep into his vision as his fingers slid over the rubbery landscape of his insides, encountering internal juices that felt too hot to be healthy.

The Skinwalker roared again, and he looked up to see more sections of the wall and door disintegrate, torn away as if no more than—

Suddenly, he had something.

Something... not right.

He'd located a spongy potato-size mass deep in his guts and pulled it out of the wound amid a river of gore.

The moment he did, the Skinwalker fell apart. The individual components of its morbid construction spilled to the ground in an avalanche, splattering across the floor with a sound Jimmy would never forget.

He stood quivering in the aftermath, too fearful to move. The pain in his stomach seemed to have dulled from the shock, but he knew he desperately needed to haul ass to a hospital.

He staggered forward.

A frightening numbness had crept into his body, and despite the fact he was still barefoot, he quickly waded through the mound of spilled viscera blocking the doorway.

Tissue squished between his toes.

Harder items poked into his heels.

He slipped twice, but managed to keep his balance, emerging from the pile only to collapse to his knees as the last of his strength fled his body.

Clear of the mess, he dropped to the floor and lay there for what seemed like eternity, one hand clamped over his gut, until he saw Sheriff Pickett push to a stand not far away. Riverwind's trio of bullets dotted the man's bulletproof vest like medals of honor.

"You alive, Cooley?"

Jimmy tried for a '*Yes, sir, I am,*' but only uttered a grunt.

The man stepped forward, eyes widening when he beheld the full extent of Jimmy's condition. "My God, son... What the hell happened to you?"

Jimmy removed his shaky hand from the wound so the Sheriff could see, realizing he still clutched the thing he'd ripped out of his body.

He uncurled his blood-splattered hand.

And almost screamed at what he saw.

"Holy Jesus," Pickett gasped. "Is that one of your kidneys?"

Jimmy dropped the organ on the floor and swung toward the mass of dismembered animal parts.

"Easy!" the Sheriff said, quickly restraining him. "We have to get you to the doc!"

"It's not dead!" he cried as Pickett lifted him to his feet. "The finger's still in me! It's playing possum, Sheriff! It's gonna try to get me again!"

He tried to break away, his mind groping for a way to burn the remains or blow up the building before it was too late, but he didn't have the strength to resist, and before he knew it, Sheriff Pickett had ushered him out the front door and into a patrol car.

"Keep pressure on the wound," Pickett told him. "We'll get you patched up in no time."

Jimmy wanted to tell him that was exactly what the witch wanted, why it had played dead and allowed them to escape, but he could only mumble something even he couldn't decipher.

The Sheriff started the car.

Switched on the lights and siren.

And as they pulled away, Jimmy thought he saw Detective Riverwind's corpse standing in the entryway of the building, the Skinwalker's four-fingered hand jutting from the hole in the man's throat, waving to him, like an old friend promising to come visit again.

Once Jimmy was healed.

Food for the Dead

MEGHAN JURADO

It's over, man. The dead have risen. People are eating each other.

It started, funny enough, with a stock report. The beef industry was in an uproar; seems cows were coming onto the slaughterhouse lines so decayed and bloated they were almost exploding from the gases in their bellies when they were cut into. Workers were being splattered with flying tripe. There was an outrage. The cattle people blamed the slaughterhouses for trying to butcher cows that were already dead, and the slaughterhouses blamed the beef people, saying the cows were up, walking, and wriggling when they were attached to the chains and hoisted. There was a lot of name-calling, a couple of corporate vandalism incidents, and on one memorable occasion, a fistfight, caught on the local news for posterity. The beef guy won, in case you were interested. Got his big cowboy hat knocked off though.

So, after a bunch of finger pointing and budget wrangling, someone finally looked into it. Turns out, the cows were dead—or more accurately, undead.

I'll give you a moment to digest that. So to speak.

A good cross section of the cattle population was showing the same symptoms: glassy, sticky eyes, lack of appetite (expect for when they took bites from each other—but that wasn't released until much later, when most of us were too panicked or shell-shocked to care,) bloating with gases usually reserved for corpses... the list went on and on.

Soon, it was *all* of the cattle. The beef industry went belly up, there were bankruptcies and suicides from the major stockholders, and suddenly there were all these *cows*, wandering through the streets. The cattle industry couldn't afford to house them; they didn't have the money to kill them either, even if they could figure out how to do it. They were rancid smelling and creepy, and it gave you quite a start to see your first undead cow, but they didn't try to attack anyone or anything dumb like that. Kids even dared each other to ride them, and it was common to see a cow corpse lurching down the street, covered in teenage riders. We just couldn't eat them anymore.

But there are lots of animals to eat, right?

It hit the chickens and pigs next. Poultry farms had been on the lookout for whatever infected the cows, and they were optimistic, at least publicly. But when it came, it came fast, and one day the news was showing rows and rows of cages, filled with dead hens, and then they would start to twitch and cluck again, and then it was business as usual for the hens, but like the cows, you couldn't eat them: the meat was as black and rotten as could be. The brood hens wouldn't lay either; their eggs just built up inside, spoiling in a nest of cooling guts. When the chickens were let loose to peck their decayed little hearts out among us regular folk, children would often chuck rocks at the dead broody hens to make the egg clutch inside explode. It was a lot like a stink bomb, but with feathers.

The pigs went down more quietly than the cows and chickens, but they received a lot more gory close-ups on the news, on account of the pink skin showing rot so well, and the fact that grown pigs are just plain scary. Soon enough, the pork industry, up to their ears in debt and floundering with this catastrophe, just let them out to wander as well, and now every time I go outside I have to shoo away one of the undead oinkers. The pigs turned a little vicious—they're more likely to give you a nip if you bug them. Their rotten snouts look like cottage cheese gone green.

The health crisis didn't infect people; as far as everyone knew, it was just animals that died and came back. We were told not to panic—*ha*—and that there was plenty of wild game still available to anyone who wanted it. Deer and bison were being trucked to functioning, sanitary (this was mentioned several times) slaughterhouses all across the nation to be killed and distributed to the American people, and to neighboring Canada and Mexico. Everyone perked up just a little. It's hard to be completely cheerful when there's an undead cow watching you with maggots in its eyes.

Then the first shipment arrived. Infected. All of it. They didn't even bother to try and kill anything; after being boxed together in the trucks for so long, the deer and bison and pheasant had all begun to rot, and many had eaten large portions of each other. The news was airing this cannibalism now.

My favorite news report of the whole disaster showed a pretty young thing with a microphone smiling and opening a truck of fresh deer. When the door opened, she peeked inside and visibly paled. Two deer stood knee deep in a pile of carcasses and gnawed bone, chewing contentedly on scraps of furred flesh. The pretty young thing lost her lunch all over her snazzy little suit, and the deer just jumped out of the truck and wandered away, leaving bloody hoof tracks. I laughed so hard I almost cried.

About the time we were thinking of eating mice or something (which wouldn't have done any good—the mice were undead too, and were twice as loud thumping in the eaves of a house,) a cause was found, too little, too late. Somehow, an unidentified mold had gotten into the feed: if an animal ate it, or if it ate another animal that had eaten it, it would be infected. It was a wonderful lesson in the food chain. Dogs and cats, hamsters and gerbils—we were warned to check manufacture dates on pet food and put poor Scruffy out of his misery if he got into some infected chow. New feed was being produced; the world would go back to normal. We scoffed, knee-deep in tuna cans. Fish were infected, but there was a run on tuna from before a certain date. Potted meats enjoyed a brief popularity too. It was a good time to be Spam.

Then, a Swedish botanist, a Dr. Hersten Ekerot, came out with *his* discovery, *Fusarium ekerotilliodes*. This mold, which the mass populace had noticed only when it directly inconvenienced them (as is usually the case with the mass populace,) had been discreetly growing on and inside all kinds of plants over the past few years. On the trees, the flowers, the bushes. Kelp had mold. *Mold* had mold. This creeping invader found a host and then made itself at home, essentially hollowing out its benefactor and filling the inside with moldy goodness. (This is me paraphrasing. The botanist said it quite differently, but it all amounted to "we're all screwed.") As soon as roots formed, the mold was there waiting. Nothing was known to kill this parasite, so plans were formed based on other strains of Fusarium mold that had successfully been eliminated. Plans were executed, plans were discarded, failure was total.

People panicked. There was nothing to eat. While the mold did not have the reanimating effect on humans, it destroyed all plant and animal life it touched. Even our pets were dead, from horse to goldfish. There was food everywhere, or what used to be food, staring at us with glazed eyes and dripping pus, *eating each other*, right in front of us, as if rubbing it in. No shortage of food for the dead.

So the only meat that wasn't infected was people.

"The Program" started right away. They called it "The Program," as not to upset the squeamish and faint of heart, but what it boiled down to was taking bodies that died of non-infectious causes, car crashes, heart attacks and the like, and testing them for contamination. These bodies were then processed into a block of pale white meat that was doled out by the government, one per house per week, extra if you have children or old people.

There were "it's people!" jokes made—funny at first, less funny on repetition, and not funny at all when you were staring at a block of someone's dead Grandpa with a fork in your hand. "Nutrio," as they called it, looked like pressed chicken and tasted like sour pork, and there were reports of people dropping dead from starvation instead of eating the stuff. The religious groups had mass sit-ins protesting Nutrio, but some gave up when they realized there was nothing for it; it was eat or die. The rest did die, slowly, and they were bulldozed into a pile and shoveled into trucks headed for the Nutrio plant. Not that they were much but skin and bones, but the ligaments could be boiled to make the Nutrio binding agent.

Black market versions of Nutrio appeared left and right (my favorite was "Pink Scrap"—available in your finest back-alley butchers,) and it wasn't safe to walk around after dark because people disappeared now. Send little Michael to the store on his own and the next time you see him is on your plate.

It's all over. The dead have risen and people are eating each other. We're struggling, but the dead are inheriting the earth. Who do you eat when everyone has been eaten? Who can you devour when everyone is already dead?

The Traumatized Generation

MURRAY LEEDER

Land sniffed at the air. He felt a kind of peace out here, so different from the city, thick with industrial fumes and soldiers. The prairies sprawled in every direction, wilder and more overgrown than they had been in more than a century, and to the west, the Rockies were lost in a pink haze. All of it sent Land back to a childhood spent traipsing around the countryside, when he didn't need to worry about what might be hiding in the wheat.

He rapped on the front door. Eventually, a woman answered in her nightgown, slightly older than him and glowering. She knew what was happening, and Land's heart sank when he realized what he was about to do.

"Mrs. March? I'm Michael Land, Paul's homeroom teacher. I'm here to pick him for today's..." He hesitated. "Today's field trip."

"I didn't give permission for any field trip," she snorted, and Land put his hand against the door to stop her from closing it.

"I'm afraid the school board doesn't require parental permission when the field trip has been made mandatory by the government of Canada."

"The government," she said. "You mean the military, don't you? Either way, I'm not about to send my son away to be traumatized by your bloodshow."

"Mrs. March," he told her, "in that car is the sergeant they sent to escort me up here. If Paul doesn't come out of this house in ten minutes, she'll have to come talk to you herself. Nobody wants that."

There was desperation in her voice. "Mr. Land, you and I remember a time before the military controlled our lives. You're an educator. How can you stand idly by and—"

"Just get your son, Mrs. March. Please. Just get Paul."

Mrs. March breathed in deeply. "Wait here," she said. "I can't believe I'm doing this."

She returned a few minutes later with the round-faced, serious little boy, dressed in unfashionable clothes and shoes that so often made him a target for jeers.

"It's good to see you, Paul," Land said, and the boy half-smiled up at him. Land knew the boy all too well: smart, shy, sensitive, and far too vulnerable for this world. Just like the young Michael Land, back when CNN reported that the dead were rising from their graves.

The car door opened, and Sgt. Hazelwood walked over to the door just as Paul was slipping on his coat. She was blond and beautiful, but to Land, she was just the kind of rhetoric-spouting career army type he had encountered too often during his tour of duty in Alaska.

"All ready to go?" she asked, wearing a false smile that Mrs. March did not return. Ignoring the sergeant's presence, Mrs. March dropped to her knees and embraced her son.

"Remember not to be too scared," she said, and Paul nodded uncertainly.

"Do something for me," Mrs. March said to Land. "Promise me you'll sit by him. Try to keep him from being too scared. He has a weak heart."

Land nodded, but before he could speak, Hazelwood interrupted. "Then we'll just have to strengthen up that heart a bit," she said, ushering the trembling boy toward the car.

As Land looked back at Mrs. March watching through the doorway as her son went away, he wanted to look in her eyes and reassure her that everything would go all right, whether or not that was true, but he couldn't.

* * * * *

The huge chain-link fence encircling Calgary was intended to keep the zombies out, which it did, but it also served to keep the people in. The rule of law didn't need to enforce this, for few wanted to leave. Officers waved Sgt. Hazelwood's car through the military checkpoint at the city's north gate, and they continued down the vacant Deerfoot Trail, bound for the Saddledome.

Built for the 1988 Olympics, the dome had served for years as sports arena and concert venue. The military had remade it into their modern-day Coliseum.

In the distance, Calgary's downtown was silhouetted against the morning sky, postcard pristine, like a snapshot from Land's childhood.

Paul was quiet the entire ride. His parents certainly taught him to avoid talking to anyone in a uniform. Land felt like he was ferrying a prisoner to an execution. He always hated this day, the worst of any school year. Nothing he'd seen up in Alaska bothered him half as much as the sight of ten thousand schoolchildren screaming for gore.

Yellow school buses dotted the Saddledome's parking lot, and Hazelwood weaved her car through the crowds of kids before they found Mr. Land's seventh-grade class. Land hoped they would arrive first, to spare Paul the humiliation of arriving under military escort, but no such luck.

"You get out here," Hazelwood said. "I'll go park in the barracks and join you inside."

"What?" Land said. "Isn't your duty here finished?"

"No." The sergeant flashed him an unreadable smile. "I'm with you the whole day."

Land coughed in disgust. She probably thought he'd let Paul slip away from the show at the first occasion. She was probably right.

The rest of the class caught sight of them as they stepped out of the military vehicle. Bruce Tomasino said something to Jason Barrows, and they sent their whispers all along the line.

"Don't worry about them, Paul," Land said softly. "Just take your place in line."

His student dutifully shuffled over to the others. Land addressed them: "I don't want to see any shoving or shouting. When we get the signal, I want us to go in a straight line inside and take our seats. Any questions?"

"I got a question," asked chubby Jimmy Conway. "Is it true... I mean, we heard a rumor that Zombie Bob will be here."

Please, no, Land thought, and he saw Paul's face grow grimmer too. TV celebrity Robert Smith Harding, or Zombie Bob, went with a camera crew behind the lines in lost cities and in infested countrysides to kill zombies in daredevil ways. His weapons of choice ranged from jackhammers to katanas. The kids loved him, wore his picture, talked about him constantly. His presence would change this field trip from a military demonstration to a rock concert.

A whistle blew somewhere across the parking lot, and the rows of students proceeded up the concrete stairs into the Saddledome. A uniformed officer waved Land's class ahead, and Land took up the end of the line to watch that they kept their course. Amid all the noise and gabbing children, he could barely hear Bruce and Jason talking about Paul. He made out one sentence: "That corpse-hugger's going to wet his pants when he sees this."

Land always marveled at how little the Saddledome had changed since his childhood. This wasn't a real surprise; though the military owned it now, it was still a sports arena of sorts. The floors were still sticky and the plastic seats still painful. The Jumbotron was still there too, left over from hockey games. Now it flashed messages like "ENJOY THE SHOW" and "THIS IS FOR YOU KIDS."

The most visible changes were the sideboards. The protective glass now went much higher and needed to be cleaned nightly of splattered blood and brain meat. As usual, a layer of freshly tilled dirt covered the arena. At one end, there was a raised platform with a few microphones, and at the other, a black velvet drape concealed the zombie cage. A trained crew with cattle prods was ready to send them out into the arena on cue.

When the students took their seats, Land called for Paul to sit next to him by the aisle. He'd wished he could have done this more subtly—*Paul didn't need to be a teacher's pet on top of a zombie-lover*—but he'd agreed to sit by the boy. As the other students chatted, he asked Paul, "What do you think of all this?"

"I don't know," the boy said. "I've never been anywhere like this before."

"Your parents didn't want you to come here," Land said. "You know that."

"But they made you get me."

Land nodded. "The military thinks it's important that you be here."

"Why?"

The question caught Land by surprise. It was a good question—why? Why did one child deserve all this special attention? He stammered, searching for an answer, before one was provided.

"Because someday you'll be called to the service, and we think it's best you know what it's all about." Sgt. Hazelwood stood in the aisle, grinning down on them both. She had changed from her green field outfit into a brown dress uniform that accentuated her curves.

That's not a real answer, Land thought, but he couldn't say anything here.

"Got room for one more?" Hazelwood asked.

Land looked at the empty seat next to him and tried to think of an excuse to keep her from sitting there. "Sure," he said. "Have a seat."

"No." She shook her head. "You sit there, and I'll sit on the other side of Paul."

Land went to protest, but thought better of it. He stood, and as she slipped past, he felt her body against his, her holstered pistol rubbing against his thigh.

She took her place next to the boy and smiled at him. "Your parents don't let you have a TV, do they?"

Paul shook his head.

"Then you don't know who Zombie Bob is?"

"Well, I know because the other kids—"

"Oh good," she said. "It just so happens that I'm a friend of Bob's, and after the show, I could take you to meet him backstage."

"Well, I don't really know if—"

"Just you, out of all these kids." She gestured at the thousands of schoolchildren around them. "That could really help you make friends, Paul. They'll want to know you for sure after that."

Land shot her a disapproving look, but she only grinned. Fortunately, the lights began to dim. He heard Hazelwood whisper, "We'll talk about this later," as a hush settled over the Saddledome.

A spotlight sprang into life, illuminating a lone figure on the platform. It was a silver-haired man in a brown dress uniform, medals dangling at his pocket. His image appeared, a thousand times larger, on the Jumbotron above.

"Howdy, kids," he said. "I'm Colonel Patrick Simonds. I recently got back from directing the troops on the coast, and the top brass asked me, 'Pat, you've just done such a great job in Vancouver. When you get back, just you name it, and it's yours.' And I said, 'I want to be the one who talks to the kids at the Saddledome.'"

The colonel wore the same politician's smile he was never seen without. Affable and grandfatherly, Simonds was just the kind of public face the military needed as it pressed its endless, costly war against an enemy that neither thought nor planned.

"Yup," Simonds went on, "that's my favorite duty because it's so important for the future. Once we recapture Vancouver and Toronto, then the real challenges will be open to us. New York, *Lost* Angeles..." he paused briefly as some of the audience chuckled at the popular pun, "maybe even London, Tokyo. That's where you kids will be fighting the zombies. You should think of this day like a '*thank you*' in advance. I think the very least we can do is show you how to do it."

Another spotlight cut through the darkness, spotlighting the black drape at the other end of the arena. Out stumbled a putrescent walking corpse, flailing its arms and staggering its way forward. Its jaw was slack, its tongue lolling out. A collective sigh filled the arena.

"Look at it," Simonds said. "I bet this is the first zombie most of you kids have ever seen. That says something about how far we've come. It's hard to imagine, but there was a time when zombies even walked the streets of Calgary. But thanks to the vaccine developed right here in Canada, none of us will ever be zombies. Remember that: kill a zombie, and that's one closer to killing them all.

"That disgusting creature you're looking at was somebody's brother or father or son once. I'm not going to lie to you about that. But he isn't no more. In fact, he's not a '*he*' at all, but an '*it*'!"

The colonel pulled his service pistol from its holster and aimed at the brightly lit target before firing. It sounded little more potent than a cap gun, but Paul twitched in his seat anyway. The bullet struck the zombie's shoulder, and it barely even noticed as it kept shambling forward.

"Ah, I didn't quite get it, did I?" Simonds said. "I've seen zombies lose all their limbs and keep on going. Their brain and their hunger drives them. They want to eat our flesh. That's all they want. And they never hesitate before they strike."

The zombie lurched steadily forward, having made it almost halfway to the podium. Many children clenched their teeth, but Land knew it would take a minor miracle for that zombie to reach the colonel.

"Now," said Simonds, "there are some who say that, because this thing was once somebody's loved one, that means we shouldn't kill it. We all know people like this. These zombie-lovers say that zombies are trainable, that maybe we can toss them the odd steak to keep them happy and teach them to fetch our slippers. But I challenge anyone to look in the eyes of the dead and see anything worth saving. Fellas, can we focus in on that?"

The Jumbotron zoomed in until the zombie's twisted, drooling face filled the screen.

"No life. No intelligence. In humans, we see some kind of spark of life; I don't know what it is, but it's always there. You don't see that in zombies. That's what zombies are: humans minus a certain spark, and that's what makes them a perversion in the eyes of God. There's only one thing to do to them!"

Simonds fired again. This time it struck the zombie square in the head, a perfect killshot. There was a splash of blood, and the creature fell. The Saddledome erupted with cheers and shrill whistles.

The house lights came up. "Pretty cool, eh?" whispered Sgt. Hazelwood to Paul.

"Now before I bring out a very special friend of mine," Simonds said, "we should all rise for the singing of our national anthem." An organ started up with "O Canada," and as they stood, Land extended his arm behind Paul's back and nudged Hazelwood.

"Sergeant," he whispered. "We need to share a word outside."

"But Mr. Land, it's disrespectful—"

"*Now*," he said, just a little too loud, and he started away from the arena. She placed her drink at her feet and stomped after him. He led her right outside onto the Saddledome's front steps, and there she began to snap at him.

"Who do you think you are that you can—"

"Who do you think you are to mess with my student like that?!" Land snapped back. "God, a military pick-up, you hanging over his shoulder... Do you think this isn't hard enough for him anyway? The other kids will never let him hear the end of this."

"Good," Hazelwood said. "I don't want him to forget today. I want him to be traumatized as hell. He'll thank us for it later."

"When? When will he thank us?"

"When he's been dropped in some hellhole and told to kill." There was absolute conviction in her voice.

"He'll be a man then, and better equipped to handle it than these kids are," Land argued. "Listen to them: they're whistling and cheering! It's just a show for them. That's just how you want them. They don't consider things. They don't think about things. The military doesn't want them to. I don't know who's more brain-dead, zombies or soldiers."

"How dare you!" Hazelwood cried, her throat hoarsening. "This isn't our world anymore! It's *theirs*! We let our guard down, and they tear our throats out! Society *must* be prepared—prepared in every way—for war! It is the only way!"

Land shrunk back at the force of her argument. "Do you remember," he said, his voice cracking, "when they used to say that watching violent movies was desensitizing, and that was a bad thing?"

For a long time, there was silence, and then Hazelwood said, "You've been wondering why all this special treatment for this one kid? What makes him so important?"

Land nodded.

"That was my idea. When I heard about Paul from your school's liaison office, I thought about the way I was before the zombies. A quiet, rural life. No TV. I'd never even witnessed violence. Then I watched as a zombie tore my father's head off while he was working the fields. You know what I did? I didn't run, I didn't scream—I just shut off. The shock almost killed me. But that made me who I am."

She was trembling slightly and clenched her fists to steady herself. Then she went on, "Maybe you're a zombie-lover too, but you earned that right by fighting for your country in Alaska. Mr. and Mrs. March never served, but their son will have to. Maybe it was noble once to be a conscientious objector, but now it's lunacy. The more they shelter Paul, the more they try to protect him, the more harm they do.

"I know you have stories like mine. We all do. We are the traumatized generation. A bit older and maybe we could have been better prepared for what was happening. A bit younger and we'd never have known a world without the zombies. If we are to spare the new generation what we went through, they must grow up impervious to trauma. Understand me: I value innocence. That's what Paul is. But in this world of ours, innocence kills." There were tears in her eyes. "What we are doing here... It's the only way. I firmly believe that, Mr. Land. So let the children cheer when zombies die. Better they cheer than scream."

Land turned away from Hazelwood and gazed at the skyscrapers of downtown Calgary, built so many decades ago and standing there like silent memorials to a dead world. "I wasn't made for these times," he said.

"None of us were."

Land wiped his eyes and turned back to face her. "They've probably brought out Zombie Bob by now. We should get back to Paul."

"Yes," Hazelwood agreed. "He needs our support."

Inside, the Saddledome pulsed with rock music. Land recognized the Doors' *Peace Frog*, which, thanks to the tastes of a certain general, became something of a military anthem. To its steady beat, Zombie Bob, dressed in full western garb with a white Stetson, wove his way between ten or so zombies, a roaring chainsaw in his hand.

It was part of Zombie Bob's appeal that it seemed like he could die at any moment.

Colonel Simonds was still on the platform, now protected by a half-dozen guards with submachine guns, offering commentary as Bob played the clown, always making it look like the zombies were just about to get him, before getting them instead.

"Careful, Bob," Simonds said, "there's another deadhead behind you." Bob did a cartoon double-take and slid the saw around to his back. Then he slid backwards on the dirt, driving the saw through the hapless zombie's midsection. Bob did a pirouette, slicing the zombie mostly in two before slamming his weapon right through its neck. A thick plume of blood shot out.

Land winced at the display. No one he had known in Alaska would attempt anything remotely like Zombie Bob's antics. He and Hazelwood slid back into their seats on either side of Paul, and Land asked the boy, "How are you doing?"

Paul March sat there in wide-eyed, stunned silence. "I... uh..." was the best answer he could manage.

"Remember," Hazelwood whispered, "there's glass between you and the zombies. They can't get you."

Zombie Bob's opponents seemed selected for maximum diversity: an old granny, a slender college girl, a middle-aged Chinese man, and so on. All that was missing was a child zombie. The media always shied clear of those.

"Wow, look at that, kids," Simonds said. "Remember, you can see Zombie Bob's adventures every Wednesday at three p.m. on CBC."

Peace Frog ended, and the music switched gears to a whimsical country waltz. Bob offered a few dance steps, tipping the white hat now splattered with blood. He pulled away from zombies to wave to the crowd, eliciting laughter as the zombies lurched up on him from behind. Then he sprang into motion, running circles around them, causing them to bump into each other, trip over each other, fall down. The crowd roared with laughter.

Paul made fists and squeezed until his knuckles were white. He was trembling hard. Land put a hand on his shoulder to steady him, and he felt the reverberations in his bones.

In this confusion, Bob rushed forward, chainsaw swinging at chest level. He caught two zombies right next to each other and forced the saw through bone and flesh. Their legs collapsed, useless, but their upper torsos were not dead and they pulled themselves across the dirt with their strong arms. Bob pulled away, ignoring them for the time.

"Two at once, Bob!" Simonds declared. "You've outclassed yourself. I don't see how you can top that."

The crowd went mad, screaming, whistling, stomping their feet, sounds echoing through the Saddledome's steel rafters. For a moment, Land felt like a kid again, listening to a crowd cheering for a wrestling match or a fight in a hockey game. Paul started making noises like little yelps. Land and Hazelwood looked at each other.

"Are you all right, Paul?" Land asked, looking into the boy's eyes. They were beginning to look glassy. Paul grasped hard onto his forearm and squeezed. Land cried out.

Zombie Bob slipped among his remaining foes so that they lurched at him from every side. Most weeks on his show, he performed some variant of this, positioning himself directly in the densest collection of zombies and fighting his way out. It was a crowd-

pleaser with any weapon, and the chainsaw was best of all. He swung it at the zombie in front of him, smoothly slitting it through the middle. On the Jumbotron, they could see smoke billowing out of the chainsaw.

Then it sputtered and died.

The camera caught the expression on Bob's face. It was real panic. This was not unusual; the TV cameras often found Zombie Bob running for his life.

"Uh-oh," said Colonel Simonds. "Looks like ol' Bob's got himself in trouble again."

Somebody cut out the music just in time for everyone to hear Bob release a stream of profanity. He threw the dead chainsaw in the face of the closest zombie and dove past it, his Stetson tumbling off his bald head. He kicked up dust as he raced away from the remaining zombies, but tripped over something, landing face-first in the dirt.

Before he could run, a strong zombie hand clamped down on one of his legs. He looked back to see a half-zombie, one of those he'd sliced in two earlier, its entrails dragging through the dirt behind it. It squeezed tighter on his leg, shattering bone and pulling away a handful of flesh. Bob's scream hit the steel roof and resonated through the Saddledome's every corner.

"Fuck!" shouted Simonds into his microphone. There was no doubt now—this was not part of the show.

The smell of fresh blood spurred the other zombies on to greater speed. Zombie Bob tried to pull himself to his feet, but they were on him in no time, ripping, tearing at his clothes and his flesh. The entire Saddledome could hear his screams. Piece by piece, they devoured him, stuffing human meat by the handful into their mouths. So here it was at last, the death of Robert Smith Harding. Everyone knew he'd die violently, himself most of all. But nobody expected it to be witnessed by ten thousand schoolchildren.

This would be remembered as the great trauma of a generation. They weren't screaming in excitement now. They were screaming in terror.

Land felt Paul's hand go limp on his arm.

"Fire! Fire! Fire! Fire!" Colonel Simonds shouted the command like a mantra, and his bodyguards loosed a hail of bullets into the zombies. Many of the bullets struck their targets, but those that didn't ricocheted off the bulletproof glass, off into the crowd. One of these stray bullets caught Simonds in the chest, and he collapsed onstage, barely noticed amid all the pandemonium.

Children and adults alike crawled over each other, fueled by the most primal surge of adrenaline, frantically seeking escape. Bodies swamped the exits and fell from balconies. Land grabbed Paul, ready to carry him out of the Saddledome, but found him limp and cold. He reached for Paul's jugular but felt no pulse.

He has a weak heart, Mrs. March had told him. She must have meant it. This shock must have been too much for poor sensitive Paul, and his little heart gave out. Hazelwood looked at him open-jawed, and despite all this noise and chaos, everything suddenly seemed so still and calm.

Then Paul's eyes jumped open.

Thank God I was wrong, Land thought first, but then he saw his eyes. He could never explain this to anyone who hadn't seen it for themselves, but the eyes of the dead were different. Simonds was right; they lacked spark, life. This was true even of the freshest zombies.

Paul sank his teeth into Sgt. Hazelwood's forearm. Her legs kicked involuntarily, knocking against the seat in front of her. Her mouth opened, but no noise came out as her eyes glassed over and she sank back into her chair, growing increasingly inert as Paul gnawed through to raw bone. Land grabbed Paul by the hair and yanked back, but even a child zombie possessed inhuman strength, and Paul wouldn't release his grasp on his prize.

The Marches, Land thought. *They live outside the city. The inoculation drives must have missed them somehow.*

Damned zombie-lovers—they didn't even inoculate their own kid against becoming one of them!

Land slid his hand down Hazelwood's thigh to her holster. He pulled out her service pistol, drove it into Paul's chin, and squeezed the trigger.

Alive Eye
for the
Dead Guy

RYAN C. THOMAS

"I told you no pink gels!" screamed Thornton Keel. "It makes them look like cotton candy, like circus clowns. I don't want circus clowns, I want goddamn zombies. You know, gray, pale, dead-looking. Jesus Christ. Who hired you anyway?"

The bald-headed lighting director bit his tongue. "Sorry, Mr. Keel. I just thought it would make things seem warmer."

"I don't want warm, I want dead. That's the point of the show, right? We need them to look drab, pathetic, then at the end, we boost the lights and they look cuddly and everyone says, 'Zombies need love too,' and go home and tell all their friends to watch this show, and I make a million dollars and buy your goddamn soul and use it to wipe my ass. Got me?"

The lighting director nodded.

"Good." Thornton smiled, happy once again to make someone else miserable. "Then fix it or you're fired."

The lighting director pulled a walkie-talkie off his belt and spoke into it. "Roger, switch out those pink gels and make 'em blue."

Some twenty feet above the floor, a young man on the lighting grid switched the gels. The television set went from the color of a Texas sunrise to the color of a New England sky awaiting a hailstorm.

"See," Thornton said for good measure, "now it looks calm, serene, dead. It looks good. Get out of my sight."

The lighting director shook his head and walked away.

Thornton walked the set once more, double-checking his mental list of daytime television show essentials: the host's desk was clean, the ensemble wardrobes were stocked, the guest mugs had bottled water in them, and the chains and shackles were tightly secured to the floor plates. He checked to make sure a handful of Weaver injection pens were stacked in the only operational drawer of the desk. He had a lot of money riding on this production, and he was not about to let some half-drunk, pot-bellied gaffers mess everything up, union or not.

"Sonofa..." he said, noticing that someone had put the potted Curculigo tree against the far wall. "Who did this?!" he yelled. The crew members looked up from whatever they were doing, but as he expected, no one answered. "This is a rare Asian Curculigo tree. It grows deep in the fucking rainforest and cost me more to ship it here than any of you are worth. It goes beside the desk so the audience can see it. If I wanted something that cost me a shitload of money to sit off-camera burning a hole in my pocket, I'd have my ex-wife come in and plop her pill-popping ass in the corner."

He snapped his fingers, and a nearby gaffer moved the tree next to the desk.

"Careful, you're knocking the berries off it!"

"Sorry, Mr. Keel."

"Yeah yeah, you're all a sorry bunch, aren't ya?"

When it was in place, Thornton shooed the gaffer away, took a breath, and calmed himself.

The latest reports told him the foyer was currently packed with a test audience eager to get inside. The promotions team was handing out shirts and bumper stickers, and a stand-up comic was warming them up with undead jokes: "Where does a zombie work? The dead letter office."

If everything went well, the network was offering a three-season contract to start.

Satisfied the set was finally in shape, Thornton pushed past some chatty production assistants and rapped on Jordan Usher's dressing room door.

From inside, Jordan replied, "Come in."

Thornton entered and stood against the wall. Jordan ignored him, preoccupied with fixing his hair in front of a large vanity mirror. Several pictures of half-naked women were taped to it, each with a scribble proclaiming some form of love or lust for him. He wore a blue-metallic pinstriped Italian suit that was tailor-made for him, courtesy of one of the sponsors. Pressing his cowlick down, he addressed Thornton in the mirror.

"You got my memo, right? I don't trust those Brutes, not with these dead fucks."

Brutes were what Jordan called the security guards Thornton hired for the show. They were big men recommended by an old army friend of his. Each was trained in advanced hand-to-hand combat and heavy weaponry. That none of their training had ever been applied to fighting zombies was a moot point to Thornton; combat was combat, after all. And besides, the zombies would be drugged. The Brutes were more or less for insurance purposes.

"I saw those fucking dead things in the pen," Jordan continued, "and they don't look happy. Where'd you find them, the zoo?"

"They were set for termination. No relatives. They were cheap."

"They look like the missing links."

"Relax," Thornton said, edging over and smoothing out Jordan's lapels. "They're harmless."

"They don't look harmless. They look hungry. Don't touch the suit."

"They'll be injected, double injected even. You'll be fine."

"They can be injected with hydrochloric acid for all I care—those Brutes aren't certified by anyone worth a damn to protect my ass. These creatures will fuck you up if they have the means. My mother is half their size, and even she kicked me in the nuts a few weeks ago when I tried to stick her."

"That's because she knows where your brains are."

"I'm not laughing, Thornton. You can triple inject them, but it doesn't change the fact they're still animals. Hiring these Brutes was a shit idea."

"Jordan, baby, don't worry," Thornton replied. "Do you think I'm some fucking asshole? I take care of my people, don't I?"

"Don't shmooze me, Thornton—"

"When you needed a gig after the drug scandal, who got you a job? When you found out that girl was underage, who put her on TV and shut her up? Me. Always me."

"Thornton, if one of those Brutes pisses me off, just looks at me wrong, I'm coming back here and jacking off while the cameras roll out there."

"Don't worry, they know what they're doing. Scout's honor. Just relax. We're making television history here."

"Oh, I'm relaxed. This show is a goddamn career-ender, but I'm relaxed."

A young production assistant with curly red hair and zits poked his head into the room. "Sorry to interrupt, sir, but you told me to tell you when the audience was coming in."

"Perfect," Thornton said. "Go check on Dr. Stafanko and see if he needs anything." Then to Jordan: "Okay, this is it. If this goes well, we're gonna be swimming in so much money we'll be able to buy God. Just remember: ratings, ratings, ratings."

"Don't worry about me," Jordan said, licking his fingers and smoothing his eyebrows. "This is my town. You want to see a zombie makeover, I'll give you a zombie makeover. The dead will get hard-ons when I turn on the charm. Let's do this fucker."

"That's my boy."

*　　*　　*　　*　　*

After the audience had been seated, the young director that Thornton hired for his overwhelming subservience said a brief hello and sat back down near the control room. Thornton came out to the set next, a lav mic attached to his lapel. He thanked the audience for showing up, introduced himself as the creator and producer of the show, and assured them what they were about to see was going to revolutionize television. He spoke with enthusiasm and fervor, and the audience cheered.

The theme music played, an upbeat jingle by a famous band hot on the charts: *"Their eyes may be glazed and their teeth all black/ But if you love your zombie, it'll love you back."* The screens in the upper corners of the stage showed the opening sequence that viewers at home would see, a cartoon zombie drinking tea while the title appeared in bold blue letters underneath: ALIVE EYE FOR THE DEAD GUY. Thornton stole the title from an archaic show that was hot at the turn of the millennium, a show that, in its day, had dared to bring a different type of taboo to the airwaves. Again, the audience cheered.

Jordan Usher rushed onstage with spunk and the kind of Hollywood smile that made girls swoon. He waved and blew kisses, caressed a young lady's cheek in the front row, shook the hand of another a few seats away, rocked his hips like a boat on the ocean. The audience cheered even louder. The stage lights danced. Still smiling, he took his seat behind the desk and waited for the music to die down. He had to wait even longer for the crowd to stop cheering.

"Whoa!" he said with his million-dollar grin. "Thank you for that warm welcome, and welcome to *Alive Eye for the Dead Guy*. Let me ask you something: How many of you have a zombie at home?"

Just about everyone in the audience raised a hand.

Offstage, Thornton smiled. Fuck the hatemail from the protest groups; fuck the church and its staunch opposition to all things undead. *Just look at that audience*, he said to himself, *they're already eating it up*. He'd have major sponsors calling him by the end of the week. Nike, Lexus, Coca Cola, Campbell's Soup: they'd all want a piece of this zombie craze.

Behind him in the studio hallway, the Brutes were wrangling the zombies toward the set, pulling them by long chain collars. Their decomposing hands and legs, although shackled, grabbed for anything and anyone within reach. A collective moan escaped their blue lips.

"Quiet those things down," Thornton said to the nearest Brute. "If the booms pick up that racket, I'm taking the looping costs out of your paycheck. The viewers can't hear them 'til we bring them out, got it?"

"Sorry, Mr. Keel," said the nearest Herculean man. "We waited to give them the shots until a few minutes ago. To cut down on the possibility of it wearing off before you finished taping. Give 'em a minute and they'll calm down."

"You waited?"

"It should be kicking in now. They'll settle down."

"Sonofa... they damn well better, or I swear..."

He noticed there were six zombies in the hallway with him, which might not have been a concern were there more than two Brutes. Weaver-controlled zombies were one thing; non-sedated ones were certainly another. Like Jordan had said, they might be loved ones in memory, but they were still animals. "Maybe you should put two back, just to be safe."

As if in protest, two of the zombies started grabbing each other, their moans rising. Thornton edged away as the Brutes tried to break it up, prayed they could get it under control and avoid any mishaps. Sweat pooled under his armpits, and his chest flared with heat. *Calm down*, he told himself, *everything is fine.*

Dr. Stafanko, an older, shorter man in spectacles, came out of his dressing room and edged past the fracas with caution. He slapped away a groping undead hand. "No! Bad! Bad zombie!" He sidled up next to Thornton. "They seem agitated, Mr. Keel. They've been given shots I hope."

Jordan 2007

Thornton smiled a bullshitter's smile. "Of course. A while ago. Don't you worry about a thing." He pointed toward the stage, toward Jordan, doing his best to distract the little man. "You ready? It looks like he's about to call you."

Behind his host desk, Jordan was clapping at one of his own jokes. He stopped and sipped his water. "Okay," he said, his tone denoting a shift in subject. "So, how many of you have a hard time getting your zombie to wear something nice for the holidays?"

Hands went up.

"And how many of you wish you could get their hair to do something stylish for once?"

More hands in the air.

"And what about that hygiene? They do hate to wash." He winked at the young girl in the front row. She smiled and looked away embarrassed. "Well, you've come to the right place, my friends. On today's show, we're going to focus on what I like to call Death Breath."

The audience moaned.

"I know, I know. It stinks. That's what you get with meat-eaters. And forget getting them to brush their teeth. Why, my mother hasn't brushed in over six months, and the harder I fight with her, the more she tries to bite me, the rascal. I can't take her anywhere. So today, we've got Dr. Myron Stafanko, a pioneer in the field of cadaver dentistry. He's going to give us some tips on how to turn those rotting blacks into pearly whites. Dr. Stafanko?"

The audience obeyed the applause sign and clapped enthusiastically. In the studio hallway, a little red light came on above Thornton's head. Dr. Stafanko, having been prepped on the cue, walked on stage and sat next to Jordan.

"Dr. Stafanko," Jordan beamed, "so nice of you to come on. Tell me, how did you get started in cadaver dentistry?"

The small man nodded, as if he knew this would be the first question. "It was my wife," he said with a heavy Slavic accent. "We were married thirty-four years when a heart attack took her from me."

"My condolences," Jordan replied, all the while ogling the girl in the front row.

"Yes. Well. We had no children, you see, and she was all I had. I applied and was approved for the Code 42, so I prepared for her return by tying her to the bed—customary, you probably know. It was only a few days later she awoke, barely decomposed and only slightly gray. I thought she looked beautiful. Naturally, I immediately gave her the Weaver shot to sedate her. Then, well, I went to kiss her, but her breath was so bad I vomited all over myself. It was then I knew that the undead needed dental care."

The audience applauded.

Jordan touched Dr. Stafanko lightly on the shoulder. "That was a touching story. Wasn't that a touching story, folks?"

The audience cheered again. Jordan pretended to wipe a tear from his eye.

"And now you're going to show us some zombie dental procedures we can try at home?"

"Oh yes, these are simple, easy methods to get your zombie's teeth to sparkle and their breath to smell clean."

Offstage, Thornton was smiling. Jordan had the audience in the palms of his hands, just as he'd hoped—the man could charm the stink off shit...

Realizing it was almost time for the zombies, he waved at the nearest Brute. "Hey, you, get ready."

The two zombies that started the earlier scuffle had been separated like disobedient children at playtime, and were now quiet. In fact, they all seemed less agitated, though they still showed signs of hunger, drooling and licking their lips. They staggered around the hallway, bumping into one another, one of them trying to eat the fire extinguisher on the wall.

Thornton heard Jordan announce the zombies, and the little red light in the hall went on. The Brutes yanked the walking dead past Thornton and onto the set.

The audience went wild.

"Here they come, folks," Jordan said, his smile nearly wrapping around his head.

They shuffled around Jordan's desk, groping at the Curculigo tree, nearly knocking it over at one point, making their way to the shackles where the Brutes chained them up. They could move, but only in a limited space. The serum was working its way into their brains, putting them in a languid trance.

From the hall, Thornton watched as Dr. Stafanko and Jordan went over to the monsters and began examining them. *I am going to be so rich*, he thought. His mind immediately veered toward merchandising ideas: shirts, lunchboxes, a line of styling products, an unedited DVD version with staged outtakes. And of course, spin-offs: interior decorating for zombies, zombie travel programs, zombie emergency room docu-dramas. *I'll make these ugly things stars*, he thought, *I'll conquer the networks.*

Even when the plague first struck, he knew he could turn it into a profit. Then, when the epidemic had been put under control, and the Weaver Serum was created to sedate the zombies and allow researchers to study the elusive cause of the plague, again he knew there was money in it somewhere. He knew that much about life—you could always make money off it somehow; you just needed some creative juices and a complete lack of ethics. When the government passed Code 42, allowing families to retain certain undead family members in controlled situations, (if they could afford the application fee,) he'd had his brainchild. Sedated zombies were a goldmine.

Owning a zombie was now as common as owning a second house. Not everyone could do it, but many could. And even if you didn't, you knew somebody who did. People were proud of their dead family members; many swore their relationships even improved after one of them died. "We don't fight anymore," was a common phrase from zombie-owning spouses.

Yes, after this pilot show aired, Thornton would be a very rich man.

"Now, is it possible to give them, let's say, gold teeth?" Jordan was asking Dr. Stafanko on the set. The little man had his hands in the mouth of a very dead old lady and was flossing her back molars. With the serum controlling it, the zombie only swayed and moaned.

"Oh yes," he replied. "It is not something to do at home yourself, but my practice could do it for you. Mind you, as the gums continue to rot, the teeth will have to be reinforced into the jawbone. Otherwise they may fall out."

"Interesting," Jordan said, staring on with a mixture of genuine interest and television showmanship. He was about to comment further when one of the bigger zombies lurched forward and grabbed for him. The host jumped out of the way as a Brute put the creature in a headlock and immobilized it for a few seconds. When he let go, it was still again.

The director winced, but did not make eye contact with either the host or the producer. Jordan, however, shot Thornton a look of disgust, as if to say, *If I get bit I'm coming after you!* There was no way viewers hadn't noticed it, so he made a joke: "Little zombie anxiety there, folks, we'll just edit that out."

The audience laughed.

Thornton made a mental note to scream bloody murder at the Brutes after the show. They should have injected the serum sooner; they should be more aware.

Jordan, ever the professional, went back to leading the segment. "Dr. Stafanko, we know they're meat-eaters. But is a meat-only diet good for their teeth? What do you feed your wife?"

"My wife gets meat, like most zombies. But I also give her plenty of calcium. Some cheese, some milk. I mix it up in raw ground beef, and she barely notices. It helps to strengthen the teeth. Ah now..."

"Something wrong?"

Dr. Stafanko pointed into the zombie's mouth. "See here, this one has some berries stuck under its gums."

"Berries? Who fed it berries?"

"I think, perhaps, it grabbed them off the tree there when it came out. I've seen them mistake many things for meat. It could cause further decay, and this is one reason they may have bad breath. What you need to do in this instance is get in there and pry it out. I prefer to use my dental pick, but you can use a toothpick. Never something too sharp; you don't want to cut the gum open. Just get in there and pull it out. I find if you press back on their forehead, they have a harder time clamping down than if you yank their bottom jaw open."

"Interesting," Jordon said again. He moved to his desk and produced a small colorful box that had been placed on the shelf underneath. After holding it up for the camera, he handed it to the doctor. "Now what's this product here?"

From inside the box, the doctor removed a clear tooth mold, filled it with a liquid, and inserted it over the zombie's lower teeth. "This is a very simple and effective whitening product I have created which I call *Corpse Paste*. It includes a bonding agent, so not only will the teeth whiten, but they won't fall out as easily. It's available on my website."

"Doctor, have you ever considered just taking out their teeth? I mean, if they were to bite you while you were in there—"

"I'm not afraid. Weaver Serum has been a blessing. There has not been a documented case of infectious zombie bite in over three years, you know. No, taking their teeth out means taking away their identity."

"Yes, but let's say for your wife, you're a lonely man, maybe she could, you know... if you didn't have to worry about teeth."

The audience groaned and chuckled like children.

In the hall, Thornton went rigid. Was Jordan going to test the censors? How dare he! Thornton would have his ass for this!

But the audience kept laughing, and no one seemed insulted. After all, the main ingredient in any good show was sex. And Thorton hadn't gotten where he'd gotten in Hollywood by not taking risks. Hell, two of the creatures were female... maybe he should have put them in bikinis. It was something to consider for a future show, anyway. For now, he'd let Jordan run with it. Later, they could discuss—

"What the...?"

Onstage, the zombies were suddenly jerking about, shuffling as far as their chains would allow, growling and reaching for the audience as if someone had sucked all the Weaver Serum out of them. They made groggy swipes at the Brutes, who in turn pushed them away and restrained them. It was uncharacteristic for a Weaver-injected zombie to still be moving like that.

Ever so slowly, Jordan took a small step back, as if he didn't want the audience to see what he was doing. The doctor filled another mold and fought to place it on his undead patient's top row of teeth. It was also acting far more agitated than it should.

Out of nowhere, a network executive in a suit that cost more than a small nation's gross income appeared next to Thornton in the hall, his brow furrowed. "Why're they still grabbing for people, Keel?"

"They were given the shots a bit late, but it's all under control now. Been almost fifteen minutes."

"Weaver Serum doesn't take fifteen minutes to kick in, Keel. It's almost an instantaneous thing."

The zombies on stage staggered about and grabbed at Stafanko. One of the Brutes stepped in and shoved the doctor out of the way. The muscular ex-soldier pushed the creature back and jammed an injection pen in its throat.

Thornton was starting to sweat. "We'll edit that out," he told the executive.

"Jesus Christ. You made the doctor sign a waiver, right?"

"Of course. Besides, he does this for a living. He knows the risks."

"If something happens to that audience—"

Thornton rested his hand on the man's shoulder. "Nothing will happen, other than you're going to have a forty share by morning. You've just got to trust me—"

Thornton stopped short. The executive's eyes were bulging, reacting to something on the set. The air was full of screaming, full of zombie growls.

The corpses were attacking.

They had broken their chains—actually torn the links apart—and were struggling with the Brutes. And for all their muscles, the Brutes were losing.

The audience was screaming, running up aisles toward the exits, while Dr. Stafanko stood in the center of the stage, shrieking, his hand missing. Thornton saw it dangling from one of the zombie's mouths, the plastic tooth mold stuck to it with saliva.

"Oh no," was all he could say.

"A... a zombie bite," the executive finally said, slowly backing away down the hall. "Jesus Christ, Keel. Look what you did!"

"What I did?"

"Holy shit. Holy shit. This is lawsuit city, Keel. This is—If I get through this alive, you'll never work in this town again. Do you hear me?! I'll see you in court!" With that, he bolted down the hall and out the back exit, leaving Thornton to wrap his mind around what was going on, to rationalize how zombies could break thick chains.

On set, Jordan let out a shrill scream and ran around the desk only to be tackled by a suddenly agile zombie. The creature bit off the host's nose with a loud crack. Blood erupted like a geyser, coating the stage in red. Nearby, the Brutes lay in their own pools of blood with large bites taken out of their bodies—definitely dead.

The doctor ran behind the tree, doing his best to evade one of the creatures, all the while looking at the stump at the end of his arm. The zombie sniffed the tree, plucked a berry off it, and ate it. Which made little sense to Thornton, but then he never really understood these animals anyway. The doctor made a break for it, heading for Thornton, but the zombie ran—*ran!*—after him and took him out like a linebacker sacking a quarterback. With lightning-fast reflexes, the zombie tore a chunk out of the small man's skull.

Two more of the zombies reached out for the tree and plucked berries off it.

What the hell is with the goddamn berries? Thornton wondered. All he knew about the tree was that it was rare, and that an article in *Better Homes and Gardens* had touted it as the garden enhancement of the stars. The berries could give you the shits if eaten, but that couldn't mean anything, could it? Could the berries be poisonous, and could the poison be affecting their brains? Could they contain some rare chemical that amped up the synapses or made the muscles stronger?

Bang!

The gunshot shook Thornton from his reverie. SWAT was spilling in from every entryway, unloading bullets into the creatures' heads. Brains went flying across the set, splotching down on the desk, the walls, even landing in the tree. Bullets zinged through the air, tearing apart the walls, the floor, the lights.

It was over in seconds. Six zombies lay sprawled on the stage, two Brutes dead beside them. Jordan was still twitching, somehow alive, but it didn't matter. He'd been bitten, and they could either kill him or wait for him to turn. (*That's an expensive contract down the drain*, he thought.) Same with the doctor, who was rocking back and forth beside the desk, his eyes staring into oblivion, a large cavity in his skull.

"You in charge here?" The detective grabbed Thornton's shoulder and gave him a little shake to get his attention. Other than the officers, Thornton was the only one left in the building, frozen in place by shock.

"Um... yes."

"You okay? You get bit? You understand what I'm—"

"Yeah, yeah, I'm fine. Jesus, look at my set. I need to call—"

"Make your calls later. Right now, come with me."

Thornton hung his head and thought, *Shit, this is not good for ratings. Not good at all.*

* * * * *

As he sat at his desk in his Hollywood office, looking over the ratings numbers from his newest show, Thornton Keel couldn't help but pat himself on the back.

"Jesus Christ," he said. "A gold mine I tell you. People love zombies."

Four months had passed since the zombie attack, four months of front-page articles about the bloodshed, about how one Thornton Keel discovered a rare berry that, when mixed with Weaver Serum, caused zombies to take on superhuman strength. The going theory was that the mixture rapidly generated adrenaline on a scale never dreamed possible in the human body. But nothing concrete had been officially reported.

The state of California and the studio both tried to sue him, of course, but the one thing Thornton knew how to do was shmooze.

He made everyone a deal.

Since the newly dead had signed waivers acknowledging the risks involved in working with zombies (and technically Jordan was still under contract,) and since none of them had any living family members, why not turn a lemon into lemonade: a new show, one that would promise loads of ad revenue, enough to fund research projects into zombie behavior. (Enough to fund certain political parties as well, especially ones that had strong ties to Hollywood, though none of that went on record. Greasy palms must stay greasy.)

At the end of the day, the complaining parties opted for the deal. Immediate money, after all, was far better than a lengthy litigious battle. And such it was that Thornton's newest endeavor, *The Dead World*, had just reached number one in the prime-time slot. The reality series focused on four zombies living in a house together, just being themselves. Kenner Toys had already called and bid on the toy line for the characters, and the studio had drawn up a contract for a four-season deal. Jordan, his mother, the doctor, and his wife were the stars, all of them already famous from the much-publicized massacre. Thornton was back in the game, and his name was gold again.

The greatest part was that he didn't even need a crew. The pseudo-house was locked inside a military-style compound, and the remote controlled cameras did all the rest. They recorded non-stop, and at the end of each week, the good bits were culled and edited together for the show. Random openings in the roof of the house allowed items to be dropped in for the zombies. It was genius.

Coca Cola bought advertising time, as did Nike and BMW. Money greased palms.

Now, sitting at his desk, Thorton turned his computer on and watched the scenes from inside the house; he had full-time access to the feed. A blow-up doll had somehow attached to Jordan's suit jacket, and it followed him around like a stalking lover. Doctor Stafanko had knocked the fish tank over and was poking a fish with a chopstick. His wife was ambling from room to room, drooling. And Jordan's mother was sitting in the kitchen sink playing with the water, splashing it at her son.

Thornton leaned back in his chair and smiled. "This is *my* town."

'til the Lord Comes

SCOTT STANDRIDGE

Timothy shouldered through the mortuary doors at 7:35, his hands cupped in front of him as if he were carrying water. It was late autumn in Winthrop County; the dark had come nearly an hour ago, and the pale moon stared from a gray-black haze of clouds that hid all but the brightest stars. The damp air chilled Timothy through his tight black suit, and his hands were cold in spite of their warm burden.

As the doors swung shut, Bob Griegerson looked up from his inventory list, his small glasses perched on the end of his long, pointed nose like a dragonfly on a branch.

"You're late," Bob said. "I've been waiting half an hour. When they told me you were slow, I thought they meant *mentally.*"

Timothy stared at the floor. "Sorry," he said.

Bob was a thin man, with a severe mouth and arched eyebrows that made him look somber and foreboding. He was hunched and unpleasant and he frightened small children, but he was still the best coffin salesman in three counties. Bob slammed his ledger shut and stood up. "You're lucky no one else wants this job. I swear, if I had one more apprentice—" He let the threat hang a moment, then sniffed, satisfied. "Come on, help me close up."

Bob and Timothy started at opposite ends of the showroom, like always. They walked down the dim aisles, closing the lids of the untenanted caskets one by one, making sure the latch on each caught before moving on to the next. Timothy never asked why they did this. Tonight, he nudged the coffin lids with his elbow, keeping his hands cupped close to his chest. It was hard to shut the lids securely this way, but he managed. He met Bob at the front door.

"Linda Redfield called me today," Bob said. "Upset with your work. She didn't much like the way you presented her mother at the service."

Timothy shrugged. "Widow Redfield was ugly," he said. "Not much I could do about that."

Bob stared at him a moment, then burst out laughing. "That's one of the things I like about you, Timothy. You might be slow, but at least you don't sugar-coat."

Timothy cringed away from Bob's slap on the back. *I ain't slow,* he thought, but said nothing.

Bob finally noticed Timothy's careful posture. "What you got there?"

Timothy held his cupped hands out for Bob's inspection. "I found her on the way," he explained. "That's why I was late." It was a killdeer, squat in its brown and white plumage, with two black bands around its neck like a priest's collar. One wing was twisted and bloody, and the left leg was badly mangled. "I couldn't just leave her."

Bob wrinkled his nose. "Christ," he said. "I work a ten-hour day and then have to stay thirty minutes late while you prance around playing Dr. Doolittle? You know I can't leave 'til you get here."

"You could give me a key," Timothy said. "Then I could come and go as I please."

"You'd like *that,* wouldn't you?" Bob jerked a thumb toward the prep room. "Busy night for you. Mary Lindquist is still in there, of course. Funeral's tomorrow, so you'll need to dress her, do her hair and makeup, the works. After her, there's Deacon Johnson, dropped this morning. He'll need to be cleaned, disinfected, and embalmed. The family wants visitation day after tomorrow, so you've got a little time." Bob pointed to the killdeer. "What'll you do with that?"

"I saved her eggs," Timothy said. "Found 'em nearby, just off the path. I'm gonna nurse her back to health."

Bob shook his head. "I hate to tell you this, son, but healing ain't exactly your business." He looked at the bird again. "Maybe you can embalm it, if you get through early. Give it a decent Christian burial."

"Just wait," Timothy said. "You'll see."

When Bob was gone, Timothy headed back toward the prep room. The workspace was crowded, as Bob had warned. Mary Lindquist lay on the slab nearest the door, nude under her thin white shroud. On the far side of the room, the corpse of Frank Johnson strained another table. The sheet draping the huge mound of his belly barely touched the slab's edge.

Timothy's Grandpa Evans had been big like that. Timothy remembered nestling in his mother's skirts at the old man's funeral, the strong smell of gardenias emanating from his grandfather's bier. Young as he was at the time, Timothy had been unable to look away from Grandpa Evans' face, convinced that any moment the eyes would open, lock on his, and wink. The memory snapped into an image of crystal clarity, then faded away like a mist. Timothy shook his head and turned his attention to the killdeer.

Mrs. Jenkins, the special ed teacher, had once told Timothy's class how a killdeer would endanger itself in order to protect its eggs. When a predator—a cat, raccoon, even a rattlesnake—approached the nest, the mother bird would chirp loudly, one wing folded to her chest as if wounded, the other extended skyward. The attacker would pursue the seemingly injured adult, who would lead it a safe distance away before "recovering" and soaring free. She was probably doing this when the car hit her, Timothy figured. At least her eggs were safe.

A tray of instruments stood between the two slabs. Timothy put the killdeer on top and rummaged in the shelves beneath. He came up with a small chrome pan lined with cotton balls. He took the three buff-colored eggs, still intact, from his loose shirt pocket and set them in the fluffy nest. Finally, he laid the killdeer atop the eggs and covered her with gauze. The injured bird twittered, but soon settled down to rest.

Timothy walked over to Mary Lindquist and pulled the sheet back from her face. The harsh work lights washed her skin bone white, and her hair shined like black water. Mary was just nineteen, a college girl, home on a weekend break. A hemorrhage hidden in her brain for years had popped a day ago, felling her in the street like a sniper's bullet.

Mary's lips, though blue now, were full and bow-shaped, and the cleft below her nose creased like fine fabric. Her hair was done

S.BLUNDELL

up in an old-fashioned style, bangs curled tight and straight tresses down to her shoulders. Her neck, an alabaster pillar, curved down into hard collarbones. Even though he hadn't meant to, Timothy found himself staring at her hard, focused on the spot just above and between her dark eyebrows. After a few minutes, Mary's eyes twitched and fluttered open, pupils milky with film.

"Hello, Timothy," she said.

"Evenin', Mary."

She rose from the table, slow and stiff, vertebrae going off like firecrackers. Timothy helped her up, pulling the shroud over her shoulder and tying it there. Mary smiled, or tried to, but her facial muscles were stiff with rigor mortis, and she managed only a stroke-victim grimace. Timothy smiled back.

"I'm having trouble... moving," Mary whispered. She twisted on the slab and threw a leg over the edge. The shift in balance levered her upright into Timothy's arms, board-stiff.

"Just take it easy," he said. "Let me loosen you up."

He started with her face, pushing his fingers into the muscles of her cheeks and jaw to stretch them over the bone. Then he moved down her neck and back. He grabbed both shoulders and pulled until he heard a crack, then worked them to and fro like rusted hinges. He did the same with her arms and fingers, legs and toes. Finally, Mary was able to stand on her own.

"Could I have some water?" she asked.

Timothy shook his head. "That's not a good idea."

"Why not? I'm *so* thirsty."

He shrugged. "Yesterday when they brought you in, I had to embalm you. Blood out, formaldehyde in. You know." He stopped to see if she'd understood. Her silence told him she hadn't. "See, inside you, in your cavities—it's all empty around the guts. There's some thin tissue, but mostly it's just air. After you die, that gas blows up. It starts to stink. You have to do something about that quick, get it out, or things can get ugly."

"Gas?" Mary said.

Timothy nodded. "Lots of it. So usually I have to aspirate. Put a tube in your belly—you can see the mark—and just suck the gas right out. Then I hook the tube to the jug of preservative and fill you up. That's why you feel so heavy now, 'cause you're full of it, top to toe."

He shrugged again. "So it'd be hard to get the water down, 'cause of the pressure from the preservative on your esophagus and intestines. That's all I meant."

Mary stared at him a moment, eyes cataract-white, then nodded. She turned and took a few steps away from him. The shroud twisted around her legs, and she pitched forward. Timothy rushed to help, but Mary turned on him with a snarl and batted his hand away. She untangled her legs and limped over to the slab from which she'd risen. Then she hung her head and leaned on the table, sobbing.

Timothy kept his distance and rubbed the blood from his wrist where Mary had clawed him. The skin around the scratches was already stinging and inflamed. Eventually, Mary stopped crying and stood motionless. The shroud hung off her like an evening gown, leaving the long white line of her back exposed and elegant. Timothy thought of a creased photo in his family album, his mother posing in her wedding gown. In the black and white snapshot, her skin was as pale as Mary's. The thought made Timothy feel strange—a tremulous rustle about his ribcage that made him queasy. He pressed his wrist tighter.

The killdeer turned on its nest and chirped in pain. Mary cocked an ear toward it.

"What's that?" she asked.

"A bird I found," Timothy said. "On my way to work tonight. She's hurt. Come here, I'll show you."

He led Mary to the instrument tray and showed her the killdeer in its metal nest. The bird twittered under the gauze shroud. Mary pulled the cloth back and leaned over it.

"Poor thing," she croaked. "It's not going to make it."

"She'll pull through," Timothy said. "I'm going to nurse her. I saved her eggs."

"Timmy, its ribs are crushed, see?" Mary pointed at the blood-matted feathers. "Massive internal trauma. I was studying to be a vet before—well, *before*. I'm surprised the little thing's lasted as long as it has."

"She'll live."

"I don't think so, Timmy. It's hurt too bad. And it's in such pain. The best thing would be to put it out of its misery. Wouldn't take much—I'm sure you've got some ether or something around here—"

"She'll live," Timothy insisted. "I saved her eggs, see? I made her a nest. I can feed her—I'll mash up some worms or something, feed her through a tube. She's got those eggs. I can keep them warm, with the cotton and all. She'll pull through. Her eggs—" Timothy fell quiet, staring at the bird's bloody wing. Finally, he looked back at Mary.

"You'll see," he said.

Mary stared at him again, silent, then looked back down at the bird. She reached to replace the gauze. As her wrist caught the light, Timothy noticed the gentle curve of her forearm, its pale fuzz a shade darker now that her skin had blanched. His mother had been like that, pale and delicate. Mary held her hand up to her face, dark eyebrows knit over blank eyes.

"I'm so cold," she said. "I hadn't noticed 'til now. That's funny, isn't it? To notice it now, after all this time? It's like I'm made of ice. And the veins, here in my hand, see? They look almost *green*. Isn't that strange?"

Timothy shook his head. "That's just the formaldehyde. It's kind of yellow, not red like your blood. So in the blue veins, the color mixes, and that's what makes it look green. It happens to everybody— at least everyone I ever worked on. The first time I embalmed someone—"

"Timothy, please. Can we talk about something else?" She started to sob again, her dry tongue clicking against the back of her throat.

"It's okay, Mary," he said, taking her cold hand in his. "I know it seems scary now, but you'll be okay. I've seen it before."

"What's happening, Timmy? Why am I like this?" She stared into his face, her milky eyes sad and scared. "I'm not supposed to be like this. I'm supposed to be like *him*." She pointed at Deacon Johnson.

Timothy put his hands in his pockets and stared at his scuffed black shoes. "They ain't all Wakers," he mumbled.

Mary looked up. "What?"

"Wakers. That's what I call them—you. When you get up, when you're dead. They don't all wake up."

"I don't understand," Mary said.

He shrugged. "Sometimes they wake, sometimes they don't. The older they are, the less it seems to happen. But it's not a rule.

Remember Doug McKinley? Big old man, I think he used to work with your dad at the foundry." Mary nodded. "Well, when he died a year or so back, I didn't think he'd wake. He was sixty years old, after all, and he'd had a stroke besides. But I was wrong. A couple nights after the burial, I heard a nose out in the 'yard, and when I got there, the McKinley crypt was open and his coffin busted to splinters on the ground. I found him near the east wall, sitting on a gravestone. His arms were all smashed to hell, what he'd done getting out. He was just looking at them.

"'*I used to be so strong,*' he said. '*I could feel the iron in my hands. Now look at my arms. They're just sticks. Just a couple of broken-up sticks.*'" Timothy scratched his chin. "Don't know why I remember it like that, but I do, clear as day. Maybe because he was my uncle—brother of my stepdad, anyway. Took me three hours to talk him back into the tomb."

They fell silent. Finally, Mary shivered.

"It's freezing in here. Can we go outside?"

"Sure," he said. "I know a quiet spot."

The sky had cleared since Timothy's arrival at work, and now the moon shone full and bright, illuminating their path as he led Mary to the far corner of the graveyard. They held hands. Mary's fingers—long, slender, and cold—interlocked with his like briars. His knuckles ached in her nerveless grip, but he did not complain. A lovely mist sat a few inches above the manicured, gray-green lawn, and its gentle glow softened the stones' edges and robbed them of their menace. The shroud slipped down Mary's shoulder as they walked, revealing her small pale breasts, globed and perfect in the moonlight.

"Over here," Timothy said.

They stopped in front of a small gravestone just a few yards from the cemetery's border. Timothy helped Mary sit on the grass and then crouched beside her, staring at the marker.

"Your mother?" Mary asked.

Timothy nodded. The grave was well tended, thanks to his nightly ministrations. A perfect brown rectangle of earth, topped by a bouquet of fresh wildflowers, lay before the simple white stone. Square letters spelled out his mother's name—*Beatrice*—and the dates of her birth and death. At the top of the stone's curve, a photo was imbedded: bangs curled over a soft white forehead, pale blue eyes showing gray in the picture, red lips like a bow. *A Loving Mother—Always Remembered.* That had been Timothy's idea.

"She was young," Mary said.

"Car wreck," Timothy explained. "My stepdad lost control. It had been raining. They hit a tree, and the gas tank caught fire. Burned her up bad. They didn't let me see her. Kept the casket closed. I never got to say goodbye."

"That's terrible." Mary stared at the photo again. "She was beautiful."

"So are you," Timothy said.

Again, Mary tried and failed at a smile. "Was she—did she *wake*?"

Timothy shrugged. For a moment, they listened to the rattling dry leaves on their branches. Mary bowed her head.

"So what happens now?" she asked.

"What do you mean?"

"What do I do? You know... at the funeral?"

Timothy pulled a weed from the grass near his mother's tombstone and sighed. "You gotta think about it this way," he said. "Think about your family, sitting there at the funeral, looking at you. They want you to be peaceful. They want to know you're at rest."

"But I'm not."

"Still, you gotta think about *them*. They're the ones still living. What would your mother do if she knew you were waking? She's already lost you once. See what I mean? And there's nothing you could do to help that. The only thing you could do is harm. You gotta think about that."

"So I just lay there? Like I'm not awake?"

"I think it's best. Just lay back and relax. Try to look as peaceful as you can. Listen to the service. Enjoy the music. Remember how much everyone loves you."

Mary nodded. "Then what?"

Timothy shrugged again. "Then we bury you."

Mary stared at him, eyes like pearls. "But I'll still be awake! It'll be horrible!"

He shook his head. "No it won't. It'll get boring, maybe, but if you just lie still and don't fight it, it'll be fine. Quiet, peaceful like. You can just lay there and rest, 'til the Lord comes."

"How long will that be?"

"I don't know. Soon, I reckon."

Mary's throat clicked again, and she sniffed, though her nose and eyes were dry. She looked at her hands again. "Do you think that's why some of us are waking? Because the Lord's coming?"

He sighed and shifted away from her. "Maybe. No. I don't think so. How the hell do I know?" He stood up fast. "Maybe it's always been this way. Maybe everybody's waking, down there under the ground, just too afraid or weak or lazy to come out. Maybe it's 'cause of toxic waste. Radioactive waves. Hell, maybe it's aliens."

They were quiet for a moment. A cricket chirped once and fell silent. Mary leaned closer to the gravestone.

"I look like your mother, don't I?"

Timothy turned around. "What?"

"I couldn't see it very well before, but I do. The hair, I guess. Isn't that funny?"

"I don't know," Timothy said. He kicked a pebble across the path. "I guess so."

Mary leaned back on her arms, breasts still exposed, brows knit in thought. "And that uncle of yours—the one you told me about— he waked too."

Timothy paced a few yards away and said nothing.

"Is it always someone you know, Timothy? Or somebody that reminds you of someone?"

"It ain't me," Timothy said.

"I'm just saying. Why wouldn't it happen around anyone else? Other graveyards, I mean. Seems like you'd hear about it. Like someone would talk. Doesn't it?"

"That's silly. You don't know what you're saying."

"Listen to me, Timothy—this is important. Why, in all the world, why would you be the only one? There's got to be a reason, right? And you—you've thought of this before. That's why you said, 'It ain't me.' Maybe that's why I'm—Timothy, look at me."

He closed his eyes and shook his head. She did sound like his mother. Telling him things he didn't want to hear—that his father had died, that she was marrying Peter Grimley, that he shouldn't apply to the state college but work close to home instead. How she and Pete were just going to drive to the movies and be back after midnight, the trip that ended in fire and pain.

"It ain't me," he said again. Then they heard the crash.

Timothy bounded down the trail back to the mortuary. He heard another crash, glass breaking and metal clanging tile, and turned the corner in time to see a wide shadow pass over the prep room window. He scrambled up three steps to the mortuary's back door, flung it open and dashed inside.

The prep room blinked light and dark. Smashed fluorescent bulbs hung like shattered bones from the ceiling. A coil of tubing slipped off an empty, dented metal table, curling to the floor like guts. Malfunctioning lights buzzed, and some desperate alarm squeaked. In the middle of the room hunched the gray bullfrog form of Deacon Johnson.

"Brother Johnson?" Timothy called over the incessant squeal. "It's all right, sir. Everything's okay."

The deacon rose to a crouch, moving slowly. He was naked, and blue veins speckled the rolls of fat around his middle. Splotchy maroon bruises spread across his shoulder blades and massive buttocks where the blood had pooled as he lay on the slab. He cast a bewildered stare at Timothy; his eyes were filmy black spots. His quivering lower lip was yellow.

"Where am I?!" the old man shouted. "Where are my clothes?!"

"Please try to stay calm, Deacon. It's me, Timothy Rogers. You're at the mortuary. I got some bad news for you."

"Mortuary?" The big man faced Timothy fully, his breasts heavy and white with fur. His whole mouth glistened with sick yellow ooze. "What? Am I—Rogers? Boy... I don't feel so... where are my *clothes*?"

"You've passed on, sir," Timothy explained. The squeaking noise seemed to fill the whole room, coming from everywhere at once. It was hard for Timothy to concentrate. "You're dead. I know it's hard to get a handle on, but if you'll just listen to me—"

Deacon Johnson watched Timothy a moment, his lips slimy and quivering. Finally, he started blubbering, though his tear ducts were clogged and dry.

"I can't feel nothing," he sobbed. "My hands—there's glass in 'em, and I don't even feel it! And I can't *taste* nothing! My tongue, my mouth..." He pointed to his lips, and Timothy saw pale buff shards of eggshell stuck in the yolk that slimed the old man's mouth. Timothy looked at the instrument tray and noticed the chrome pan emptied of gauze, next to a small pool of clear liquid. A short distance away, its mangled wing pinned under the weight of the overturned cart, the killdeer sent out its incessant chirp. Timothy stared, his lips a tight line. Then he turned back to the deacon.

"You ain't alive no more," he whispered. "You're gonna have to lay down, so we can get you ready. Your funeral's in two days."

Brother Johnson's lips continued to shake, but his eyes widened as Timothy's words sank in. "I'm not dead. I'm not! Look, I'm as alive as you!"

"No, you ain't," Timothy said. "You're gone, and you have to be buried."

Johnson's eyes narrowed. "You ain't burying nobody, son."

"Yes, sir," Timothy replied. "I am."

With a roar, the old man sprang on Timothy, fingers clawed like a tiger's. Timothy sidestepped him, and Deacon Johnson sprawled to the floor, skidding on layers of fat. The old man tried to stand, but his limbs were already stiff and he couldn't get leverage on the slick tile.

Timothy picked up one of the heavier chrome pans and struck the old man at the base of the skull. The metal sang as Timothy swung it again and again, until finally deacon's corpse was still. Timothy stood, panting.

The killdeer's chirping had stopped. He turned to the instrument tray, where a tuft of brown feathers lay still under the cart. He put his hand to his face and brought it away, wet. When he looked up, he found Mary staring at him from the outer door.

"What happened?" she whispered.

Timothy wiped his nose on his wrist. "Come on. Help me get him on the table."

Timothy did the embalming as quickly as he could, but Brother Johnson was a big man, and it took a lot of preservative to fill him. When that was done, Timothy turned the body over and took up one of the scalpels. He traced the tendons on the back of Deacon Johnson's legs, pressing two fingers into the soft flesh on either side of the hamstring until it stood out like a piano wire. He severed it cleanly, with one stroke, wincing only a little as the tight rubbery tissue went *pop!* under his blade. Then he cut the rest of the tendons—legs, feet, arms, hands, front and back. Finally, he cut the cords connecting the old man's neck to his collarbone, taking care also to sever the windpipe. That finished, he sutured the straight, bloodless wounds with care.

"Timothy," Mary croaked from the doorway. "Why?"

"He ain't restful," Timothy explained. "And I ain't got time to go through it with him. It's after three already. I can't have him waking when Bob comes in. And the funeral—he'd sit up in his coffin, sure. Think of his family. He's got a daughter not much older than us."

"But Timothy—this is awful."

He shrugged. "He don't feel it. And after a while, he'll get used to the idea. It ain't so bad."

Timothy took some lighter thread and set to work on the deacon's face. He sewed the eyelids shut, folding the lids back to hide the stitches. Then he used some of the thicker filament to close the old man's mouth, looping it through the gums. He couldn't cut the facial muscles—he'd never be able to cover the marks—but by the funeral, the deacon would be so stiff that it wouldn't matter. After breaking off the last stitch, Timothy turned around to find Mary on the other slab.

"What's this?"

"Do me now," she said. "Like him."

Timothy threw the scalpel onto the tray. "Ain't no reason to," he said. "You'll be at peace. You won't cause a ruckus like him."

"I might, Timothy. You don't know me that well. The thought of that lid closing, the dirt coming down—I don't want that. Nobody does. And all that time, waiting, just sitting there in that box—I'm going crazy just thinking about it!"

Timothy shook his head and kept shaking it. "No reason for that, Mary. No reason at all."

She turned her eyes on him, cloudy white and blank. "I'm not supposed to be like this, Timmy. And maybe it's your fault. Maybe if you forget me, then I can rest. Maybe I'll just fall off dead, like I'm supposed to. But you won't forget before Friday, and I don't think I can stand it."

Timothy started to object again, but Mary shut her eyes and crossed her arms over her chest. She lay perfectly still, perfectly beautiful.

"Please," she said.

Timothy went to the tray and picked up the scalpel.

*　　*　　*　　*　　*

Both funerals went off without a hitch. Even Bob had to say that Mary Lindquist looked good. "Like a statue, or a painting, or something. Like the god-damned *Mona Lisa*." Others complimented Timothy on his artistry, including Mrs. Lindquist, who hugged him and whispered a tearful thank-you. Deacon Johnson's funeral two days later also ended quietly. A few of his relatives mumbled that he looked uncomfortable even in the plush pillows of his coffin, but most thought he looked fine. After that, things were quiet for a while.

Timothy buried the killdeer in the flowerbed just behind the small room that he rented from Mrs. Orson. He used a large box, much larger than was needed for its tiny, crushed frame. He packed some gauze and cotton in it as well, together with the shards of eggshell he'd cleaned from the floor of the prep room. He buried it only a few inches below ground, right outside the window of his bedroom.

He decided to take some time off from his job at the mortuary. Instead of tending to the dead, Timothy took some time to look over his old college application materials. He mostly succeeded in not thinking of his mother, restless in her grave. He tried not to think of Mary either, her kind eyes and beautiful dead flesh. When such thoughts started to creep in, he thought instead of the killdeer and its unselfish devotion to its young. Then he would peer out his window, over the dew-kissed petals of the flowers beneath him, and listen to the killdeer chirp—calling him away, away, away from the broken eggs that were her mother's hope.

Ravenous Angels

A. KIWI COURTERS

"The victim wasn't violated." The tiny blonde dame in the pink dress orbited the body as the crime scene boys outlined the victim with chalk, mostly just making a ravine in the dust that covered the floor of the warehouse. One of the techs picked up a pistol, dangling it by the trigger guard at the end of a probe. The dame kept talking to herself, taking verbal notes—real irritating, like. "Killed by a man filled with rage; filled with hatred toward her."

The blonde had a speech impediment that made her pronounce *rage* as *wage*, *hatred* as *hatwed*. It added to her little girl countenance in a way that made me a tad uncomfortable—a tad too intrigued.

"Because he covered her face?" I asked.

"Because he ripped her arms off." The blonde gave me the pathetic-old-man look.

I gave her the hick-town sheriff shrug. "Maybe crazy, or on drugs?"

She didn't look at me, just kept circling, each step puffing powder into the air.

The victim lay a few yards from big cold-storage units, doors dented and smashed in. A rag covered the vic's face, her legs splayed. She wasn't from around here. But then, neither were the feds. And the broad? What was a woman doing at a crime scene like this? I got the call at a fundraiser for the varsity basketball team. I wasn't expected, but I wasn't excluded, either.

"Kinda looks like an angel," I said, noting the shape.

The dame asked, "What do you make of all the footprints?"

I saw lots, way too many for an abandoned building miles from town. Bending close, I pulled on my specs. The dust had an odd, crystal look to it, like fine salt. I could feel it at the back of my throat. "Different shoes, mostly the same size. He wasn't working alone."

"Anything else?"

I pulled my light from the ring on my gun belt, casting around without stepping past the crime scene tape. Most of the room hadn't been gone over yet. Even with the overheads and the six-cell Kel, gloom filled the big chamber. As the flashlight beam probed the lunar-like surface of the floor, I could see that most of 'em weren't fresh. They'd gone soft around the edges with the fall of more dust.

"None of her footprints. Maybe they carried her in?" I examined the outline of my oxfords, size ten—I saw it. "Awful small feet."

"Uh-huh." She started out, and I followed.

Flintman, the coroner, waited just outside, arms folded. "Can we move her?"

"Not until we're finished securing the scene." The blonde continued through the parking lot, to a yellow turbo Beetle. She beeped the doors open and slipped inside. I caught a glimpse of thigh. In the glow of the dome light, her round forehead, high cheekbones, and cupid-bow lips made her look even that much younger, or more vulnerable. I looked at the car instead.

"It's a rental," she said. I saw a flush in her cheeks.

Desert air flitted through acres of empty parking lot, gritty and cold. A gulf of dry night separated us from Hatchet, the town that elected and employed me; an ocean of high desert scrub and sand from Elko, the nearest what you might call civilized place. Somewhere in the vast emptiness, a coyote complained. I started to brush all the dust off my uniform and sneezed.

"What was this place?" the blonde asked.

I gazed at the shadowed carcass of the warehouse and factory behind. "Used to be Graham Consolidated, manufacturer of the world's supply of Fairy Rings. I was a driver for them, back when I was a kid." When they laid me off, I ran for sheriff. Thirty years later, here I was.

"Any problems out this way recently?" She tugged at her dress, trying to hide the ripeness of her figure.

"Serious vandalism. Place was totally busted up. We locked it up tight after that."

"Vagrancy?"

"We're surrounded by hundreds of square miles of nowhere."

"Make a hell of a hideout." She looked out her windshield, pursing her pouty lips. "I need a place to stay in town."

I tore my eyes from her to look at the dark, abandoned piles. "Take 228 to Prospector Road. First left will take you to the Motor-Go Motel. It ain't much, but it's clean."

"I'll be in touch," she said and held out her card.

I took it. "Blanche Hillor, FDA Enforcement Officer" was all it said, with some phone numbers and a government e-mail. "Food and Drug Administration?"

"My cell's on the back."

I dug in my uniform pocket for my own card, but she said, "I can find you if I need you." She dismissed me, and started her car.

* * * * *

Morning arrived with me still in my dusty uniform, waiting for the first pot of coffee to brew at Dahlia's. No one else occupied the diner at five a.m., and very few would walk through the door during the day. Old-timers would come by with the *Star,* get their daily cholesterol before seeking their daily alcohol.

"Up early, or up late Billy-Joe?" Dahlia put her elbows on the counter and leaned over enough for me to look down her blouse. Her bra was light blue.

"Late."

"Sounds like trouble."

"Yep."

"Wanna talk about it?"

"Nope."

With half a scowl, she grabbed a cup and held it under the drip. Ben Callahan came in with a stack of the *Hatchet Star,* and I grabbed the top one. No murder headline. Thank Christ.

"Morning, Billy-Joe. Up early, or up late?"

"Late."

He lifted his eyebrows. "Uh-oh."

Dahlia slid the cup at me. "He ain't talkin', Ben."

He shrugged. "I got my route anyways."

Dahlia headed behind the grill to throw around some eggs, potatoes, and bacon. I gazed down Prospector at the town hall façade lit by the earliest, orangest sunlight. Harriet usually came in early, and I knew there was no point trying to sleep until I visited her. Just around the bend that sent Prospector toward West Bullion, the Motor-Go Motel lot held several cars, all hidden in the dim, but one vehicle looked brighter and rounder. My breakfast arrived with a clatter, and I wolfed it down.

Dahlia looked at my empty plate with a smirk. "Refill?"

It felt like I hadn't eaten anything. "Yeah, another No. 2." I watched Earl, my deputy, arrive early for his shift, and watched Deputy Bill leave early. The sky came to life in pale lemon, violet shadows shouldering the structures downtown as my second breakfast arrived. Betty Silver's piece-of-shit Dodge roared down the road loud as a helicopter. Her teacher's salary didn't seem enough to keep a muffler on that beast. She headed north, and her place was north, so I figured she'd been shacked up with Skip Meyers again since his wife took off last year. Skip was a nice enough fella, but I knew he'd been busted for picking up transvestite hookers in Vegas.

Anyone in town with a penchant for vice eventually came under my scrutiny, and that turned out to be almost everyone important: the mayor, the council, school board members like my idiot nephew, Bobby-Lee; the Lions, and the chamber of commerce. One night, I'd be eating with them at a fundraiser, as all good elected officials did, and the next, I'd be throwing one in the drunk tank.

None of the miscreants and perverts in charge of Hatchet seemed capable of murder. Knowing the people, knowing their occasional forays into lawlessness, gave me that much insight.

The light in the town hall came on, Harriet Briggs, town clerk, arriving early for another hot, dry day of filing. I finished my second breakfast and headed down the street. Hatchet started cold in the mornings until the sun fired her up like a coal fire in a furnace. Already, the first slanting rays of sun left an arid, prickly passage on my face.

"Morning, Billy-Joe."

"Harriet." I tipped my hat.

"Must be something serious, you in here at this hour." She sat in a chair that must have been as old as the town hall building itself, one of those wooden office chairs on castors. Next to the computer was a can of nuts, and she kept digging into them, chewing noisily. My gut should've felt like it was going to explode, but I grabbed a handful and tossed them back.

"Just need to see the deed on the old GC buildings."

She gave me an odd look. "Graham Consolidated owns them."

"Didn't they sell them back in '80?"

Harriet rolled herself to a file cabinet, flung open a drawer. "Yes, they did sell them. But they bought 'em back. Your nephew's the agent on the property."

Which would explain his new truck. "Thanks, Harriet. Any idea why they'd want the buildings back?"

She shook her head.

I thanked her and walked out into the increasingly warm morning. Why the hell would a defunct corporation buy back a bunch of buildings in the middle of nowhere? My nephew, Bobby-Lee, might have that answer. But I decided to stop in at the office first.

"Morning, Sheriff. You up early or up late?" Earl got the day shift because he did respectful things like call me "Sheriff" and such.

"Morning, Earl. Up late."

"Something going on?" He had a big bag of fast-food breakfast that he kept dipping into. In spite of my large morning meal, the smell made my mouth water.

"Yeah, we had us a murder last night out to the old GC compound."

"A murder?"

I snuck a nugget of hash brown. "Ain't had one before."

Around a mouthful, he said: "I sure don't remember one."

"The feds're here looking into it, and we'll be as cooperative as we can so it can get solved. Anything else happening?"

Earl cast around, coming up with a pink phone message. "Blanche Hillor called."

That was quick. I took the note from him. There was a greasy thumbprint in the middle. "I'll call her from the car."

"Where you going to be at?"

"Bobby-Lee's. Shouldn't be long."

Dora Gibbons, the receptionist and part-time dispatcher, came in the front door with an open box of donuts, powdered sugar stuck to her makeup. "Morning, Sheriff. You up early, or up late?"

I snagged an old-fashioned and headed out.

* * * * *

Just as I made a dusty turn onto Argent Street, the radio crackled. "Sheriff, we got a 10-103mj down to the high school, or maybe a 415c, come back?"

What the hell was a 10-103mj, or a 415c? "In English words, Earl."

"A disturbance, involving a juvenile, probably mentally deranged, over."

Ah, shit. I made a U-turn, heading back into town, lights and sirens. "On my way."

"Sheriff 10-38 Jefferson High, 10-4."

Ten minutes later, I pulled alongside the red curb outside the school, behind an ambulance. Teenagers were standing in lines with teachers at the head of each.

"In the cafeteria," Betty Silver pointed.

I went in the lobby doors, the cafeteria on the right; a banner over the doorway still announced last weekend's band boosters pancake breakfast. EMT radios chirped, and guys in blue jumpsuits stood talking in low murmurs near the lunch line doors. Breakfast smells hung in the air, making my stomach growl. One of the serving women stood nearer the exit, a diamond of sweat rolling down into the valley revealed by her V-neck. She swiped a damp, curly lock from her eyes as I came in.

"He's loco." She nodded toward the kitchen.

I slipped past the knot of ambulance drivers.

"Careful, Billy-Joe," one of them said, though none moved to help.

Cornered, a doe-eyed cafeteria gal looked at me with relief. One hand was gloved in plastic, holding the other hand, bare and coated in red. She huddled between a huge dishwasher and a long griddle, whimpering, eyes going from mine to something in front of her.

Sidling around the cash register, I got a good look. Tim Fields, Marty and Sherry's boy, crouched, surrounded by ripped-open cardboard in front of the open doors of the shiny new stainless steel freezers. As I came around, I saw the server gal's missing glove, fingers full of blood, dangling from his mouth.

When he turned his eyes on me, I saw nothing of the boy with the straight, wheat-colored hair, the two-time winner of the annual spelling bee and roast beef dinner fundraiser; it was gone, wiped

away by the feral gleam of a trapped beast. He chewed on the glove with a squelchy sound, blood dripping from his chin. Snarling, eyes wide, his little body tensed. My first instinct was to draw my gun and kill it, kill the filthy, snarling thing.

Tim scrambled backward, his head hit the freezer door behind, and he whirled around with an inhuman cry. I pounced, grabbing up his arms. Sneakers slammed into my hip, and I almost lost him. Bloodstained teeth snapped, nearly biting my nose, feet pumped and kicked. But savage as he was, he was also a kid. Wrapping one arm around both of his, the other around his legs, I hauled the squirming bundle out to the EMTs.

"Jesus, Billy-Joe!"

"Shut up and give him something to knock him out."

One of the older men injected the boy, but he only struggled harder. A stretcher came rolling in, medics running around, bringing the wounded server out of the kitchen.

"I'm getting too old for this."

Three techs grabbed the boy, trying to strap him to a gurney, and that was about as much as I could take.

I headed back to Bobby-Lee's place. The drive was long enough to make a phone call.

"FDA, Hillor."

"It's Billy-Joe. You called?"

"We ID'd the vic."

"Do tell."

"Prints on the weapon came back to Ann Blevins, driver for GC."

"Driver?" I made the turn. "Where's her truck?"

Hillor paused. "We're looking into it." She disconnected.

I pulled into the long, dusty drive of my nephew's place, parked next to his new monster truck, Ford F-350. Bobby-Lee had my sister's looks, fat head, pear-shaped body, and lank brown hair. It worked better on my sister. He answered the door.

"What's up, Uncle Billy-Joe?"

"Not working today?" Not an unusual situation.

"Kid home sick." He leaned on the doorframe, chewing on a hotdog covered in ketchup.

I shifted the hat on my head, feeling dampness in the band. "I need to ask you about the GC buildings."

"Oh, that?" He didn't invite me in. "GC wanted to buy 'em back. I thought they might start up the plant, get some jobs around here again." He stuck the remaining dog and bun into his mouth, making his cheeks puff out.

"Why you, and not some big firm in Vegas?"

His mud-colored eyes looked past my shoulder. "Well, they want to keep it under the hat a little. Asked me to fill out the paperwork at the courthouse, no listings, that kinda thing."

"You didn't think it was fishy?"

"I'd do business with Charley the Tuna for a sale. What's the big deal, anyway?"

"Woman murdered up there."

"What? When?"

"Found her last night. Been there a while."

A hank of hair peeled itself from greasy clutches, falling over his brow. "Well, I wouldn't know anything about that. There's no work going on there, far's I know."

"Far as you know. What else do you know, Bobby-Lee?"

"Look, I don't know what their plans are, they didn't tell me. But I figured, hell, if they opened up again, be good for everyone, y'know? We scratch their back, they scratch ours."

He was talking faster—he was up to something. It was time to bluff him, see what I could get. "What about all the trucks up there?"

He blinked, swallowed, and took the lure. "They were just there moving stuff out. A lot of stuff left behind I guess. Clean up, y'know?"

"So you do know what's going on."

He waved his hands in the air, getting worked up a little. Bugs do that, too, when it gets hot out. "No, that's it. I don't know nothing."

I took a step toward him. The house had central air, the cool oozing past my nephew with the smell of cooking dogs. "So how do you know they were cleaning up?"

"I don't. I mean, that's what it looked like."

He backed up a couple steps, and soon I was inside, closing the door behind me. I felt my sweat ice over. "How often you been up there, Nephew?"

"Once. Maybe twice."

"Dad, you're letting the cool out, you idiot." Jimmy-Bob shuffled into the living room in pajama bottoms and a stained T-shirt.

"J.B., go cook up some more wieners or something. I'm talking business with Uncle Billy-Joe."

"Whatever." The boy folded his arms.

Bobby-Lee's mouth wadded up, his eyes squinched at the bottoms. "Please," he said, making it sound like an insult.

Jimmy-Bob shuffled back out, murmuring, "Asshole."

I looked at Dad the asshole. "Talk to me, or so help me, I'll bring you to the station. We don't have AC there."

"Okay, okay. Here's the whole of it. The sale hadn't gone through yet, but the GC boys wanted to take a look for themselves. They were getting a good price, but as-is, y'know. They asked me if maybe they could use the place to store some stuff. I said they couldn't, not 'til the sale was final."

"But they passed on some green persuasion."

"Well, yeah, favors exchanged, y'know. It didn't do no harm. Look, I needed this sale, Uncle Billy-Joe. If for sale signs were tombstones, this town'd be a cemetery. How'd I put Jimmy-Bob through college?"

"Your boy's about as smart as an opossum, and maybe half as fast."

His mouth bunched up again, but he got it smoothed out quick. "That's what I know, Billy-Joe. And that's all."

I knew that wasn't all, but I had work to do and sleep to catch up on, so I headed back to the office.

*   *   *   *   *

Behind my sunglasses, I figured no one could tell I was catnapping. I had the phone forwarded, feet up on the desk, the remainders of a double cheeseburger next to the phone. I nearly fell out of my chair when something roared by. I got through the door just in time to see a herd of dark blue sedans roaring through downtown, little gumball lights on the dashboards, and squeal their tires around the bend of Prospector Road, heading north. At the rear was a new yellow Beetle.

"Son of a bitch."

I hurried out to the Jeep, lights and sirens again, and followed the flock of feds. Near the turn-off to 229, I found myself in a cloud of their dust. We drove past the GC compound about two miles. A semi sat on the side of the road, blinkers on, slow and weak. I pulled over and jumped out of the Jeep. "Goddamnit, Hillor."

Blanche Hillor jumped out of the Bug. "Sheriff, this is a case involving interstate commerce, and it clearly falls within federal jurisdiction." The pink party dress had been replaced by a boring brown suit. But put money in bags the same color and it still won't keep your mind off the goods inside.

Hillor stuck a finger in her mouth, chewing on the nail. In the light of day, crows feet stretched out from her mirror sunglasses and threads of silver mingled with the gold of her hair. Instead of detracting from her looks, it only made her seem more attainable. Especially when she called me "Shewiff." But I was there on business.

"I don't care if you're with the FBI, the FDA, or the goddamn KKK: this township is my responsibility, and if you drive like that through town again, I'll toss all your asses in the pokey."

Her mouth formed a thin, unattractive line, a blush rising from her collar. "Murder is a little more important that a traffic ticket, Sheriff."

"Murder?" I looked over at the semi. It leaned awkwardly on the shoulder, as if ready to tip over. Tires on the passenger side were flat. Dark-suited men closed on the vehicle, like ants on a dead snail. Some I recognized from the previous night, though they'd lost the unlettered jumpsuits in favor of business attire. No logos adorned the panels of the container or the doors of the cab.

"I'm sorry, Sheriff. We had no reason to tear through your town like that."

She was leaning against her rental car, looking tired, biting her nails.

I got the feeling she didn't want me looking too closely at the truck. "Fine," I said. "Don't let it happen again. But I'd still like to know why you think this is a murder case."

"Hey, you men stay away from there until the vans arrive!" The suited men stopped short, each throwing a sheepish look Hillor's way. To me, she said: "We've seen two other semis stopped in this area, drivers gone missing. The woman in the warehouse was the first body we've found."

"And you think the same happened here?" I squinted at the Freightliner, heat shimmering up from the road. It looked like a rusty handprint marred the windshield, but I couldn't be certain.

"Both of the incidents occurred near Hatchet."

It was my turn to work up a blush. "I haven't heard about any truck driver murders until last night."

"And you don't want to." Blanche said it in a harsh whisper. She took off her mirror sunglasses and looked up at me. "Let us clean this up so you can go back to tossing drunks in a cell and chasing teenagers out of lover's lanes and all the other dull, wonderful things you do in town. You don't know how serious this is. You don't—"

"Agent Hillor." One of the clean-cut feds came up on us silently. "The vans are here."

Before Blanche Hillor put her shades back on, she gave me a long look, holding my eyes until I nodded in agreement. I went back to the Jeep and U-turned toward town. But as I drove away, I wrote down the license number of the truck even as a man with a battery-powered drill-driver crouched to remove the plate.

When 228 swooped to the southeast enough to lose me from sight, I called it in.

"I'll run a check, Sheriff. You need it right away?"

"Better make it now, Earl."

Earl didn't say anything for a while. Then the radio crackled again. "Sheriff, plate comes back to a commercial vehicle owned by Hardenton Systems out of Carson City."

"Reported stolen?"

"No, sir. Should be on a run to Phoenix."

So what was it doing outside of Hatchet, Nevada? We were a good piece off the beaten path to Arizona. "You know anything about Hardenton Systems?"

"No, sir, but I'll find out."

"I'll be in the office shortly."

"Sheriff 10-19 HQ, 10-4."

Christ, he loved his codes.

*　*　*　*　*

Earl waved me over excitedly when I walked in the glass front doors. The fans were on so high I had to hold my hat down. "What you got, Earl?"

"Check this out, Sheriff." Earl had another greasy fast-food bag in front of him, and I stole his fries. "Hardenton Systems is a multinational corporation, and they do everything from military applications to shipping. They don't own anything in the state. Except one of the corporations they own under the Hardenton Systems umbrella is—" Earl dramatically pressed the mouse, but nothing happened. He fiddled with the computer a few minutes. "I can't find it anymore."

"Can't find what?"

"The multinational watchdog page listed all the companies Hardenton Systems owns, but they're all gone."

I wasn't surprised. "Go to the DMV and run that plate again."

"Sure thing." Earl went to the Nevada Department of Motor Vehicles and logged in. When he ran the plate, it came up as an unassigned number. "Damn, that's weird. I swear it said—"

"I believe you, Deputy. Now," I said over a mouthful of fried potato, "what was the name of the corporation they own that had you all excited?"

"Graham Consolidated," he said.

GC repurchased their plant on the outskirts of Hatchet. Hardenton owned not only GC, but the trucks that people seemed to be dying in around these parts. And somebody wanted what was in those trucks, wanted it so bad that they'd kill the drivers to get it. With Hillor being from the Food and Drug Administration, I figured it to be some kind of pharmaceutical, something with a street value. OxyContin, maybe, Dilaudid or Vicodin. But that didn't explain why that truck was so far off a route to Phoenix.

"Oh shit."

I looked over Earl's shoulder. A pop-up for penis enlargement filled the screen, followed a second later by one for a porn site. Then they came up faster than you could read them, one after the other. Earl clicked with the mouse, and then punched the keyboard, but they kept on, a flicker of illegible ads. "It must be a virus, a hijacker."

I reached behind the machine and pulled out a blue cable. The ads stopped. Earl looked up at me, swallowing hard. "I don't go to these, I mean, the office computer—"

"I know. Just shut it off before Dora sees it. Then put her on dispatch. I want you out on patrol."

"Yes, sir. Where will you be if something comes up?"

Sleeping. "In my office. But unless the whole town is falling apart, don't bug me."

The computer screen went blank. "Okay, Sheriff."

Let Blanche Hillor and her FDA, or whoever, boys deal with it. I was too damned beat. Foregoing appearances, I spread out on the worn sofa and put my hat over my eyes. The fries sparked hunger in me, but I was more tired than anything. It didn't seem like I'd been asleep more than a minute when I heard Dora's gentle voice.

"Sheriff, I think you'd better wake up."

I removed the hat from my eyes, finding my office dark. "What is it?"

"Earl's on the radio, says there's a 10-35 down to the high school."

"What's a 10-35?"

"I don't know, but he sounds plenty shook." Dora led the way back to the front office, where Earl's voice squawked from the radio. She pulled a donut from the box, and turned up the base station radio.

"We have a 10-35 at the high school, a 10-103 by the looks of it."

"Earl!" I grabbed the mic. "English!"

"A 187—" A loud bark of a scream came over the speaker, just a second's worth of sound, but a sound of sheer horror. I ran for the door.

"Bill on yet, Dora?"

"On his way, I imagine. Should I get on the blower and send him code-three to the school?"

"Yeah, do that right away." I was out the door.

I returned to the school, a ten-minute drive from downtown. I made it in five, code-three, lights and sirens—they were getting more use than they had in ten years.

I pulled behind Earl's black-and-white, silhouetted by a lit marquee announcing the basketball team's spaghetti dinner fundraiser. He wasn't inside. The seats, the floormat, even the ceiling was painted in red. It dripped from the steering wheel, off the radio handset.

Checking the ground, I saw nothing but undisturbed concrete. A few yards away, I found a single, fat drop of blood, then another, all leading toward the front door of the school.

Two feet from the façade of the school, I saw a trooper hat lying on the concrete. A wedge of light came from the door, giving the hat a long shadow. The door was propped open by something. I pulled my gun and hurried forward.

"Murder, 187." Earl managed to get out as I crouched down. His body held the door open, or, at least, the top half of his body. His hands clutched and unclutched, eyes staring up at nothing. Like a fish, his lips gasped for air, but a chunk of his neck was missing. Below his belts, his pants lay flat and dark with blood, a pool of it extending across the lobby, footprints leading away into the dark school building. I pulled my gun with one hand, my radio with the other.

"Dora, you there?"

"You'll need to speak up, Sheriff."

I couldn't raise my voice much more. "I want every sworn officer down to the school. Call everybody on staff, and get 'em down here. Now."

"Copy that. Bill's 10-19, ETA five minutes."

I put the radio back on my belt, grabbed a flashlight. As an elected official, I hadn't trained as a cop, but I got to seminars as often as I could. Holding the light away from my body, making a target away from me, I stepped over the wide, red pool and down the hall. Other than the lit trophy display in the lobby, the school was dark save the red glow of the exit signs. Light switches were operated by a key.

Noises came from deeper within, a loud bang, murmured words, shuffling. It wasn't a good idea, but with Bill on the way, I ran toward the sounds. I nearly stumbled over something in the dark, nearly dropped the gun and the light, but I caught myself. A pale hand lay on the floor, the arm trailing into a storage closet, the body hidden by a mostly-closed door.

Shoving it open, I saw a young man, face down. I turned him over and revealed a face splattered in red. Jack Fields. His brother Tim was the boy who went crazy in the cafeteria. Maybe it ran in the family. The boy wasn't breathing. In spite of the blood, I found no obvious fatal wounds. I squatted, reached down to his white throat to take his pulse. My fingers shook, but I held them fast to his carotid artery. Nothing.

Shining my Kel-light around, I found racks of stainless steel pans and lids, stacks of trays, containers of silverware. Piles of similar items lay against another door. Holding the light under my chin, I turned the knob. Slowly, I walked into the kitchen side of the cafeteria.

A clang issued from the dark, and I switched off the light, waiting. Counting twenty heartbeats, I stepped inside, squinting hard, holding my breath to listen. What I heard was the distant wail of a siren.

Shit.

Holstering my weapon, I slipped back into the storage closet and closed the door. "Adam-three, you copy?"

"Adam-three, go."

"Proceed code-two to the rear of the school. Copy?"

Immediately, the siren died. "I copy."

"Suspects are inside, Bill. Come in the back and meet me in the cafeteria. Bring the Remington."

"Jesus. Okay, I'm two minutes out."

Another loud bang came from the other side of the door, and another. Voices drifted, but I couldn't make out what was said.

Something bumped my leg.

Shining the light down, I saw Jack Fields licking my shoe like a dog. His eyes were glazed over, as if he were stoned. Under the light, his lips pulled back in a snarl, revealing bloodstained teeth.

"Fucking cops!" The sound was a roar in the closet. He leapt up, hands going for my eyes. I kicked out, hard, shoving him back enough to give me time to free my gun. Thumbing off the safety, I aimed dead center at his torso.

"On the floor, now!"

But he came again, fast, arms out.

I fired, once, twice, three times, the 9mm punching holes in his body. Jack staggered, but he was on me. I put the gun in his face, pulled the trigger. And again. The closet filled with strobing light, blindingly intense. I had nine in the magazine; I refused to carry one in the chamber. How many had I fired? It didn't matter.

His hands found my throat, and I pressed the muzzle to his neck. In the flash, I saw a rain of blood. Then we were wrestling. Jack was on the varsity team, and he wrapped me up expertly. Together, we hit the floor, his nails digging into my throat, my face.

I tried kicking him, but his legs wrapped around mine. I still had the gun. Taking my finger from the trigger, I hammered at him. We slid around the slick floor. I felt my skin tear. Hammered him again, hearing a satisfying crunch. But the boy wouldn't let go.

Finally, I got both my arms between both of his. Making one big fist, I punched upwards. His hands ripped away from me, painfully, but I was free. Scrabbling backwards, I found the flashlight rolling around. The lens was covered in red. I saw him coming again, dead eyes, slack jaw, but determined.

With six D-cells, a Kel-light is the policeman's best friend because in addition to the bright light, it makes one hell of a club. I swung, putting some hip into it. It crashed into the boy, knocking him back a step.

Fumbling, I reached out, grabbed his shirt, pulled him close. Fingers brushed my face, but I slammed out with the light, hearing a wet snap. Then, something came over me. I brought the light down, hard, over and over. Even when I felt the youth's weight in the hand grabbing his shirt, I kept swinging. With every strike, my target felt softer, each blow had more give until it felt like I pounded away at nothing.

Letting the boy drop, I pulled myself together. The other end of the rugged light showed a ragged figure, covered in blood, forehead dented in. Normally, I would've been sick. Adrenaline pumped through me, hyping me up. I opened the door into the kitchen.

I heard a shout, echoing off the stainless steel equipment, and hurried through the dark room.

"Get on the floor or I'll shoot! I swear I'll shoot!"

Ducking beneath the cash register, I slipped from the serving area. Shadows lingered on the far side of the room, past a dozen Formica islands. "Bill, shoot!" I ran, darting between the tables, light bobbing in front of me. My shin barked against a chair, sending it scooting across the linoleum. Bill faced down two small figures, each of them lunging at him in turn. One wore a letter jacket.

Bill raised the shotgun, then saw me. "Billy-Joe!"

Both figures turned my way only an instant before I tackled the closest one. I took him at the knees, like they taught me a hundred years ago when I played. Letter-Jacket folded, going down immediately. Not fooling around with this one, I pulled my cuffs, pressed my knee into his spine, slapped one wrist, then the other. Good.

The second figure grabbed my neck, both hands circling. A blast shook and lit the vast, dark room. I ducked down, rolling away. Behind me, a body fell, most of its face gone.

"Bill, Jesus Christ."

"I can't believe it, he was trying to kill you."

I couldn't catch my breath, my body shook everywhere, and I couldn't stand up. The deputy gaped, shotgun still pointing at the floor. "I can't believe it." Bill then turned green, leaned over, and puked on the linoleum.

"Call the EMTs and get more back-up. There may be more."

Bill tried to pull it together. "I can't believe it."

"Shut up and believe it. They got Earl, ripped him apart. I want every man we got in here, dogs if we can, to lock this place down. You hear me?"

"I can't believe it, they're—they're just kids!"

I was too tired to get angry. "Bill, get it together."

"Jesus, Billy-Joe, you look like shit."

We had twelve deputies who worked split-shifts, and ten of them showed up. Three ambulances arrived, and two EMTs pulled me to my feet after hovering like mother hens. Still breathing hard, I limped out to the parking lot behind the school. I didn't see the familiar yellow VW anywhere, or any late model sedans. Blanche Hillor was acting as if this wasn't related to her murders, but I suspected otherwise. Betty Silver's Dodge was parked behind a line of doorless freezers.

I leaned against one of the stainless steel shells. The old appliance looked about as old and useless as I felt. After I finally started to breathe normally, a stretcher rolled through the lot. A body struggled against the restraints, spitting and growling.

"What's your name?" I demanded before they put him in the back of the bus.

Glassy, fish-like eyes rolled toward me. "I ain't telling you shit, you fascist."

"You're Skip Meyers' boy."

"I want my phone call. I want a fucking lawyer."

"You're lucky you still have a mouth to swear with, boy. You see your friend in there?"

With jerky motions, the Meyers boy sneered, eyes twitching in opposite directions. "He was a pussy. You can't hold me like this. I want my dad!"

One of the medics reached over to take his pulse. He would've lost his fingers if the boy's head weren't strapped to the gurney. Muscles stood out in his neck as he tried to turn his head to bite the attendant.

"I don't know why this kid's so hyped up. I can hardly feel his pulse."

"Feel this, faggot."

The punk's bullshit was getting old. "How about I take a look in Betty's car? She's not the one who parked it here, is she?"

"Fourth Amendment, asshole."

I walked over to the beat up K-Car, found a bloody handprint on the trunk. "Plenty of probable cause here." Walking back, I patted Zack Meyers down, finding the keys. "What am I going to find in the car, boy?"

"It's not my car, fuck-face."

"Get him out of here." As I walked back, I heard the ambulance doors close over a string of cussing. Opening the trunk, I found a stack of two-by-fours, nails protruding. Tatters of black rubber remained on the spikes. Unbelievable as it seemed, our local boys were responsible for hijacking trucks, for murdering drivers. On the dashboard, a shipping itinerary from Hardenton Systems pretty much sealed the case. Now I knew who, and I knew how, but I still didn't know why. But I knew who did.

"You really ought to let us take you to the hospital, Billy-Joe. You need stitches."

I continued to the Jeep, watching as more kids in restraints were rolled, kicking and screaming, into waiting ambulances. How many had been involved? I tallied up at least seven, five living, before I pulled out of the parking lot.

In five minutes, I pulled into another lot, and saw Blanche Hillor hurrying to her rental car, suitcases in hand. Pulling diagonally behind her, I jumped out.

"What's in those trucks, Hillor?"

She didn't stop loading her car. "Sheriff, you need to evacuate the town."

That stopped me up. "What?"

"Get everybody out. You've got a major contamination problem."

I grabbed her arm before she could put the second case in the trunk. "Contamination from what? We just arrested the juveniles responsible for the truck murders."

"They're not the responsible ones." She looked up at me, her big, blue eyes wide.

But I'd seen the evidence, seen how those boys reacted. They were obviously on something. "So who is Hardenton Systems?"

She took a deep breath, looking as if I slapped her.

"Were they shipping some kind of illegal drug?"

"We all crave certain things, things food companies have exploited since mass production started. Simple, basic things like salt, sugar, some more brain-related like alcohol and caffeine. Hardenton was testing a long-chain molecule that breaks down in the body like sugar and salt, but affects the dopamine receptors in the brain. They wanted to make an addictive food. That's why they bought a broken-down snack company, to test the chemical on a wide market. Sodiummethalglucosine turned out to be so addictive that their tests backfired. We had... incidents in Carson City. People exposed to SMGC would do anything to get more, eat anything. Anything."

"Jesus Christ."

"We caught on to what Hardenton was doing, but it was too late. They broke down the chemical plant and shipped it out of the country."

"In trucks," I said.

"Out of the forty-seven semis, we tracked down twelve. Three were here, in Hatchet Township. We found the first in November, the second last night, and the third yesterday morning. But we were too late. Somehow, the SMGC contaminated people in town."

An idea began forming in my head.

"The victims will eat anything at hand trying to satisfy the addiction, like sharks. Their bodies will shut down until they get more, lying dormant, waiting for the next dose of SMGC. I suggest you, and everyone not affected, leave here."

I wasn't buying it. "What are you leaving out, Blanche?"

"What do you mean?"

"If you're so worried about contamination, why haven't I seen any biohazard suits? You and your boys are walking around a hot zone in your civvies."

With a quick motion, she produced a gun. "Hands on the car, Sheriff. You move, I shoot."

Shit. I put my hands on the VW. In the trunk, I could see strips of rubber studded with hundreds of tacks, far more professional equipment for stopping trucks than the two-by-fours in Betty Silver's trunk. I heard a distant jingle. She'd tossed the keys across the parking lot, then locked up the Jeep.

"Get on your radio and start the evacuation. I'll be listening. You come after us, I'll kill you." Blanche, the same dead look in her eyes as the kids in the school, shoved me away from the car and closed the trunk. In a moment, she pulled away, tires screeching.

Once she was out of sight, I got the spare key from the magnetic holder under the rear fender. I glanced at the shipping itinerary from Betty's car. The route for A. Blevins was halfway down the list, and according to the schedule, she drove strictly at night, resting away the daylight. I knew her rest stop was the GC warehouse. But that wasn't the end of the story.

I knew one person in town connected both with the warehouse and the school. As I drove, I saw police strobes on every street, the radio crackling with Dora's voice—more kids converging on the school. I ignored her, heading toward Argent.

No lights showed in the windows of the big ranch style, though his old cars and new truck were parked. I tossed the screen door aside and kicked in the front door. "Bobby-Lee!"

In the dark living room, he sat facing away from me, looking at an infomercial on TV. He didn't say anything. I reached for my handcuffs, and remembered I left them on Zack Meyers. I freed my weapon.

"I know the school board didn't get the freezers at the high school replaced until just before Christmas break. You put it all in the freezers in the GC plant, didn't you? All their food. Getting your back scratched, right?"

I raised the 9mm as I sidled around the room.

"Just saving the district some money, right? You were selling the place, had the keys."

In the blue light of the TV, the blood covering his body looked purple. His face was gone, his neck ripped open. I took a step back, nearly dropping my gun.

"So what?"

I whirled around. Jimmy-Bob, a miniature duplicate of his father, looked up at me from under lank brown bangs, his features twisted in a snarl, half-hidden by drying blood. His eyes strayed to the gun, as if he were considering something. And it came together.

Aiming at his face, I said: "That's when you came in."

"Fuck you, pig." Jimmy-Bob took a step, stopped when I raised my gun, eyeing the barrel like he was making a decision.

I wanted to kill him, blast a hole in the murdering shitbag. But I wasn't an executioner. I clenched my teeth and tried to keep my head together, tried talk it out.

"You and your asshole friends went joy riding in Betty Silver's car. Swiped your dad's warehouse keys."

He shuffled forward, making my finger twitch impatiently on the trigger. Again, that calculating look at the 9mm. I wanted to squeeze and splash the place with blood. But I kept talking, even when the sweat ran down my back and my tendons ached with the urge to fire and kill. Holding back made me want to cry.

"You found a semi parked inside, opened up the container, found some packages. The stuff in the packages was sweet, wasn't it? You started eating it, and found you couldn't stop, you and Zack Meyers, Tim and Jack Fields. Then you went a little crazy, started busting up the truck, the whole warehouse." I knew how crazy they got. I'd just beaten a boy to death with a flashlight, tackled another one from across the room. And now...

"You got hooked," I said, still trying to distract myself, "but when you went back, none of your keys worked anymore. But you knew when the next truck was due." Without moving the gun or looking away, I pulled the itinerary out of my pocket. Jimmy-Bob's eyes got wide.

"By then, your dad'd moved all the food to the new freezers at the school. Bought that great big new truck to do it. The buildings were sold, but you had to bust in—you were junkies. That truck driver caught you, and even though she had a gun, you boys did a number on her. Like you think you might do on me, right?"

My nephew showed me some teeth. I wanted to see some brains.

"Her hands were covered in the chemical, weren't they? Made her flesh irresistible." Words tumbled from me in a rush to get out. I felt a growl in my gut, almost painful.

"When you busted up the freezers in the warehouse, the packaging on the school's food got contaminated."

"So?"

"A lot of people eat at the schools, not just kids. I ate at a fundraiser just last night. But I've had more than a taste."

It was all over the warehouse, looking like crystalline dust, so good that Jack Fields licked it off my shoes; Tim Fields was jonesing so bad he ate cardboard off boxes, ate the glove off a cafeteria worker. Half the town had been dosed a little. But me, I got a really big dose at the crime scene, just like Blanche Hillor and her boys must've got.

I took a step toward him, and he took an uncertain step back. There was a scent in the air, redolent of glazed, fatty meat, pleasant and homey, making my stomach clench.

"You know what that means?"

Jimmy-Bob shook his head.

"It means that you and your asshole friends have the shit in your blood. You're the best-tasting criminals in town. You made everyone real hungry."

Jimmy-Bob turned as he realized what I was saying. I put one in his spine, one that he felt. His legs kicked a few times as he tried to drag himself away with his arms. I stepped on his neck, and he snarled. His hands would be the best part, the most saturated. And once I was done with him, I would visit Zack in the psych ward where he would be strapped down tight. And what had Blanche said? How many more trucks still out there? I had the itinerary: I could find those trucks faster than her bunch of addicts.

Kneeling on his back, I twisted the boy's hand around. That wonderful aroma rose from Jimmy-Bob's sweat. He whimpered as my teeth found his fingers, fat as sausages.

Misfortune

VINCE CHURCHILL

Phil took a hand off the steering wheel and flexed it to get back the feeling. He had been clutching the wheel as if his white-knuckle grip would save him. Unfortunately, the world was too far gone for such simple salvation.

Clutched between his other hand and the wheel was his lottery ticket. He glanced at the numbers: 6, 12, 18, 24, 30, 36, and the bonus number 42. The show that announced the numbers had been interrupted by emergency programming, but he knew his numbers were the winners. Fucking living dead cost him over twenty million dollars. He slammed his fist against the horn and then tossed the ticket on the passenger seat. It landed on the family portrait, covering his wife's face. She'd always said playing the lottery was a waste of time. She would have probably laughed herself to tears when he'd won.

The faded red Ford Escort flew down the highway, on occasion swerving to avoid cars that hadn't made it out of the lanes. Phil ignored the vehicles, fighting the urge to glance into passing windows. He'd learned the hard way not all of them were abandoned. His stomach knotted at the nightmares he'd witnessed only half a gas tank ago.

*   *   *   *   *

When the outbreak swept over Springfield, Illinois, like a wildfire, children were still sitting in their classrooms. A lot of innocent people were massacred while those in the know scurried out of town like vermin. Phil probably stayed a day or two too long, foolish for listening to the authorities. He locked himself in his basement and ignored all the pounding and screams and grotesque noises, some right on the other side of the ground-level windows. Being hard of hearing finally came in handy.

He thought he'd played it smart. And for once in his life he'd actually thought he'd gotten a little lucky. He had a ton of canned goods and bottled water stocked up already for tornado season. The basement had once been a play area for his daughter so it was more than habitable. He was set to ride this situation out until the Army or National Guard or Steven Seagal came to save him.

He did his best to not draw unwanted attention. He stayed quiet, using headphones for his radio and TV. There he was, staring at a five-inch black-and-white television he used to take camping when the giant plasma television he'd ordered was sitting in a warehouse somewhere. He was never going to see the Cardinals and Albert Pujols on his big screen. He was never going to enjoy all the stuff his millions were going to buy him. He pushed the Playboy-esque prostitute images out of his mind.

He played a lot of solitaire, but never won, at least not without cheating. Even when he threw his pair of lucky dice, he hadn't remembered rolling a single seven since the dead pulled themselves out of the ground. He might as well have been back in Vegas, maxing out his credit cards and trying to get lucky with tired, air-headed nightshift cocktail waitresses.

At night, he only used his light in the crawlspace under the basement stairs so he wouldn't attract those things. It wasn't until the third straight day of automated emergency broadcasts that he finally decided he should make a run for it. It was also the day when his luck took a turn for the worse. Sort of.

Word was, the living dead preferred darkness or minimal light, so he waited through the cloudy morning and into the sunnier afternoon, pressing his ear against the basement door, listening for any movement. He endured a long period of silence, hearing only the quiet pounding of his heart. Yet the former surgical nurse turned handyman couldn't shake the feeling of a bloodthirsty cadaver patiently waiting for him on the other side, blind milky eyes staring at him through the door, drool spilling from a grotesque, lipless mouth like a starving, rabid dog.

Aluminum bat cocked and ready, he eased the door open and moved through the house, careful to stay out of sight of the windows, forgetting he'd pulled all the shades before retreating to the basement. He was relieved to find the house empty and undisturbed, with the exception of a broken bathroom window. He stood and stared at the shattered glass, bloody shards still in the small frame. He could only wonder if the intruder had been one of those things trying to get inside, or if it had been a desperate neighbor seeking safety.

Suddenly, a long hard squeal of tire rubber on asphalt filled the room, freezing him. The smash of metal into something solid jolted him to action.

He ran toward the living room windows that faced the street. A loud boom surrounded him. The house shook and he lost his balance, stumbling to the hardwood floor his first wife had loved so much. He grunted with the impact, pieces of plaster and wood raining around him. He crawled the last several feet, one hand floating above his head for protection. Phil jerked back the curtains, his mouth yawning open in disbelief.

A beer delivery truck had smashed into the power pole at the corner of his property. Even though he couldn't see its full length, the pole had obviously fallen onto his home.

As the zombies swarmed to the doors of the truck, the driver screamed inside the cab. But the screams seemed to fade a little as Phil stared at the truck's side panel. *Mountain Top Beer: Straight from Mother Nature to you.* He glanced back toward his kitchen. He'd drunk his last Mountain Top just after the dead had started to rise. He'd barely licked his lips when the acrid smell of burning electricity attacked his nostrils.

The electrical pole... his house... FIRE!

He spun from the window, forgetting the besieged driver of the truck.

He grabbed some clothing and food and water, and he threw it into the back seat of his car. Thank goodness for his attached garage. He was just about to start the car when a thought flashed into his mind. He made a final dash into the house, grabbed his lottery ticket and a picture of his family, and then jumped behind the wheel again.

Here he was, firing up the old Escort when he should have been out shopping for a Jag or a Beamer. Hell, he could have afforded a limo and driver if he wanted; even high school students would probably have turned their noses up at his car. He glanced around the inside of the Escort and his focus landed on the picture of his family, which he had tossed into the front passenger seat along with his lottery ticket. As he stared at the photo, tears welled up.

It was one of those department store studio shots. He and his wife Kathryn stood smiling behind a seated, moon-faced Roberta. He'd worn his only suit, which barely fit him. His hair had been much fuller and less gray. Back then he didn't have the jowls or the hollow, haunted eyes he did now, or the flabby midsection that now rubbed against the bottom curve of the steering wheel.

Kathryn looked beautiful; her eyes were shiny and bright, while her hair was long and dark. A cheerleader in college, she had maintained both her figure and her enthusiasm throughout the years, but it had been her quiet, compassionate wisdom that fueled the family's happiness. And it had been Kat, once she'd discovered she was pregnant, who'd argued they should move to a small town for a better environment to raise a child. But Phil had convinced her his job was more important, especially with those all-important medical benefits. For a moment he rued the decision, and wondered how their life might have turned out differently.

In the photo, they each had a comforting, steady hand on their daughter's shoulders, but their loving guidance hadn't been enough. Unfortunately for Roberta, his wife's great genetics hadn't passed on. A big girl from birth, Berta had been a bullying troublemaker throughout her school years.

Kat had dismissed chemotherapy as an option to treat her breast cancer. Against the doctors' orders, she'd attempted a holistic route of treatment. It was a bad bet. When Kat lost her life to a recurrence a decade ago, their daughter Berta had shed all aspects of kindness and self-respect, lashing out at the world and herself in the process. No matter what steps Phil took to help her, his daughter continued down a self-destructive path.

She started using hard drugs. It wasn't long before Phil made his first shameful trip to the police station to bail out his daughter for charges of solicitation. Because she was still a minor with no record, they had released her into his custody after the first offense.

It wasn't long before Roberta, calling herself *Rose*, had moved out of the house and was doing God knew what. Phil was too busy wallowing in grief to care much. Fighting took more energy than he could spare. So when the caller ID indicated that the Springfield Police Station central booking was calling for the eighth occasion, he didn't bother to answer. He'd lived alone ever since.

Phil winced starting the car, knowing the noise might attract unwanted company. He didn't have a full tank of gas, but it was going to be enough to get him out of the Land of Lincoln.

He scanned the AM/FM but all the stations were either off the air or just broadcasting the same emergency instructions that had been looping for days. Disgusted, he snapped the radio off.

With the car warmed up, Phil took a deep breath and pressed the garage door opener. The panels of the door raised, the sound filling his ears like an earthquake. The rising door seemed to take forever, exposing more and more of the outside world like a striptease. Terrified a mob of undead would be waiting for him just out of sight, Phil gunned the vehicle out of the garage, scraping the car's roof against the bottom edge of the rising door. The Escort burst into the bright sunshine.

Phil braked with a skid at the end of his driveway. He needed to go left and west for the quickest access to the highway, but the sight of the beer truck made him pause.

He hadn't thought of it before—he'd been too distracted by the crash—but nobody was stupid enough to still be on the job this deep into the shit. Maybe the driver was using the truck to plow his way to safety or something. Staying on the road might have helped.

The passenger side door of the truck hung open, an ominous sign. The quivering torso of a zombie woman was wedged between the bumper and the power pole, but Phil didn't see any more of the walking corpses. Maybe the driver had made a run for it, drawing the dead after him.

A loud popping sound startled Phil, and he threw the gearshift into park. He stepped from the car and stared up at the roof of his house. Flames danced and black smoke drifted skyward, joining similar plumes in the distance.

"*Jesus H. Christ,*" he muttered. Slowly, his attention slipped back to the beer truck. He glanced around, double-checking that the coast was clear. He hissed, "Screw it," and then sprinted to the wrecked vehicle. On the driver's side, he quickly jerked up the roller panel. The frosty air was refreshing.

He managed to pull three cases free when he heard odd noises coming from the far front bumper. Despite the blaring of his flight instinct, he couldn't ignore the sounds. He padded quietly along the truck, leaning out as he got close to the wrap-around bumper.

A half dozen ghouls were making a picnic of the driver's midsection.

Phil dropped a case of cold beer. The crashing bottles hardly disturbed the gory feast. A case handle clutched in each fist, Phil ran back to his car and screeched away, a combination of electric scorch and freshly defiled human organs haunting his nostrils.

* * * * *

Eerily, everything looked normal for a block or two.

He lived on Springfield's west side in a nice upper-middle class area. Bigger houses, well-kept lawns, nicer cars in driveways or garages. The neighborhood kids went to private schools, and dogs were walked on leashes.

The further he drove, the more Phil realized how much the world had decayed. Thick black smoke preceded the burning homes and cars. Emergency weather sirens blared in the distance.

"Jesus Christ," Phil whispered. "I wish it *was* a fucking tornado."

The devastation continued to worsen the closer he got to the highway. Bodies littered the ground like autumn leaves. Many of the remains had the appearance of butchered, broken dolls. All Phil could do was turn away from the continual images of death. Forced to drive over bloated corpses, he felt his stomach lurch with each bump. He hadn't seen many of the walking dead, and those he had seen shambled along in the distance to unknown destinations.

The last half mile to the highway was a parking lot of abandoned cars. Phil could see the onramp as the Escort crept along the barely passable shoulder. He fought the urge to glance into the open vehicles until he neared the late-model maroon minivan blocking his path.

He steered the Escort into the gap between the minivan and the cars sitting in the lanes, focusing on the highway straight ahead. Subtle movement from the minivan's driver window caught his eye. He couldn't help looking as he pulled alongside.

Part of the lightly tinted window was badly cracked, but Phil could see through it. A woman's face was pushed into its center. Her eyeglasses were tilted off the bridge of her shattered nose and her mouth was a bloody mess. Without thinking he stopped his car and stared.

A little blood-smeared face rose up from the throat of the woman and glared blindly through the glass. Phil's blood froze as he stared at the small monstrosity.

It was a little girl, just a few years old, with white-blonde hair. Her eyes, beneath the deathly opaque film, might once have been as blue as the ocean. Her maw dripped with blood and man meat as if she'd been lapping up a strawberry pie. Grue hung from her light-colored bangs like hellish tinsel. The little girl snarled, pieces of the woman's throat spilling down her front. Then the woman's eyelids sprang open, and for an instant—an eternity of a second—their eyes locked. The woman's lips trembled a silent plea, but Phil could only slap his hand over his mouth as his stomach attempted to turn inside out.

The little girl dove back into her meal, and the woman pawed weakly at the window, her eyes rolling slowly into her head. Phil stomped the accelerator and screeched away, not caring as his car scraped loudly alongside the minivan.

Now, with more shadows than sun, and his car low on fuel, he neared the Illinois/Missouri border. He didn't want to get caught out on the road with an empty gas tank. And if Springfield was any indication, St. Louis might truly be hell on earth.

*   *   *   *   *

The sun burned sherbet-orange as it slid into the horizon. Phil turned on his headlights. God, where had the day gone? The Escort zoomed past a sign. *Mule Flats, 2 Miles*. He glanced at the gas gauge. Just a quarter of a tank. He didn't see any cars behind him—or, at least, no headlights.

He looked across the grassy median. In the distance, only a couple of cars headed east toward Springfield—which meant they had no idea what they were doing. He tipped the aluminum can to his lips, the cool beer splashing into his mouth. It would have been better ice cold. He glanced into the back seat, frowning at the cases of his favorite beer. He probably wouldn't live to drink even half of it.

Phil slugged back the last swallow and tossed the can out the window. He glanced up at the rearview mirror and watched the can bounce on the pavement. It would be just his luck if the last cop alive pulled him over for littering. Phil passed another sign: *Next Services 39 Miles*. Hell, Mule Flats should be safer than a metropolitan area. At least there should be fewer dead to deal with. He glanced at the photo on the passenger seat and nodded at the decision. Kat would agree. Small towns were safer.

Phil took the exit, veering off to the right, leaving the highway behind in the growing darkness.

He drove the connector road toward the lights of the small town. In less than a minute he approached a large truck stop. He slowed, watching. All the lights were out, including the tall pole lamps along the road. Bad sign. A couple of empty cars were pulled up at the pumps. A handful of big rigs were parked in a paved lot off to the side, but no indication of life. He cruised on toward Mule Flats, hoping for a lit-up gas station with a similar lack of activity.

Phil followed the signs and turned onto the town's main drag. The two-lane highway appeared to pass through the village's meager downtown. The abundance of streetlights and business signs fueled his hope. Hell, he might even get lucky and find a place for a quick bite. The thought caused him to chuckle. Keeping his head on a slow swivel, he obeyed the posted speed limit of 30mph as he entered the city limits.

*　*　*　*　*

Local businesses lined each side of the road. Most of the streetlights worked, though dimly. Deep shadows filled the spaces between buildings. He passed a storage facility, a car wash, a snow-cone stand, a bank, and a bar called *Rebel's* before easing into a brief stretch of residences. He rolled his window down, listening hard. Silence filled his ears. There wasn't even the song of crickets.

The Escort rolled past *Floyd's Hair Emporium*, and Phil did a double-take. The name of the establishment touched off some vague memory, but the sight of two signs further down the road grabbed his attention. The first was a simple black and white sign with POLICE spelled out vertically. Just beyond it on the same side of the street was a *Gopher Gas* sign. Phil sighed with relief. Then he peeked at the rearview mirror.

Numerous figures had silently drifted out of the darkness and were filling up the street. The same was happening down the road.

Phil stopped the car and took a good hard look around. Zombies seeped out of their hiding places like pus oozing from an infected wound. They crept in from all sides.

"Christ," he hardly heard himself whisper. Stunned by the simplicity of the trap he'd stumbled into, he glanced back through the rear window. An amazing number of walking dead came to welcome him to Mule Flats.

"Screw this." He gunned the car, barely turned forward again. He only had an instant to see the thin man in the tan uniform in front of his car. But in that split second a horrendous snapshot seared into his mind.

The man had thrown his hands away from his body, a revolver in one hand and a large black flashlight in the other. His eyes bulged from his thin face; his officer's hat jostled half off his head. The Escort's headlights reflected off the shiny badge pinned on the man's chest.

Then the man disappeared with a sickening *whomp* under the front of the car. A short distance beyond, a young woman clutched at her face and started screaming.

Phil jerked the wheel to the right, avoiding the woman. The rear wheels rolled over the officer's body—and then Phil ran into a light pole.

* * * * *

His own groan filled his ears until he heard the creak of his door.

"Come on, they're coming!" Hands clutched at his arm and shoulder. Something was pressed against his face. A soft click and the pressure was gone. Then he was falling. His eyes opened just in time for his face to hit the pavement. Air refused to enter his lungs, and he groaned into the asphalt. When he opened his eyes again, he was staring at the crumbled remains of the policeman he'd run over. Zombies closed in to feed on the still warm flesh. In the shadowy street, the deputy's gun lay between Phil and its owner's gnarled hand.

"Get up!" the young woman screeched. "We gotta get out of here! Now!" Her hands slipped under him, lifting, and he managed to get to his feet. Then his right arm nearly popped out of socket from her jerking grab. He shrugged free and managed to dive back into the front seat of the car, searching. He spotted both the family portrait and the lottery ticket on the passenger floorboard. His eyes locked on the picture, but his hand shot out and grabbed the lottery ticket. He pushed himself out of the car and stumbled after the woman, his legs feeling like melting rubber bands. After a few seconds he glanced back. The deputy had been swallowed up by a group of starving ghouls.

She slammed through a door and Phil glanced up at the POLICE sign as they entered the small Mule Flats police station. An electronic doorbell sounded. A large number of zombies closed in.

The cavernous main room of the Mule Flats jail had only a single weak and flickering fluorescent light. The woman ran into the shadows at the rear of the office. Phil propped himself up on the edge of a desk, fighting for breath. His head was pounding from the collision. Thank God the Escort had airbags.

Sounds from the dead grew closer to the entrance. Pain flared in his head as he straightened up. His hand brushed a large keyring with a pair of overly large keys. He grimaced at another wave of pain.

He called out, "I think they're coming!"

"No shit," she said from out of sight. "You're pretty observant."

Phil peered back into the darkness of the street. "You drug me in here. They're practically at the front door."

Suddenly there was a crash like a window breaking, then silence. Phil took a couple of steps forward.

"Hey, you okay?"

She reappeared a few seconds later. She tossed one of the two shotguns she carried toward Phil. He made a fumbling catch, managing not to drop his winning ticket. The shotgun was much heavier than he would've imagined.

"They're forcing their way through the back door."

Squinting through the pain, Phil finally got a look at the young woman. She was short, with long wavy brown hair pulled into a loose ponytail. Her jeans and the Mule Flats Athletics tank top displayed a budding figure. Her heart-shaped face was Midwestern attractive, smooth and wholesome.

"How old are you?" The question popped into his head and out of his mouth faster than he could stop it. She stared at him.

Then the electronic doorbell went off and the moans of the dead filled the room.

Phil froze, mesmerized by the invading zombie horde. Like individualized human car wrecks, it was hard not to stare at the things.

"What are we gonna do?" It sounded like she really needed to go to the bathroom.

Phil pried his attention from the oncoming creatures and scanned the room. Where would they be safe? There really wasn't much to it. Desks, computers, file cabinets...

There. Off to the left.

He didn't even bother to call out his intention as he staggered toward the prisoner holding pen.

*   *   *   *   *

He stumbled into the cage and dropped the ticket and the shotgun to the concrete floor. As soon as the young woman darted inside, Phil grabbed the barred door and pulled.

"Hey, wait a minute—" was all she could blurt before the metal lock clanged shut. She looked at him. "Uh, you do have the keys, right?"

He didn't. They were still on the desk where he'd seen them earlier. She followed his gaze. Phil coughed to clear his throat as he reached down for the gun and ticket.

"I think they're over there," he said.

She started to speak several times, but kept deciding not to. She mostly shook her head and cursed him under her breath. He winced every time he heard the phrase, "stupid fucker."

They watched the dead flow into the small jail. Even as the first zombies closed on the lone holding cell, there seemed to be an endless stream of walking dead. Phil and the girl stepped back toward the center of the cell as the zombies surrounded the cage and began to reach and claw at them from between the bars. The moaning and groaning filled the small police station until the hellish chorus was almost deafening.

The young woman snapped her shotgun up against her hip and tilted up the barrel. She took a couple more steps backward but lifeless fingers raked at her shoulders. She was lucky to swing around before her ponytail was grabbed.

"Brilliant idea," she cursed, turning and pointing the gun at the dead crowded around the cage. She raised the shotgun to her shoulder and pulled the trigger. Phil flinched in anticipation.

Nothing. She shucked the pump on her shotgun, but there were no shells.

"No!" she cried out. "How could they not be loaded? No, no, no, *no!*"

Stunned, Phil stared into the crowd. The jail was filled, and still more zombies forced their way through the door. The safe space in the center of the cage was hardly a few square feet. He and the girl stood shoulder to shoulder, not speaking.

He wasn't sure how much time had passed when he felt the young woman's eyes on him. He turned and looked into her face. Tears streamed down her cheeks. Her lower lip trembled.

"Because of this, I'm going to miss out on everything! We didn't even have a prom. I'm never going to see New York or Paris or L.A. Jesus, I'm going to die without seeing my parents again, or my boyfriend Jake. I've never even done it!" She lunged at him, swinging wildly at his face. He fell back a couple of steps, just enough for a few hands to rake at his shirt. He twisted away, grabbed her in a bear hug, and waltzed her back into the middle. She struggled in his arms, but soon she was sobbing. He stroked her hair with a trembling hand and tried to soothe her.

"I'm sorry. I'm so, so sorry..."

She suddenly wrenched herself away from him. "Get your hands off me, you perv! You're as bad as Barney! He protected me from those things, and then the first time I dozed off he tried to get in my pants! If he hadn't been such a loser, I might have, you know, gone along with it. But he was nothing like Sheriff Andrew, and neither are you! You're just another pathetic old man with sick end-of-the-world fantasies!"

Phil started shaking his head. "No... no... I would never—"

"Fuck you! I'm not dying in here!" She raised her shotgun like a batter and threw herself forward, using the butt of the rifle to strike at the ravenous undead reaching through the cell door. The sound of the wooden stock crunching bone made Phil cringe.

"Stop it," he said, looking at his feet. The wails of the dead easily drowned out his words. "Jesus Christ! STOP IT!"

Suddenly, the single overhead light flicked off, and darkness nearly swallowed the room. The faint glow from the outside police sign seemed miles away.

The girl cursed. Phil froze. Long seconds passed before the dim light flickered back on. Still flailing the shotgun, the girl struggled against the mauling, pulling grips of several zombies. Another couple of feet and they would have her against the bars and in easy range of their drooling, snapping teeth.

Phil jumped forward, the lottery ticket fluttering to the ground. He swung his shotgun like an axe, chopping down at their arms. Still they tugged her closer. Her angry deluge was quickly turning into pleas. When he'd managed to bat a few hands off her, he dropped his gun and grabbed her. One hard tug and she was stumbling back, free. Her shotgun remained tangled in the crowd.

Phil struggled to fight away the clawing hands, then had to lunge back into their midst when one of the mob lifted his shotgun from the floor. A scream burst from behind him as he fought. The young woman had fallen back across the cell into the waiting arms of other wanton undead. Their fresh grip on her was much more severe.

"Hold on!" Phil yelled, trying to wrestle the shotgun free by the barrel. Straining, he dropped to a knee for better leverage. Suddenly it jerked up and away from him—and then it went off with a nerve-rattling boom.

The teenager wailed behind him. Phil jerked the shotgun free and spun to see the gaping wound in her left side. Her screams became gurgly as bright red blood sprayed from her lips.

Gnarled dead hands gripped her ponytail. They pulled her head to a gap between two bars and began to force it through the impossibly small space. Phil spun away from the sight, careful to stay in the cell's safe center. He slapped his hands over his ears, almost thankful for the deafening wail of the mob to cover the sickening sounds of the girl's unnatural consumption.

Phil slid to his knees, sobbing, almost wishing he had been her so the nightmare would be over.

* * * * *

Phil sat in the center of the cell, arms wrapped around his knees, lottery ticket in his hand. Rocking slightly, he tried not to notice the thick smear of blood and gore where the dead had forced the rest of the young woman's body through the bars. The light had been sporadic, but all he did during the dark times was close his eyes and remember how wonderful his life had been before Kat got sick.

He glanced at his watch. It hadn't even been two hours since he'd left the highway. He stared into the masses surrounding him. It was a packed house and he was the only show in town. They continually clawed at him with a ravenous urgency only the devil could instill. He looked at the shotgun on the floor beside him. He picked it up and turned the barrel toward his face.

"I'll see you soon, Kat." He slipped the barrel between his lips until it touched the roof of his mouth. He shut his eyes and pulled the trigger before he could think about it.

The trigger clicked harmlessly. Empty.

Phil's body sagged. He pulled the barrel from his mouth and tossed the rifle across the cell in disgust. He looked up into the flickering overhead light.

"I can't even kill myself." He closed his eyes and wrapped himself into a tight ball, clutching his ticket. The low chorus of the dead acted as a grotesque lullaby.

A scream jolted him awake. For an instant he thought he'd imagined it until a second painful cry broke the silence. Phil sat up, rubbing his eyes. He glanced at his watch and marveled at the time. It was morning.

Blinking away sleep, he looked around the holding cage. The crush of zombies had eased considerably. A few still strained their clutching arms through the bars, but he was no longer surrounded. Perhaps they were giving up. The scream might have signaled easier-to-reach prey.

Those screams also offered a spark of hope. Maybe there were townspeople just waiting for the dead to withdraw from the sunny morning. Maybe there were survivors aware of him in the jail. Last night's crash, the screams, gunshots. Someone might have heard. A cautious smile leaked onto his face even as his stomach growled. All he had to do was sit tight. Help might be just down the block.

A few minutes later, Phil heard the electronic doorbell. Absently, he looked toward the front door, but even with the thin crowd of zombies, it was impossible to see.

Phil rose to his feet from the cool concrete floor. He couldn't help but look into the faces of the damned. As much as he wanted this torture to be over, he really didn't want to become one of those things. Jesus, no. He'd be better off starving to death.

Staring into the heart of the thinning mob, he almost missed the movement at the bottom of the cell door. His eyes drifted down and locked on the bug-eyed stare of the Mule Flats deputy he'd accidentally run down. Actually, the stare came from only one of the deputy's bulging, bloodshot eyes. The other eye drooped onto his cheek as if it had crawled from the socket as far as its stalk would allow. Most of his face had been chewed away, and his throat was all but severed from his shoulders. It should have been impossible for the man's head to even stay up. But it did.

The deputy used the bars to drag himself up from the floor. His legs were missing, and the edges of his torso and uneaten organs hung in bloody tatters like the cords of a wet mop. Somehow his leather utility belt remained cinched around his narrow waist. His metallic nametag came into sight: *Barney.*

When Barney had pulled his ravaged torso midway up the cell door, he pawed at the lock with his ragged, three-fingered hand. A smile gradually spread across Phil's face.

"You can't get in, you piece of shit! It's locked!" He danced a little jig. Barney didn't respond, except to periodically jam his hand against the lock. Phil slid to the floor and pulled his legs up to sit Indian-style. He kissed the lottery ticket like a good luck charm.

Hours passed and Barney continued his assault on the lock. Most of the remaining zombies floated away from the cage and searched elsewhere for food. More than half the room had emptied when Phil noticed Barney had stopped banging at the door.

"Finally give up, half pint?"

Barney didn't react to his voice, continuing to stare beyond him. Curious, Phil turned to see what the deputy was looking at. Phil's jaw dropped open.

The keyring was still lying on the corner of the desk.

"Jesus Christ," Phil whispered. "No way. No fucking way..."

Barney was now staring at him, the remains of the lower part of his face flinching. Slowly, the deputy let himself slide to the floor, and then he started to crawl toward the desk.

"No," Phil muttered. "No, no, no."

Phil flinched when Barney reached up and knocked the keys to the floor. He watched with moistening eyes as the deputy slowly pulled himself back around the cell. A few of the remaining zombies wandered behind the crawling deputy, gathering at the cell's door. Barney pulled himself back up the bars of the cage, the keyring looped around the bony wrist of his three-fingered hand. The zombie lawman's stare never left his prey.

Phil closed his eyes when Barney reached the height of the lock. He began to utter his wife's name over and over and over like a protective spell. Hot tears slipped down his face.

It seemed like an eternity as Barney fumbled to get the key in the lock. When the key finally slipped home and caused a quiet opening click, it sounded like a gunshot. The sharp scent of Phil's own urine filled his nose. He pressed the lottery ticket to his chest. Had he been in Vegas, he'd have just rolled craps.

Who said having bad luck was better than no luck at all?

He screamed at the first cold, dead touch.

SKIN AND BONES

D.L. SNELL

One

The cemetery was dark, and the freshly turned earth yielded to his shovel. It was autumn and cold enough for his breath to steam, yet his palms sweated. He wore black gloves though, so his grip on the shovel's handle was firm.

No, he thought. *Not firm. Stiff.*

He tittered.

The bulge of his black corduroy crotch ached, and he wanted to molest it, but it would ruin everything. So he kept flinging dirt, clearing out the rectangle so he could open the coffin. To distract himself, he thought of what he'd find inside.

Like him, she lived by the cemetery and frequented the grounds. She was beautiful: onyx eyes and sable hair, the mournful face of a granite angel, her fingers mere wisps of smoke. Watching her drift through the graves always brought tears to his eyes. He would stop trimming trees, cutting grass, or whatever he was doing to rub the throb in his crotch.

That's why he had killed her. So they could be together, so his mourning could end.

Shoveling, he moaned. The ache had returned. He wanted to massage it.

No. Wait for her.

It wasn't his voice (it rarely was,) but this one he didn't recognize. It was a phantom whisper, barely an autumn chill.

His gloves grew slippery against his palms, flesh against flesh, so sensual. His heart fluttered, as did his breath.

Wait for her.

Occasionally, he'd strike sparks from a rock. Otherwise, it was easy work; she'd been buried earlier that day. He had watched from behind an Oregon white oak, breathing deep the smell of tears. Her husband had attended, though he hadn't wept. Tall and skinny in a black suit, silver hair whispering on his shoulders—nearly a walking corpse, all cold and beautiful.

The gravedigger had followed him to a gray house on the cemetery's outskirts, the only residence among the cypresses. He'd watched from behind a bush, hoping to see the man through a window. After half an hour, he gave up. He planned to return, but never did.

He heard a noise. A leaf crunching. The digger skimmed the yard. Nothing but crosses and tombstones.

Camouflaged in all black, he wasn't afraid of being seen. Police rarely patrolled the grounds, sticking mainly to domestic disturbance calls, DUIs, and *The Jelly Donut*. But he did fear other grave robbers.

Recently, someone had stolen several corpses, some a century old. The gravedigger had filled the holes and had patched the top with sod. He didn't want attention drawn to the cemetery. It could interrupt his own practices. So he stopped digging for a week. But then he saw *her* and decided it was safe.

It was still smart to keep an eye peeled. The other robber might become territorial and attack, or tip off the police. The gravedigger needed time to escape. Luckily, he knew every inch of the cemetery, having maintained it for over six years.

It didn't look like he would need to escape tonight though.

Satisfied, he resumed his dig. Finally, a hollow thud. He knelt and cleared the remaining dirt from the lid.

Moonlight trickled through rusty oak leaves and splashed the ebony wood. The digger touched the glossy surface, so much like her hair.

Open it, the phantom ordered. *Behold my bride.*

The gravedigger dug a trench beside the coffin and stepped down. The lid creaked as he lifted it. He shuddered.

Moonlight flooded the casket's red velvet interior. It draped the woman's cheek and added silver highlights to her hair. She appeared to be asleep, hands folded below the swell of her breasts, wispy fingers interlocked. She wore a fiery ring on her wedding finger, but the gravedigger glanced at it only as an afterthought.

He touched her chest, braless and firm beneath her gossamer black gown. His bulge twitched. He knew she would be cold inside, and he grew harder.

Kiss her. Feed her.

Using snips, the gravedigger cut the suture that sealed her mouth. Her jaw dropped open, and he scooped out the cotton. He bent to her neck, where makeup covered his strangulation marks. He kissed her artery, tempted to bite. If she still pumped blood, he might have.

He nibbled the woman's lips and pressed his own against their plush rose, one hand still on her breast, unaware that her nipple was erect. He probed her cold mouth with his tongue and slid his hand down her belly, toward her pelvis.

She became his wife, lying motionless in bed, the empty wineglass and half-empty aspirin bottle sitting on the nightstand where she'd left them. He took off his glove and pulled her gown up to her belly. Her navel was cold and soft beneath his fingertips.

Her arm twitched. He was too absorbed in fantasy to notice. He could clearly see his wife, face slack and staring at the ceiling as he made swirls and figure eights in her pubic hair, moaning as he kissed deeper. He inched between her legs, fingers poised and ready to part.

She twitched again.

A cold claw seized his wrist.

There was a sharp pain and a warm coppery flood as his tongue was caught in a guillotine of teeth.

The digger pulled away, drooling blood. Some spattered the woman's face, black ink on soft parchment. She flinched. Her eyes snapped open, the eyes of a snake.

The gravedigger tried to scream, but the woman's other hand clenched his throat. He gurgled.

She sat up and bit his neck, tearing away muscle and artery. Blood sprayed her jaw line, and she opened her mouth to catch the squirts.

The phantom voice addressed the woman. *Rise*, it said.

She hauled the gravedigger from the pit and dragged him by the hair. He would have followed willingly, but he was too weak. All his strength flowed down his black sweater. His vision dissolved. So did his hearing.

Rise.

A hand burst from a grave and snatched the gravedigger's corduroys. A few scraps of leather clung to its fingers. His mistress kicked the hand with a black high-heel boot, and the bones crumbled.

Another hand shot up.

Then another.

Several burial plots began to move.

Two

Sy looked at the analog clock above the glowing red soda machine. Almost nine. Almost closing time.

A plastic bag scooted between the two rows of gas pumps. Past that, the green, red, and amber lights of Grants Pass bejeweled the night. A few cars buzzed up 7th Street, subwoofers thumping hip-hop beats, but the town was otherwise desolate, smelling of concrete and spilled oil.

He sighed and glanced back at the clock.

Only seconds had passed.

To hell with it.

Sy approached the pumps to total their meters. He heard the tinny growl of an approaching car and expected it to pass, until he saw it. The convertible flashed silver beneath the lampposts. Lacy Walker was driving, and Sarah Finch sat shotgun.

Sy felt like dashing inside to shut off the station's power—the lights, the pumps, everything. He would hide in the restroom until the convertible drove away.

But then Sarah stood up. She braced her pelvis against the windshield and waved her arms. Her black hair flowed, and her letterman jacket flapped. Underneath, a black half-shirt rippled over her bouncing, unbridled breasts and showed the firm, tan curve of her belly.

"Macky!" she called, still waving her arms.

Sy waved back, feeling awkward, feeling trapped. Lacy pulled the convertible between him and the pumps. Sarah sat down as they came to a stop, pulling her shorts out of her crotch.

"Hey, Macky." She smiled, lips a violent red against perfect white teeth. Everyone at school called him "Macky," short for his last name, McFarlin. Sarah knew he hated it.

"Hey," Sy said, fixing his eyes on Lacy.

She offered a warm, subtle smile. Her blonde hair was windswept and gorgeous, sapphire eyes embedded in sandy skin. Sy had never noticed the spray of freckles on her nose and cheeks. The gas station lights always revealed things otherwise hidden, and he wondered if she could see the scars from his pubescent acne attacks.

"Hey, Sy," Lacy said.

With her eyes on him, he couldn't check her out, but he saw enough to know that, under her unzipped sweatshirt, a white tank top showcased her cleavage. Her tits were perky, not as big and braless as Sarah's, but Sy figured her nipples were finer, aureoles without bumps or stray hairs that had eluded the tweezers.

"Need gas?" Sy asked, amazingly cool in the face.

Before Lacy could answer, Sarah said, "Fill her up." It sounded suspiciously like, "*Feel* her up," and Sarah's grin widened. Her green eyes twinkled with mischief.

Now a little warm in the cheeks, Sy said, "You got it."

He stuck the nozzle into the car, and Sarah winked at him, offering a sultry smile. Then she turned forward and lit a cigarette. A Marlboro 100, the smoke wispy and pale. The coal reddened as she took her first puff.

Sy enjoyed the aroma. He didn't want to say anything, but the tang of gas was much stronger. He quit pumping, and the nozzle hitched in his hand.

"Hey," he said. "No smoking."

"Really?" Sarah arched one perfectly plucked eyebrow and blew smoke in his face. He'd heard somewhere that when a girl does that, it means she loves you, but coming from Sarah Finch, a.k.a. *the Cinch,* the gesture meant nothing. He had dated her long enough to know she didn't love him. Hell, he was the only one she hadn't laid.

"C'mon, Sarah," Lacy pitched in. "Sy's right. You could blow us up."

"*Blow us up?* What are we, sex dolls?"

Lacy arched her eyebrows.

"Fine." Sarah crushed her cigarette in the ashtray, where it sent up one last smoke signal. "Happy?"

Sy reengaged the pump. He felt stupid just standing there. He thought about washing Lacy's windshield, but the glass was already sparkling.

Sarah clicked her long black nails, and Lacy stared toward the soda machine, daydreaming.

Sy peeked at Sarah's legs. It was damn cold outside—Sy himself wore his work coat, gloves, and a pair of Dickies over thermal underwear—but Sarah wore shorts. He could see her tight thighs and smooth knees, both toasted bronze from the sun box.

It didn't feel right peeping with Lacy nearby. Besides, Sarah was like a succulent turkey glazed in the drool of a dozen mutts. But that didn't stop Sy. Neither did the sick sensation in his stomach. He could still feel Sarah's smooth skin, even though a year had passed since they dated.

Sarah sighed and slapped her knees.

Sy pretended to watch the meters.

"We're gonna be late," Sarah said.

Lacy looked at the clock. "It's only nine."

"The party starts at nine."

"It's not that far."

"Yeah, but I wanted to get there before Willy."

Willy—or William—was Sarah's new boyfriend. It was *his* letterman she wore. *O'Connor* was embroidered in golden cursive on the left breast.

"You're not still pissed at him, are you?" Lacy asked.

"He had sex with that bitch. What do you think?"

"I don't know."

"Yeah, I want to get there and fuck someone and have him find us together."

"Jesus, Sarah."

She craned around again. "Hey, Macky. Wanna go to a kegger?"

Lacy winced. "Sarah, don't—"

"Shut up." She smiled at Sy. "So what do you say?"

Lacy offered him an apologetic smile and shrugged.

"I don't know," Sy said.

"C'mon."

"Ah—I smell like gas."

"Lacy's gotta change, too. You can shower at her pad."

"No clothes."

"Really? Then what's in the backpack?" She pointed a long black nail at the bag slung over Sy's chair.

He hadn't planned to go home; his dad was getting drunk at the Lantern again and would be in one of his moods. Now Sy looked like a prick for lying.

"Fine," he resolved.

"You'll go?"

"Yeah. Just let me close up."

Sarah winked at him. "You won't regret it."

When he finished cashing out, turning off, and locking up, Sy grabbed his backpack and walked toward the convertible. Sarah had lit a new cigarette, and the cherry burned a red hole in the darkness. Sy hopped in back and tossed his bag on the seat beside him.

Lacy pulled out of the station, hair flickering gold in the lamplight.

Sarah turned around and exhaled. The smoke smelled good.

"Got a spare?" Sy asked.

She took a long puff and offered the leftovers. Red lipstick ringed the filter. Maybe even herpes.

"You got another one?" he asked.

Sarah exhaled. "Last one. But you can have it."

He took the cigarette, but didn't smoke it. Seconds later, Sarah lit a fresh one. Sy kept quiet. He tossed his cigarette over the side and watched Lacy's hair stream in the darkness.

Three

Mitchell pressed Lacy's bra to his nose and breathed in her peaches as he masturbated. In the darkness behind his eyelids, she danced around, topless, mouth spread in a naïve and joyous smile. Then Mitchell's alter ego, Walker, ran past and swooped a knife across her belly. Her intestines spooled on the floor, and Walker pranced in them.

Mitchell's orgasm mounted. He took one last whiff of peaches and cupped the bra against his crotch. He shuddered and gasped.

A car pulled up to the house. A dozen bras lay at Mitchell's feet. *Shit.*

He stuffed the braziers into Lacy's dresser and slammed the drawer on a purple shoulder strap.

Outside, a car door clapped shut.

Mitchell crammed the strap inside the drawer. He glanced around Lacy's room for anything misplaced, shut off the lights, and jumped into the hall. Through the skylights that flanked the front door, he could see several figures approaching. He heard the jangle of kcys.

Mitchell dashed down the hall into his father's room. He made it dark and locked it. He listened for movement, trying to ignore the steady pounding of his heart.

The front door opened, and three people entered. From the footsteps, he identified his stepsister Lacy, her friend Sarah, and a stranger, a man. Not his father. His father was heavier. This was a slim-built man. A *nervous* man, treading lightly, conscious of his every step. And—was he wearing something on his back?

"Mitchell!" Lacy called, flicking on the front room light. "Mitchell!"

"Maybe he's jerking off," Sarah suggested.

Mitchell envisioned her tits—full and jiggling, aching to be free of a tight shirt. He touched himself. Walker touched himself as well.

"Jesus, Sarah," Lacy said. "That's my brother you're talking about."

Stepbrother, cunt.

"Hey, Macky," Sarah said in a different tone. "You gonna shower, or what?"

Mitchell focused, waiting for the guy's answer.

"Um, yeah," Macky said. "Where's the bathroom?"

Lacy gave him directions, and footsteps filled the hall.

"Oh, no no no," Lacy said. "That's Mitchell's room. It's the next one. Sorry."

"It's all right," Macky replied.

Guy sounds like a dipshit, Walker hissed.

Mitchell agreed.

Macky went into the bathroom and shut the door. The shower squeaked on, and at first, the spray laid static over Lacy and Sarah's conversation. Then they went into Lacy's bedroom, right next door, and their voices clarified.

Mitchell crept to his father's closet. He opened the mirrored door, which slid on thoroughly lubed tracks. On the wall behind the shirts, a piece of tape covered a peephole. Mitchell peeled it back and peeked.

'*It's for you, son,*' his father had said the day he drilled the hole. His hand had been on Mitchell's shoulder. '*Just put the tape back when you're done, or light will shine through. And make it dark in here before you peek, okay?'*

What a present. *I see London, I see France, I see Lacy's underpants.* Mitchell even had his own cleanup rag stowed between the boxes. It was crusty with semen.

Although he'd seen Lacy's breasts through the hole only once (just a sandy curve, no nipple, mostly shoulder blade,) spying always aroused him, until lately. Lacy was too much of a prude, freezing water to a man's genitalia.

The light came on in her room, and in his own closet deep within Mitchell's head, Walker pressed his eye to the peephole. A ray illuminated his crazed and bloodshot eye.

Lacy walked past, just a streak of gray, but Sarah stopped in line with the hole. She wore a jacket and a tight black half-shirt. Her nipples jutted from the cold.

Mitchell felt himself growing.

"Why'd you invite him?" Lacy asked.

"Maybe I miss him."

"Whatever. You're using him."

"So what? It's not like Willy didn't use that freshman bitch from North Valley. Mary Golbrath, or whatever. Christ, Lacy, he made her deepthroat—she puked."

"I didn't want to know that."

Just like Lacy to ruin a good thing.

"Besides," Lacy continued, "that has nothing to do with Sy."

"He pumps gas, Lacy. What do you care?"

Sarah's nipples seemed stiffer, more prominent through the black cloth. Maybe fighting aroused her. Or maybe she was watching Lacy, who was changing her pants from the sound of it. Sarah was turned the wrong way for that, though, facing the large mirror above the peephole.

"So what if he pumps gas," Lacy said. "Willy doesn't even work."

"He plays football, doesn't he?" She was putting on eyeliner now.

"He doesn't get paid for that."

"Yeah, but he gets scholarships."

"Whatever. I just think you're being immature."

"Whatever you say, Miss Virgin." She was leaning in close to the mirror, applying blood-red lipstick, so her voice was low as she said it. Lacy still heard her.

"Fuck off, Sarah."

Ooh, Walker crooned. *Miss Prude said the f-word.*

Sarah stepped back and gave her breasts two good hoists. Mitchell wondered what all that flesh would feel like, all heavy in his hands. He unzipped and fished his hand inside, still spying on Sarah, applying his X-ray vision: her breasts heaving and crisscrossed with welts; a drop of scarlet blood glistening on a nipple; Walker, catching the drop on his tongue.

"Are you ready yet?" Sarah asked.

"Yeah." Lacy opened a dresser drawer. "Just need a bra—*ah*, what the hell? Mitchell! *Mitchell!*"

Lacy stormed through the hall and pounded on his bedroom door, one room up and across from his father's.

"Mitchell! Open your goddamn door!"

"Told you he was probably jerking off," Sarah said.

Mitchell suddenly understood why Lacy was pissed. He had squirted into one of her bras and had stuffed it back in the drawer.

"Mitchell!"

"Forget it, Lacy. Just get dressed. We're gonna be late."

"Get your hand off me." Lacy stomped back into her bedroom. A second later, the bathroom door opened.

"Someone need in?" Macky asked, probably hanging out the door, steam billowing over his head.

"Never mind," Sarah answered. "You almost done?"

"Yeah."

"C'mon, then. We're outta here."

There was some shuffling, murmurs, footsteps, doors slamming, and soon, Lacy's car peeled out of the driveway.

After the engine faded, Mitchell went into the bathroom. Macky had used their shampoo; the smell still lingered in the air like spring rain. Mitchell sniffed the towel wadded in the hamper. Macky had also used their soap: Ivory.

At least the asshole didn't leave watery footprints, Walker observed.

Mitchell went into Lacy's room. She would've locked it, that bitch, but her door locked from the outside. Even the laundry room was more secure.

He found the soiled bra in Lacy's wire-mesh wastebasket. It no longer held the subtle scent of peaches, just the mineral stink of semen.

On the floor by Lacy's dresser lay the pair of white panties she had just changed. They tasted unripe. Mitchell dropped the panties and went to the mirror above the peephole, which was concealed in shadows.

Instead of his reflection, Sarah stared back, red lips spread in a provocative grin, mimicking a sexual orifice. Her hair was midnight-black, and her eyes sparkled green. She moaned, tweaking her nipples through her shirt.

Mitchell kissed the lipstick she'd applied. He could taste her lips, like ripe cherries. He put everything back the way it was and took the soiled bra outside to dispose of the evidence. He torched it with his dad's lighter, huddling around the warm, orange glow.

A trashcan was pushed against the trellis siding of the front porch. Mitchell discarded the bra's metal supports and looked out across a small field, through the woods and toward the cemetery. He expected his father to walk out of the trees, done with his grave-yard shift, pockets full of riches, shovel on his shoulder. But the field was desolate, a skeletal gray, barely touched by the yellow orb of porch light.

He'll be here soon, Mitchell thought, exhaling a ghostly breath. He lingered a moment longer and went back inside.

Four

The gravedigger woke to a strong pang in his stomach. He smelled warm flesh and lurched forward to seize it. He couldn't; he was crucified against a stone wall, wrists and ankles clamped into metal cuffs.

Somebody moaned.

Across the basement, two people writhed beneath gray blankets on a four-poster bed: his mistress, with her flowing black mane, and a man with silver hair. She was straddling him, and the blankets huddled around her buttocks.

Other people stood around the bed, watching, drooling, naked. Some were skeletons with black crust clinging to yellowed bones. Others had sagging, bruise-colored skin, and a few looked quite fresh. They had piled their burial suits and dresses in one corner.

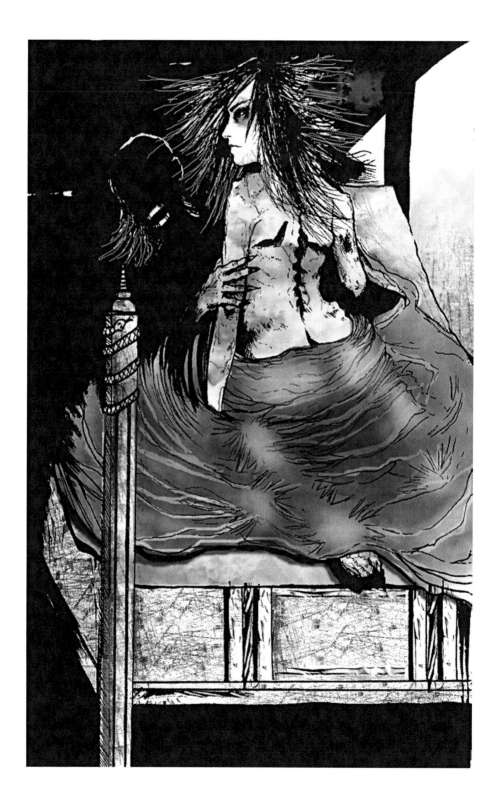

For a moment, the gravedigger saw through his mistress' eyes, almost as if he possessed her body. Her lover's face was bony and long, his irises gray like open urns. His chest heaved beneath her hands, hairless and taut against his ribs. He was skeletal, yet his flesh smelled tender and alive.

The gravedigger felt the man buck against his mistress, felt a hot thrusting shaft, flesh stabbing flesh.

He could see through the eyes of the onlookers as well, just as they could see through his, their vision fragmented into a fly's-eye grid. They were all bound in a psychic network, a web of silk filaments and lightning; the skeletal man held the ends. He was their puppet master. He controlled them, their hunger secondary to his command.

The skeletal man moaned again. He shuddered, mouth agape and eyes rolled up to the bloodshot whites. The mistress tossed her head, exposing her graceful throat. The gravedigger felt through her again, and the man's shaft thrust deep and exploded inside her.

The onlookers gasped, sharing their mistress' pleasure. The man yelled, thrust hard, gushing, gushing. Then he withered, and there was dead calm.

The mistress rolled off and lay next to the man, her chest still of breath.

A phantom whisper drifted through the crowd; it was the skeletal man's voice, the one from the cemetery that had called the corpses to rise. A blonde with large breasts and wide hips answered his call. She stepped to the bed, holding a silky black robe. The skeletal man stood and let her drape the robe over his shoulders. He didn't tie the sash, leaving the front to flap.

As he walked away from the bed, the skeletal man allowed his mistress and the blonde to feast on a male corpse. They dragged him onto the mattress and pinned him.

The gravedigger lurched against his restraints. He tasted through their mouths. He tasted cold meat; he could feel it between his teeth. It wasn't enough to soothe the ache.

"I see you've come around," the skeletal man said, standing in front of him. The phantom translated his words in an underlying whisper. "You want her, don't you?" He gestured toward his wife. "You can almost taste her. All you crave is sex and sustenance, the skin and bones of human desire. But you will go unsatisfied."

The mistress bit the dead man's neck, tearing away a strip of skin and a limp vein. The blonde ate the corpse's arm like a drumstick.

"My name is Bones," the skeletal man continued, "and she is my wife. You killed her, and now you suffer." He grinned, resembling a skull. "You, and the ones you love."

An image flashed through the gravedigger's mind, a picture of his son and daughter, both smiling. Bones grinned and made the gravedigger feel sorrow, something he could not feel on his own, being dead. Bones controlled his very thoughts.

"I know you intended to use the girl like you did my wife. You didn't love her like you did the boy. But you were possessive, jealous. I'll be sure to defile her while you watch. And she'll be dead and cold, just as you prefer. As for the boy? I'll make you torture him. To the edge of death and beyond. You will feel all his pain."

Bones turned, showing his long, silver hair. On the bed, the mistress was straddling the man and gouging his eyes. The blonde had gnawed his arm to ligaments and bone. The rest of the zombies watched, hungry but patient.

"Finished, my dear?"

The mistress smiled at him. Strands of meat stuck between her teeth.

"Come to me."

She crawled off her victim and walked toward him, curvy hips swaying. Bones welcomed her into a side-by-side embrace.

"This is my wife, Venice. Venice, I'd like you to meet the gravedigger—or as I've come to call him, *Digger*."

Venice's eyes fluttered down Digger's body like raven's feathers. He saw himself through her eyes, saw the blue-veined love handles and the gouge on his neck, surrounded by a hickey of crusted blood. He saw his own face, haggard and drawn with starvation. He could also feel Venice's craving, a frantic heat in her breast, and he knew that she wanted him.

Venice caressed his chest, coaxing the ache into the pit of his stomach.

Bones pushed her hand aside. "This one's mine," he said. "Leave us."

Venice lingered for a moment, still staring, licking her thick lips.

Then she went to the mattress and gnawed on the dead man's femur, moaning and twisting a nipple as she ate.

Bones smiled at Digger. "You can see through her eyes, can't you? Taste what she tastes? You all can. You're connected, a shared consciousness, one mind.

"And soon, your children will hear a pounding on the door... and the walls... and the windows... You won't miss a thing."

He walked away, his mad laughter echoing, his robe billowing around bony legs.

Five

"Damn," Lacy said as she nosed into the driveway, headlights gleaming off countless chrome bumpers. "Looks like the whole school's here."

Sarah stood up. "See Willy's car anywhere?"

Sy didn't know about the car, but he had a nice view of Sarah's ass, her shorts snug against the curves and cleft. It rotted the pit of his stomach, so he glanced away, even though his crotch swelled.

"Sit down," Lacy said. "I'm gonna back out."

"What?"

"I have to park, don't I?"

"Oh." Sarah sat down.

Sy gazed through the windshield. Most of the cars were white Jettas and silver BMWs, here and there a red corvette. He searched for a rusty beater, just one century-old Volvo or shit-brown station wagon, any indication that he knew someone here, not just faces he'd glimpsed in the hall or names he'd seen on the honor roll.

All the cars seemed brand new.

Sy sat back.

He shouldn't have come. By now, he could have found an unlocked car to sleep in or a newspaper to rest beneath. Hell, listening to his drunk dad ramble about how the crash hadn't been his fault—he'd only had a few drinks that night, the steering wheel had slipped in his hands, and Sy's mother hadn't been wearing a seatbelt—all that seemed better than this.

Lacy craned around and reversed. A white scrunchee bundled her hair, and moonlight bathed her face. Her sapphire eyes twinkled as she scanned her path.

They parked in a gravel turnaround beside the main road, which was good because they could leave at any time.

Sarah hopped over her door. Lacy opened hers, and Sy did likewise, stretching his muscles as he stood.

"C'mon," Sarah said.

She led the way, and Sy took the rear. The moon was full, but misty clouds and towering pines filtered its light, so he could barely make out Lacy's backside. In loose-fitting jeans, her rump wasn't as defined as Sarah's. It was still a better view.

They made their way through the cars toward the thump of music. Lights were on in the house, but beige curtains veiled the interior. Inside, people guffawed and cheered, noises Sy associated with football games.

He shivered and put his hands in his pockets, fumbling with his buck knife. His fingers traced the engraving on the wooden handle: '*To Sy, Love Mom.*'

He shivered again.

Should've brought his coat, but it reeked of gas and would've burst into flames the moment he lit a cigarette. As it was, he wore a T-shirt and jeans. He cursed himself for not packing a sweater. After all, he had planned to sleep outside, and autumn in Grants Pass could freeze you. At least he was better off than Sarah, with her flirtatious shorts. Lacy was the only smart one.

At her house, she had donned a white T-shirt beneath her gray sweater. Nevertheless, she crossed her arms and walked stiffly, as if cold. Now Sy wished he'd brought his coat to warm her, but its stink was too terrible.

Taking his hands out of his pockets, he rubbed warmth into his forearms and biceps. He could smell marijuana, with skunk-like potency, but the only clouds came from his and Lacy's breath. No dome lights glowed in the cars, and no lighters flickered orange.

"Look," Sarah said, pointing at a red Mustang. "Willy's car." She cupped her hands against the driver's-side window and peered in. "What the hell are *you* doing here?" she asked, talking to someone in the back seat.

Sy could see the person through the rear windshield. She glanced at him, a porcelain face, cheeks a livid red.

Lacy had a better view. "Don't look. She's naked."

Sy's first instinct was to peek, but Lacy was there, and he didn't want to seem like a pervert, so he watched from the corner of his eye.

Sarah tried the door handle, but the car was locked. She pounded on the window. "Get outta the car! I don't give a shit about your shirt! Just step out!"

"Who is it?" Sy whispered to Lacy.

"I don't know." Her voice was soft, so only Sy could hear. "Some freshman chick... This is Willy's car, you know."

"I guessed."

Still badgering the girl to get out, Sarah didn't notice the massive silhouette creeping around the front bumper. Sy whipped out his buck knife and stepped forward.

The silhouette raised its arms over Sarah's head.

Sy shouted, "Sarah!"

The silhouette brought its hands down: "Boo!"

Sarah looked up from the window. "Burger, what're you doing?"

The hulk chuckled. It stepped forward, and moonlight draped its fat grin. "What's up, Cinch?" Brian 'Burger' Borgerson flicked ashes off his joint. "Picking on my freshie, here?"

"This is *your* slut?"

"That's right. But I'm done if you want her. She's tight. Got nice tits."

Sarah scowled. "You're a pig, Burger."

His grin broadened so his cheeks wadded up. "And you're a cinch." He puffed the joint between his thin lips. The coal flared red and lit his beady brown eyes. The breast of his jersey was stained with mustard.

"So," Sarah said, "what's she doing in Willy's car?"

Burger exhaled a puff of smoke that smelled of dank lungs and beer. He smiled. "Is this *Willy's* car? Shucks, I didn't know."

Sy folded his knife and slipped it in his pocket. He glanced at the car. Burger's freshie had already put on her shirt. She was staring at Sy but looked away when she noticed his glance. He looked away too, focusing on the conversation again, thankful Lacy hadn't seen him peek.

"I don't care if you're parked by the road," Sarah told Burger. "Just get her outta there before she leaves a snail trail on the upholstery."

"Whatever you say." But Burger just stood there, puffing his joint. He looked past Sarah for the first time. "What's up, Lacy?"

Lacy crossed her arms as if to hide her chest. "Hey, Burger."

"Who's that behind you?"

"Oh, Sy."

"You mean Macky?"

"Uh... yeah."

Sy stepped forward, and Lacy looked thankful.

"Macky, that you? What're you doing here, man?"

Before Sy could stutter, Sarah said, "Hey, fat-ass. You gonna get this bitch outta my man's car, or what?"

"Well, maybe Macky wants a go." Burger smiled at him. "Whaddya say, Mack-dad? You into freshies?"

The air went thick. Sy could feel everyone's eyes on him, especially Lacy's, awaiting his answer. Once again, Sarah saved him: "He's with me."

Burger's smile disappeared. "But, you and Willy—"

"Just shut up and get this cunt outta the car, okay, Burger? Christ."

"All right, all right. Here, hold my joint."

Sarah stomped it into the pavement.

"Hey," Burger cried. "That was Panama Red. Why'd you—?"

"Just shut up and do it."

"Jeez, Cinch." Burger fumbled out a set of keys. "Didn't have to stomp my doob."

Once he'd found the right key, Burger bent to the keyhole. Sy winced at the sound of scraping paint.

Sarah snatched the keys from Burger and unlocked the door. "Get out," she told the freshie.

The girl was probably no older than fifteen, and her wrists tinkled with bracelets. Her dishwater hair was mussed, and her lipstick was smeared. Burger didn't have any of the makeup on his mouth, which meant she had smeared it elsewhere.

The girl stood up, glancing around.

"Go on," Sarah told her. "Get outta here."

The girl turned to Burger.

"Go," he said. "It's cool."

"Where's my beer? You promised me beer."

Sarah made a snotty sound and crossed her arms. "I said get outta here, you little slut."

The freshie looked at her. "*You're* the slut. You're that cheerleader that sleeps with the jocks."

Sarah grabbed the freshie's hair and pulled her head back. The girl let out a small whimper.

"Hey," Lacy said. "Maybe we should—"

"Shut your mouth, Lacy." Sarah bent to the freshie's ear and spoke in an intimidating, confidential voice. "Listen, you little freshman bitch. You better shut that pretty little mouth of yours before someone else decides to fuck it. Slut." She gave the girl's hair a nasty jerk and released her.

The freshie's face was completely red, and tears streaked her eye shadow. She glared at Sarah. "Whore." The girl ran off through the cars, away from the house, bracelets clicking together.

Lacy crossed her arms and looked after the freshie. "Jeez, Sarah. You didn't have to be so harsh."

"Christ, Lacy, you'd think she was your sister." Sarah turned to Burger, who was rolling another joint. "Where's Willy?"

"Inside." He licked the adhesive strip and glued the joint together.

"Show me."

He was busy lighting up. Sarah slapped the joint out of his hands, sending up firefly sparks.

"Take me to Willy, goddamn it."

"All right, all right. Here..." Burger took a bag of blue plastic cups from his pocket. "Might as well take one of these." He offered everyone a cup.

Sy declined the offer.

"What, you don't drink or something?"

"Nope."

Burger's eyes widened. His lips opened and closed, trying to form words.

"Where's the keg?" Sarah asked.

Burger answered her, but he was still gawking at Sy. "It's inside. Willy's guarding it."

"Really? Show me."

"Okay..."

"*Burger.*"

"Oh... yeah. Follow me."

Burger waddled off between the cars. Sarah picked up the joint and took a hit. She passed it to Lacy, who coughed up smoke and gave it to Sy. He took a puff, savoring the trace of Lacy's watermelon lip balm, holding the smoke until his vision blurred. Then he, Lacy, and Sarah followed Burger toward the house. Sy's stomach trembled with the thrum of loud music.

Six

Something shattered outside.

Mitchell pulled his hands out of his pants and jerked his head around, away from the zombie movie where a bunch of old corpses surrounded an 80's punk with a short red dye job, pushing her down to eat her alive. The living room lights were off, but the TV cast a reflection on the two sidelights flanking the door.

Mitchell clicked off the TV via remote control. He listened—*Walker* listened.

Silence. Then a clumsy footstep.

Not his father's either.

Mitchell focused harder on the darkness outside. He thought he saw a silhouette that didn't belong. Much too gaunt to be his father's. Sy, maybe? That faggot that defiled the bathroom? What was he doing here?

Another footstep.

The silhouette moved away from the sidelight, and the doorknob began to turn. The door was unlocked.

Slowly, Mitchell stood from the chair, grimacing as it made sounds of relief. He stepped toward the hall, and a board squeaked underfoot. He glanced back at the door.

The knob stopped moving.

The house settled and groaned.

Bravo, Walker said. *Why don't you just jump and yell?*

Mitchell went down the hallway as fast and quiet as possible. At the far end, the laundry room door breathed darkness. Someone could be hiding in there, waiting with a knife.

Mitchell sidestepped into his father's room. He locked it and stood in the dark, listening.

The front door creaked open.

Mitchell gasped and held his breath.

No movement from the front room. Maybe the prowler had fled. Maybe he had seen Mitchell's father returning from the graveyard and had bolted for the woods.

No, Mitchell thought. I would've heard him running.

Okay. Maybe he snuck away to avoid Dad's attention.

THUMP.

The prowler stepped inside. Definitely not Sy. Unless he was drunk.

THUMP, THUMP, THUMP.

No. Not Sy, not Dad, not Lacy. A burglar.

The gun, Walker suggested. *Your dad's gun.*

Mitchell tiptoed to the bed and felt under the mattress. He touched the glossy paper of his dad's autopsy pictures and prodded the spongy dildo. He searched deeper. Nothing but space.

He didn't take it with him, Mitchell thought. He never takes it with him.

The intruder stopped moving. Maybe he heard Mitchell rummaging. Maybe he was right outside, ear pressed to the door.

Mitchell plunged his arm in to the shoulder, groping. Nothing, nothing—something cold and metal.

Yes!

He yanked out the gun and nearly stumbled as his arm pulled free. He steadied himself on the nightstand. An empty glass sat on top. It toppled, making a hollow rocking sound on the wood.

Mitchell swiped for it, knocked it over. He caught it before it could clunk and maybe shatter. Sighing, he set the glass on the bed.

The air was thick with silence and hard to breathe. Mitchell got the creeps, like someone was watching him. He whirled, pointing the gun, finger itching the trigger.

Darkness lunged at him.

Its threat was empty. The door was locked, the window was locked, and the blinds were drawn tight: not even moonlight could intrude.

Mitchell lowered the gun. He focused on the throbbing darkness, listening hard for any movement. The only sound was the beating of his heart. He relaxed and let his arms hang at his sides. Then he heard a footstep directly ahead.

THUMP.

He almost screamed. His arms sprang up immediately, shaking as he tried to steady the gun.

THUMP.

Lacy's room, Walker said. *He's in Lacy's room.*

Mitchell tiptoed through the dark, avoiding the noisy board at the foot of his father's bed.

Inside the closet, he peeled the tape, trying to limit the crackle of parting adhesive.

Lacy's room had no windows, but on the far wall by the door, a nightlight cast a dim blue sphere. And there, just outside the sphere, was a human figure.

Mitchell's heart lurched. He pressed his eye tighter to the hole. The figure stood motionless. It was skinny. Too skinny. Mitchell could see its arm, thin as a stick.

That's just a shadow, he rationalized. Trick of the eye. No one there.

Bullshit, Walker said.

But the longer Mitchell stared, the more the figure resembled a bedpost draped with a skin-tight sweater. He let out his breath and pulled away from the peephole.

Could he have imagined it all, the footsteps merely the wind buffeting the house?

Mitchell took one last look, just to be sure, just to silence Walker's cynicism. Another eye stared back at him, wide, crazed, and hungry.

Seven

Digger stood in a dark room lit only by an orb of blue light. The room smelled of peaches and perfume, but undermining this was the reek of flesh and blood.

In some recess of his brain, he remembered the peephole. He remembered his pride that his son was becoming a man.

Digger went to the mirror, where the smell of flesh was most potent. He bent and pressed his eye to the hole. Another eye stared back, inky, wide, and terrified. Digger could almost taste the blood pumping through its veins.

He slammed his fist against the wall. The eye disappeared, and Digger woke in Bones' basement, still cuffed to cold stone.

He moaned and looked toward the bed.

Venice and the blonde were feasting on another corpse. In a chair nearby, Bones watched. More zombies lurked in the shadows, idle.

Through a mouthful of fatty curd, Venice moaned, and Digger shared her senses again, squishing lard and crunching gristle.

As he returned to his own body, he felt a dull cramping in his stomach. The smell of Bones' flesh was sharp and ripe. Underneath it was the smell of someone else's flesh, someone miles away. A boy, locked in a room, trembling, terrified of what he'd seen through the peephole. It was Digger's own son. And a zombie was in his house.

He felt a twinge of guilt, a sagging in his heart. But his hunger was right there with it, gnawing through the cartilage and bone encaging his last shreds of humanity.

Bones walked to the bed and pulled the blonde's buttocks over the edge. He flipped open the front of his robe, but before he could slide inside, Venice pushed the blonde onto the floor. Venice lowered her head to pleasure Bones, but he stopped her.

"No," he said, phantom voice hissing. "Dine."

Venice glared at the blonde. She stalked out of the room, and Bones did nothing to stop her. She couldn't escape. Digger knew this somehow, and he could feel the heat of Venice's frustration as she realized it too. He couldn't see through her, couldn't see what kind of obstruction waited in the next room.

Bones summoned the blonde back to the bed. When he finished pumping against her, he approached Digger, his robe billowing, exposing his narrow chest. The blonde returned to the corpse and continued to eat.

"Do you feel it?" Bones asked, smirking slightly. "Do you feel the hunger and the pain? I know you do. You see your son, don't you? You smell him."

Digger trembled and shut his eyes. He was in his house again, staring at a closed bedroom door. A tormenting scent drifted up from beneath it, the scent of tears, flesh, and blood.

"Yes," Bones crooned as Digger opened his eyes. "His flesh is so tender, so sweet. Oh, don't worry. The zombie won't kill him. And I daresay you'll see him before he dies. In fact, you may be holding the very blade that spills his blood."

Digger shuddered as a wave of desire, guilt, and anger surged through him.

Bones' smile broadened. "Be calm," he said. "You will feast soon enough. And I'm sure your son will be delectable."

Digger snapped at Bones' face, missing his nose by inches. The man laughed and walked away, disappearing into the next room with a swirl of robe. He emerged shortly, with Venice trailing behind him.

On his command, she went to the bed. The blonde looked back at her, and Digger felt hate flare through Venice's breast. She slugged the blonde and broke her nose. Then she lunged and took her down, gnashing teeth and raking her nails across the woman's sallow face.

Bones stood to the side, watching, arms crossed, thin lips curved into a smile. He turned and left the room. There was a phantom whisper as Bones told someone to let him pass, the sound of bare feet ascending wooden stairs, a trapdoor slamming shut, and then the basement was no longer cold with Bones' presence.

Digger looked to the bed, where the blonde lay limp. Her legs dangled off the mattress. Venice clamped a scrap of the blonde's cheek between her teeth and pulled, trying to tear it from the bottom jaw. She called two men to the feast, and they peeled back the blonde's stomach and dug through her intestines.

Digger's belly cramped. He shut his eyes, but didn't find peace. He found himself in that house, trying to break down the bedroom door so he could kidnap his son, huddled inside, trembling and smelling delicious.

Eight

Burger, Sarah, Lacy, and Sy were greeted at the door with whoops and hollers and thumping loud music, that rap shit Sy hated.

Immediately, someone passed a joint to Burger, who took a cheek-swelling pull and passed it on. He exhaled heavily and started to hack. People cheered and slapped his back as Sarah prodded him through the crowd.

The dark-lit living room was twice as large as Sy's, and it teemed with people, everyone grinding to the music, holding blue cups and slopping beer onto the carpet.

Looking over the partygoers through a halo of smoke, Sy saw a silver flat-screen TV mounted on one wall. A horde of zombies attacked a roadblock, and a naked chick with short red hair grabbed one of the cops, opening wide to eat his brains. Sy also saw a couple dry humping on a huge leather couch. The guy was on top, feeling up the girl's shirt, his mouth suctioned to hers.

Sy didn't recognize anyone in the living room. He figured some must've attended school in Hidden Valley and North Valley instead of Grants Pass High.

Burger led them to a doorless entryway, congested with guys in Quicksilver shirts, talking about stockcars and holding half-empty cups.

"Excuse me, boys," Burger said, shouldering them aside. He held up the sack of blue cups. "On official keg business."

The guys sucked up against the white-spackled walls, holding their cups next to their cheeks as Burger waddled through. They eyed Sarah and Lacy as they passed and nodded at Sy. He nodded back and stepped through the entryway, into a sparkling kitchen.

His own kitchen was ugly in comparison: sink overflowing with food-crusted dishes; counters stacked with beer cans; fruit molding in a bowl on the table and attracting flies; cereal bits, crumbs, and wrapper scraps littering the sticky and stained linoleum floor.

Besides a few blue cups on the shiny black counter, this place was immaculate.

In the center of the kitchen stood a square oak dining table, where partygoers were playing strip poker. Willy sat at the head of the table, wearing nothing but his jockeys and a cloud of smoke. He was the only guy at the table. The rest were girls in various stages of undress, one girl giggling and barring her breasts with a forearm, holding her cards in her free hand.

Another girl stood behind Willy, massaging his shoulders and his sculpted, hairless chest. She was Latina, with straightened auburn hair, black eyes, and a white top.

Willy looked up from his cards as everyone entered the kitchen. All the girls looked around too. Sy had a hard time keeping his eyes off the topless girl, whose breasts jiggled as she laughed.

"Burger," Willy bellowed, a cigarette clenched between his perfect white teeth. "Come, join us."

Burger hesitated, glancing at the topless chick.

Sarah pushed past him.

"Oh," Willy said, catching sight of her. The Latina stopped rubbing his shoulders and stood erect.

"Sarah," Willy continued. "You can join us too. You, Lacy, and uh... who's that behind you?"

Everyone except Sarah turned to Sy. The half-naked girls at the table looked him up and down, probably assessing his attire. One girl, who was still wearing a blue bra, raised her eyebrow and curled her lip.

Sy's face felt warm. He wanted very much to step out of the kitchen, away from the smothering silence and the scrutinizing eyes.

Burger finally broke the quiet. "That's Macky."

Sarah crossed her arms and nodded at the Latina. "Who's the skank?"

"I'm Carmen," the girl retorted, crossing her own arms. "Who the fuck are you?"

"Now, now," Willy said, "let's not start calling names, okay? Sarah, baby, why don't you come get a drink, cool down, have some fun, huh?" He rocked the keg, which sat in a trashcan full of ice.

"Wait," Carmen said, glaring at Sarah. "I know you. You're that star cheerleader from Grants Pass. Cinch or something."

Sarah never looked at Carmen. She kept her glower on Willy. "Okay, babe." She held out her cup. "You win. Fill me up."

Willy gave her his sparkling, square-jawed Mister America smile and extended the keg spigot to her cup, priming the keg's pump with his other hand.

"I thought you'd see things my way," he said around the cigarette. He pulled the trigger on the spigot, and amber beer gushed into the container. Foam bubbled above the rim, and he released the trigger. He smiled as Sarah took the first drink.

"Mmm," she hummed.

Sarah swished and spit the mouthful back into the cup. She cleared her throat and let a thick string of mucus ooze into the beer. One of the strip poker girls said, "Gross," and Willy watched, smile tightening and quivering at the edges.

"What're you doing?" he asked through clenched teeth.

Sarah ignored him and gazed into her drink. "You know what, babe? I don't think I'm the one who needs to cool down. I think *she* does."

For the first time, Sarah met eyes with Carmen. She splashed her soiled beer in the Latina's face.

Cursing, Willy lurched forward to dodge the splash. His knee hit the table, and all the cups atop it fell. The cigarette ejected from his mouth and sizzled in the spreading puddles of beer. The topless girl screamed, scooted back, and tossed up her hands as if to stop the beer from pouring into her lap. Sy stole a glance at her quivering, unbarred breasts. The nipples were hard, aureoles pink and puckered.

Carmen stooped, holding her arms away from her body. Her face glistened, and Sarah's spit hung in her hair. The front of her shirt was wet and clinging. "You stupid bitch."

Lacy stepped around Burger, who was gawking at Carmen's wet shirt. She laid her hand on Sarah's arm. "Hey, maybe we should—"

Sarah pulled away. She got in Carmen's face and spoke in the same confidential voice she'd used with Burger's freshie: "Oh, and the name's Finch."

She turned and marched past Lacy. "Let's go."

"Bitch!" Carmen lunged after her, but Willy caught her and held her around the waist. "Fucking whore! Fucking cheerleading slut!"

Sarah barged through the Quicksilver guys at the entryway. Lacy turned to Sy. "C'mon," she said.

Everyone was gawking at him. The topless girl was so shocked she'd forgotten to hide her breasts; her mouth hung open in a pink-rimmed O.

Carmen screamed and spit and writhed against Willy's hold. He shut his eyes and roared, "Sarah!"

Burger let out a short chuckle. "Later, Macky."

"Yeah."

Sy followed Lacy back through the living room. The music still thumped, but most of the people were crowded around the kitchen, spectators. Some stared after Sarah, who stormed out the front door.

Lacy and Sy excused their way through the crowd, which was trying to mend, murmuring uncertainly.

On his way through, Sy glanced at the leather couch. The couple was gone, only a bra left behind. On the wall-mounted TV, red credits scrolled across clips from the zombie film, clips from some kind of medical supply warehouse and a graveyard.

No one cheered to see them off, and no one passed a farewell joint. They just walked into the cold, where their breath steamed. Sy shut the door behind them to muffle the crappy rap and to blind all those staring, curious eyes.

*   *   *   *   *

By the time Sy and Lacy arrived, Sarah was leaning against the convertible, just a sexy silhouette, her cigarette burning in the dark.

"I slashed his tires," she said casually.

"What?" Lacy walked up to Sarah and put a hand on her shoulder. "With *what*?"

Sarah held something up. It looked like a straight razor. "With this," she said.

"What—where did you get that?"

"Doesn't matter." She threw the razor like a knife. The blade glinted as it flipped over the road and through a moonbeam. Then it crashed through the brush and disappeared in the opposite ditch.

Lacy caressed Sarah's arm. "I'm so sorry, Sarah."

"Whatever." She took a drag and exhaled. "That asshole's been cheating since before we started dating."

Dating wasn't exactly what Sy would have called it. It was more a prolonged one-night stand, a series of *Wham, bam, thank you, ma'ams* and hand-jobs in the school darkroom. Sy's time with Sarah had been closer to dating, though they never went on a date. Sarah had just used him for free gas, let him feel her legs now and then, nothing else, and he had only kissed her once. A short peck of the tongue and she had pushed him away. Still, it was closer to dating than what she and Willy had.

"Well," Lacy said, "that doesn't give him the right."

Sarah shrugged off her hand. "Oh, get off it, Lacy. You're so naïve."

She flicked her cigarette into the road. It blazed right past Sy's face, spitting sparks, and he caught a whiff of smoke. It eased his stomach, and he wanted more.

Lacy crossed her arms against the cold. "What now?"

"I need cigarettes," Sarah said.

"Okay. We'll stop at 7-11 after we let Sy off."

He winced at the thought of going home—his father was probably just barging through the front door, reeling toward the toilet with a bladder-full of beer, dwelling on the car accident and on Sy's mother.

Even worse, Lacy would see his house. Strays had toppled the trashcan and had strewn litter across the lawn, which grew in brown patches; three cars rusted on cement blocks in the driveway; and the trailer's pus-yellow siding was streaked with years of grime, its slat windows cracked and sealed with duct tape, its roof covered with an old black tarp to keep out the rain.

After Lacy's fresh home and the luxurious party-pad, Sy's trailer resembled a tramp-inhabited railroad car, like the ones parked beneath the bridge in downtown Grants Pass. He would rather walk home than face that humiliation, but before he could say anything, Sarah said, "No, Sy stays with us. We'll crash at your house."

Lacy arched her eyebrows. "He can't—Gary won't let him stay over. He flips out when I talk to guys on the phone."

Gary must be her stepfather, Sy guessed.

"He'll let him," Sarah said. "I'll ask. You know he can't deny me."

"But—"

"Just shut up and let's go. I need a cigarette."

Lacy sighed. "Fine. Let's go then."

They got in the car and pulled onto the road. Sy sat quiet in the back seat, fingering his knife. At least, he thought, a warm house beat the streets.

Nine

Mitchell cowered deeper in the closet as the intruder hammered the bedroom door. He clenched the gun and tried to stop sobbing. Not that the intruder didn't already know where he was.

That goddamn water glass. That had given him away. And the peephole. Mitchell had found someone staring back at him. He'd lurched backward, squirting urine into his jeans, and he'd knocked over the boxes stacked in the closet. There had been a moment's silence afterward. Then the banging. On the wall in front of him first. Then on the bedroom door.

The closet was the only place to hide. The bed was close to the ground, and Mitchell was too big to squirm underneath. Plus, fear had liquefied his innards like spider venom. He was too afraid he'd knock something over, that the intruder would break down the door and slit his throat, or kidnap him, knock out his teeth and peel off his eyelids so he would have to watch his own torment.

The pounding stopped. Mechanisms clicked as the intruder tried the knob. Locked. He hit the door and shook the frame. Mitchell flinched. Another squirt of urine heated his crotch.

The intruder shuffled down the hall, through the front room and into the kitchen, both part of the same space, separated by a bar. The intruder pulled out a drawer, clattered through it, and slammed it shut. He opened another drawer and rifled.

What's he doing?

Knives, Walker said.

Oh shit.

The clattering stopped. The footsteps stopped. The wind moaned, and a board in the hallway creaked. Mitchell held his breath, listening, hearing nothing. Snot stung his nostril. He smeared it away on the back of his hand.

Gone, he thought, but Walker shook his head: *He won't leave until he's got you.*

Mitchell dried his sweaty palms on his pant legs and got a better grip on the gun.

C'mon. Where are you?

The wind moaned, and something banged shut. Just the front door. Did the burglar leave? Or is it Dad? Jesus, please, *please* let it be Dad.

You know better, Walker said. *Your dad's dead.*

The wind shifted the house again. The same board creaked in the hallway.

Mitchell slid open the mirrored door and peeked out. He could discern the corner of the bed, and past that, the door. On the knob, the alarm clock's light glowed red.

I could run for it, he thought.

Walker said nothing. Probably wanted to watch him try and fail. Walker would be glad to have Mitchell's eyelids removed, so he could peek as the intruder tortured him.

I could run, find Dad in the graveyard.

He hefted the gun: Or I could deal with it myself.

Yes, Walker urged. *That's it.*

But Mitchell had never fired a gun. What if he accidentally shot himself? Ricochet or something.

Pussy.

God, he had to pee! His bladder throbbed.

Pee your pants. Oops, too late. At least it'll keep your corpse warm. Pussy.

Okay. Go to the door and listen then. Figure it out from there.

Mitchell crawled out of the closet. He took a step forward—onto the squeaky board between the closet and the bed. No wind masked his mistake.

Something moved in the hall.

Oh shit, oh shit.

Silence.

Mitchell lifted his foot off the squeaky board and crept to the door. He listened a moment longer, then pressed his ear against the cold wood.

Something chopped through.

Right in front of his face.

A blade.

He staggered backward, screaming. The edge of the nightstand dug into his upper thigh, just below his hip. The gun thunked to the floor. Mitchell dropped to his knees and groped for it, whimpering.

The blade pulled from the door, squeaking against the wood. It struck again. Wood splintered, and the blade came through.

It's a cleaver, Mitchell realized. Jesus Christ.

Yes, Walker said. *Yes!*

The intruder continued to hack through the door. Mitchell scrambled around on his hands and knees, searching, piss dripping from his crotch. The gun was nowhere. A splinter from the door pricked his finger. More showered his hair. He yelped, recoiled. He fell over backward and sat on something hard. The gun!

Mitchell stood, aiming at the door. He couldn't keep the pistol steady.

Shoot it, shoot it!

Mitchell whimpered.

I can't.

Shoot the goddamn gun!

No!

His finger tightened around the trigger. He winced—but nothing happened. The trigger was locked in place.

Mitchell ran to the closet. He slammed the door and curled in the corner, clutching the gun to his chest, cringing each time the cleaver struck, releasing the last of his urine.

Nice job, Walker said. *Next time, why don't you just point your cock at him and forget to piss.*

Finally, the hacking stopped. With a chafing, cracking sound, the intruder pushed his arm through the door. A hand thumped and scuffed the wall, then rattled the doorknob. Clumsy fingers fumbled the lock, turned it. The arm pulled out of the hole. The doorknob turned. The door sighed open.

Just then, the drone of an approaching car hummed through the house. The intruder hesitated in the doorway. The hum strengthened until the car was right out front. Then it shut off.

The intruder stood still.

That's Lacy, Walker said.

Lacy. Shit. Mitchell had to do something, had to warn her somehow.

No. Let that bitch get what she deserves.

Mitchell nodded and cowered deeper into the closet, hoping the intruder would take the bait.

══ Ten ══

He was almost through the door. As he chopped with the cleaver, he could smell the boy's tears and urine. Hunger knifed through him, and he chopped harder. He cut a hole and stuffed his arm through, searching for the knob. He found it, unlocked it. He pulled his arm out and opened the door.

The room stank of gas, a mixture of fear and adrenaline.

He stepped across the threshold—and stopped mid-step when he heard the engine. He looked down the hall to the front room, flooded with yellow headlight. The car parked near the porch, the engine stopped, and the headlights clicked off. He heard voices, but he'd shattered the porch light and could see only darkness.

Hide, the phantom whispered. *Help is coming.*

He stepped back into the room's fragrant gloom and waited with his cleaver.

* * * * *

A rubbing sensation disturbed Digger's dream, and he opened his eyes. Venice stared back at him, her eyes black and ravenous.

She wore obsidian lipstick and a seductive smile. She stroked his chest and moaned. Digger could feel her lust, a hot throbbing in her chest and groin, a fever in her brow.

He groaned and looked past her. Zombie corpses sprawled on the mattress, intestines strewn about, a disembodied head lying on the pillow, one eye staring blankly, bite marks on its neck. Pieces of the blonde were scattered: an ear here, a swatch of hairy scalp there. Venice had laid waste to them all.

And Bones was still gone.

Digger looked down at Venice's nudity. Her skin was so pale, like the moon, except for dark bruises on her biceps and thighs. More surfaced on her milky breasts in the shape of fingers and palms.

Still rubbing Digger's breast, Venice went down on him, tickling his chest hair with kisses, circling his navel with her tongue. He moaned as his bellyache intensified.

Venice smiled up at him. Then she bit into his stomach. She gnawed through skin and fat and muscle, ripping with her hands until she could grab the slimy rope of an intestine. She tore the membranes that held it in place and pulled out a huge sausage link of Digger's digestive tract. She chomped into it and tore off a scrap.

In the other room, the trapdoor opened and shut. Venice looked up as Bones stormed in. A crew of skeletons clattered behind him. His face was furrowed, red, and scowling.

Eleven

Lacy parked on the concrete pad in front of the house.

The porch light was off. Sy swore it had been on when they left. He started to ask about it, but stopped. He didn't want to sound like a pussy. But when Lacy killed her headlights, he saw how dark it was, not only outside but inside as well.

"No porch light?"

"My brother probably turned it off," Lacy said. "He's always pulling creepy stunts like that."

"You've got a brother?"

"Well, stepbrother actually. No blood at all."

"Yeah," Sarah added. "Name's Mitchell. A little pervert too. Nutted in one of Lacy's bras earlier."

"Shut up," Lacy said.

Sy wasn't sure he'd heard right (he did *what*?), but Lacy was embarrassed, so he didn't ask. He felt stupid for worrying in the first place.

"You should've seen it," Sarah continued. "You were in the shower, and Lacy was changing. She found his cum in one of her bras—"

"Shut up, Sarah."

"Lacy pounded on Mitchell's door, pinching that bra between her fingers like toxic waste."

"Knock it off."

"It was hilarious."

"I'm getting out now."

"Ah, come off it," Sarah said. "Your brother's a pervert. No sense hiding it."

"Yeah, but you don't have to announce it, either." Lacy crossed her arms and shivered. "I'm going inside now. Bye."

She stepped out and slammed the door. Sy tried to follow, but Sarah held his arm.

"Let her be. Let her blow it off."

Sy looked through the windshield. Lacy ascended the porch steps, swallowed in darkness.

"It's okay," Sarah said. "She'll be fine. Just let her cool off. Wanna smoke?"

Lacy opened the front door and turned on the living room light. No one jumped out and grabbed her. No one yanked her inside.

Sy settled into his seat. Sarah was right; Lacy needed a few minutes to herself, just long enough to let the red fade from her cheeks. And Sy needed a cigarette. He'd smelled Sarah's smoke all the way here, and it had added an anxious pang to the flutters in his stomach.

"Here," Sarah said, offering him his very own cigarette. On the way to Lacy's, she had bought a pack of Marlboro Reds at the 7-11 in Grants Pass. She usually smoked 100's, but Sy wasn't complaining.

He stuck the cigarette between his lips, savoring the raisin-like flavor of dry tobacco. Sarah lit her own cigarette, and the lighter's orange flame illuminated her face, except the hollows of her temples and cheeks; shadows danced everywhere. She reached over her seat and lit Sy's. He puffed until the coal was strong and bright, and then he inhaled deeply.

The tension drained from his abdominal muscles, and he leaned against his seat, listening to Sarah's exhalations. Lacy had rolled the top back onto the convertible, and the smoke clouded the roof, mimicking the sky. A crisp breeze rolled through the open window and cooled Sy's brow.

"So how'd you like the party?" Sarah asked.

"It was all right."

"It sucked," Sarah said. "Just a bunch of jocks and preppies boning drunk bimbos and freshman lushes, just like every other party."

"I guess." Sy took another drag.

She reached forward and tapped ashes into the ashtray. "You know, I can't blame you for staying away from those things. You're better than that."

It was a strange compliment, and it made Sy hesitate. "Thanks," he said, and then he sucked more smoke.

"I always knew you were different."

He glanced toward the house. The front deck was dark. Why didn't Lacy turn on the porch light?

He took one last drag off his cigarette and leaned forward to put it out in the backseat ashtray. Sarah turned. For a moment, their faces were so close Sy could smell her red lipstick, could feel her warm breath glide across his cheek. He pulled slowly back, cigarette still burning between his fingers.

Sarah gazed into his eyes, her own glittering green with reflected light. "Why'd we ever break up, Sy?"

His stomach fluttered again. His palms began to sweat.

"We had some good times," she said. "I mean, you're not like those other assholes that play football and dick anything with two legs. I miss you, Sy. I miss us."

She grazed her long black nails across his cheek, sending chills down his spine. Her knuckles brushed his skin. They were cold and bony, as if she were dead. It felt wrong, but he swelled anyway, surging with a gritty tingling. Sarah traced a nail down his chest and belly, which seized and recoiled. Her fingers flitted over the taut denim of his crotch.

Slowly, as if in a dream, Sarah leaned over the back of her seat. Her lips parted, and her breath quivered against Sy's mouth. She unzipped his pants, and their lips brushed.

He pulled back, and she pushed forward. Her hot tongue probed his lips. Her hand snuck inside his fly and massaged him through his briefs. The fabric abraded his glans, and he flinched. He tried to take her hand out, but his arm was too weak.

Sarah's kiss deepened. Sy's mouth opened submissively, and her tongue slipped inside, coiling, lolling, flirting with his. Cold fingertips wiggled into the opening in his briefs.

A scream shattered the darkness.

Lacy.

Sy pushed Sarah away, threw open his door and flew out. Glass crunched underfoot as he pounded across the porch. Sy barely heard it beneath Lacy's shrieks.

He slammed through the front door, scanned the front room.

Nothing.

The hallway.

It was dark, and Lacy was struggling with someone. A man. He had ripped off her sweatshirt and was clutching at her breasts as she tried to escape. In one hand, he held a cleaver.

"Help!"

Sy rushed forward, whipping out his knife. His thigh hit the arm of a recliner. He staggered.

With a rip, Lacy escaped the man's grasp. She blundered forward, shirt torn to reveal a slash of belly and bra. She stumbled and fell, throwing out her hands to deflect the impact. The man lunged into the light and landed on her.

He was bloated and gray, flesh wadded on old bones. He yanked on Lacy's bra strap and cut it with the cleaver.

Sy roared as he bore down, trying to scare the man off. The attacker glanced up. Cataracts glossed his eyes, and strands of dead hair veiled them.

Sy punted him in the teeth. The blow knocked him off Lacy, who tried to scramble away on her hands and knees. The man caught her ankle. She screamed. Sy stomped his arm. There was a dry snap of bones, and the hand released. Lacy crawled away.

Dropping the cleaver, the man clamped onto Sy's calf. He started to pull himself up, but Sy stamped his face. He grabbed the attacker's fleshy throat and dragged him into Lacy's room and left him there. He slammed the door. There was a lock on the knob. He turned it.

Curled against the wall, Lacy whimpered, gaping at her bedroom door. Her hair was mussed, half of it pulled from her scrunchee, and tears glazed her eyes. One of her breasts poked from the tear in her shirt. As her chest hitched, the flesh shuddered. Shame flushed Sy's cheeks.

He wanted to put his arm around her. He stepped forward, hesitated, took a step back.

"What happened?" Sarah asked. She stood inside the front doorway, looking from him to Lacy. It must've seemed suspicious: Sy looming over her with his zipper down, a knife in one hand. He receded a step and lowered his blade.

Something smashed behind him. Sy whirled, slicing his knife through the air, dreading a face-to-face with cloudy eyes. Something jumped out at him. Just Lacy's door, shuddering as the bloated man pounded it.

"What is that?" Sarah asked. She took a step forward, glancing at Lacy, then at Sy. "Is that Mitchell? Did that little creep try to rape her?"

"I—I don't... I'm not sure—"

Lacy suddenly gasped and seized Sy's arm. "Mitchell," she said. "Where's Mitchell?"

Twelve

Don't answer, Walker said as Lacy called Mitchell's name. *And if someone pokes their head in here, shoot it.*

Lacy shouted again. The intruder thrashed inside her room, and something shattered behind Mitchell's head.

There goes Lacy's mirror.

Someone flicked on the bedroom light. A yellow line appeared at the seams of the closet.

"Who busted the door?" Sarah asked.

"Don't know," Macky said as he stepped into the room.

Mitchell could see him through the seam. He pointed the gun at the door and tightened his grip.

Don't forget the safety, Walker said.

Mitchell clicked it off.

"Mitchell?" Macky asked, taking another step.

C'mon, Walker crooned. *Stick your faggot face in here. I'll give it a makeover.*

Sarah stepped forward, too. "Mitchell," she called. "Come out, you little shit!"

Why don't you come in, bitch? Bet you've never seen a gun as big as mine.

I can't do this, Mitchell whined. I can't shoot them.

Shut up. Walker leaned closer to his peephole into the world.

Macky checked under the bed. Good thing Daddy didn't hide anything there. Under the mattress, though...

"I don't think he's in here," Macky said.

Dumbass.

Sarah crossed her arms. "What about the closet?"

In another part of the house, Lacy yelled Mitchell's name. The intruder pounded on the wall behind him.

Macky fidgeted with something in his pocket. "Uh, maybe one of us should stay with Lacy. She—"

"What was it?" Sarah interrupted. "What attacked her?"

Macky hesitated. "I don't know. It... it looked human, but... it was all *bloated*."

"What do you mean, *bloated*?"

"Look, I don't know. Just—Lacy shouldn't be alone."

"Well then are you gonna check the closet, or should I?"

"No. That's—I'll do it."

Walker leaned forward. *Get ready.*

I can't do it. It's murder.

Who's to say he isn't another intruder? Best not take any chances. Shoot him.

The door slid open.

Shoot him!

BAM!—the gun bucked.

Macky recoiled. Gunpowder had burned his cheek.

Before Macky could regain his balance, Mitchell pushed past. Sarah tried to block the door, but he bulled through her. His bedroom was dark. Inside, he slammed the door and locked it. He trembled all over. He dropped the gun: *thud.*

In the hall, Lacy called out, making sure everyone was okay.

You missed, Walker said. *Point-blank and you missed.*

"Shut up," Mitchell whispered. "Why'd you make me shoot?"

Because. Kill Macky, and the girls are ours. We could tie 'em up, play all sorts of games.

In the hall right outside his door, Lacy asked what happened. Sarah ranted in response.

Kill Macky, Walker repeated, *and the girls are ours.*

You're crazy.

Am I?

They won't just let me tie them up.

Who says they have to?

How else am I gonna do it?

You still have the gun, don't you?

Lacy knocked on Mitchell's door. "Mitchell?" She tried to sound calm, but he could hear the waver in her voice. "It's okay. Sy's okay. No one blames you. We're... we're just glad you're all right. Please, just come out? Lay down the gun, and... and just come out, okay? Mitchell?"

Mitchell, Mitchell, Walker scoffed. *Is that your name, Mitchell?*

He picked up the gun. It was heavy, a comfortable weight. He pointed it at the door and pretended to shoot, mouthing quiet gunshots. No, he thought. My name's not Mitchell. It's Walker. And yes, I *do* have the gun.

Thirteen

"You bitch!"

Bones' skeleton crew waited by the entrance as he bore down on Venice; she was kneeling in front of Digger, feeding from his guts. Bones slapped her, and she sprawled on the concrete.

As she propped herself up, Digger felt her emotions—a flash of shame, hate, and regret. Bones jabbed a finger in her face, where a black handprint slowly focused.

"I *ordered* you to stay away from him! I *ordered* you!"

Venice snapped at his fingers. He recoiled, barely evading her bite. Then his hand shot forward and throttled her neck. He got in her face, cheeks quivering. "You will *not* defy me again."

Bones squeezed harder, making her feel the pain. He threw her down and marched out.

After he slammed the door, his skeleton crew clattered to the bed and filled garbage bags with dismembered bodies. One worker draped a redheaded scalp over its skull as a wig.

Venice pushed the skeletons away and swiped a detached arm.

She chewed off the meat and used the bone to bash in the blonde's cheekless teeth, striking so hard the corpse jiggled.

Digger closed his eyes.

For a moment, he could see through Venice, and he watched the blonde's face crumple and crunch. Then Digger sank through Venice's lava flow. He traversed a plane of darkness, into a cemetery. Bones' face peered down from the skeletal moon, nearly veiled by silvery wisps. His phantom chanted on the wind, compelling Digger onward, through the gravestones and into the trees.

Others followed, their skin mostly black with putrefaction, their burial suits disintegrating and drooping on sunken frames. They shared a hunger, they shared a stomach, and beyond those trees sat a house that packaged four tender adolescents. Two were to be abducted and kept alive, but the other two? They were expendable, rewards for those who brought Bones his prize.

Fourteen

Sy stooped into the closet, careful not to kneel in the wet spot that stank of urine. He fingered the flap of duct tape hanging from the wall. A blue laser pinpointed his hand, coming from a hole in the plaster. Sy pressed his eye to the opening and peeped into Lacy's room. A blue nightlight illuminated shadowy hulks. The *thing* he'd locked in there had fallen silent. Nothing moved. Sy thought he saw a stick figure and pressed his eye closer.

"Hey," someone spoke behind him.

Sy whirled around.

Sarah stood near the foot of the bed. He hadn't heard her because his ears were still ringing from the gunshot.

"Lacy's freaking out," she said.

Sy could hear her, still pounding on Mitchell's door. "Did you, uh... her bra—"

"I got her a shirt, yeah." Sarah frowned and crossed her arms. "So what's going on here, Macky, huh?"

"I told you. I don't know."

"What is that thing in there?" She nodded toward Lacy's room. "Lacy, she's too freaked. She won't tell me. You got the best look at it. What the hell is it?"

Sy glanced back at the peephole. He wasn't sure what he'd seen. Adrenaline and shock had distorted his memory into caricatures and animations. The guy could've been disguised in a Halloween mask, or he could've been obese and blind. The remaining possibility was insane: a corpse couldn't walk, let alone attack someone.

Sy finally turned to Sarah. "It was dark. I didn't get a good look."

"That's bullshit, Sy. That thing in there, it tried to rape her, maybe even kill her. You saw it, and I wanna know what we're up against."

Sy fidgeted in his pocket with his knife. He glanced at the peephole again.

"What?" Sarah asked. "What're you looking at?" She took a step toward the closet.

"Nothing." He hadn't decided whether to tell anyone about the hole. Lacy was already upset, and knowing that her stepbrother and stepfather spied on her would make things worse.

Sarah gave him a suspicious look and stepped to the closet. "Smells like piss."

"Hey," Sy said, "maybe we should call the cops."

"What's this?" Sarah stooped over. "Is this a fucking *peephole*?" She pressed her eye to the wall. "What—" She stopped and looked up at Sy.

He heard it, too.

A truck had just squealed to a stop outside.

"Who is it?" Lacy asked as they exited the bedroom.

Sarah pushed past her, and Lacy turned to Sy. Her eyes jittered in swollen flesh, and her hair was frayed, but at least she wore a shirt. Sy would've felt ashamed copping a glance when she was so distraught.

"Who's here?" she asked.

"I don't know."

In the living room, Sarah peeked through one of the sidelights. "Who the—*shit*."

She threw open the door and stomped to the top of the stairs, resting her hand on a cocked hip. The front-room light barely illuminated her backside.

"What do you think you're doing here?!" she shouted.

A car door slammed. Willy's voice followed. "Hey, babe. What was that shit at the party, huh?"

"I don't know, Willy, you tell me." She paused. "Why'd you bring fat ass along?"

Burger spoke up next, doing his best Cartman impression. "Hey, I ain't fat. I'm big-boned."

Lacy groaned beside Sy. "What're they doing here?"

He shook his head.

"Well," Willy explained, creeping up the stairs toward Sarah, "someone slashed my tires, and Burger here was nice enough to give me a lift. Ain't that right, Burger?"

"Sure as shit."

"So," Willy said, stopping on the step below Sarah, "aren't you gonna invite us in?"

Before she could retort, Willy swiped her into a dip and planted his mouth on hers.

"Go, bro!" Burger cheered as Willy's hand brushed Sarah's breast.

She slapped him and wiggled away. He simpered up at her, rubbing mindlessly at the handprint on his cheek. Sarah stomped inside, and Willy ambled after her, still grinning. Burger followed, smoking a joint.

Lacy took Sarah's arm and said, "Tell them to leave."

Willy interrupted. "Jesus, what happened to you, Lacy?"

Sarah said, "Someone tried to rape her."

Willy flexed his jaw and nodded at Sy. "Him?"

"No. The guy's in there." Sarah pointed at Lacy's door. "Sy locked him in."

Willy nodded at the room. "In there?"

"That's where I'm pointing, isn't it?"

"Who is it?"

"I don't know."

"Well, how about we take a look-see?" Willy glanced over his shoulder and said, "Burger?"

"Right behind you, bro." He flicked his joint into the night and strode toward Willy, who was reaching for the doorknob.

"Wait." Lacy caught his arm. "Don't."

Willy gave her a stony look. "It's all right, Lacy. We just wanna take a look."

"Yeah," Burger said. "And if he tries anything, Willy and me'll cream him."

Lacy thought about it, then shook her head. "No. Nuh-uh."

Sarah sighed and crossed her arms. "C'mon, Lacy. Just let them open it."

Willy's face went calm. "Let go of my arm, Lacy."

She held his gaze, but finally released him. "Fine."

"That's a girl. Now stand back."

Lacy stood with Sarah near the mouth of the hall. Burger moved behind Willy, and Sy stood by the axed bedroom door, fingering his knife inside his pocket. His stomach was trembling, twisting. He dreaded another encounter with that bloated face and those white eyes, but he needed to *see*, needed to prove the thing wasn't some horror show zombie. So he gritted his teeth and clenched his knife.

Willy turned the lock. "Ready?" he asked.

Burger assumed the sumo wrestler stance. He took a deep breath. "Ready."

"On three: one..."

He turned the knob.

"Two..."

Burger braced himself.

"Three!"

Willy yanked open the door. He gagged and plugged his nose. "Jesus. Smells like your jock strap, Burger."

"Screw you."

With his free hand, Willy fanned the air and peered into the room, barely lit by the nightlight. "I don't see anything."

Burger leaned closer. "Me neither."

Lacy said, "Maybe we should call the cops."

"Screw the cops," Willy replied. "Hey, Burger, feel for the light switch."

"No way, man. You do it."

"Just do it, Burger. I got your back."

"Shit, whatever."

Burger stuck his arm into the darkness. His hand thumped the wall as he searched.

Lacy stepped forward. "Seriously, guys, let's just forget about it—"

Sarah pulled her back. "Let them be," she said, fixated on the darkness.

Burger was still searching.

"Got it?" Willy asked.

"Does it look like I got it?"

"It's up higher," Sarah added.

Before Burger could find the switch, something jerked his arm. His chest slammed into the doorframe.

"Holy shit, get it off me! Get it off!"

Willy took a half step into the room and jabbed at the attacker. He pulled Burger back, and the enemy emerged.

Lacy screamed. Sy gasped. It was official now: the thing latched to Burger's arm was a zombie. It snapped its teeth, which were red with Burger's blood. It had already taken a chunk out of his forearm.

Willy punched the zombie again. It released Burger and fell to the floor. It farted gasses. Willy stomped its head until the cranium collapsed, but the thing kept coming, clawing at his pants with its good hand. Willy managed to kick and shove it back into the room. He slammed the door and locked it.

"Jesus Christ, what was that?"

"A zombie," Sy replied.

Everyone looked at him.

Willy furrowed his brow and curled his lip. "A what?"

"I think... I think it was a zombie."

"You're nuts!"

"It bit me," Burger said, grasping his forearm above his bloody wound. "I'm gonna die. I'm gonna die and become one of them."

"That's bullshit, Burger. That wasn't a zombie."

Sarah crossed her arms. "Then what the hell was it, huh, Willy?"

"I don't know. Some freak in a mask."

"You stomped its head in, Willy. It's still *alive*."

Sy could hear it, a feeble thump, as if the corpse was dragging itself around Lacy's room.

"That's death throes or something," Willy rationalized. "Like when you cut the head off a chicken."

"I'm gonna die!" Burger sobbed.

Sarah ignored him. "You're a meathead, Willy, you know that? A true dumb shit."

"At least I did something. Your pussy boyfriend here didn't do shit! Just stood there and watched that freak take a bite out of Burger's arm!"

Sy knew Willy was referring to him as Sarah's boyfriend. He fingered his knife and glanced from Willy to Sarah.

"Sy locked it up in the first place!" she yelled. "You should've never opened it!"

"Christ, you begged me to do it!"

Before Sarah could argue, Lacy stepped forward. "Shut up! Just everyone, shut up!"

Willy and Sarah stopped squabbling, and Burger hushed to a whimper.

"We need to call the cops. We need to get Burger to a hospital."

Sy stepped forward too. "Lacy's right."

Willy shoved him back. "I ain't taking orders from no pussy. I'm in charge now. Burger, let me see the bite."

Burger held his arm against his chubby breast. He cringed as Willy reached for it.

"Let me see." He grabbed Burger's wrist and pulled his arm straight. The bite had gone through the muscle on the side of his forearm, the side you'd slit when committing suicide. The wound had nicked a vessel and left a bloody pit, fringed with the cottage cheese of fatty tissue.

Willy dropped Burger's arm. "It's a flesh wound. I had it worse when I scraped my shin on the bleachers—ah, quit crying, you faggot."

Burger strapped his arm against his chest, and tears streamed down his jowls. "I don't wanna die. Please... don't let me die."

"I said shut up."

"Knock it off," Lacy told Willy. She turned to Burger. "It'll be all right. But you need a bandage. C'mon." Lacy turned to Sy. She was still frayed, but a calm had settled over her eyes, like wind rippling across a blue lake. "Call an ambulance, okay?"

Sy nodded. "Okay."

"What am *I* supposed to do?" Willy asked. "Play with my dick?"

Lacy offered him a chilly stare. "You and Sarah watch the door."

"Whatever."

Lacy led Burger into the bathroom, leaving a trail of blood. Sy tried to squeeze past Willy into the front room, but Willy grabbed his arm and got in Sy's face. His eyes were stony, and his breath smelled like beer.

"You'd best stay out of my way, Macky."

Willy released him, and Sy left the hall. He scanned the living room: the chair he'd nearly tripped over, the cream-colored couch, a big-screen TV, a stand with a gardening magazine and a coffee ring on top, but no telephone.

Sy turned to the bar separating the front room from the kitchen. On the bar's green-tiled surface sat a black phone.

He picked up the receiver and was about to dial when something caught his eye. Across from him, the kitchen drawers were half open, their silvery contents strewn. One drawer sparkled with chef knives and other huge blades, probably where the zombie got its cleaver.

Sy put the receiver to his ear. He went to jab 9-1-1, but there was a click, and the dial tone died.

Sy pressed the hang-up lever on the phone's cradle. Silence. He pressed the lever again. More silence. He thwacked it repeatedly with his thumb. Still, silence.

Just as he went to try again, darkness swallowed him.

Willy growled in the hall. "Macky! Turn on the goddamn lights! Macky?!"

Sy stared at the front door. Burger had left it open. Sy ran over and slammed it.

"Macky! Where's the goddamn lights?!"

"Power's out!" he yelled.

Sarah cursed, and Willy punched a wall.

Sy turned back to the door. He cupped his hands against the left skylight and peeked out. Moonbeams highlighted the deck railing. Darkness obscured everything else. But Sy sensed something lurking. He knew this wasn't a simple power outage. Something had snipped the phone line and had tripped the breakers.

Something was out there, and it was hungry.

Fifteen

Mitchell peeked through a tiny hole into the bathroom. Lacy was rifling through the medicine cabinet. The fat guy, Burger, was weeping on the toilet.

I wanna see your wound, Walker said. *Show me your wound.*

But Burger hugged his arm to his chest, and all Mitchell could see was his broad back and the side of his face.

Lacy finally closed the cabinet. She had a sack of cotton balls and a roll of gauze.

"Let me see," she said.

Burger hesitated, then extended his arm, dripping scarlet from a cavity.

That's it, Walker hissed. The smell of Burger's blood and tears excited him.

Suddenly, the lights went out in the bathroom. Walker cursed. Lacy cussed too. Mitchell could barely discern her silhouette, but from her movements, he knew she was bandaging Burger's arm in the dark.

Turn on the lights—turn on the lights!

"There," Lacy said, "all fixed."

Damn it!

Burger wept. "I'm gonna die."

"Don't say that."

"That zombie bit me." His voice began to rise and crack. "It bit me, and I'm gonna become one of them."

What a pussy, Walker sneered.

But Burger had a point. Mitchell had watched a zombie movie earlier, and everyone bitten turned into living dead. Like that one guy's nephew, Freddy. And the thing in Lacy's room? Mitchell had watched beneath his bedroom door as Willy had stomped in its head. He'd seen the bloated face and the milky eyes. Definitely a Freddy.

Lacy stroked Burger's good arm. "You'll be fine."

Burger buried his face in his hands, and Mitchell turned away from the peephole.

In the hall, Willy and Sarah blamed each other for Burger's accident. Willy shouted and punched a wall.

We'll have to watch that one, Walker said, meaning Willy.

Mitchell agreed. Before, only Macky stood between him and the girls. Now Willy was here, and his voice alone had turkey-sized biceps.

Burger's a pussy, but Willy... We'll have to take him out first— by surprise.

I could shoot him right now, Mitchell thought. Through the wall.

He put the gun to his door, honing in on Willy's voice.

Do that and the others might run. Just wait. We'll get our chance. Meanwhile...

Under Walker's instructions, Mitchell pressed against the wall where Sarah stood and held the gun to her head.

I'm gonna rape you, bitch, Walker whispered. *Then I'm gonna kill you and rape you again. Just wait. We'll get our chance.*

Sixteen

Digger moaned, and his head lolled. He dreamt about his house. He stood outside, in the night, by the open fuse box. He tripped the circuits. He had already snipped the phone line.

The wind smelled of flesh, and Digger followed the scent to the front of the house. Through the deck railing, he could see the front door. It was agape and exhaling bloody breath.

Stomach growling, Digger approached the house. He heard footsteps and froze. A ghost face appeared in the doorway, and the door slammed shut, stilling the house's breath. People yelled from inside, then the ghost face pressed against the sidelight. There was more shouting. The face disappeared.

As the dream shifted, Digger was lost in dark currents: swirling, flowing, blind. He surfaced in a pitch-black room. He was on the floor, stuffing his face into a hamper of dirty clothes. He was trying to lick the crotch of a woman's panties, but he had bit off his own tongue. His face was crushed. There was fresh meat out in the hall. He'd tasted it, a chunk, and he wanted more, but he was trapped in the room now. The panties were all he had, so he stuffed them into his mouth and chewed.

* * * * *

Pain slashed Digger's chest. The dream dissolved, and his eyes snapped open to another slash of pain.

Bones grinned at him, holding a knife in one hand. "Rise," he said. "We have business."

A zombie stood behind Bones. His flesh was black and runny, and red worms squirmed in his eye sockets. His lipless teeth chattered endlessly.

"Meet the Castrator," Bones said.

He stepped aside, and the Castrator knelt. He chomped into Digger's penis, biting off hotdog rounds. Digger tried to scream, but an invisible band strangled him.

"She's rotting," Bones said, whispering in Digger's ear, gazing to the bed where Venice was tied spread-eagle. "Quicker than usual. See the dark splotches? You have them too. Pretty soon, you'll both look like the Castrator. It's the necromancy. It's not supposed to be used like this." He shook his head. "Venice tried to perfect it, tried to tamper with the summoning spell. But of course, you know that. You covered the graves for us. I bet it was strange, wasn't it? Finding graves without corpses?" Bones chuckled to himself.

The Castrator took his last bite. Digger's head hung, and all he could see was the grisly nub of his missing penis, the dried apricot of his scrotum.

Bones handed his knife to the Castrator. "Stab him."

The Castrator plunged the knife into Digger's wound so the handle protruded like a black dildo. All Digger felt was the impact, a throbbing deadness.

"There," Bones said. "Now when your son arrives, you can sodomize him."

Laughing, Bones left the basement with the Castrator.

Digger groaned.

From the bed, Venice stared at him. The spots on her body were darker, larger, ink infusions on pale paper. The ripest ones were slick and sagging. Something wriggled beneath them.

Digger felt the rage that simmered in Venice's chest. He saw her fantasy: Bones, naked and skeletal and crucified on the wall, his skin stripped from the waist down and wadded in the corner like khakis.

Venice's anger heated Digger's brow until the image faded, leaving him empty and exhausted. His head dropped, and his eyes fluttered shut. He floated into the satin currents of the dream world, that big web of psychic lightning that connected him to his brethren, and he waited for the house to spill its human guts.

Seventeen

"Burger needs a hospital," Lacy said.

Sy couldn't see her in the darkness of the hall, but he could hear the distress in her voice, like a balsa wood tower in a press, creaking to its breaking point. He could smell her anxiety too, a mixture of tears and propane. Luckily, Burger was weeping in the bathroom and unable to sense her concern.

God, he wanted to comfort her, hug her, kiss her.

"Burger doesn't need a hospital," Willy argued. "It's a scrape, that's all."

"The bite nicked an artery, Willy." Lacy sounded like she was talking to an idiot. "He could bleed to death."

"Then why don't *you* take him?"

"I can't. I can't leave my brother. Not with that thing in there."

"Then I'll stay. Sarah, too. Won't you, babe?"

Sy didn't need to see Sarah to know her arms were crossed. He could hear it in her voice.

"Just take him, Willy. You brought him here. He's your responsibility."

"And who's gonna stay and protect you? Macky?"

Sy didn't like the silence that answered. It was heavy with responsibility.

"Whatever. I'll take him. Happy?"

"Yes," Sarah said.

Willy pounded on the bathroom door. "Burger! Get your ass out here! You're going to the hospital!"

Silence.

Willy pounded again. "C'mon, Burger! Wipe your ass and let's go!" He reached for the doorknob. "Christ, Burger, do I gotta carry you out?"

"Wait!" Sy grabbed Willy's arm. "He's not answering."

"Yeah? So?"

"What if... he could've died. He might... he might try to attack."

"Get your hand off me before I break your nose."

Willy threw open the door. Sy jumped back, expecting a bulk to lunge out and gouge Willy's throat. Nothing happened, and Willy disappeared inside.

Sy peered in and saw the silhouette of Burger sitting on the toilet, crying.

"Get up," Willy said.

Burger tried, but plopped back down.

"Jesus. You're helpless."

Willy slung Burger's arm over his shoulder and lifted him.

"I'm dying," Burger mumbled as they shambled into the hall. "I'm gonna pass out."

Lacy caressed his arm. "You'll be fine. Willy will get you to a hospital now."

In a voice that was purposefully strained, Willy asked, "Someone gonna help me carry him out?"

Sy stepped forward, but Willy pushed him back.

"Nuh-uh," he said. "Not you. Sarah."

Sarah crossed her arms. "He's your responsibility. *You* carry him."

"Bitch."

"Just leave, Willy. Nobody invited you."

"*I'll* help you," Lacy offered.

"Thanks, but I got him."

Glaring at Sarah, Willy helped Burger to the front door.

"Oh, and don't come back," Sarah said. "It's over. We're through."

"Whatever." Willy opened the door, and he and Burger shambled down the steps.

Sarah followed them onto the porch. "I hope you crash!"

"Love you too, babe!"

"I hope you die!"

*　　*　　*　　*　　*

Mitchell nearly wet his pants. He couldn't believe it. Willy was leaving.

Walker grinned. *Now we'll have the bitches to ourselves. Just take out Macky, and we'll have a ménage á trois.*

Mitchell tightened his grip on the gun. He was pressed against the wall beside the door, ready to pop into the hall and fire. He would put enough rounds into Macky's face to obliterate his skull and still have plenty to control the girls.

Be patient, Walker said. *Wait until they leave.*

Mitchell felt his crotch growing. In his mind, he saw Macky's face crumple, saw his brain matter make art on the wall. His crotch grew harder.

I could make the girls play with his corpse, he thought. If I wanted to.

He'd leave that up to Walker.

*　　*　　*　　*　　*

In his dream, Digger waited as two men came down the steps. The strong man was arguing with a woman in the doorway. The other man was injured, and the smell of blood sweetened the night's chill.

Digger salivated.

On my mark, the phantom ordered, but before it signaled him, Digger went forward. The other zombies closed in too, staggering out of their dark pockets as the men headed for a beige truck. The phantom ordered them to wait, but they kept going, now under the command of their hunger.

*   *   *   *   *

"Holy shit!" Willy shouted.

Sarah screamed. Sy ran forward and pushed past her.

In the moonlit driveway, a horde of zombies closed in on Burger and Willy. One zombie staggered forward and latched onto Burger's injured arm. Willy planted his shoe in the zombie's stomach. The corpse's spine snapped, and its upper body folded and slouched against its legs, held together by its three-piece suit. The thing kept coming, swiping for Burger's calves.

More zombies lurched forward, gurgling, groaning. Willy and Burger headed for the Chevy. Burger stumbled. Willy tried to hold him up, but he hit the pavement anyway.

The broken zombie grabbed Burger's hair and yanked back his head. It sank its teeth into his cheek. He squealed and kicked.

"Oh my god!" Lacy put a hand to her mouth. "You've gotta help them!"

"No!" Sarah clutched Sy's arm. "He's not going out there!"

"He's got to! He's gotta help them!"

"Fuck them!"

Sy was shaking. He wanted to slam the door and lock it, but he didn't want to disappoint Lacy. He didn't want *her* to try to help them. Not with those things out there.

Sy pulled away from Sarah, but before he could descend the steps, Willy barged past.

"Move!"

Lacy blocked the door. "What about Burger?!"

"He's dead!"

Willy tried to sidestep her, but she blocked him. "Bullshit! You can't just leave him out there!"

Burger screamed and tried to stand. His cheek bled, and his molars were visible. Zombies dragged him down.

"He's dead, Lacy! Get inside!"

Willy tried to muscle her out of the way, but she struggled.

"Sy! Do something!"

Sy's belly was in knots. He turned to the stairs, but Willy clamped down on his neck and pushed him into the house. Sy collapsed. Lacy hurried over and helped him up.

"Are you okay?"

"Yeah."

Willy slammed the door. His eyes shined in the dark. "Are you all fucking crazy?"

"Go to hell," Lacy said.

"What do you want from me, huh?"

"You should've done something."

"I kicked one of those things in half! What else could I do?"

"You could've saved Burger!"

"Burger's dead!"

But he wasn't. He was out there, crying for help.

Sarah covered her ears and paced back and forth. "God, won't he stop?"

Willy tried to caress her arm. "Calm down, babe."

She shrugged him off. "Don't touch me."

"Someone should go for help," Lacy suggested.

"Fuck that," Sarah said, still pacing. "Fuck that."

"You wouldn't make it past those things," Willy added. "Not without a gun."

Suddenly, Sarah stopped pacing. She turned to Lacy, and her eyes were feverish. "Your brother. *He* had a gun."

Willy said, "What? Where is he? Does he still have it?"

"We don't know," Lacy said. "He locked himself in his bedroom."

"Oh he has it," Sarah chipped in. "Nearly blew Sy's head off."

"So let's get it from him." Willy tromped toward the hallway, but Lacy barred him.

"Let me do it," she said quietly. "I'm his sister."

"Whatever. But if he gives you shit, I'm kicking his door in."

"Just—stay here." Lacy turned to Sy. "C'mon."

She took his hand and led him into the hallway. Her palm was cool and smooth against his, and it felt good, though Lacy probably meant nothing intimate. She was just guiding him through the dark. She released his hand to knock on her brother's door.

"Mitchell," she said, her voice warm with milk and honey, soothing even to Sy. "Mitchell, you need to come out. There's been an accident. We need to go."

The silence behind the door seemed to breathe and scheme. Burger had stopped mewling, which was a relief, but Sy had a bad feeling.

What if Lacy's brother had *intended* to shoot him but missed? What if he was in there right now, waiting? From what Sarah said, it wasn't too outrageous. The creep had ejaculated into Lacy's bra, for God's sake. He had a peephole into her room.

"Mitchell, honey, I know you're scared, but we need you to come out. You're not in trouble. We just... we need to leave, okay? *Please* come out?"

In the living room, Willy cursed. Sy heard metal clanking from outside.

"Hurry! They're killing the cars!"

Sy could imagine the zombies under the hood of Lacy's convertible, tearing out wires and cracking the coolant tank. Obviously, Lacy imagined something similar, because she knocked harder.

"C'mon, Mitchell. We need to go. We need to—"

"Goddamn it, Lacy, hurry up!"

Lacy glanced at Willy, then back at the door. "Mitchell, please—"

Willy bulled Sy aside and stepped behind Lacy. "Move it."

She ignored him.

"I said *move.*"

Willy spun her by the shoulders and pushed her. She would've hit the wall, but Sy caught her.

Willy faced Mitchell's bedroom.

"Don't!" Lacy screamed, but it was no use.

Willy reared back to kick down the door.

* * * * *

In the dark, Mitchell waited, crouched behind boxes, gun pointed at the entrance.

Check the magazine, Walker said.

Empty. One cartridge in the chamber. His dad must have forgotten to reload.

Don't miss, Walker hissed.

I won't.

The door exploded inward.

Eighteen

When he woke, Digger still tasted the fat man's flesh, still felt his warm, slippery insides. He heard his brethren destroying the cars, heard the phantom giving directions. But he followed a different voice, one that wrapped around him like a greedy lover, one that kissed him and shared his feast. It was a serpent's hiss, a lullaby tainted with venom.

As the dream faded, the voice stayed with him. It came from the bed where Venice was tied, staring at him, luring him with her black-hole eyes. She spoke to him with her mind, told him to test his bonds. Locked and drilled into the concrete, the cuffs were unbreakable, inescapable, unless he severed his hands and feet.

Venice tested her own restraints. They were tight and strong, but when Bones had made the knots, Venice had flexed, leaving slack when she relaxed. She wriggled one hand free and worked on her other.

When she stooped to unleash her ankles, Digger saw the contusions on her back, plum-colored sweet spots. Her wrists wore black tattoos where the rope had bruised.

Loose, Venice slid off the bed and strode toward Digger, hair flowing like ink around her now sagging face. The dark splotches on her thighs had encroached her abdomen, which sagged like a ripe eggplant, glistening and pregnant. Mascara-colored bags pouched beneath her eyes, and on her cheek, Bones' handprint had blackened. The darkness was creeping into her veins.

Venice pressed against Digger and kissed him. He yearned to bite her tongue, to chew the spongy tissue, but she controlled him. Using one hand, she grasped the hilt of Digger's new phallus and raped him with the blade. Too soon, she pulled away, stealing his breath.

With a fingertip, Venice traced the lock on Digger's cuffs. Her neck came close to his mouth, close enough to nip, but she wouldn't allow it; she had control over him now. She withdrew her hand from the cuff and placed a cool palm to Digger's forehead. There was a burst of light, and then a flashback: Bones, depositing a silver key into his robe pocket.

The scene flashed, and Digger was in the graveyard, among a group of corpses. One carcass lay on the ground, and the others stripped slime off its bones, stuffing the muck into their mouths. More zombies joined in, some fresh from the ground, others journeying from somewhere else in the cemetery. For every five that came, one sacrificed itself.

A cordite-black snake slithered through the fallen oak leaves toward the rabble. It coiled around a nearby cross and fixed its obsidian eyes on the group. *Come,* it hissed in Venice's voice, its forked tongue flickering like blood. *Feed.*

The serpent wriggled back through the leaves, and the zombies followed, under Venice's spell, snipped from Bones' puppetry.

When Digger came to, Venice was staring at him. Her eyes were those of the snake: black and rapacious. She kissed him. *Soon,* she breathed, *we will be free.*

Nineteen

Willy's kick cracked the doorjamb and forced the door inward. Lacy grabbed his arm and tried to pull him back, but he pushed her away and stepped into Mitchell's room.

A gunshot shattered everything. Sy heard the bullet ping off a pipe in the wall. Lacy screamed and ran into the room. There was struggling, Willy grunting, Mitchell squealing, shrieking. Something crashed to the floor.

"Stop it!" Lacy trilled. "Leave him alone!"

Sy didn't want to get too close to the doorway, afraid another bullet might shear off his head. Lacy was in there, though. She could get shot.

Sy took a step forward.

Willy roared, and a small figure pushed past Sy. The bathroom door slammed shut. The lock clicked.

Willy barged into the hall, holding the gun. He pounded on the bathroom door. "Come out, you little shit!"

Lacy pulled at him. "Leave him alone! You've got the gun! Just let him go!"

"He *bit* me!" He held up his gun hand, which dripped blood from a crescent of punctures.

"He's scared! Just forget him!"

Willy punched the door. "I'm gonna kill you, you shit." He stomped into the front room.

Lacy sighed. "Jesus."

In the other room, Sarah said, "Willy? What're you doing?"

"Let go of me."

"Don't you open that door! Don't you open *that door!*"

Lacy and Sy exchanged a worried glance. They hurried into the front room, where Willy and Sarah were struggling. Willy smacked her, and she stumbled back. Sarah's eyes went wide and dazed. She rubbed her cheek.

"You bastard."

"I told you to let go."

Sarah wailed and lunged at him. He blocked her, hurled her to the floor. She prepared to spring up, but Willy pointed the pistol in her face.

"Sit."

Sarah hesitated, glowering. She lowered herself to the floor.

"Good girl. Now stay."

Lacy said, "What do you think you're doing?"

Keeping the gun on Sarah, Willy gave Lacy a sideways glance. "I'm getting outta here, that's what. You guys can stay if you want."

Lacy crossed her arms. "I'm not gonna leave my brother."

"Whatever. I'm leaving." Willy grinned at Sarah. "Later, babe." He turned to open the door.

Burger was at one of the sidelights. His gut was hollow and gaping like a shocked person's mouth, fringed with the blood-drenched tatters of his jersey. His cheek was ripped back into a crazy grin, and his eyes were blank.

More zombies flanked him.

Burger lifted his hand.

He held a rock.

"Oh shit." Willy stepped back, aiming the gun.

Burger swung his fist at the window, and Sy heard a dry click as Willy pulled the trigger. Then glass shattered everywhere. Fangs of it.

Screaming, Sarah scuttled into the corner. Willy roared and pulled the trigger: *click-click-click.*

Burger stepped halfway through the window and swung the rock. Willy kicked him in the crotch, knocking him back.

Burger caught himself on the window frame, dropping the rock and cutting his hands on shards of glass. No blood ran from his wounds.

Willy kicked him again, and Burger fell backward, plowing through the crowd of zombies. One eyeless ghoul cracked its teeth on the porch banister as it fell.

Willy turned and pushed past Sy. "Outta my way!"

Lacy grabbed for him. "Where're you going?"

Willy didn't answer.

Sarah followed him down the hall.

"C'mon," Lacy told Sy. "The window!"

She ran to the couch, but Sy stared as Burger pawed at the railing, trying to sit up. Burger's lungs had started to slump into his abdominal cavity, withered sacks blackened from cigarettes.

The other zombies recuperated, too, groaning, gurgling, getting up.

"Sy!" Lacy shouted, hunkered at one end of the couch. "Help me!"

Trembling, he went to the opposite side of the divan and grabbed the bottom edge.

"We've gotta block the window!"

He nodded.

On the count of three, they lifted. Sy's back groaned, and the muscles in his arms and neck pulled tight. The hard, wooden edge bit into his fingers. Lacy grimaced. Sy got a better hold and made sure to bear most of the weight.

They scuffled sideways, and Sy stumbled over his own feet. Burger stood again, swaying. A kidney glistened far back in the cave of his gut.

Sy bumped into a coffee stand. It toppled, and he twisted his ankle in its supports. His end of the couch landed on the floor. Then his chest hit, too. A dull thud reverberated through his jaw.

"Sy!" Lacy squealed. "Get up! Get up!"

Burger was halfway through the sidelight again, one hand on the frame, the other held out for balance. The others massed behind him, pushing him onward.

As pain corkscrewed through his ankle, Sy got up and grabbed the couch.

"Tip it up!" Lacy ordered. "We've gotta tip it up!"

Before they could maneuver, Burger plopped down on the cushions. The bottom edge grated Sy's fingers, and he lost his grip. Lacy released her side, and the couch tipped, spilling Burger into the front room.

He swiped for Lacy's ankle.

She jumped back, out of his reach.

Ignoring the zombies that clambered over the couch, Sy kicked Burger in the face. He stubbed his toe, but he heard a crack as the zombie's eye socket fractured. He kicked again, this time knocking out rotten fragments of Burger's molars.

"Sy!" Lacy shrieked.

Another zombie, this one naked with gray, hole-filled tits, lunged at him over the couch. Her jagged, dirt-packed nails clawed at his eyes.

Crying out, Sy punched her. The woman's jaw went crooked, and her teeth bit through her leathery cheek. Sy slammed into her chest, and her sternum snapped. She tumbled backward over the couch. More zombies swung at him. He tried to deflect, and one grabbed his arm.

Using the coffee stand like a bat, Lacy turned the back of Burger's skull into a mush of hair. The eye above his torn cheek bulged from the pressure. He groped for her leg. She tried to jump over him to help Sy, but Burger seized her ankle. Lacy fell on the couch. The zombies grabbed her hair and hauled her toward the window.

"Sy! Help—*help me!*"

The undead jammed hands under her armpits and pulled harder, suspending her over glass daggers caught in the windowsill. Her one foot was wedged in the couch cushions, gripping the edge, keeping her from tumbling outside.

Sy head-butted the putrid corpse snapping at his cheek. He crunched bone and split skin. He tried to escape, but the intruders held his shirt. The neckline pulled against his throat, and the hem began to rip.

He lunged forward, and the shirt ripped a little more. Lacy screamed. Her foot began to slip. Zombies gnawed on her arms.

Surging with adrenaline, Sy tore away and stumbled back. Burger crawled toward him, snarling, leaving a blood trail on the carpet. Bulging eye, dangling cheek, exposed teeth.

Sy punted him in the nose. Cartilage crumpled, but no blood escaped.

As Burger recovered, Sy leapt and grabbed for Lacy's ankle. Her shoe slipped off in his hand. Lacy screeched and fell into the zombies.

"Lacy!"

Sy stumbled back, out of Burger's grasp. Someone shoved past him. Willy. He had the gun. And a box full of bullets.

Twenty

Ear pressed against the bathroom door, Mitchell heard Willy shout, "Die, you motherfuckers!" Three gunshots followed. Sy yelled for Lacy, and she cried back. More gunshots ensued.

Okay, Walker said. *It's our time. Don't screw it up.*

Mitchell peeked out the bathroom door. The hallway was dark, unattended. Sy, Willy, and Lacy battled zombies in the front room, and Sarah stood at the mouth of the hall. She would be the first one to hide if zombies penetrated the hold.

Mitchell's eyes fell upon Lacy's bedroom door.

Do it, Walker said.

Mitchell stepped into the hall. He unlocked Lacy's room and let it swing open.

A hand shot from the dark.

It grabbed his ankle and pulled. Mitchell bent to pry off the fingers, but a head popped over the threshold—a crushed eggshell of a head. The zombie bit the flesh between Mitchell's thumb and forefinger. He almost yelped, but Walker stifled him.

And took control of his leg.

Like a puppet, Mitchell stomped the corpse's bloated neck. The teeth slid out of his hand, and he yanked it back; he held it to his chest and rushed to the bathroom.

Sarah had not seen him.

And the zombie crawled toward her down the hall.

Twenty-One

For a moment, Digger was back in that pitch-black room, munching on a peach of panties, waiting by the door. Gunshots exploded, loud yet muffled by the walls. Except now, the shots were growing louder, clearer, and the smell of meat had strengthened too.

Casting aside the panties, he reached out and found someone's ankle. He bit and found flesh—a hand. But before the blood could saturate his tongue, the darkness swirled and hatched a moon.

Pale gravestones erupted from the ground in an explosion of dirt and grass, and the warm stink of flesh melted into the wind's cold breath. Venice's followers materialized from the dark. They were still following the black snake as it twisted across the grass, across the leaves.

Climbing through a rift in the cemetery fence, they followed the serpent toward a gray house. Three of Bones' puppets stood guard on the porch, their suits full of holes and smeared with soil. The dead sentinels brandished steak knives, and as Venice's mob swarmed them, the sentinels lashed out, stabbing throats, chests, and withered eyes.

Parrying, Venice's pack shouldered through the guards and bashed open the door, splintering the frame. Inside, black candles glowed on granite plant stands and in cast-iron holders. Scarlet drapery billowed from the walls and ceiling.

In the center of the room, Bones stood, muttering incantations. His phantom voice commanded the invaders, tried to stop them, but the corpses advanced.

In a whirl of robe, Bones disappeared behind a red tapestry, through a door. Venice's onslaught pursued, and as they disappeared behind the tapestry, Digger spiraled through the darkness, back into the basement.

Venice stood in front of him, smiling. The black spot on her cheek had liquefied and was melting, infested with red worms. The organisms nested in the runny handprint on her neck, as well.

Bones stormed in, his eyes sizzling and bulging, his hair frayed. Tendons stood out on his neck. Muscles bulged on his jaw. And in the center of his forehead, a forked vein pulsed.

With a snarl, he lunged at Venice, punching, splattering the gooey spots and making new bruises. Venice scratched his cheek, clawing for his eyes. He kneed her in the stomach. Her dissolving skin burst and spilled loops and streamers of intestines. Red worms wriggled in the slime that coated the innards.

Bashing her on the nape of the neck, Bones drove her to her knees. "Traitorous bitch!" He yanked back her head, uprooting hair and peeling back swathes of scalp. From the pocket of his robe, he pulled a silver blade. He stabbed through Venice's eye. Bone cracked.

Tearing her own scalp, Venice plunged her head into Bones' crotch. Digger heard the clack of teeth through soft, spongy flesh. There was a red spray. Bones howled, and Venice's intruders breached the basement. They crowded around Bones, and the floor ran with his blood.

Twenty-Two

Willy ejected the gun's magazine and thumbed in fresh cartridges. Burger's corpse lay immobile on the floor.

"Help!" Lacy cried, still in the clutches of the zombies.

Sy grabbed her hands. He pulled, and she kicked, trying to free her legs.

Willy slammed the loaded magazine into the gun and took aim. "Outta the way!" The gun boomed, and lead whizzed past Sy's face, downing three zombies.

"Stop!" Lacy screamed. *"Stop!"*

But Willy kept firing.

Lacy finally kicked free, and Sy hauled her over the upturned couch, still flinching at the gunshots.

Lacy stood and doubled over, holding herself as if punched in the gut.

"C'mon!" Sy said, dragging her away from the sidelight, away from the zombies clambering over the couch.

Something warm and damp spread across his stomach. Lacy began to sag against him, and he had to bear her weight. He got her behind Willy, behind the gun.

Lacy brought her hand away from her belly. "I—I think I've been shot."

As she said it, a coppery scent permeated the air, and Sy realized what was soaking his shirt. It was blood.

Lacy's blood.

"Sy... please."

She grew heavier, and Sy's knees weakened.

Willy ran out of bullets and shuffled to reload. Zombies pushed him back. "Shit!"

Sarah blocked the hallway. "Lacy, what—?"

Something grabbed her from behind. She screamed. It was the zombie. The one from Lacy's room. The one that had attacked her. The one that had torn her bra. Its head was crushed like an eggshell, leaving only its teeth. That's all it needed.

It bit into Sarah's neck and ripped away a chunk.

Willy roared: "Sarah!"

He shoved past Sy and pistol-whipped the zombie's skull. He beat the corpse until it released her. Then he shot it in the head. It twitched, trying to get up. It wasn't dead. And Sarah was fading fast. More zombies were halfway across the living room, filling the house with their stink.

Willy shot them, but couldn't stop the horde as it clambered toward the hall.

"Fuck you!" Willy said. "Fuck you all!" He knocked Sarah down and shut himself in Lacy's bedroom.

Sy looked down at Sarah. She grew pale, and blood dyed her shirt. Clamped over the wound, her hand barely stanched the flow.

Getting a better hold on Lacy, Sy staggered toward the door at the end of the hall.

Sarah screamed at him.

"Wait," Lacy said. "Don't... don't leave her—"

"I'll come back, I'll—I'll come back."

The room at the rear of the house smelled like detergent and boxes. Sy laid Lacy on the floor in front of the washer and dryer. She grabbed his hand before he could leave.

"What about... what about my brother?"

"He's safe."

Sarah screamed again. Sy ran to the hall. Zombies swarmed her, gnawing her arm and face. She swatted them, kicked, but they dragged her to the floor and kept eating.

One zombie opened Lacy's door. Willy shot it, but others were right behind it, scrambling inside.

More shambled toward the laundry room. Sy shut the door and locked it. Willy's gun boomed. Sarah continued to scream.

Sy sat by Lacy and held her hand. He compressed her wound, and hot blood bubbled against his palm. She had teeth marks all over her.

"Sy," Lacy said. "Burger, he... he got bit. He—"

"Don't worry." Sy squeezed her hand. "That's not gonna happen to you."

"Promise?"

He didn't say anything.

"Do you promise?"

"I can't do that. I can't—I can't—"

"You have to."

Lacy began to sit up. Sy tried to stop her, but she still had strength. She pressed her lips against his.

At first, Sy pulled away, shocked. But Lacy tasted so good, like watermelons. He sank into her kiss and held her. She laid her head on his shoulder and wept.

"You have to," she whispered. *"You have to."*

In the hall, Willy stopped shooting and began to scream. The zombies pounded on the laundry room door. They had a knife or something and were hacking through.

Amidst it all, Sarah had fallen quiet. She was probably out there, walking around. She had been bitten, just like Burger. She had been bitten, so she must have come back from the grave.

Lacy moaned. She lay down and took Sy's hand. She squeezed it, and he squeezed back.

He pulled out his knife, and for the first time in a long time, he cried. Silently. Biting his lip until it bled. He gripped his knife and opened the blade.

"To Sy, Love Mom."

The zombies were almost through.

Twenty-Three

Bones was nothing but a skeleton, stripped of his skin and gutted. His intestines were strewn across the concrete. His liver glistened by the bed. The zombies ate, crunching gristle, squishing fat.

Venice watched them from a puddle of black stew. Her organs and skin had sloughed off to steam on the floor, some still clumped on her bones. The red worms squirmed in the mess, wriggling, eating, dying—turning gray.

Digger was dissolving too. His lungs hung from his stomach cavity, and his skin dripped, thick and black.

All the other zombies were falling dead, snipped from Bones' strings. Venice was the only force that allowed them to stand. Digger could feel her brain dissolving, trickling down her nasal cavities. His was too.

Venice grinned at him for the last time before her lips warped into a scream. She blinked, and then her eyes stayed open. They ran from her skull, and the lights went out. Digger's head fell against his chest.

Before his own eyes liquefied, he saw the other zombies collapsing to the floor. Venice's snake hissed one last time, and then everything went dark.

Twenty-Four

Walker woke in his closet of the mind.

Sometime last night, Mitchell had crawled inside. He cowered in the corner, drenched in piss and hugging his injured hand: "It's okay. Gonna be okay. Gonna be just fine."

Through the peephole, Walker saw the bathroom, flooded with daylight. He listened. No noise except the chirp of birds outside. That and Mitchell: "Gonna be just fine."

Somehow, Walker had fallen asleep. The zombies had been banging at the bathroom door, and he had drifted off. Now the zombies had stilled. The whole house smelled dead.

Walker got up, wincing as his muscles ached. He looked down at Mitchell. Pitiful.

He opened the closet and stepped out, into the bathroom, locking Mitchell inside.

The bathroom air was crisp and cool. Pieces of gauze and cotton littered the linoleum from when Lacy had patched Burger's zombie bite.

Burger: he had worried about infection, about becoming the undead. Grimacing, Walker flexed his new hands. The one with the teeth marks was stiff and sore, punctured by the zombie's canines. But the skin looked peachy around the crusted blood. No contamination. And he felt very much alive.

He chuckled and tested his legs.

Everything would be just fine.

At the bathroom door, he listened: nothing.

He stepped into the hall. Skeletons littered the floor, simmering in black ooze. Sarah's body lay beneath one. Most of her face had been eaten. White patches of skull showed through the muscle and flesh.

In Lacy's room, Walker found more skeletons. And Willy. They had eaten his bowels and his crotch, leaving nothing but bone and shreds of meat threaded with tubes. The room smelled of urine and excrement.

Walker chortled and went to the laundry room, stepping over ribcages and bones, slicks and puddles of grue.

The zombies had almost ruined the door, butcher knife wedged in the wood. Walker didn't need it. He stuck his arm through a hole and disengaged the lock.

In the middle of the floor, Lacy and Sy lay in a slant of light from the window. Around her midriff, Lacy wore a shawl of blood. Her wrists were slit, as were Sy's. He held a knife in one hand. In the other, he held Lacy's.

Together, they slept.

Walker sneered. There was a can of gas in the shed. He would douse their bodies and burn them. Seemed fitting.

But first...

Walker stole Sy's knife and went to the hall. He unburied Sarah's body and stooped to examine her. He kissed her, feeling the ragged edge of her eaten lip, feeling the ceramic surface of exposed teeth. The kiss tasted like blood.

Walker grinned.

Then he dragged her into his room. He shut the door and drew the blinds, **welcoming the dark.**

DYING TO LIVE
a novel of life among the undead

After wandering for months in a zombie-infested world, Jonah Caine discovers a group of survivors. Living in a museum-turned-compound, they are led by an ever-practical and efficient military man, and a mysterious, quizzical prophet who holds a strange power over the living dead. But Jonah's newfound peace is shattered when a clash with another group of survivors reminds them that the undead are not the only—nor the most grotesque—horrors they must face.

"*Dying to Live* is not just a thinking man's horror novel, it's a zombie book for philosophers. There's plenty of action—and we enter the story while it's already in gear—and we get inside the head and heart of a moral man trying to understand the cosmic implications of the apocalypse."

—Jonathan Maberry, author of *Ghost Road Blues*

Chapter One

I AWOKE TO find a lone zombie underneath my little hideaway. The tree house I had spent the night in was poorly constructed—the bottom was just a square of plywood, reinforced with a couple boards, with plywood walls on three sides and the fourth one open. It had no roof, but the sky was clear, so no bother. All the pieces were irregular and unpainted, with big gaps between them in many spots, and the walls were only between two and three feet high. But it was higher up than most, a good twelve feet off the ground (the kid's mom must've been one of the ones we always called a "cool mom," to allow such a dangerous playhouse), so I was even more surprised to see my unwanted visitor.

I scanned the surrounding field and trees and saw that the zombie and I were alone; my heart slowed down. In a few moments, my situation had gone from peaceful morning reverie, to possible or near-certain death, to minor inconvenience. In that respect, this was a typical morning.

Tree houses, and any other little platform above the ground, were my favorite places to catch a couple hours of sleep at night as I made my way across the country. Going inside a building required a careful search, and later on, as you tried to sleep, you'd start to worry that maybe you had missed some hiding place, from which the real Boogie Man, who doesn't need sleep, would rise up during the night. And building the necessary barricades on the doors and windows often made so much noise you could end up with a growing crowd of the undead, whose moaning and clawing at the doors would probably keep you up, on top of the danger they would pose when you tried to leave your shelter in the morning. Unless you were in a group, a building was not a good choice for your little motel in hell.

Little platforms above ground, on the other hand, were ideal. Not comfortable, but ideal. You usually had to lash yourself to them so you wouldn't fall off in the night, and you almost always had to sleep sitting up, but that was nothing for a few blessed hours of relative peace of mind. The undead are by nature incurious and almost never look up, so the chances of being spotted once you were in your little eyrie were low. For exactly the same reason that hunters once used them, back when humans were the hunters rather than the hunted, your scent wouldn't usually carry down to the creatures below, either. The tree houses always made me a little sad, 'cause they reminded me of my kids, but what could you do? All in all, my little sky boxes were the best places I had found to spend the night, so long as the living dead were afoot. But best, of course, had never been the same as perfect, and that was infinitely more true now.

One reason the zombie and I were alone this morning was that it lacked the ability to make sound. Like so many of its kind, its throat was torn open, leaving its windpipe a ragged hole, and the front of its suit stained brown with blood.

It looked up at me with its listless, cloudy eyes that lacked all expression—not hatred, not evil, not even hunger, just blanks. It was chilling in its own way, like the stare of a snake or an insect. Its look would never change, whether you drove a spike through its head, or it sank its yellow teeth into your soft, warm flesh; it lacked all capacity to be afraid, or to be satisfied. Its mouth, however, had a great deal more bestial expression to it, for it was wide open, almost gnawing at the bark of the tree as it clawed upward.

I stood looking down at it for a few moments. It was times like this—and there had been several in the last few months—that I had always wished that I smoked. In a few seconds, I would fight this thing and one or both of us would cease to exist—"die" is obviously the wrong word here—and just to stand here and con-template that inevitability cried out for some distraction, some mindless and sensual habit like smoking, to make it less horrible. I

2

guess I could've chewed gum, but that would make the whole scene ridiculous, when it was really as serious, overwhelming, and sad as any that had ever occurred to a man.

With nothing to distract me, I just felt the full weight of a terrible and necessary task, and the tediousness and unfairness of it. I had just awakened from a relatively peaceful sleep, and I already felt a crushing weariness coming over me. Again, it was developing into a pretty typical morning.

People had come up with lots of names for the walking dead in the preceding months. While we weren't fighting them off or running like hell, we usually came up with humorous labels. "Meat puppets" was a popular one. Somebody came up with "Jacks and Janes," like they were just some annoying neighbors from the next circle of hell, or as a variation on "Jack-offs."

Sometimes, when they'd get especially noisy and rambunctious, but didn't pose any immediate threat, we'd call them "the natives," as in "the natives are restless." Maybe that was a little racist, I don't know. "Walking stiffs" was pretty accurate. But mostly we'd go for the tried and true—zombies. That's what they were, and we'd always be one breath away from becoming one—a mindless, shambling bag of flesh without a mind.

My zombie this morning looked to have been a middle-aged man in its human life, slightly graying, average build. Its suit was intact, and other than its throat wound, there were no signs of further fights with humans or other zombies. Decay had taken its toll, and it looked more desiccated than gooey, a brittle husk rather than the dripping bag of puss that some of them became.

At first, I looked it over to size up its threat and plan my attack, but that quickly turned into contemplating its human existence. Maybe his kids had built the tree house, and that's why he'd been hanging around here, almost as if he were protecting it, or waiting for them to come back. Or even worse, maybe his kids had been the ones to tear out his throat, when he had rushed home in the midst of the outbreak, hoping against hope they were still okay. Or, just as bad, maybe he'd been bitten at work or on the way home, only to break in to his own house and kill his kids.

My mind reeled, and I clutched the wall of the tree house. I'd heard of soldiers in other wars having a "thousand yard stare," a

3

blank look that signaled they were giving in to the hopelessness and horror around them, soon to be dead or insane. As for me, I was suffering the thousand yard stare of the war with the undead: once you contemplated the zombies as human beings, once you thought of them as having kids and lives and loves and worries and hopes and fears, you might as well just put your gun in your mouth and be done with it right then, because you were losing it—fast. But, God knows, if you never looked at them that way, if they were just meat puppets whose heads exploded in your rifle's sights, then hopefully somebody would put a bullet in your brain, because you had become more monstrous than any zombie ever could be.

I shook myself free of my paralysis. I'm not exactly sure why, but I wasn't ready to give up yet. I tossed my backpack beyond where the zombie stood. It turned to see where it landed, then immediately looked back up at me. Its head lolled from side to side, and I was again glad that it couldn't vocalize, as it was clearly getting worked up and would've been making quite a racket if it could.

You never used a gun if you didn't have to, for its noise brought lots of unwanted attention, so I pulled out a knife, the one I carried with a long, thin blade, like a bayonet, as that would work best. I stood at the edge of the plywood platform. "I'm sorry," I said, looking right in the zombie's eyes. "Maybe somewhere, deep down, you still understand: I'm sorry."

I took a step forward and started to fall. I tried to hit it on the shoulder with my right foot, but its arms were flailing about, and my boot hit its left wrist, sliding along its arm. I sprawled to the right and then rolled away as the zombie was shoved into the tree.

As it turned to face me, I scrambled up, took a step forward, and drove the knife into its left eye. Its hands flailed about, either to attack me or to ward off the blow. The blade was long and thin enough that it went almost to the back of its skull. The whole attack was noiseless, without so much as the sound of a squish or a glitch as the blade slid through its eyeball and brain.

As I drew the blade out, I grabbed the zombie by the hair and shoved it downward to the side, where it fell to the ground and lay motionless.

And that was that. Like everyone, I always used to imagine deadly fights would be much more dramatic. But in my experience,

4

there were seldom any Chuck Norris flying, spinning kicks, or any *Matrix*-style running up the wall while firing two guns on full auto. If anyone's ever around to make movies about the wars against the undead, maybe there will be such moves in them, I don't know. But usually, like this morning, there were just a couple of savage, clumsy blows, and it was over.

I was barely breathing at all, let alone breathing hard, the way I felt someone should when they kill something that was somehow, in some small way, still human. A few months ago, I would've at least felt nauseous, but not anymore. Looking down at the creature from the tree house had been much more traumatic than delivering the killing blow.

I bent down over my would-be killer and cleaned the blade on his suit jacket. I then reached into his pocket. It was a little ritual I still followed when I could, though the horrible exigencies of a zombie-infested world usually made it impossible. I pulled out his wallet and got out his driver's license. Rather than look at the bloody horror at my feet, with its one undead eye and one bloody, vacant socket, I stared at his driver's license picture—smiling, happy, alive, years and decades of life ahead of him. I cleared my throat to speak clearly. "I have killed Daniel Gerard. I hope he's somewhere better now."

I cast the wallet and license on top of his motionless body, scooped up my backpack, and hurried away.

It had been close to a year since all the worst parts of the Bible started coming true. Armageddon. Apocalypse. The End of Days. God's righteous judgment on a sinful humanity. Whatever the self-righteous jerk who railed at you once a week from a pulpit used to call it. Well, he might have been self-righteous and a jerk, and now he was probably lurching around like most everyone else, drooling on himself with half his face torn off, but it sure seemed as though he had had some inside information that we all wish we'd gotten a little sooner.

For most people, I assume it started like every other day. Brush your teeth. Kiss your spouse without any feeling. Go to work.

Grab whatever it is you grab to eat on your way to work. Eat it, not really noticing or enjoying it. But then at some point that blessed, kind, comforting routine goes horribly awry and someone—maybe your neighbor, or coworker, or worse, your kids or your spouse—staggers up to you with a blank look and tries to tear your throat out with his teeth. If he gets you, then you don't have to worry anymore, because you'll be dead, and then you'll get up and wander around like him, with no more thoughts or feelings, just shuffling around trying to bite people. If you get away from him, then you'd be one of the survivors, at least for a little while, and then you'd have lots of worries, and your only feeling would be fear. Either way—welcome to hell.

Theological assessments aside, the automatic assumption was that the dead were rising and killing because of some infection, and the infection was spread by their bites. The next logical assumption—since there was not much reliable evidence of zombie infestations before the 21st century (horror movies notwithstanding)—was that we had tinkered with viruses and DNA and had brought all this shit on ourselves.

Here again, a theological assessment was hard to avoid. We had created a hell on earth through our own arrogance and ignorance, and now we were reaping what we had sown—with a vengeance. Worse than any couple who ate an apple or any bozo who slapped some brick and mortar on the Tower of Babel, we'd messed with The Man's prerogatives, and either He'd given us the biggest damn smack down of all time, or we'd just set off something that only He could control. Shit, you didn't need to believe in the Bible to see how much sense it made. You remember that crazy Greek myth you read about in fifth grade—Pandora's box. Same damn thing. A box full of walking cannibal corpses who wouldn't let you close it once it got open.

Now, how that box got opened, that was a hot topic of debate among survivors, when we weren't fighting to prolong our miserable existence and could afford the luxury of conversation or discussion. Outright warfare or a terrorist attack was probably the least popular theory, though it had vigorous proponents. I don't know why more of us didn't subscribe to that hypothesis. I suppose it's funny to say, but I think we didn't because it was the least comforting of all our speculations. It was too horrible to imagine that even terrorists could unleash the hellish plague of undeath on the whole world, even their own people, including women, children, and the elderly. And at the same time, the theory made it too pat and simple, like it was just some crazies who did this, some tiny band of malcontents—horror of this magnitude seemed to require a more powerful, far-reaching source.

That's probably why more people bought into the paranoid, conspiratorial theory that the disease had been released by our government or someone else's as a horribly botched attempt to test it on a real population. Proponents of this theory almost delighted in its vindication of every real and imagined form of government-sponsored terror, from Andersonville to Tuskegee to Gitmo to putting fluoride in the tap water. Their tales could almost be the bedtime stories of the apocalypse, lulling us to sleep with some tiny and bizarre shred of hope that even now, the world made some weird kind of sense, that undeath was not a new and incomprehensible kind of evil, but just a continuation of this world's madness and brutality, like Jackie scrambling on the trunk of the Lincoln to grab the big chunk of her husband's head that was sliding around back there, or like bulldozers pushing mountains of emaciated bodies into pits in Dachau. Strange comfort, that, but it was often all we had.

But the most popular theory—the one I personally advocated, though without much conviction—was simply that there had been a horrible accident. Nothing malevolent or calculated, just plain old human error. Somebody dropped a test tube somewhere. A lab monkey bit through somebody's glove. The kind of thing that happens a thousand times a day for thousands of days with no fatal outcome. It was the most blackly humorous theory, I suppose, for it made the misery and violent deaths of billions of people just the result of a stupid mistake, but it had its own cold comfort. If all this was just some blunder, then maybe, if we could ever shoot every zombie in the head—the only way we had found to kill them permanently—or if they would just eventually rot and fall apart—what everyone had hoped for initially—then we could go back to life like it used to be. We weren't evil, just stupid and clumsy. Like poor Pandora.

That's how some of us theorized that it had begun. But whatever had happened—and I've left out the more exotic theories, like an extra-terrestrial source of infection—we ended up in the same place. Almost one year after the first corpse rose, the world was ruled by the undead, who wandered about with no discernible goal other than to kill and eat living people. The undead were everywhere, the new dominant species that took the place of the old, extinct one. Places where there had been large human populations were especially thick with the walking dead, though they never took any notice of one another.

The living, meanwhile, as was their wont, almost always congregated in little groups. The government or society or culture had imploded or disintegrated with terrifying speed as the infection spread. Within hours, there had been no telephone service, no police or rescue response to the terrified calls for help. Within days, there was no power or television. And within weeks, the last organized military and government resistance collapsed, at least in the U.S.

But groups of survivors quickly came together into little groups, little communities with a pecking order and rules and authority, but also some of the little perks of being around other people—companionship, conversation, sex, someone to hold your hand when you die, someone to put a bullet in your brain when you went to get back up as a zombie. (And if you've ever seen a zombie—and God love you, I hope you haven't, but if you're reading this, I suspect you have—then you know that last perk is by no means the least important one.) You didn't have to be a damned philosopher to know that we're social animals, and would be till the last zombie bit the last human and dragged us all down to hell, which, judging by the zombies, looked like it was going to be the most unsociable place imaginable.

Yes, humans always build their little communities in order to survive, and in order to make surviving a little more bearable. Except me. I was alone. And it sucked. It was dangerous and it sucked.

By midday, I was moving closer to what looked like a small-sized city. I had thrown my maps away a few days ago when I had failed to find my family. After that, I figured, I didn't have much need for maps: if I didn't have any place to go anymore—and I had decided that I didn't—what difference did it make where I was at the moment? Besides, the end of civilization had wreaked a lot of havoc with the things depicted on maps: I guess the rivers and mountains were still there, but cities were gone, roads were clogged with wrecked cars, bridges and tunnels and dams had been blown up to try to stop the rampaging hordes of the undead. So long as I was out of reach of those things, and had one bullet for myself if it came to that, I was in about the best location I could hope for.

It was a late spring day, bursting with a sunshine that didn't make it hot, but just made things seem better, brighter, more alive than they were on other days. I still had the instinct to call it beautiful as I looked around and forgot the obvious shortcomings of the day for a moment. One shortcoming I couldn't forget, however, was the gnawing hunger I felt.

Never one for breakfast, I had definitely been put off from eating anything this morning after killing Daniel Gerard, a man who, after all, had only been looking for something to eat, just as I was. I had some supplies in my backpack, but if I was near an area where I could forage for more and conserve what I had, that would be the much wiser course.

The undead weren't exactly afraid of sunlight—they weren't afraid of anything—but they did seem to avoid it unless aroused and provoked. Maybe it hurt their skin or eyes, or maybe they could sense that it was speeding their decay and that brought them some discomfort. Whatever it was, during bright daylight, you could walk through places where the walking dead were nearby without immediately attracting a crowd, so long as you were quiet and downwind. Still, I never went too far into an urban area. Right now, I just wanted to find some food and get back out to the sticks before nightfall.

From what I'd seen, many cities had burned more or less to the ground, once fire crews were no longer there to put out the inevitable fires. But here, for whatever reason of wind or rain or luck, many buildings were still standing. Some were gutted or damaged by fire, and all had the usual marks of looting, ransacking, and the final, desperate battles between the living and the dead. There were few unbroken windows.

In the street, wrecked or abandoned cars were everywhere. There were a few bodies and pieces of bodies in extremely advanced stages of decay, and paper and dead leaves rustled about on a light breeze.

The sight of the burnt-out remains of a city was almost as overwhelmingly depressing as the human wrecks that wandered everywhere as zombies: this place should be bustling and alive, and instead it was—quite literally—a graveyard.

I always wondered why there weren't more animals around now, since zombies didn't eat them, but everywhere I went, it always seemed like there were even fewer animals than when people had ruled the earth. I almost never heard a bird sing. I seldom saw pigeons or squirrels. It was almost as though even the animals fled from such horror, fled when the ruler of the animal kingdom died, and left the king's mausoleum in peace, until it could completely crumble away and they could reclaim it after a suitable mourning period. I know it seems almost delusional in its anthropomorphism, but sometimes you can't help thinking like that when you're alone in these dead places.

I checked the remains of a couple stores, barely venturing inside the darkened buildings, for fear of the dead hiding in ambush. The inventories of a clothing store and a jewelry store were barely touched: it was funny how quickly things had been re-prioritized in the final, chaotic days of the human race.

I looked at what appeared to be hundreds of thousands of dollars of diamonds, now mixed in with the smashed glass of the cases that had once displayed them: both sparkled in the sun, but their value had been radically and traumatically equalized a few months ago. I imagined that during last winter—the first winter of a world that would now remain more or less dead in every season—the snow too had sparkled just as brightly when it blew in and covered the diamonds that, in better times, would've adorned hundreds of brides.

A quick look into a liquor store revealed much less remaining stock—human nature and appetites being what they are—but there was a bottle of some bad bourbon just a few feet inside the door, so I reached in and grabbed it. I didn't know when I'd be able to drop my guard enough to partake, but since I wasn't carrying that much, it made sense to take it.

I knew I was getting too far into the dead city, but on the next street was a convenience store where there might be food. It was facing perpendicularly from the stores I had examined, so at least it would be brighter inside. The big front windows were still intact, but the glass of the front door had been smashed. Looking up and down the street and still seeing no movement, I went inside the store.

I was looking for snack cakes. When the final crisis of humanity had begun, people had instinctively stocked up on canned food: I guess Spam is forever etched in our collective consciousness as the foodstuff of the apocalypse. People at first had bought up everything canned, and then, within just a couple days, as cash became utterly worthless and stores weren't even open, the stronger smashed and grabbed from the weaker. I had never seen a can of food in a store since I had started foraging: you could only find cans in people's houses, and even then they were getting pretty rare at this point. So, for now, snack cakes were the way to go. What I would do when those finally went bad and the last few cans ran out—that was a question still a few months off, and therefore way beyond any reasonable contingency plans.

I don't know if all the old urban legends that Twinkies and those pink Snow Ball cakes could survive a nuclear explosion were true, but they and their kind definitely had a shelf life well over a year, if the box wasn't opened and you weren't fussy, which I clearly wasn't at this point.

There was a treasure trove of them in the second aisle into the store, and I smiled when I saw there were no chocolate ones: I guessed some priorities remained effective right up till the last gasp of humanity. I made my way quietly to them, tore open the boxes, shoveled a bunch of the wrapped ones into my backpack, and proceeded to gorge myself on what I couldn't carry. I was licking white crème filling off my fingers when I heard the crunch of a shoe stepping on broken glass.

ABOUT
THE
AUTHORS

Eric S. Brown is the author of the zombie novel/novellas *Cobble, The Queen,* and *The Wave* as well numerous other collections and chapbooks. His latest book, *Zombies: Inhuman,* will be out in 2007. One can find most of his work on www.amazon.com or www.nakedsnakepress.com. He is 31 years old and lives in NC with his family.

*   *   *   *   *

Freelancer **Vince Churchill** writes regularly for Daystar Studios and The Hacker's Source magazine. Recent stories have appeared in The Undead and in The Horror Library, Volume One. He has two novels: *The Dead Shall Inherit The Earth* and *The Blackest Heart.* He is currently working on a pair of projects for Daystar Studios: writing and editing duties for an upcoming horror/sci-fi/dark fantasy comic anthology called *The Realm,* and a horror novella entitled *Condemned.* Vince's next novel, a dark, end-of-the-world love story called *Good Night My Sweet,* is slated for completion in early 2008.

*   *   *   *   *

Following an accident that left her homebound, **Adrian Kiwi Courters** opted on a career where she didn't have to leave the house. She lives in the San Francisco Bay Area with her (understanding) husband, Neil; (computer crashing) sons, Skip and Bobby; and (just feed the damn thing) cat, Frisket. This is her first published piece, (outside of angry letters to the press and some terrible poetry.)

*   *   *   *   *

David Dunwoody lives in Utah with his wife and two cats. Recent publications featuring his short works include *Read by Dawn 2* from Bloody Books, and Permuted Press' novella collection *Headshot Quartet*. He also writes fiction and reviews for the magazine *The Hacker's Source*. In 2006 David serialized a novel online, which can be read at EmpireNovel.com.

*   *   *   *   *

Philip "Evil Avatar" Hansen is the owner and webmaster of the popular video game news page, *Evil Avatar - Daily Gaming News... With Attitude*. (http://www.evilavatar.com) Philip is the author of several Bradygames official video game strategy guides. He lives and works in Phoenix, Arizona. When not playing or writing about video games, Philip is hard at work on a perpetually unfinished novel of the old west.

*   *   *   *   *

Matt Hults lives with his wife and two children in Minneapolis, Minnesota. His fiction appears in the anthologies Echoes of Terror, Fried; Fast Food, Slow Deaths, and Horror Library, Volume 2. His first horror e-book, *Skinwalker*, will soon be available from Wild Child Publishing. Sample more of Matt's work at his web site, NewHorrorFiction.com.

*   *   *   *   *

Meghan Jurado is a horror writer from Colorado. She lives there with her husband and three hairless dogs. Her works have been included in *The Undead, The Travel Guide to the Haunted-Mid-Atlantic Region, The Shadowbox Collection*, and the online zombie magazine *Revenant*. You can see more of her upcoming projects at: www.demonnurse.com.

*   *   *   *   *

Born in a comparatively zombie-free Calgary, **Murray Leeder** is currently pursuing a Ph.D. at Carleton University in Ottawa. He wrote *Plague of Ice* and *Son of Thunder* for Wizards of the Coast, along with about twenty published horror and fantasy short stories, most recently in anthologies *Sails & Sorcery* and *Blood & Devotion. The Traumatized Generation* debuted in *Open Space: New Canadian Fantastic Fiction,* receiving honorable mention in Datlow and Windling's *Year's Best Fantasy and Horror 2004.*

*   *   *   *   *

Kim Paffenroth teaches Religious Studies at Iona College, after receiving degrees from St. John's College (Annapolis, MD), Harvard Divinity School, and the University of Notre Dame. He has written numerous non-fiction works, including *The Truth Is Out There: Christian Faith and the Classics of TV Science Fiction* (co-authored with T. Bertonneau; Brazos Press, 2006), and *Gospel of the Living Dead: George Romero's Visions of Hell on Earth* (Baylor, 2006), which won the 2006 Bram Stoker Award for Superior Achievement in Non-Fiction.

*   *   *   *   *

Eric Shapiro and his wife Rhoda live in Los Angeles. His fiction has appeared in *The Elastic Book of Numbers* (British Fantasy Award Winner, 2006) and *Corpse Blossoms* (Bram Stoker Award Nominee, 2005), among many other publications. His apocalyptic novella *It's Only Temporary* was on the Preliminary Nominee Ballot for the 2005 Bram Stoker Award in Long Fiction.

*   *   *   *   *

Matthew Shepherd is a professional writer splitting his time between marketing, comics and traditional prose: he's the author among other things of the Slave Labor Graphics series *Dead Eyes Open* and *Dust and Steel*. He writes the online comic *Man-Man* and can be contacted through his perpetually run-down Web site at www.shep.ca.

*　*　*　*　*

D.L. Snell is an Affiliate member of the Horror Writers Association and an editor for Permuted Press. Award-winning author Brian Keene "dug the hell" out of Snell's short zombie/vampire story, "Limbless Bodies Swaying," which Snell expanded into his first novel, *Roses of Blood on Barbwire Vines*, available from Permuted Press. For more information and to read sample chapters, visit www.rosesofblood.com.

*　*　*　*　*

Scott Standridge is a writer and editor from Little Rock, Arkansas. His work has appeared in *City Slab, Whispers from the Shattered Forum*, and many other small press magazines. In addition to writing fiction and nonfiction, he recently completed his online "Sonnet Project," for which he wrote a sonnet a day for a full year. You can view the results, many of them horror-themed, at:
http://thesonnetproject.blogspot.com
He is also Fiction Editor for *City Slab Magazine*. Read more of his stories and post comments on his website:
www.scottstandridge.com

*　*　*　*　*

As a librarian, **Joel A. Sutherland** is well-prepared for the fast-approaching zombie apocalypse. His fiction has appeared in many small press magazines and anthologies, and his first novel will be published later this year by Lachesis Publishing. He lives in Whitby, Ontario, with his wife, Colleen, and his Goldendoodle, Murphy. Read Sutherland's blog at:
http://joelasutherland.livejournal.com

*　*　*　*　*

Ryan C. Thomas works as an editor in San Diego, California. His first novel, *The Summer I Died*, was released by Coscom Entertainment in 2006, and has become a cult favorite among extreme horror fans. His short stories have appeared in numerous markets over the years. You can usually find him in the bars on the weekends playing with his band, The Buzzbombs. When he is not writing or rocking out, he is at home with his cat, Elvis, watching really bad B-movies. Visit him on the web at:
www.ryancthomas.com

* * * * *

David Wellington is the author of the zombie novels *Monster Island* and *Monster Nation*. His vampire novel, *Thirteen Bullets*, will be published by Three Rivers Press in the Summer of 2007. He lives in New York City with his wife, Elisabeth. For more information please visit www.davidwellington.net.

ABOUT THE ARTISTS

Stephen Blundell lives in Brisbane, Australia. He is zombie-like due to "working" excessively on his computer and rarely showers. He has no interests in life but is often found flashing little old ladies down at the local park. As a chronic liar, you shouldn't believe a single thing you've read in this bio. Truthfully though, he lives with his long-suffering wife Joanne, and despondently tolerates her three spoilt cats. They look forward to welcoming their first child in July, 2007. You can find more of his art at:

http://djdyme.deviantart.com/gallery/

And can keep up to date with his music at: http://opus.110mb.com/

* * * * *

Paul Campbell is an accomplished professional in both the writing and illustration fields with more than 15 years experience. He currently has over 75 published stories and countless illustrations. Some of his more recently renowned work would be his illustrations for Baen's Universe produced by Baen's Books where he's illustrated stories written by but not limited to: H.G. Wells, Joe R. Lansdale, and Bob Shaw. Having previously owned and operated a publishing company with a readership of over 50,000, Paul has once again decided to step back into the field of publishing with a new venture: RAZAR Magazine.

www.RazarMagazine.com

* * * * *

Blake Clouser is a film maker and visual artist living in Chicago, IL. He has studied drawing and painting in Italy under the renowned landscape painter Daniel Lang. His previous works have been diverse creations in the form of poster art, websites, album cover design, videogame character design, music, screenplays, and comic book art. He is the eldest of 4 boys in his family.

* * * * *

Bret Jordan is a 39 year old Texas resident. He is married and has four children, all girls. By day he programs computers for a local business, and by night he works as a freelance artist. When not working, drawing, and spending time with his family, he reads and writes stories. Samples of his artwork may be seen at:
www.bretjordan.com

* * * * *

Clint Leduc is an artist and aspiring amateur filmmaker. He lives in a small town outside of Worcester, Massachusetts where he attends college as a Graphic Design major. His work for *The Undead: Skin & Bones* and *Flesh Feast* marks his first foray into illustration.

* * * * *

Jesus Riddle Morales is an illustrator and Graffiti-Art-Style muralist. He is also a freelance commercial artist and Internet author. He, along with his counterparts in the Synoptic Knight Templars and "BTB" crew, co-created a system of stylized art called "Hyper-gothics." Hailing from Chicago's Southwest Ghetto, "Riddle's" work is well known throughout the U.S. His "Zombie Bible" tales are a staple in the West Coast college scene and his alluring, Hyper-Gothic art can be found in many underground books, web-sites, and other forums. Visit Riddle's art-page at:
http://www.myspace.com/darkriddle

* * * * *

A member of Golden Goat Studios since 2003, **Joshua Ross** has published a number of projects and worked with clients such as Ape Comics, Breygent Marketing, Warner Bros, Digital Webbing and **Permuted Press**. He is best known for numerous NightmareWorld.com contributions, his weekly online comic *Tales of Mr. Rhee*, and his graphic novel *Put Some Pants On*. For more of Josh's art visit his website at: artronin9.com

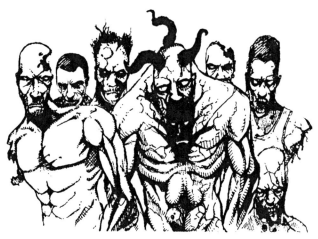

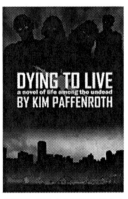
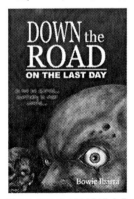

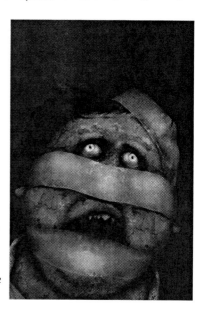

Printed in the United States
142620LV00004B/83/A